Mad Kestrel

Mad Kestrel

MISTY MASSEY

A TOM DOHERTY ASSOCIATES BOOK
New York

MAD KESTREL

Copyright © 2008 by Misty Massey

A Tor Book
Published by Tom Doherty Associates, LLC
175 Fifth Avenue
New York, NY 10010

www.tor.com

Tor® is a registered trademark of Tom Doherty Associates, LLC.

Library of Congress Cataloging-in-Publication Data

Massey, Misty.
    Mad Kestrel / Misty Massey.—1st trade pbk. ed.
        p.   cm.
    "A Tom Doherty Associates Book."
    ISBN-13: 978-0-7653-1802-2
    ISBN-10: 0-7653-1802-4
    1. Women sailors—Fiction.   I. Title.
    PS3613.A81935M33   2008
    813'.6—dc22
                                            2007046721

First Edition: March 2008

Printed in the United States of America

0   9   8   7   6   5   4   3   2   1

For Todd,
who never doubted

ACKNOWLEDGMENTS

This book wouldn't exist in the first place if it hadn't been for The South Carolina Writers Workshop: Craig Faris, Norman Froscher, Kim Harrison, Virginia Wilcox, and most of all Faith Hunter, who insisted I let my inner novelist roam free, and never let me forget for a second that she believed in me.

Thanks are due to David Hartwell, my award-winning editor; Denis Wong, for his suggestions and support; and my wonderful agent, Holly McClure, whose faith and confidence in me never wavered.

My beloved sister, Alicia Barton, and my oldest friend in the world, Jan Schumann, held me up when I was down, made me laugh when I needed it, and kept me sane.

My parents, Dr. Donald A. and Anne Swetnam Barton, raised me to be a lover of the written word. They gave me so much throughout my life, but the gift I value most was the permission to read anything I chose, without censor or judgment. It sounds like such a simple thing, but it was truly the greatest privilege anyone could have offered me. I love you both, and I thank you from the bottom of my heart.

And finally, the two men who ran errands, did housework, cooked their own dinners, rescued me from weird computer glitches, endured multiple viewings of old pirate movies for atmosphere, put up with me suddenly saying "Aye" and "Avast ye" all the time, and blocked fight scenes so that I could see what I was writing.

Bleys, you're the best son I could have ever hoped for.

Todd, you're my world, and always will be.

Mad Kestrel

One

And now the storm blast came, and he
Was tyrannous and strong;
He struck with his o'ertaking wings
And chas'd us south along.

—SAMUEL TAYLOR COLERIDGE

Cold waves splashed across the railings, nearly knocking Kestrel over. She gripped the wet wood tighter, squinting into the rain-whipped darkness. Lightning split the sky, and Kestrel began counting under her breath. *One . . . two . . . three . . . four . . .* Thunder rumbled suddenly, loud and gut-shaking, but one second farther away than it had been moments ago. She breathed out in relief. Whether they were outrunning the storm or it them, they were finally on the safe side.

The storm had been a killer, whirling out of the night like some giant beast and taking the crew of the pirate sloop *Wolfshead* completely by surprise. If they'd only changed course, they might have been able to skirt its edges, but the captain was insistent. Changing course would put them an extra day away from their destination, and he refused to consider any delay.

They trimmed the sails and battened down to ride out the fury. Sheer luck that they'd lost none of the men over the side. As soon as the weather began to ease, she relieved as many as she could afford to. Some of them had tucked themselves into their hammocks for the night, the rest were belowdecks cleaning up and resecuring crates and barrels that had shaken loose.

"Kestrel! Get up here!"

The captain's bellow was a beacon through the pounding rain and roaring wind. Kestrel moved cautiously across the main deck to the bow, grabbing lines as she went to steady herself. She'd kicked her boots off below long before the rain started. Her toes had gone numb, so she stepped carefully across the slick deck. The worst of the weather was over, but the sloop was still a bucking horse in the wild seas the storm had churned up.

"Kestrel! Damn your eyes, where've you got to?" Captain Artemus Binns was holding the wheel with both hands, his big arms straining to keep it steady. He shook his head, flinging rain-soaked strands of his gray hair out of his face, and caught sight of his quartermaster. "Nice to see you, lass," he yelled. "For a time there, she was fightin' me so hard I almost thought she wanted to go to the deeps."

"Need me to spell you for a while?" She reached for the wheel, but he didn't let go.

"Storm's easin' up; I can handle her fine. Unless you think you can whistle me up a prevailin' current?"

Kestrel glanced around, but no one was close enough to have overheard. "Artie!" she scolded.

He laughed. "Just toyin' with you, my girl. I thought I saw somethin'. Be my eyes," he said, turning his chin toward the long brass scope tucked under his left arm.

Kestrel took the scope, slipped behind him, and braced herself against his broad back. "Where am I looking?"

"To starboard."

"And I should see what?"

"Another ship."

"Is she foundering?"

"Nay, I think not. I'm not in the business of rescuin' anyway." He grinned. "Tell me whose colors she's raised, if any."

"Aye, Captain." Pushing her black braids away from her face, she raised the scope to her eye and peered into the distance. The *Wolfshead* was still rocking hard up and down, her timbers groaning in an eerie music Kestrel knew well. Rain had smeared the telescope lens, but neither that nor the rolling seas disguised what she saw.

A huge three-master, painted black and red with vast red sails, matched their course. She cut the choppy water smoothly, looking for all the world like a queen making her entrance. The flag fluttering heavily from atop the ship was a red field with a black flaming eye.

"Damn, Artie, she's sporting twenty gunports on this side alone. Fancy painted or no, she's a powerful beast."

"Can you see her crew?"

"Aye. Fellow on the quarterdeck appears to think he's in charge."

He was tall, his honey-gold hair flying loose in the breeze, mimicking the flap of the dark cloak that hung from his broad shoulders. His legs were wrapped in boots that came halfway up his thighs, and a glint of steel winked from his hip. One foot was propped on the railing. He stared into the distance, looking like a posed painting.

Suddenly he turned his face in her direction. Very handsome, as far as she could tell from the distance, with a devilish cast to his smile. Stepping down from the railing, he crossed his arms and squared his chest, staring at her so intently that she grew uncomfortable. It was as if he could see her, out here in the dark, without a glass to aid him. Cocking one hand rakishly on his hip, he raised the other in front of him, making a "come here" waggle with his finger. Kestrel's eyes widened. Slowly she dropped the glass to her side.

"Well? Whose colors is she flyin'?"

Kestrel swallowed. "No colors I've seen before, Artie. I'd have called her a merchant ship, except she's armed to the teeth. If she's a warship, she doesn't belong to any navy I've heard of. And that captain of hers turns my stomach."

"The captain?" he asked. "What's wrong with him?"

Without the glass, the ship was a shadowy bulk in the water, the people aboard only moving shapes with no way to distinguish them. So why did she still feel that bold stare, like an unwelcome touch on her skin? She could think of only one reason the other vessel's captain could see her so well without a spyglass. Or stayed so dry.

She didn't fear much of anything, but magic, and the men who practiced it, made her skin crawl. Popular rumor insisted the magi never set foot off land, one of her prime reasons for choosing a life on the water. But rumor had been proven wrong before.

"Take the wheel," Binns ordered, before she could phrase an answer. She did as he said, handing him the scope. He raised it to his face and whistled appreciatively. "Damn fine ship, that."

"Could he be someone who's just come to the seas?" she grunted, the wheel pulling against her grip.

"Mayhap. That's a lot of money to spend on a ship. If he's not a merchant, and not a warrior, there's only one other kind of sailor I know. Men with cash enough to afford a vessel like that usually don't go on the account." He chuckled. "I wish you could see this, Kes. He's wavin' at me, as if we're friends passin' in the street!"

"Passing is exactly what we ought to do."

"Yonder boy doesn't even know who he's facin'!" Binns grinned suddenly, and Kestrel's heart dropped. She knew that look in his eye too well.

"Captain, with the weather like it is . . ." she began, but he interrupted her.

"Could be entertainin' to show this amateur a thing or two." He quirked an eyebrow at her. "Don't you think?"

Kestrel groaned. Binns was a fine captain, kinder and fairer than most in the Nine Islands, but his greed was a source of infinite frustration. He'd been on the verge of losing the *Wolfshead* when she met him. Serving under Binns was a far better life than she could ever have hoped for back on Eldraga, and he'd kept her secret even in times when it could have benefited him to reveal it. But it was moments like this when she wondered if she shouldn't have stayed ashore.

"We're not in any condition to take a ship, least of all that one. Look at her—she's got forty guns at least!"

He turned to her with a wounded look. "I don't intend to take her. I figure on playin' with her a bit. Just a warnin' shot, across her bow. To watch the jackanapes dance."

"And what if he's not some fop?" Kestrel snapped. "What if he decides to blow us out of the seas?"

"His ship's a monster, Kes, I'll grant you that. But it's too big. Even tore up like we are, we can still outrun him easy. Besides"— he raised the glass again and licked his lips—"I'm the captain and it's an order. Pass it down."

No way around it. Binns would listen to her opinions, just as he would any member of the crew who had one to voice. But once he gave an order, he expected it to be obeyed without further question. Argue the point too far, and she'd risk a public flogging. "Aye, Captain."

Returning control of the wheel to Binns, she crossed carefully to the midpoint of the deck and leaned over the hatch. "Get Shadd up here, you lads!" A moment later, a great blond bear of a man poked his head through, blinking at the stinging rain.

"Aye, Kes? What's the word?"

"Roust your gunners, tell them the captain needs their ladies warm and willing."

"Aye, Quarter. Got a target in mind?"

She pointed in the direction of the three-master. The rain had abated enough for an easy view across the water, and Shadd frowned. "We're firing on her? Is he out of his wits?"

"No more than usual." She clapped him on one massive shoulder. "It's an official order, so best get to it."

"Aye, Kes, that I will." He dropped back down the skinny ladder, roaring the order as he descended. Rising to her feet again, she returned to Binns's side.

"Ready when you are, Captain."

He rubbed his hands eagerly. "Relax, lass, this'll be a bit of sport, is all. Somethin' to boast about in the pub tomorrow." His eyes narrowed. "Fire starboard guns."

"Fire starboard guns!" Kestrel cried. The order was echoed down to the waiting gunners. Binns raised the telescope.

With a heavy deck-shivering thump, the guns answered the command. Smoke belched from the gunports, sweeping over the deck in a wave of warmth. Kestrel drew a long breath, enjoying the smell of the spent powder.

Binns was watching the big vessel intently. He barked a laugh, and turned to his quartermaster. "Kestrel, lass, I think this is somethin' you'll want to see."

"Me?" She took the offered telescope, and warily placed it to her eye.

The three-master's gunports remained closed. The cloaked fellow had moved to the main deck, and was standing with both feet on the railing, only the length of line he held onto keeping him from tipping over into the black water below. He touched one hand to his lips, then with a gallant sweep of his arm, waved it her way.

Blood rushed into Kestrel's cheeks. The nerve of him—blowing her a kiss as if she were some bar wench. She dropped the telescope. Binns was chuckling, careful not to look her in the face.

"You think that was funny?" she snapped. He glanced toward her, and exploded into full-out laughter, bending over and slapping his thigh.

"He was . . . pointin' toward you, lass . . . wanted me to . . . give you the scope . . ." he managed to force out between breaths. "I wish you . . . could have seen . . . your face . . ."

"I'll show him where he can plant those lips," she muttered, raising the glass again. The warship's captain, wisely for him, had climbed down from the railing. As she watched, he strode across his deck toward his helmsman, waving his arms. The warship responded to the helmsman's turn of the wheel, steering off and away from the *Wolfshead*.

The deck crew began cheering, some shouting insults at the retreating ship, others launching into random verses of drinking songs. Binns chuckled. "See, Kes? Just a rich popinjay with more money than sense. You were worryin' about nothin'. One little howdy-do shot and he runs like a baby."

Kestrel didn't say anything. Running he seemed to be, but that fellow hadn't acted like a coward. She couldn't believe he'd take Binns's insulting shot without an answering volley.

"Come on, girl, he's gone." Binns nudged her shoulder. "Go below and get a cup of rum, warm your bones."

She was about to drop the scope, and do as her captain suggested, when, to her horror, out of the rainy darkness, the warship reappeared. Bearing straight for them, a monstrous red juggernaut cutting through the water at top speed. Ramming speed. It was big enough to slice the *Wolfshead* completely in half and never even feel the impact.

Kestrel leaped toward the railing, not waiting for Binns to give the order. They had mere seconds before the warship crushed them under its keel. "Shadd!" she screamed. "Fire starboard guns!"

The giant man, head and shoulders out of the hatch, didn't repeat her order down the line. He was staring transfixed across the water.

"Fire guns!" Kestrel swung herself over the railing and ran for the open hatchway. She grabbed Shadd's hair, yanked his head back, and let go. "Damn your eyes, wake up, man!"

Shadd's head snapped forward, and he seemed to focus on her for the first time. "What'd ye do that for?"

"We're going to die!"

"No, we're not. There ain't nothin' there." He pointed, and she turned to follow his shaking hand.

Kestrel's eyes widened. She scanned the horizon, looking left and right. The big ship was gone, vanished into the stormy night as if it had never been there at all.

Two

And now this spell was snapped; once more
I viewed the ocean green,
And looked far forth, yet little saw
Of what had else been seen.

—SAMUEL TAYLOR COLERIDGE

What did I tell you? Didn't I say there was something strange about that boat?" Kestrel's rain-soaked braids swung as she paced the cabin, flinging tiny droplets every time she turned. Long hair was a liability on board a ship. Instead of cutting it off, she twisted it into dozens of tiny braids, tying them all back in a queue when she was done. Any other time, she would have taken her hair down to dry it out properly, but in her current mood, she'd probably end up ripping half of them off her head. "Leave it alone, that's what I said, but oh no, you had to go and get his attention."

Binns offered her a cup full nearly to brimming with black rum. "Have a drink, there's a good lass. Drink up, and we'll think this through."

"Oh, now we'll think this through? You just shot at a magus of some kind. He could've turned you into a turtle."

With his free hand, Binns reached over his shoulder and patted his back. "Nope, no shell there."

"Artemus! It's not just your life we're talking about."

He shoved the cup in front of her again. "Drink, Kes. No harm's come of it, and you bein' so frighted will only upset the others."

The three-master hadn't sunk; they'd have seen wreckage or survivors scattered in the water. Nor had it missed them and sped away. They would have seen it, felt the force of the upset seas in her wake as she passed by. First it was there, and in the next instant, it was gone.

The crew, when they got over the shock and regained use of their tongues, were crossing themselves and muttering oaths of protection against ghosts, demons, and any other sort of supernatural being they could come up with. It was the only time Kestrel could recall being thankful for a storm; the agitated seas and damaged sails kept the crew too busy to do more than gossip. Binns ordered Red Tom, his navigator, to take the wheel and tack them into Eldraga as soon as he could, then hustled Kestrel into his quarters, for a drink and a chat.

She took the proffered cup, and threw back a swallow of rum. She hadn't wanted a drink at all, angry as she was with her captain's foolhardy posturing against the mysterious ship. Closing her eyes and enjoying the calming feel of the liquor's warmth coursing down her throat, she had to admit it was helping, at least a little. The heat spread through her chest while the sweet fumes drifted up, filling the hollow behind her face like gentle smoke turning inside a hookah pipe. He was right—as quartermaster, the men looked to her almost as much as they did the captain. She didn't have the luxury of panic.

"I know why you're so gut-twisted. You think he was usin' magic, don't you?"

Kestrel nodded, not trusting herself to speak.

"How do you know he wasn't some sleighter?"

"Sleight of hand, at that distance?" She scowled at the memory. "Blew me a bloody kiss."

"Ah, lass, that proves my point. He knew good and well we were all lookin'—we'd fired on him. He lucked up on you bein' at the scope at the right moment." He shrugged. "You think the lad was Danisoban."

The very word sent an icy chill through her heart.

"I heard they can't be so close to the sea. And I've sure never seen one on my ocean." He sighed heavily. "Any chance he might be one like you?"

One like her. A Promise. What the magi called children with magic abilities. All taken by the age of four or five, trained up and set loose on the world as the vicious, coldhearted Brethren. The Danisobans never let a Promise slip through their fingers.

For as long as she could remember, Kestrel had been able to control the air around her. If she needed a breeze, or wanted to move things without touching them, she'd tap out a simple rhythm, dance, whistle . . . all of it called up the power. She used her abilities as little as possible. The magi had ways of detecting such power, and might come looking for her. And even if they didn't notice her, she lived among pirates, men who were known for their readiness to sell out a comrade for the right price. Binns was the only one aboard ship who knew what she was, what she could do.

Could it be? As far as Kestrel knew, she was the only one to ever escape the clutches of the Danisobans. She'd spent years praying for a companion, someone who understood the burden. Ordinary street urchins had come and gone, in her years living in the dark places of Eldraga, but never anyone who could do the things she could do. She'd given up wishing long ago. The chance of there being another . . . it was too much to hope for. And too painful to continue talking about.

"Firing on a ship so big . . . it wasn't the smartest thing you've ever done, you do know that."

Binns was pouring himself another cupful; he offered the bottle, but she shook her head. A little went a long way, especially when there was still work to be done. He replaced the stopper and put the bottle in his sea chest, which was standing open at the foot of the tiny bed.

The captain sat down on his mattress, took a long pull at the cup, and nodded. "You're right. I'm not as young as I used to be, but I keep takin' a young man's risks." He ran a hand through his rain-darkened gray hair. "Maybe I should retire by year's end. Leave piracy to someone younger and smarter."

"And what would you do?" Only minutes ago, she'd been ready to chastise him like a fishwife for endangering the *Wolfshead* so rashly. In the nearly two years since she joined his crew, Kestrel had come to admire her captain's energy and tenacity. Binns was always the first one up in the morning, and the last to settle down, never asking more of his men than he was willing to give himself. Hearing the word "retire" slip from his lips wasn't what she'd expected at all. It was as if the mere word had raised a curtain from her eyes, and now she saw her captain for what he was—a man well past his prime and feeling the years weighing on his back. She shivered, not liking the image a bit. "Sailoring is all you know."

He raised a finger to his mouth, as if to shush her. "I've kept a secret or two from you, my girl."

"And you're choosing now to share them?" she snorted.

Binns tilted his head, gazing at her with a look she couldn't name, as if he was searching her face for something that wasn't there. The sudden scrutiny was bringing the hairs up on her arms. What was he looking for? She was about to reach out and push him, anything to break the stare, when he blinked, shook his head, and grinned at her in the usual way.

"Nah, not yet. Maybe after this season's over."

She smacked him gently. "That isn't fair."

"See, I knew you were curious." He chuckled. "All right, here's something you've never known about me. I never told anyone, but before I went on the account, I was a barkeeper on Bix. A damn fine one, according to my customers. And I got that job after apprenticin' to a brewmaster when I was a wee pip." He puffed his chest out, and held the rum cup up as if making a toast. "I could have made an honest living, on land with a roof over my head."

So many evenings they'd spent together, drinking and talking, and he'd never told her about his youth. She wondered why it had never occurred to her to ask. Kestrel sat down on the deck, crossed her legs, and placed her cup in front of her. "But the call of the sea was too strong for you?"

"Nah, 't wasn't like that at all." He relaxed, leaning his elbows onto his knees. She noticed the lines on his face—when had they gotten deeper? Even the hair on his hands and arms had grayed.

She shook her head, trying to push away the age she saw hanging on her friend. *If he starts telling me where to hold the wake when he's gone,* she thought, *I'll box his ears. Even if it does mean a flogging later.* It wasn't something she wanted to think about. Not now.

"The girl had taken sick that week," he said, his face lost in the memory. "Master Burgan was gone on a trip to Eldraga—he was a merchant, owned the pub on the side. I had to handle the bar by myself three nights runnin'. At closin' time on the third evenin', I tossed the last drunkard out and hid the day's take under a board in the storeroom, same as I always did, then locked up and walked to the room I rented. During the night, someone stole the money." He crooked his mouth into a wry smile. "Me bein' so busy, working alone those three days, I figure the thief must've watched me for a while, learnt my ways. He knew just where to look. Didn't even break the lock on the door when he picked it open."

"Did they catch him?"

"They thought they had." He shook his head. "Around about dawn, I'm wakened by stompin' feet on the stairs. I'm still blinkin' the sleep out of my eyes when they kick in my door, haul me out of bed, and toss me in a cell. A whole day longer before I even found out what I was accused of doin'." He tossed back the last of his rum, and rolled the empty cup between his hands, back and forth. "Never got a proper trial. I was dragged before the magistrate, declared guilty, and sentenced, all before I could offer a word in my own defense. They bustled me onto a ship, chains 'round my hands and feet, bound for the Continent to mine salt."

Kestrel's eyes widened in surprise. "You've seen the Continent?" she asked in amazement. "And you never told me about it?"

"Never told you because I never got there. Nearly a week out from Bix, Flingo Naile waylaid us. He killed most of the guards and gave all us that was left, guards and prisoners alike, the choice." He shrugged. "Join his crew and adopt their goals as our own, or be killed where we stood. Some of the others fussed and cried that they weren't criminals, but I actually didn't mind so much. In the days we'd been aboard the ship, I'd come to love the smell of the ocean and the rolling deck under my feet. Being locked up had been the worst thing that ever happened to me in all my short life, and Naile boardin' us seemed like a miracle from the gods. Sure, I'd be an outlaw, but accordin' to the authorities, I was one already. I didn't see that workin' for Naile could be any worse of a death sentence than minin' salt, and at least I'd be under the open sky."

The wind whistled, a lonely sound punctuating their lulled conversation. Binns was staring at his empty cup, his face far away and lost in a past that he could never reclaim. Kestrel dropped her gaze to the cup on the floor, not wanting to give in to the emotion that threatened to rush over her. He'd thought about this for a long while, that much was clear. The question wasn't whether he'd retire, only when. She was already missing him, but this wasn't the time for tears. "What'll you do, then?"

"Been considerin' that very question," he said. "I have a bit of coin squirreled away."

"Do you now?" she asked, thankful for the chance to tease him. "You've not been holding out on us, have you? Keeping more than your share?"

"No, lass. I've just had a few independent opportunities along the way. P'raps I'll share some o' them stories next time." He scratched the knuckles of one hand absently. "Thought I might open a little pub on the docks somewhere. That way I could keep my eye on you sea rats."

"So where's this pub of yours to be, old man?"

Binns chuckled softly. "Well, I daresay not on Bix."

She joined him in his laughter. As it died away, she got to her feet. "Thanks for the drink, and the tale," she said, handing him her empty cup.

"You feelin' better now, lass?" he asked, squinting at her.

"I suppose. That ship could still be out there, waiting for us to let our guard down."

"Aye, that it could. Could be they're aimin' at us right now, lookin' to blow us out of the water. But what's the use in frettin'? What's comin' is comin', and what's not is not. Worryin' about it before it happens only tires a man's brain." He set the two cups on the floor and stood up. "On decks with you. Eldraga is waitin' for us."

Kestrel nodded. "Aye, Captain." She trudged out of the cabin, ahead of Binns.

The sky was clearing. Every so often, a star peeked out from the wind-chased clouds above them. The air was flavored with the sharp, clean tang of rain, but the downfall had ceased and the waves were calming.

Unlike most sailors, Kestrel didn't believe in sea monsters—they always turned out to be whales and squids, seen through the sun-blinded gaze of men too long at sea. As for ghost ships, maybe they roamed the oceans and maybe they didn't, but the only ghosts that had a grip on her were the specters of memory and loss.

She barely remembered her parents. They'd been murdered, leaving her orphaned, before she was five years old. Living on the streets, she'd learned to protect herself, to be wary of anyone who stepped too close. There hadn't been time to fear much of anything. Except the Danisoba Magi.

Kestrel scanned the dark water to either side of the sloop, but the only thing in sight was the distant glimmer of the harbor at Eldraga. A frisson ran down her back—she could feel his eyes still on her. Pursing her lips, she whistled softly, a song she'd often heard in the pubs but never learned the words for.

She always half expected to see blue lightning running along her arms whenever she tried her tricks. Tiny needles of power tickled her skin. Her feet tingled, and she felt the breeze playing at the loose hairs close to her face. She raised a hand, brushing her fingers toward Eldraga. The wind changed direction, strengthened. It filled the remaining sails, pushing the battered ship toward the far-away glow. Kestrel heaved a sigh. As much as it scared her, magic was useful now and then. Too bad that it came at such a price she'd never be able to use it in the open. She'd never tried anything stronger than a soft whistle, for fear of what might happen. Or who might notice.

Now that the storm had cleared, the seas were clear from horizon to horizon. No huge ship lurking anywhere. *I don't know where you went, and I'm not even sure what you are*, she thought, *but I know you're out there. Magic at your fingertips or not, you'd best stay away from this ship. You're not the only one with tricks up your sleeve.*

Binns was speaking quietly with Red Tom, their heads close together. The breeze ruffled his hair, and he looked up, catching Kestrel's eye.

"Wind's changed, Tom. And I have a feeling my quarter's ready for shore leave," he said, grinning.

Looking at him, his face half-lit by the hooded lantern, she could easily imagine him tapping kegs, rubbing a gleaming bar with a cloth, and holding court over a smoky room until the wee hours. But the look he'd given her before revealing his secret ambition was still bothering her.

A secret or two, he'd said. She thought she knew him inside and out, better than anyone else on the seas or the land. She'd even trusted him enough to share her own secret, one that, if it became common knowledge, would result in a fate worse than mere dying. He'd proved worthy of her trust. But if the strange way he'd stared at her was any indication, he was holding his most dangerous secret back. She just hoped he wouldn't wait too long to share it.

Three

It is an ancient Mariner
And he stoppeth one of three,
"By thy long gray beard and glittering eye
Now wherefore stopp'st thou me?"
                —SAMUEL TAYLOR COLERIDGE

Trimming the sails, the *Wolfshead* slowed as she entered Eldraga harbor. It was a huge, deep water lagoon, surrounded
by the embrace of the Spits, long arms of land that wrapped in a
wide curve forming a protective wall. A dozen other ships of various allegiances were anchored already. Eldraga, being the largest
and busiest trading port in the Nine Islands, existed under a flag of
truce. All were welcome, whether merchant or pirate, but enmities
had to be left outside the boundaries of the island.

The water, stained golden pink from the rising sun, was dotted
with small rowboats ferrying men to and fro. In between the rowboats and the bigger ships, mastheads rose from the surface of
the harbor like flagpoles, the only evidence that remained of
ships whose histories had ended in this harbor, whether by the
fury of storms or the mischief of men. Kestrel carefully maneu-
vered between them, choosing a spot and giving the order to
weigh anchor.

The shore was studded with docks, most of them busily
crowded with landbound merchants doing illicit business with the
pirates under cover of darkness. According to the law, buying
goods from anyone who didn't wear a merchant's mantle was pun-
ishable by heavy fines and sometimes even public flogging, but it
went on just the same. Once, when he was thoroughly in his cups,
Binns claimed the king himself had purchased the occasional trinket

from him. Whether it was true or not, Kestrel didn't know, but she wouldn't have been a bit surprised.

Once the *Wolfshead* was solidly anchored, Kestrel gave the order to drop sail. The deck crew sprang to obey. The sooner they were done, the sooner they could make ready to go ashore. Three men had already volunteered to stay aboard this first night. They'd be busy stitching the tears in the sails, stowing cargo that had been shaken loose, and inspecting the lines for problems no one caught the first time. It wasn't the favored job, having to wait a whole day while their crewmates were in the taverns carousing, but they received an extra share for their willingness. Kestrel had three others lined up to spell them the next night. No one would feel completely cheated of his shore leave.

A few sudden catcalls caught her attention. Kestrel turned to see what was going on and choked back a laugh. Shadd lumbered out of the hold, waving a hand back to whoever remained below. His wild hair was sticking out around his head, curls exploding in every direction, the usual result of washing without benefit of a combing. He'd scrubbed the gunpowder shadow off his face, beard, and hands, and he was wearing a bright blue shirt and a purple satin doublet over yellow breeches. He looked behind him, grinning at the whistles that still echoed from the hold. "Just remember this later, when all the ladies are hangin' on my arms and ignoring you filthy beggars."

Binns's master gunner was one of the biggest men Kestrel had ever seen, and the hairiest. Most of the sailors kept their hair in tarred pigtails for convenience, but never Shadd. Thick, curling golden locks covered his head in a mass of tangles that only got combed out and washed during shore leave, and then only because it made the tavern wenches happy to do it. Well over six feet and with the bulk to match, she'd always been surprised that he didn't suffer from the close quarters of the ship.

Kestrel planted her hands on her hips, speaking slowly so as to avoid laughing out loud. "You're looking comely. Where did you get your hands on such a splendid set of clothes?"

"Traded for 'em, on Pecheta." He stopped in front of her, extended his arms, and rotated his body. "Ain't I the lordly gentleman?"

"Indeed, you are, Shadd my lad," she agreed. "But your hair could do with some attention."

He grinned, pulling a huge fishbone comb from his pocket and holding it out to her. "I was savin' that job for you."

"I'd have to be out of my wits. Who can tell what's nesting in that mop?"

Shadd slid the comb back into his pocket, pouting dramatically, but Kestrel couldn't miss the twinkle in his eye. "Ye don't know what ye're missin', lass. There's ladies in port be waitin' in line for the chance to run their hands into m' hair."

Shadd was a popular man on Eldraga, especially among the wenches of Camberlin's Inn. It would take much more than the previous night's fright to stop him from donning his finery and going ashore to visit them. And he wasn't the only one—most of the gunners, having secured the heavy cannons during the storm, were now emerging on deck, washed and dressed in the motley assortment of finery they'd managed to acquire from past conquests. Stripes and plaids mixed with bright silks and linens; under the bright morning sun, the combinations they made were almost painful to the eye.

After setting the wind the night before, Kestrel had stolen a quick opportunity to change into dry breeches and a red silk shirt, with generous sleeves and ruffles at the neck. She'd pulled her boots back on, and taken her hair out of its braids so it could dry out completely. The tight waves left by the braiding made her long black hair feel soft as a cloud as it tumbled over her shoulders. As lovely as it felt, she couldn't go out on decks with her hair loose, so she tied it back into a tail with a bit of leather lace. She almost wished she felt comfortable wearing a dress into town.

The surest way to start trouble on the ship was to let the men remember she was a woman, even if for only a moment. It had taken her most of the last two years to prove herself as one of them, working twice as hard as any one of them did just to reach some semblance of equality. Now that she had it, she wouldn't risk losing that power. On the ship she stuck with breeches and billowy shirts that hid her feminine shape. Besides, she'd never really been comfortable in skirts—all that material sliding in between the feet and hanging heavily from the waist made her feel slow and ungainly.

"Come by Camberlin's, later," Shadd urged her, putting his comb away. "Olympia'll want to chat ye up, see how ye're doin', and all." He grinned. "But make it a good bit later, since I'm of a mind to keep her busy."

"Get away with you. Tell me too much, and you'll make me sorry I ever introduced you to my friend."

He sauntered away, gathering his gun crew around him as they headed for the rope ladder being lowered. Several hackney boats had already pulled up alongside the *Wolfshead,* their rowers crying out for customers to pile in and be taken to the docks. Kestrel watched Shadd and his fellows disappear over the railing. As she turned back to her duties, she heard them begin singing, a rousing tune about ale and blood and a rolling chariot. Apparently there were three or four different melodies, each man attempting to howl his chosen tune louder than his companions. More of the crew was arriving on deck now, joining the musical fray as Shadd and his men rowed away. *Maybe they can't sing like angels,* she thought, *but you'd never convince them of that. And they certainly do make up for it in enthusiasm.*

"All right then, Quartermaster, what's the damage?"

Binns had apparently been in his cabin cleaning up as well. He'd slicked his hair back into a tidy, gleaming gray ponytail. He was wearing his red silk breeches, his best black boots, a black silk tunic, and a purple and red brocade frock coat he'd picked up two seasons ago. He held a black leather hat in one hand, and was attaching long, fluffy red and purple feathers to the crown with the other.

"Well, you're the dandy indeed," Kestrel said. "Up 'til now I thought Shadd had you beaten."

Finally getting the feathers where he wanted them, Binns

dropped the hat on his head and struck a pose. "Never, my dear."
He straightened. "Let's have the ill news."

"Not so bad as I first feared." She pointed forward. "There's
tearing in the jib and fore topsail, but they're not unmendable.
Dreso says he and his men'll have it stitched up by morning. We
lost a bit of line, and as far as I can tell, only one barrel of our fresh
water was tainted. We could do with a few crates of biscuit, maybe
a keg or two of rum to tide us over. Other than that, we came
through the storm fair decent."

"Good, good." Leaning closer, he whispered, "Any palaver about
ghosts this fine morning?"

"Not a word. I saw Dreso passing out luck pendants to the other
two staying on board with him tonight." She shrugged. "No more
reaction than that, so I count us lucky." Knowing how close sailors
held their superstitions, she was surprised the crew had cast off
their fears so easily. Maybe it had all happened too fast. More likely
it had been the lure of shore leave.

"Excellent!" The captain rubbed his hands together, then bent
his arm, offering it to her. "In that case, may I invite you to accompany me to the docks, my dear?"

She glanced around her at the nearly deserted decks. The last
boatload of pirates was loading, and only Dreso and his companions remained, watching their fellows with envious eyes and paying
no attention to their captain and quartermaster. She smiled, and
inclined her head toward Binns. "After you, Captain."

Bowing low, she swept an arm out for him to precede her to the
waiting ladder. A hackney boat with the last few crewmen waited
below, bobbing gently, bumping against the *Wolfshead*'s sides.
Binns threw a leg over the rail, and climbed down. Kestrel glanced
over the deck once more. She stopped suddenly, her heart leaping
into her throat.

The ship from the night before was tacking slowly into the harbor. It was even more garishly red in the light of day, and the eye
seemed to wink at her as the ship moved over the water. She was a
good ways away, far enough that her crew seemed like black ants

crawling over her decks, but Kestrel shuddered, remembering the touch of the strange man's gaze in the dark. Was he chasing them? Had he followed them here for some nefarious purpose? Or was it all the greatest of coincidences? She stared, trying, even though she knew it was impossible from this distance, to see if she could pick him out from the other tiny black specks. Somehow she couldn't believe that anything about that ship and her captain could have anything to do with coincidence.

"Come on, lass, get a move on," Binns called from the boat. Kestrel swallowed the lump in her throat, and climbed down the rope ladder. Reaching the end, she hopped, surefooted, into the waiting boat and sat down, leaning forward to try to catch a glimpse of the newcomer.

The rowers pushed off, and began pulling their oars through the water. Binns touched her hand. "What's the matter, my girl?" he asked, his concern plain. "Your face is whiter'n a new-bought sail."

"That ship, the red monster," she muttered. "From last night."

"Aye, what of it?"

"It's here."

Binns turned in the direction she pointed, his eyes widening. "Well, so it is." He smiled, patting her hand and sitting back up straight. "Guess that proves it isn't a ghost."

"I never thought it was," she said. "Why is it here, though?"

"Could be her captain needs a few things after survivin' that storm, just like we ourselves." He shook his head. "All ships stop in Eldraga, lass, sooner or later. Don't worry yourself so." He puffed out his chest. "P'raps we'll even meet the young pup. You'd like that, now, wouldn't you?" He let out a hearty laugh at the shocked and indignant look on her face. "Come on, Kes, sing with me."

She raised her eyebrows. Whistling was dangerous enough— she'd never been brave enough to actually sing a song out loud. "Are you wanting to add a few vessels to the bottom of this harbor?"

"One of these days, my girl, you'll be singin' loud enough to change the world." He winked at her. "Sure you don't want to join in? I'll bet we can even overpower yon gunners if we try." He launched into the rollicking song the other boatload of men had been singing.

Kestrel smiled but didn't join in. She couldn't help the feeling they were rowing into a trap.

BY the time they finished their negotiations at the dockmaster's office, she'd almost convinced herself to relax. So the magus was anchored in the same harbor they were. Why should she fear? It was a big island, and the chance they'd run into each other at all was a small one. The *Wolfshead's* sails would be stitched up clean by tomorrow, one more night on shore, and they'd be well away from here before the magus even knew they were gone. Even if they did somehow meet up, what could he possibly do to them here on Eldraga? Peace was the law, and it was kept no matter what the cost.

Binns spent nearly half an hour in heated discussion with the dockmaster, an ancient curmudgeon who drove a viciously hard bargain. When the smoke cleared, Binns had paid out four gold octavos in exchange for two nights' anchorage. "Four octavos," he murmured to his quartermaster as they were leaving the office. "And they call *me* a pirate?" He looked up and down the streets, then clapped his hands. "So, lass, where shall we visit first?"

Kestrel drew a long breath, savoring the odd mixture of tar, seasoned wood, and low tide muck that always permeated the docks. Even she couldn't claim it was a pleasant odor, but no matter what harbor she was in, it always smelled like home to her.

The market had opened shortly after sunrise; people were still running back and forth from ships to the street, carrying loads of goods for the eager buyers, yelling to announce their presence. Her heart quickened at the sight of the riches being traded. Being a pirate had opened her eyes to so many exciting treasures, fabulous jewelry, and rich foodstuffs, all hers for the taking. But whenever the chance to visit the market came up, no plunder could compare.

Growing up in the muck-filled alleys of Eldraga, she and the other castoff children had devised ways to steal what they needed—

an apple off the fruit cart, bread from the baker. They never took more than they could easily carry, nor so much that the merchants might complain to the guard. It was an unspoken rule—take only enough food to keep from starving, and leave the trinkets behind. Even if she did have the ability to snatch things from a distance.

But every now and then, Kestrel would sneak away from her cronies and wander through the stalls and carts, hiding in the shadows as she admired the fabrics and tapestries, filling her lungs with the heady scents of spices and incense. She would watch, envious, as shoppers opened fat purses, trading gold coins for the shining treasures she could never own. And she promised herself—one day, she would have a purse with coins in it. She would buy things just because they pleased her eye while the merchants climbed over each other to gain her custom.

That had been so long ago, and things were better for her now. She didn't have to waste her hard-earned coin. Almost everything she could purchase in the market could be gotten, without cost, from the ripe merchant ships they plundered on a regular basis. That didn't make a difference. It wasn't about possessing the things she bought. Hunting through the carts and booths, digging around to see what fantastic prize she might discover, up until then overlooked by all those who'd been there before her; the search was entertaining, and even somewhat satisfying. But paying for the privilege, and finally feeling respected, that was the real reward.

Her intention must have showed on her face, because her captain sighed. "You're goin' shoppin', aren't you?"

She hid the grin that threatened to pop out. "I told you a few crates of biscuit were fouled in the storm. And we could do with a bit more rum." She wiggled the hilt of her sword. "And I thought I'd drop by Jack's, see what new blades he's come up with since last year."

He nodded, making the brightly colored feathers on his hat bounce merrily. "I'll leave you to it, then. Had a bit of walkin' around I wanted to do myself. Shall we meet up this evening for supper?"

Kestrel thought for a second. No sense suggesting Camberlin's.

Since the night they met, Binns refused to set foot in the place. "Bad luck is too easily awakened when you go back to where you last saw it," he always said. She'd have to take time to visit Olympia Camberlin while she was on her own.

"How about the Cup o' Gold?" she finally suggested.

Binns nodded his approval. "Fine choice. We can get rooms there as well." He swept his hat from his head and dropped a low bow. "I'll see you at dusk, my girl." Replacing his hat, he strode away, waving left and right as if he was some wealthy noble surveying his holdings.

Kestrel watched him until he had blended into the crowd, then turned toward Market Street, joining the throng making its way to the colorful stalls and the treasures they contained within. The street was crowded with people, buying, selling, and browsing. The well-monied merchants owned space inside the Markethouse, a breezeway constructed of marble bricks running the length of the street. Every few yards the wall was broken by arched doorways, letting customers step in and out as they needed. Despite the openings, it offered cover on the rainiest days. Less well-to-do businessmen set up tented stalls on the outer edge of the street, while bakers and pickle sellers pushed carts up and down, weaving their way through the crowd and crying their wares for anyone who'd stop them.

Everywhere she looked, it seemed she was surrounded by the treasures of legend. Gems of every shape and color sparkled in the brilliant morning sunshine, bright green springstones, rich red drops-of-blood, midnight opals as deep purple as the last moment of a summer sunset. Bolts of Pechetan silk stood side by side with baby-soft wools from the Continent in fabulous hues, the cut ends fluttering in the morning breeze off the water. Intricately carved boxes, delicate glass bottles full of perfumes, handpainted playing cards and toys—as far as she could see, paradise itself wouldn't be able to compare with the riches surrounding her on the street.

A hand grabbed her left arm. Long fingers, bony and cold as ancient death. Kestrel's hand crossed to her sword hilt.

"None of that, now," a voice hissed. Its owner was a skeleton with tight, pasty skin, garbed in a suit of leather clothes that probably weighed half again what he did. Wisps of graying hair sprouted from his head in sickly patches. Kestrel drew back in disgust, but the creature laughed.

"You needn't fear me. What's wrong with me ain't catching." His teeth were filmed with yellow gunk, and the whiff of decay floating from his mouth made Kestrel gag.

"If it's coin you want, beggar, you'd best let go of my arm."

He leaned closer. Kestrel turned her face partway, trying to avoid the stench of him.

"No coin for me. I'm paid well enough. So if you don't mind me earning my pay," he dropped his voice to a murmur, "I've got a message for you to carry to your master."

"My master?" she asked, and laughed at the thought. "Are you talking about Binns?" Captain he was, leader and friend, but hardly her master.

The leather-clad cadaver frowned. "Keep your voice down." He tightened his grip on her wrist, pulling her up sharply. "You tell him: the blush is on the rose, but thorns have grown up 'round the foot of the mountain. Do you have it?"

She stared at him incredulously. "Are you drunk? What's that supposed to mean?"

"Not drunk yet, but plans are in motion to get me there." The tramp released his grip on her. "Don't you get drunk and forget what I said, now." Raising his long, bony fingers to his forehead, he tipped an imaginary cap to her, and faded into the crowd.

Kestrel stared at the spot where he'd been standing, then suddenly patted herself down. In a crowd like this, paying attention to one beggar the way she had was a sure and certain way to get herself robbed. Even though it was already tied in the special knot she'd learned would thwart most pickpockets, no knot in the world could hold against a passing cutpurse's blade.

The purse hung at her waist, still heavy with coin. So he hadn't been a thief. She blew out a frustrated breath. Just a tramp. Must have seen her come ashore with Binns, and thought he could play a game with her. She grinned. Binns would enjoy the story tonight, over mugs of ale.

Kestrel stopped at a baker's cart, and purchased two nut pastry squares, each one sticky with honey. She had him wrap one in several layers of paper, and tucked it carefully in her pouch. The other she nibbled as she strolled, careful to lick her fingers clean after every bite. It wouldn't do to have some merchant screaming that she'd ruined his offerings with her honeyed touch.

She swallowed the last bite, sighing as it went down. *Nothing that tasty on board ship,* she thought. Turning, she headed down the street toward Gentleman Jack's Armory. She'd known Jack since her days working the tables at Camberlin's—he always treated her squarely.

The crowd thickened, slowing her progress. She glanced around, keeping a sharp eye on anyone standing especially close to her, and tightened her hold on the purse at her side.

Out of the corner of her eye, she saw a quick flap of fabric. Not an unusual sight in a marketplace, where bolts of cloth were bought and sold continuously, but for some reason, the movement drew her gaze. She stopped, staring in shock.

It can't be, she tried to tell herself. But there he was, clear as the morning sky. The handsome captain of the red ghost ship. Close up like this, he looked even less like the usual Danisoban. Too well dressed, for one thing, with a hardy color in his cheeks that implied time spent in the sun. Magi preferred the shadows of their ateliers, rarely venturing out-of-doors. Then again, the Danisobans never went to sea, either.

He was standing on the opposite side of Market Street, the river of people separating them as surely as any real one could. Somehow, among the hundreds of people around them, he'd recognized her. He was looking directly at her, a sardonic half grin twisting his mouth and emphasizing his sharp-cut cheekbones. He raised his hand, and touched his finger to his lips suggestively, as he had done the night before.

Her heart pounded, a frightened bird trying to free itself from the cage of her ribs. The air was suddenly thick, hard to draw in, and dizziness threatened to overcome her. It was a spell, it had to be. She'd been right all along. But she didn't have time to crow about it. Tearing her eyes away from his, she licked her dry lips and whistled a sharp note in his direction.

Needle pricks of energy teased along her arms and scalp. Air moved around her feet, spawning tiny dust devils that swirled through the street. Kestrel sucked in more breath through her nose, and whistled again. This time, she turned her attention directly toward the man watching her.

Her whirlwind strengthened, and caught up the loose ends of fabric from the bolts to either side of him. Brightly colored silk whipped up in front of his face and wrapped, like slithering serpents, around his arms. He stumbled backward, struggling to free himself.

It was the distraction she'd hoped for. Kestrel began pushing against the crowd, fighting to get inside one of the brick archways, into the shadows and away from his sight. If he couldn't see her, he'd have a harder time casting any more evil magic her way.

Ignoring the grumbling and protests of the other folk around her, she managed to slip between bodies and finally reached the sanctuary of the somewhat less jammed brick Markethouse. She blinked at the change of light, but chanced to look behind her. The throng had reasserted itself, moving in fits and starts as it had before. The man was nowhere to be seen.

"Fresh tubers, mistress?"

Kestrel's heart jumped into her throat at the unexpected voice. She turned, her hand on her sword. A plain-faced man was smiling at her. He was dressed in loose-fitting dun trousers, with a long-sleeved tunic belted over. A farmer, if she was going to lay money on his occupation. He waved a hand at the vegetable booth behind him. "Finest produce you'll see all day."

"Sorry. I'm not buying." She shot another look toward the street.

"Are you looking for someone? Haven't lost a child, have you?" The man was persistent, but most merchants were.

"I'm quite all right," she said. "Good luck with your booth." The fabric bolts seemed to have settled down, but the man was gone. Time for her to be gone as well. She quick-stepped as best she could down the coolness of the shaded breezeway. She'd get to Jack's, buy what she needed, and head for Camberlin's. If anyone could tell her who the mysterious man was, it would be Olympia Camberlin.

Four

This riddling tale, to what does it belong?
Is't history? Vision? Or an idle song?

—SAMUEL TAYLOR COLERIDGE

Kestrel reached Jack's safely, despite the ominous feeling of being watched that made her spine twist the entire way. Once inside the armory, she spent a relaxing hour discussing with Jack what she needed and how much she was willing to pay for it. At the end of their time, she left a deposit of three octavos on a new *sinistre*, a short blade designed for fighting double-handed. It was balanced to match her fighting style perfectly. Jack assured her he would work the night through if necessary, to have it ready for her by sunset the following day.

It was just past midday, and her stomach was rumbling. She cast a thought toward the pastry wrapped in her pocket. Perhaps she could share a meal with Olympia while she dug for any gossip about a new magus in town. As long as Shadd wasn't keeping her too busy.

Camberlin's was the most popular public house on Eldraga. Freshly painted every year after spinstorm season, it was a bright blue and white two-story house, its glass windows covered from within by genteel lace curtains. Situated at one end of Market Street, the house loomed like a palace, drawing visitors from all walks of life. Some came for the rousing musical shows, some to try their luck at the numerous gaming tables, and not a few fancied the companionship of the Camberlin Wenches, known throughout the Nine Islands as the loveliest and most accommodating ladies of pleasure one could hope to find.

"Well, well, well, look what the wind's blown our way!"

A tall man, dark of hair and eye, with a vicious scar running from temple to cheek, stood before the swinging doors of the house. He was dressed in black leather armor, studded in various places with dull steel. An assortment of blades were sheathed on his legs, arms, and hip, and in one hand, he held a long, wickedly pointed pike. "If the sun hasn't blinded my tired old eyes, then I have to say it's my darlin' Kestrel! Where's my kiss, lovey?" He opened his arms wide, letting the pike rest in the crook of his elbow.

"Ahoy, Sabas, you always greet your friends with your big pike showing?"

Lean and well muscled Sabas had guarded the door to Camberlin's for as long as Kestrel could recall. The pike was a prop. Let a fight break out, and the long polearm would be tossed aside in favor of one of the many smaller, sharper blades he kept hanging from his person.

"You call this big?" He stood the pike against the wall behind him. "I've got a much better weapon I can show you upstairs in me chambers." He wiggled his eyebrows lasciviously. "If you're of a mind to play with it, that is."

Kestrel laughed, letting him sweep her into a crushing hug that nearly took her off her feet. "So, where's your mistress, Sabas?" she asked as soon as he'd put her back down.

He waved a hand toward the bright room past him. "Holding court as always. You want I should announce you?"

Kestrel shook her head. "Not this time. Shadd beat me here already, I reckon?"

"Aye, you should 'a seen it! He does nothing but walk in the door. At sight of him, Olympia prances and jigs like a drop of water on a hot iron skillet." Sabas's eyes twinkled merrily as he swept his arm wide, pushing open the door for her. "Actually, I think he's in the bath right now. You can likely get an audience with our lady."

Striding into the main room, Kestrel paused to let her eyes adjust. Standing on the raised hearth were two musicians, playing something rousing on drum and lute. The room was crowded with finely dressed gentlemen and raggedy sailors alike, some pounding their mugs on the wooden tables in time with the music, and others dancing or flirting with the wenches. Against the back wall stood the bar. It was almost twenty feet long and four feet wide, made of dark, lustrous wood and covered in writhing, lifelike carvings of serpents and beasts only spoken of in legend. Olympia liked to tell people that it had once been a church altar, stolen long ago from the Temple of the Nameless Lord on the island of Cre'esh before the Great Cataclysm.

Behind it were kegs of various ales and wines propped on stands, each bearing a label listing its name and place of origin in the four most common languages of the Islands. On top of the bar, at the far right end where it met the side wall, stood a massive chair, made of the same dark wood. Bloodred velvet covered the seat, back, and arms, and similar carvings danced over the exposed portions.

Olympia Camberlin was relaxing in her throne atop the bar, a drink in her hand and a pleased expression on her pretty face. Her daintily crossed feet peeked out from beneath layers of skirts. Her long chestnut hair, streaked with strands of silver that in no way detracted from her charm, draped in silky waves over her bared shoulders, her chemise pulled low for maximum effect, as usual. She was tapping her wooden mug in time with the music, but her eyes were sleepy, and she hadn't so much as glanced toward the door.

Olympia had been a country girl once, the daughter of a MelaDoana farmer, until her sparkling smile and tight-laced bodice caught not only the eye of Forbert Camberlin, lord of the manor, but his hand in marriage as well. When he died, leaving her a substantial fortune and a crowd of vengeful, would-be heirs, Olympia sold the land holdings and moved to Eldraga, opening her successful inn and living happily ever since. She'd been Kestrel's savior when the *Candela's* captain beached her.

Back then, she'd been serving aboard the merchant ship *Candela* in the guise of a young boy. When the quartermaster found out her secret, he'd offered her a choice—warm his bed or be tossed to the sharks. She pretended to go along with him, letting him hustle her to his small cabin. But as soon as his breeches were down to his ankles, she drove a knee into his manhood, followed by a hard fist to his jaw. The quartermaster's howling brought the watch running. Before she knew what was what, she was standing in the captain's cabin, being berated for her duplicity.

Women aboard ship were considered ill luck. Even female passengers received the blame for everything from sudden storms to maggoty biscuits. No merchant ever hired a female sailor. Though she'd managed to do her share of the work well, the *Candela's* captain had made no exception. He put her ashore as soon as they reached Eldraga. The story spread like wildfire among the crews in port, effectively wiping out her chances of working aboard any other merchant vessels.

She'd been down to her last few coins when she met Olympia Camberlin. With no other prospects in sight, Kestrel came to the gut-wrenching decision that she had only one thing left to sell. She demanded an audience with the madame of Camberlin's and begged for a job. Olympia, perhaps recognizing the seawater in Kestrel's veins, refused to put her to work on her back. She hired Kestrel to work behind the bar instead. It had been an equitable arrangement, saved her from starvation, and Kestrel never missed a chance to show her gratitude.

She sidled to the right-hand wall, and crept along it, staying out of Olympia's direct line of sight. She stopped a few feet away. Crouching down, she pulled out a small parcel from her bag, and slipped it into the pocket of her breeches. She removed the honey and nut pastry, unwrapped it, and placed it in the palm of her hand.

"My, my, my," she said, rising to her feet again, "look at this treat I brought all the way from town for Mistress Camberlin. And she can't even spare me a glance! Guess I'll have to eat it myself."

Olympia's head whipped around, her eyes alert and her body straightening. "Kes!" she shrieked. She sprang to her feet, and waved her mug at the bartender, who managed to take it from her without being drenched, then lifted the hem of her dress up to her ankles. "One of you men there, come help me down! Quick now!"

At her command, two sailors drinking at a nearby table leaped to offer their hands. She was by no means a small woman, but graceful nonetheless, and with the sailors' assistance, she landed softly on her feet. Once off the bar, Olympia threw herself into Kestrel's arms, nearly knocking her over.

"Easy!" Kestrel laughed. "I'll drop this sweet I brought you."

Olympia backed away, her lip poked out in a sudden coquettish pout. "You go off to sea, become a pirate, spend the last two years divesting rich folk of their fancy gems and dresses, and all I get is a pastry?"

Kestrel grinned. Setting the pastry on the bar, she reached into her shirt and pulled out the parcel. Affecting an innocent look, she said, "Oh, you mean you'd rather have something like this?"

The pout instantly was taken over by a giggling smile, as the chestnut-haired woman took the parcel from Kestrel's hand. She unwrapped the fabric, and squealed. "It's so beautiful!" she cried, waving the pearl and ruby necklace in the air. Tossing the wrapping to the floor, she unhooked the clasp and offered the necklace to Kestrel again. "Oh, do put it on me, please."

When they first met, Olympia's wanton behavior had grated on Kestrel's nerves—her high-pitched cadence and batting eyelashes were all well and good for the gentlemen who visited her, but she couldn't fathom why Olympia spoke that way over breakfast or in the market, times when no customers were near. Eventually, Kestrel had learned it was simply Olympia being herself—flirting was as natural to her as breathing. Underneath it she was strong and capable, a born businesswoman. The veneer often threw off competitors enough to afford her the advantage in tricky negotiations.

Kestrel took the necklace and fitted the jewels around Olympia's smooth neck, snapped the clasp and patted her shoulder. "There you go. I still think the pastry was the best part."

Olympia pressed her chin down in a vain attempt to see the necklace. "Oh, pish! I can't see how it becomes me!" She pressed her fingers against the string of gems, and marched to the bar. "Billy, fetch me the glass." The bartender didn't speak, but bent down and retrieved a huge silvered platter. Setting the edge against the bar's lip, he angled the flat surface so Olympia could admire herself. She cooed as she turned one way, then another, tilting her head. "It's so beautiful!"

Her face was shining with delight as she took Kestrel by the hand. "Come on, my darling, tell me all your adventures. Billy!" she called out. "Bring ale! Bring food!" She led the way to a small, unoccupied table.

Almost immediately, mugs appeared, the tea-brown froth at the top indicating it was Camberlin's Dark, brewed in the back rooms during the storm season, when business was slow. Kestrel helped herself to a long draught, and sighed in satisfaction.

"I hear you ran afoul of a ghost ship last night."

"Shadd didn't waste any time." Kestrel took another swallow of the ale and set her mug down.

"Terrible gossip, that man. Were the ghosts all wearing bloodied sheets, moaning and howling and rattling their chains?" Olympia stage-whispered, her eyes wide.

"You have to remember, it was raining and we were being tossed and slung like a leaf on the wind. And her captain . . ." She stopped, an involuntary shiver running over her skin. "He was no ghost. A sure and certain man, that one was." If she'd had any doubt before, his sudden, unnerving appearance in the market had put those to rest. She'd seen him, in the light of day, as solid and real as she was herself. She wondered if she wouldn't have rather he'd turned out to be some phantom who dissipated with the rising of the sun.

"Shadd says it just disappeared. There one minute, gone the next."

"Shadd's right. Artie ordered a shot across her bow, just playing with her he said. But next thing we knew, she was gone. Not sunk, not running away, just gone."

Olympia wrapped her arms around herself, as if she felt a sudden chill. "So what do you think it was?"

"Here's the thing. She was a big girl, forty guns if she had one, but running no flags I've seen before. And the way her captain acted, and the fact that she's in port this very minute . . ."

"Here?" Olympia's eyebrows shot upward. "The ghost ship is here?"

"Dropped anchor this morning, on the far side of the harbor," Kestrel said. "Like I told you, she's no ghost. But I have a bad feeling I know what is going on."

Olympia crossed her arms on the table and leaned closer to her friend, all pretense gone. "And what might that be?"

Kestrel looked up. No one was near enough to overhear—the few customers were busy with their own conversations, as far as she could tell. "It's a new magus. Young, strong-bodied. And he's taken to the seas."

"I heard he's quite the charm for the eye, as well." Kestrel almost groaned at the light that sparked in Olympia's face. "Handsome sea captain, with a disappearing boat? Sounds like just the man you've been waiting for, darling."

First Binns, now Olympia. Let a fine-looking man wander by and they were all trying to match her up. If she'd let them have their way, either or both of them would have had her married off ten times already. "Didn't you hear me? He's a magus."

Olympia rolled her eyes impatiently. "I heard. I'm just wondering what his dabbling in magic has to do with anything."

Of course she wouldn't understand. She hadn't grown up in hiding from the Danisobans, afraid to use her own meager power for fear they'd locate her and take her away. Kestrel was as close to Olympia as she was with Binns, but she'd never shared that one facet of herself. Enough that Artie knew. A secret didn't remain a secret when everyone knew it, and she'd kept her secret too long to give it up so easily. Even to a trusted friend.

"His dabbling, Olympia, has everything to do with it. The Danisobans use children for their experiments! They rip families apart. And for what good reason?"

"Calm down, precious." She resettled herself, and smiled brightly. "So was he wearing a silver band on his left wrist?"

"I only saw him a couple of times, and then not up close. I wasn't looking at his arms."

Her friend's grin widened. "Too busy looking at his mighty spyglass, perhaps?"

Kestrel tightened her eyes in a deadly squint. Olympia held up both hands in mock surrender. "Easy now. I'd say that your vanishing captain couldn't be a magus, though," she said emphatically. "The magi almost never go to sea. Have you ever seen what seawater does to silver?" She grimaced. "They can't be away from their native soil. Only the most powerful ones even try ocean voyages."

"I'd think someone who could make a whole ship vanish would have to be strong, wouldn't you?"

"Any trickster can make things seem to disappear." Olympia shook her head, smiling in an irritatingly maternal way. "Powerful equals old, darling. Very old and no longer handsome."

"Maybe he's spelled himself to look young. To throw people off," Kestrel protested.

"Kes, dearest to my heart," Olympia murmured, reaching out and taking her friend's calloused hands between her own soft ones. "You saw this man? So he was on the deck, yes?" She squeezed Kestrel's hands gently. "On the extremely rare occasion that a Danisoban ships out, he has to cart along a crate of dirt to keep him healthy throughout the trip. He'll sleep on that dirt, and sit on it. But he will never, never walk around on deck. Too close to the sea. No, your fine-looking sea captain certainly sounds like he's up to something, but he's no Danisoban."

Kestrel's gut twisted with deeper fear. "What if he's a rogue? Not trained by the school but come to his power some other way? Not bound by the rules, few as they are, free to act as he pleases, menace who he wants?" *Someone like me*, she thought, despising the idea of having anything in common with the man.

Olympia put a dainty hand to her mouth. "That would be a danger," she admitted. "Who would have trained him, besides the school?"

Kestrel shrugged. The Danisobans had been awarded a charter

by the current king's grandfather, in an attempt to put a halt to the petty skirmishes between rival wizards that had been killing peasants and burning crops. They had taken their new responsibility seriously, hunting down and killing those few wizards who refused to join their ranks. No one had heard of any rogue magi for over a century. She couldn't guess how the fellow could be so accomplished, since there'd be no one to teach him the magical arts in the first place. Then again, there'd been no one to teach her. And she'd managed well enough, although she was sure she couldn't make a ship disappear. She could imagine the treatment she might receive if the Danisobans caught her. It was the stuff her nightmares were made of.

"Tell you what I'll do," Olympia said. "I'll put the word out, ask the right questions, find out if there's been any talk of a magus running away from the school or such like that. I'll have my girls keep their ears open, too. When do you ship out?"

Kestrel shrugged. "Tomorrow, the day after at the most. We just stopped long enough to mend some sail and give the boys a rest. Between the storm and that vanishing ship, they needed a bit of dry land, to get their heads turned right again."

"Olympia!"

The sudden bellow from the stairs made both women jump. Olympia smiled. "Speaking of your boys, I think one's finished with his bath." She rose. Crossing to Kestrel's side, she hugged her again. "Come by before you weigh anchor. P'raps I'll have some good information about your mystery man by then."

Kestrel ordered a drink, and found a quiet spot to enjoy the music, although she never joined in the singing, nor tapped her foot in time. Stretching her legs across the chair next to her, she took a long swallow of ale. She tried to convince herself she was in no hurry to rejoin her captain because the entertainment was of such high quality, but inside she knew she was avoiding the streets for a different reason. After an hour or two, Billy appeared at the table with a laden platter of food. It was enough to feed three sailors and still leave plenty for later. "Compliments of the house," he said with a grin. She grinned back, and helped herself to the sumptuous treats before her.

"Well, hello again!"

Kestrel glanced away from her plate. A man was standing next to her table, a man who looked vaguely familiar. Then it came to her . . . the vegetable merchant. A tankard in one hand, he was pulling back a chair with the other. Kestrel sighed. Lucky her, to have found one of those men who believe two words amount to the beginnings of romance.

"Isn't it a coincidence, us meeting again here, like this?" He settled into the chair. His mug tipped, a few drops of ale sliding over the side and trickling down his fingers. "I'm Jaeger." He wiped his hand on the front of his tunic, then held it out toward her.

"Kestrel." She nodded, keeping her own hands busy with fork and knife.

After a moment, he withdrew his hand, lifted his mug, and took a deep draught. "Beautiful day out there, wasn't it? Excepting that little windstorm that shook the market."

Kestrel's heart thumped. Had he noticed her whistling? Made the connection? She kept her eyes down.

"Didn't bother me, though, not a bit. I had a fine morning. Sold everything I brought with me." He patted the purse hanging at his side. "Certainly wouldn't mind someone to help me spend it all."

Kestrel put down her cutlery, and sighed. Such a fool, to be making so much of his full purse in public, he deserved to be robbed. *Damn me for having a soft heart.* "First time at market?"

He raised his eyebrows. "My brother Dieter usually handles the selling, but he broke his leg and couldn't come. How'd you guess?"

"You're taking an awful risk, showing off your purse. I'm surprised no one's lifted it from you already."

"You mean a pickpocket? Dieter warned me about them. That's why I hung it in front of me."

"But you didn't tie it closed. In the right crowd, a thief could easily slip the neck open and help himself to a handful of your coin.

And that lanyard you're using to tie it off is easy as butter to cut through."

He paled. "What should I do?"

Kestrel got up and joined him on his side of the table. "Take it from around your waist, and I'll show you what to do."

Jaeger loosened the smooth rope and handed it, and his purse, to her. He chuckled. "You're, uh, not going to run off with that, are you?"

She rolled her eyes. If she'd wanted to rob him, he was making it awfully simple. Lashing the ends of the rope into a tight square knot, she showed him how to close the mouth of his purse with a strangle-snare. "The harder they pull, the tighter the knot. And this bit of fluff is fine for now, but I'd recommend buying a length of something tougher in the morning. Until then . . ." She settled the circle of rope around his neck. "Drop your purse into your shirt. And leave it there."

He pulled open his collar to drop the purse inside, and something caught Kestrel's eye. A twist of color, red and blue, twining over his breastbone and ending she knew not where. Farmers weren't commonly wearers of skin etchings—sailors and soldiers were. Kestrel couldn't help a stab of curiosity, which probably showed on her face. She turned away quickly, while Jaeger covered up.

"You're very kind," he said. "Let me buy you a drink, please."

"I drink free, here. Friend of the owner." Kestrel hesitated. "I'm sure you're a pleasant enough fellow, but I'm not looking for companionship right now. I won't even be in port two nights from now."

"Sailor, are you?" Jaeger wrinkled his forehead. "But you're a woman."

"Aye," she said. "How's that for a peculiar story to take home with you?" She'd already shared too much with this stranger, innocent as he seemed. "I have to be going. Keep your purse close."

Olympia hadn't come back downstairs, so Kestrel bid Sabas farewell and stepped into the cool of the evening. The market had

long since closed down, and the crowds gone home. Shadows began to lengthen along the cobbled stones of the street, casting
eerie shapes into the nooks and side alleys. It would almost have
seemed romantic, had she someone with whom to stroll along, arm
in arm, heads close together, whispering in the way that lovers always seemed to do. Not tonight. Tonight she remembered her
childhood all too well—running with others from one merchant's
back door to the next, begging for food or coin, and avoiding the
deeper shadows in which a flesh-hunter might lurk, hoping to grab
a stray child to sell to the slavers. Or to the Danisoba Magi, for their
experiments.

The Danisoba School was located on the windward side of Eldraga, a sprawling complex of black stone buildings. Kestrel had
only ever seen the School from the safety of the *Wolfshead*'s deck.
No one visited it. Even the nobles who employed the magi on a
regular basis used a system of colored flags to summon them.

The Danisoba used their skills to locate the Promises, children
with magic potential, throughout the Nine Islands. Once a child
was found, the Factors were dispatched to take possession of the
child. The parents' feelings were of no consequence. If they gave
up their children without complaint, the Factors awarded them a
generous stipend, to help dull the impact as screaming sons and
daughters were torn from their arms. Those parents who objected
were punished. Once installed at the complex, the children didn't
leave until they had grown to adulthood.

But they were the lucky ones. After graduating, many of the
magi established workshops in town, to be close to any supplies they
might need. They had often walked the streets when Kestrel was a
girl. When a magus was about, even the deadliest cutthroat slipped
into shadows rather than be noticed. The alley children had been in
the most danger from them, being lured time and again with sweet
words and candy to follow a magus into his atelier, never to be seen
again. She'd grown up hearing the whispers about the uses to which
the stolen ones were put.

She shuddered, and laid a hand on the hilt of her sword, relishing the power that small gesture returned to her. No longer was she a defenseless little girl. So the man from the ship might be a magus. Just because he'd smiled at her twice now didn't mean he could do her any harm. He was still a man. Probably under the misconception that she was a free and easy tumble. Well and good for him. He'd have to get past her steel first. And not many men had managed that. She smiled. Maybe she'd never been the strongest of Binns's crew, but she was certainly the best with a blade. She had a natural grace and accuracy, so much so that Binns now left it to her to teach new crew members who never had experience with swords before.

Squaring her shoulders, she glanced down the quickly darkening street. *I'd better get my feet moving,* she thought, looking left and right at the pockets of shadow that now seemed no more threatening than the darkest places in the hold of her own ship. *Artie's waiting, and he'll worry if I don't step lively.* She strode forward, hand on her sword hilt, her confidence restored, and ignored the tickle on the back of her neck.

Five

And all who heard should see them there
And all should cry, Beware! Beware!
His flashing eyes! His floating hair!
—SAMUEL TAYLOR COLERIDGE

B y the time she reached the Cup o' Gold Inn, sunset had given
way to twilight, the early stars just starting to peek from the
midnight-blue of the sky. Warm light poured from the windows of
the inn, and as she neared the door, she was surrounded by the delicious aroma of roasting meat. She stepped inside, letting her eyes
adjust to the brightness and checking the room for familiar faces.

The room wasn't very crowded. A lively game of cards was going on at the largest table by the stone hearth. At another table two
men were dicing halfheartedly with a cup. The stakes couldn't have
been high—they both seemed more interested in the crowded
room than the results of their game.

Binns was leaning backward against the far end of the bar, resting on his elbows. He raised a hand in greeting when he caught
sight of his quartermaster. "Over here, my girl!" he called out, then
turned and signaled to the barman.

"Food, too!" she called, making her way over to her captain. The
barman nodded, delivering her mug and waving a hand toward the
harried serving wench.

"How was your afternoon, lass?" Binns asked nonchalantly. "See
your friends, did you?"

She took a long swallow of her ale, to keep from grinning at
him. She'd met Binns for the first time at Camberlin's. Back when
he was a regular customer.

Artemus Binns was playing cards at Camberlin's one evening almost a year after Kestrel took the job. He'd joined a game against a professional gambler who always let his marks win a few hands first. Binns had been so excited, so sure that the next hand of cards would be the winner, he'd bet his ship. He was as delighted as a child, all his attention focused on the cards in his hand. He didn't see what the dealer was up to.

But Kestrel had. The cardsharp was taking advantage of the pirate's excitement to switch cards from his sleeve to his hand. It wasn't her problem, and she certainly knew better than to involve herself in anyone else's hardship. Something about the situation rankled her. Maybe it was the sweetness in the older man's expression, or maybe the fact that no one had ever stood up for her. For whatever reason, she found herself sneaking behind the dealer. With a cry, she pretended to trip, and dropped her mug of ale over his shoulder and into his lap. He leaped to his feet, flinging cards everywhere and exposing the fraud.

Binns had been more than grateful. "I'd have been left stranded on the docks, watching my sloop sail into the sunset without me," he'd declared. "Tell me what I can do to show you my gratitude."

She hadn't hesitated. "Take me with you." At his shocked expression, she rushed to explain. "I'm as good a sailor as any man on board. Give me a chance."

Pirates, it seemed, didn't hold the same superstitions about women on ships. It hadn't been easy at first—pirates were a more accepting lot, but they were, for the most part, still men. She'd managed to fight off the tickles and grabs, proving herself first to the crew and then to the captain. Over the last two seasons, she'd managed to become not only quartermaster, but Binns's trusted confidante.

Having narrowly escaped losing possession of the *Wolfshead*, Binns decided he'd tempted fate close enough. He convinced himself that by so much as setting foot inside Camberlin's, he would gain fate's undivided attention, and it would take the opportunity to grab the ship it had been cheated out of by Kestrel's quick thinking.

He hadn't even walked past the place on the same side of the street since that night. He tried to pretend it didn't matter to him, but he never missed a chance to ask how things were at that end of Market Street.

"Everyone's fine. Sabas said he's got some time in the morning, if you'd care to share a drink and a chat." Kestrel elbowed him in the ribs. "I'll bet Olympia would let you have a romp with the girls at no cost, if you go by and ask."

Binns squinted, tilting his head as if he was thinking ahead to the next day. "Temptin' offer, that. Olympia's a fine woman, very generous. But I fear I won't have the time to dally. All that work to do on the ship, and us without even one prize in our hold as yet." He tsked, and shook his head sadly. "Maybe next time we're in port."

Same thing he said every time. Kestrel grinned into her ale, and said nothing.

The serving girl swung out of the kitchen, platters arranged along her slender arms. She stopped by the two pirates. With the grace common to serving wenches the world over, she placed a plate of steaming meat and bread in front of each of them without spilling a drop of juice from the other plates she carried.

"Damn my eyes!" Binns commented, watching the girl move smoothly into the maze of tables, "If I didn't know better, I'd swear that girl could fly!"

Kestrel tucked into the food before her. The meat had been roasting for hours, and was as tender as melted butter. Too soon, the plate was empty. She sopped up the last drops of juice with her bread, popped the last bite in her mouth, and leaned against the bar.

"That was excellent, Artie," she sighed. "Beats biscuit and salt fish any day."

Binns was picking at his teeth with a bit of splinter. "And what, may I ask, is wrong with salt fish, madam? Full of salty goodness, keeps your blood red, it does."

"Ale keeps my blood red," she countered, waving at the barman for another round.

"That's a foul myth, perpetrated by the ale makers to sell more of their brew." He pushed his own mug forward when the barman approached. "But just in case I'm wrong, fill me up, too."

Holding his bit of wood between his lips, he stepped back from the bar and stretched his arms out, squeezing his face tight and letting himself relax with a great whooshing sigh. "Breaks m'heart we ain't got cargo to sell. The crowd in the market today was throwin' down coin like sand. We'd have made a kingly fortune indeed."

The market crowd. Something about the words teased at Kestrel's memory. There was a message she was to deliver. It flashed into the forefront of her thoughts like a bolt of blue lightning.

"Artie, I ran into the oddest fellow today, in the market." She laughed. If only he knew how many odd fellows she'd met today. "All skin and bones, and dressed in leather clothes. Half-bald and missing a good many of his teeth. Probably from the drink, that. He reeked of ale." She leaned close to Binns with a conspiratorial wink. "He gave me a message for you. Want to hear?"

Binns took a long pull at his mug, then wiped away the foam from his lip. "Let's have it, then."

Looking to the left, then the right, Kestrel dropped her voice to a dramatic whisper. "The blush is on the rose, but thorns have grown up 'round the foot of the mountain." She chuckled and picked up her own mug for a swallow. "He swore he wasn't drunk." She waited for his appreciative laugh.

Binns was staring at the tavern door, his face a mask of serious consideration. Kestrel elbowed him gently. "Is something wrong?" He was still as stone. She wished for a moment she'd never remembered the old beggar and his ramblings. "Don't pay him any mind, Artie. It was just a foolish prank. No need to take it so serious."

He turned his gaze upon her. She'd never seen him so grim. The cold of fear was seeping into her pores, and she wrapped her arms around her body reflexively.

"There's somethin' I need to tell you, lass. Something I should have told you last night, when I had the chance. But I can't do it with so many interested ears."

He glanced around the room, then stopped short, his head

turned away from her. "By all the spines on Pantheus's back." Binns looked at her once more. The old grin was back, as if the strange moment hadn't happened at all. "Maybe this'll all turn out as it should."

She quirked her eyes in the direction Binns was looking. Her chest tightened with the now-familiar tension.

A young man leaned against the opposite end of the bar, nursing a mug and watching the room. Tall and long-limbed, with long brown hair that was pulled into a lock over his shoulder, and dressed well—boots that rode halfway up his thighs and a black cloak that fell nearly to the floor, almost hiding the jut of a sword hilt at his hip.

Bloody Grace and all her whips, she thought. *How the hell did he find me? And what does he want?* She couldn't use any of her tricks to get away this time. Too small an area—too easy for people to notice what she was doing. He hadn't looked at her yet, his gaze seemingly fixed straight ahead. He looked innocent, a man just stopped by for a drink, nothing more. It was that casual attitude that made her trust him only as far as she might trust an angry cat. Her skin crawled.

"Don't say anything to him," she whispered.

Binns leaned closer to her. "Why not? What's he goin' to do here, in front of a dozen witnesses?"

She chanced another glance. The man still hadn't seemed to notice them at all, his attention apparently drawn by the slightly noisy game of cards going on in the far end of the room. The dice players were gone, their cup and dice abandoned on the table. "He'll wait until we're on the street, turn us into rats, and keep walking like nothing happened."

"Nonsense. So he could see you without a spyglass. How do you know he doesn't just have good eyesight or somethin'?" He sat up, and signaled with three fingers to the barman.

"What are you doing?" she asked.

"Buyin' my new friend a drink."

He was out of his mind. She wondered if she should have told her captain about seeing the man in Market Street earlier. Even after Olympia's assurances that he was no magus she'd ever heard of, his effect on Kestrel alarmed her. Danisoban or rogue or even ordinary sailor, what he was she didn't know. What she did know for certain was that he was trouble. If Binns couldn't be talked out of his dangerous course, she wouldn't be a party to it. "Suit yourself," she muttered, "I'm going back to the *Wolfshead*. And when you're never seen or heard from again, I'll come into town and start hunting for a gray-haired rat. Maybe I'll find you before a cat does."

Before she could walk away, her captain grasped her elbow, pulling her closer to his side. "Belay that thought. You're stayin' right here."

The barman finished filling the three mugs, and set them down. Binns flipped a coin to him and slid a mug into Kestrel's hands. "I value your opinion, lass, but you tend to think you're right a little too often. Not everyone's a villain, and not every situation's a trap." He flashed another coin, catching the barman's eye. "Carry this last mug down to yonder gentleman, with my compliments."

The barman nodded. Picking up the freshly drawn mug, he delivered it to the young man, waving a hand toward Kestrel and Binns. The man looked surprised, then turned toward the two pirates, raising the mug and smiling in a gesture of thanks.

Binns grinned at his quartermaster. "See? Just a sailor, same's us."

If he's just a sailor, then I'm Bloody Grace herself, she thought. He certainly looked harmless enough, leaning on the bar and sipping his ale, his boots polished and his hair, freshly washed and combed, gleaming like old gold under the warm light of the taproom. By all appearances, he was a fop, a danger to no one but himself. But that was no indicator—any magus worth his salt could pretend to be innocuous to suit his purposes.

She squeezed the handle of her mug tightly and closed her eyes. So many years since she'd even seen one of the magi, and she was still reacting like the frightened alley child she'd been. This was ridiculous. She was a warrior, able to defend herself. It took a magus a little time to prepare a spell, time in which she could easily slit his gullet open. How many men had died at the end of her sword? And what was a magus but a man with secrets at his beck and call? Her fears were groundless. She was a grown woman now, and a pirate to boot. Time to behave like one.

Opening her eyes again, she saw Binns stride forward, approaching the mysterious man. She tilted her chin haughtily, and followed her captain, tucking her left thumb into her belt so her hand was inches from the hilt of her main gauche. Let the dandy try to cast some spell. She'd have her blade at his throat before he could utter a word.

Binns had reached the stranger, taking his hand and shaking it vigorously. "A fine evening to you, my good man," he sang out, in an exaggerated upper-class accent. "I'm Artemus Binns, captain of the *Wolfshead.*"

"Many thanks for your kindness." Slipping his hand from Binns's grasp, the young man swept his cloak around him and dropped into a courtly bow, his long hair draping gracefully over his shoulder. "Philip McAvery, late of MelaDoana and presently captain of the vessel *Thanos.*" He rose again, his eyes twinkling as they met Kestrel's. "Would this be your daughter, sir?"

Binns clapped her on the shoulder indulgently. "Would that she were, lad. This is Kestrel, my quartermaster and"—he winked at her—"policy advisor. A finer sailor you'll never find in all the Nine Islands."

McAvery reached out a hand, but Kestrel crossed her arms and took a step back. Whether he'd intended to kiss her hand or merely to shake it, she wasn't letting him touch her.

After a tense moment, McAvery withdrew his waiting hand. "I'm pleased to meet you face-to-face, mistress. I have to admit I thought you were a fine-looking woman when I saw you last night. Even better this morning in the market. But until this moment"— he raised an eyebrow—"I had no idea how lovely you truly are."

Binns quirked his lip. "You ran into each other this morning? Funny, Kestrel never mentioned it."

Kestrel ignored him. "How did you manage to see me last night?" she demanded, her curiosity getting the better of her.

"Why, with my eyes, of course. How else does one see things?" He widened his eyes innocently, then laughed. "I had a telescope, same as you."

"You had no glass in your hand."

"My hands were wet, and the glass kept slipping from my fingers. It's a wonder it isn't broken, as often as I dropped it."

"See, Kestrel? All just a mistake." Binns chuckled indulgently. "Same as us thinking he was some dirty pirate." He turned back to McAvery. "That ship of yours, the way it was painted all red and black . . . I've had trouble with pirates before. Then when you appeared so suddenly, coming in close like you did, I fired at you before thinking."

A mistake, Binns said. But she knew what she'd seen. That had been no clumsy boy dangling from the rigging of the ship. He couldn't drop what he hadn't been holding in the first place.

"What about your ship? You tried to ram us, then vanished into thin air." She cocked her head toward her captain. *Even you can't say I made that up, not with a shipload of witnesses*, she wanted to say, letting her eyes speak for her.

"I'm new at this. We veered away from you, but the helmsman said we were coming up on a reef or something, so he spun the wheel and we ended up running straight for you. Thank the gods, we barely managed to slip past, and we fell far behind." He took a long draught of his ale, and sighed. "I have to assume that's why you lost sight of us."

Who did he think he was trying to fool? His explanations might have sounded plausible to some tavern wench who'd never even wandered down to the beach. That ship hadn't changed course—it had vanished. This McAvery was hiding something. Maybe he wasn't a magus—he certainly didn't behave like any she'd known—but he was no farm boy either. There was definitely a secret he was keeping. That suited her fine. He could have his secrets, as many as he wanted, as long as none of them got in her way.

"So, my boy," Binns's voice interrupted her thoughts. "You say you're new to sailoring. How've you come to adopt a life on the water?"

McAvery continued to watch Kestrel, but answered Binns in a companionable manner. "I grew up on a farm, on MelaDoana. I hated it. Up every day before the sun, milking cows, gathering eggs, plowing, sweating, and always the same thing day after day. I promised myself a little adventure someday. When my father died, I sold it all. Took a trip to Pecheta to see the sights, and while I was there, I bought the *Thanos* from a merchant who had to pay off some gambling debts. What was left I used to hire a few men, and went to sea. A wild impulse, seemed smart at the time, all that sort of thing."

Binns was listening, his eyebrows raised. "A farmer? And you went to sea, just like that?"

"Just like that," McAvery agreed. "Stupidest thing I ever did. I've got no sea legs, so I spent the first few days hanging over the rail. Even later, when I stopped being sick, it was no good. I'm a landlubber, heart and soul." He sighed. "What I wouldn't do to be back on the farm."

Kestrel rolled her eyes. She'd never heard a story so contrived in all her life. Poor farm boy gone to sea . . . surely Binns could hear how ridiculous it was. She leaned forward to catch his eye, and her heart sank.

He was wearing that expression, a combination of childish delight and jaded avarice, the one he always wore when he thought he was going to win big. It was the look she knew too well. He thought he could get something from McAvery. But what?

"It's a sad story you tell, young man," Binns said. He laid a sympathetic hand on McAvery's shoulder, and shook his head. "Many's the time I've heard it, too. The life of a sailor isn't meant for every man."

"It certainly wasn't meant for me," McAvery said. "That's why I came here. I decided days ago to sell the ship, release the men, and go home. I can't recoup what I paid for the *Thanos,* I know, but I figured I stood a better chance for a fair price here on Eldraga than I would at home."

Binns slapped his own knee. "I'll be damned! If I didn't believe in fate before this day, I do now. As it happens, I've been considering trading up for a bigger ship myself. Only so much my sloop can do, you know, so little room in her hold for . . . uh, cargo." He leaned in close. "So what were you thinking to ask for the *Thanos*?"

Kestrel let go of the breath she hadn't realized she was holding. So that's what he was up to. Take advantage of the callow farm boy and get his hands on the better ship for the price of a rowboat. Pure larceny, simple and plain. As long as the farm boy really was as callow as he pretended.

"I wouldn't want to cheat you by asking too much." McAvery was looking at the ceiling now, his brow furrowed. "What's the market value for a forty-gun warship?"

A slow smile spread across Binns's face. "Let me buy you another drink, lad, and we'll talk it over."

The young man leaned down, and hefted a cloth bag from its place between his feet. He tucked it securely into the crook of his elbow. "I suggest we seat ourselves. This could take a little while."

THE negotiations lasted long into the night. Kestrel found herself once or twice nodding, despite her best efforts to stay alert. By the time the bell rang, signaling last call, the two men seemed to have come to an agreement. Repairs to the *Wolfshead* would be finished in a day's time. The day after, Binns and McAvery would meet with the dockmaster to formalize their exchange and then each would go his separate way. Binns had generously offered to take on any of the men who had sailed with McAvery. On a ship the size of the *Thanos*, every able body would be necessary.

Kestrel couldn't help wondering what McAvery wasn't telling them. Assuming that even a fraction of his story was true, which she didn't, there were gaping holes in the tale that begged for filling. Farm boy dreaming of a life at sea? Possible. Selling off the family farm and buying a ship with the proceeds was a little harder to swallow. The part about the debt-ridden merchant could have happened, although that left open the question of the debt collectors. A crafty man with a gaudy ship like the *Thanos* would know that unloading the ship on an unsuspecting fellow would set the dogs to following, giving him time to escape into anonymity with enough coin to make a fresh start.

Binns always teased her that she was too suspicious. Maybe she was inferring too much into the situation. Both men seemed determined to come to an agreement about the trade, and so far the arrangement was beyond equitable for her side. She couldn't rid herself of the tiny niggling kernel of doubt that tickled at her conscience, but she decided to ignore it. For her captain's sake, if nothing else.

Six

*. . . within what space
of time this wild, disastrous change took place?*
—SAMUEL TAYLOR COLERIDGE

Shortly after dawn, when the sun's light was still only a minor an-
noyance, Binns pounded on the door of Kestrel's room. "Breakfast is downstairs, my girl!" he yelled through the thin wood, likely
waking every other tenant at the same time. "Just because you be
sleepin' like a duchess doesn't mean you'll be gettin' fed like one!"

Kestrel stretched, extending hands and feet as far away from
each other as they could go without pulling her apart. Her shoulders were tight and achy from the night spent on a plain mattress.
Sleeping flat after weeks in her hammock never worked out well for
her. Binns insisted on spending a night or two on land whenever
they were in port anywhere. "Good for the digestion," he would
say. "Lets your stomach have a bit of respite from all that tossin'
and rollin'." Kestrel didn't know whether her stomach was func-
tioning any better or not, but she knew for certain her back was
missing her hammock on board the ship. She sat up and crossed
her arms in front of her, wincing at the pulling stiffness of sleep-
dulled joints, then swung her legs over the edge of the bed.

As she usually did when she was on land, she'd slept in her short
clothes. She'd rinsed her breeches and silk shirt out the night before, laying them across the chair to dry. Her other breeches and
shirts were still in her sea chest aboard the *Wolfshead*—she hadn't
figured on needing more than one set of clothes. She fingered the
clothing, grimacing. Her shirt was dry, it being too fine to hold water

long anyway. But the sturdy black breeches were stubbornly damp, especially along the seams where they were thickest.

She sighed. Nothing to do but wear them anyway. More than likely they'd dry out enough by midmorning. She'd only have to suffer for a little while. She tied the waistband and slipped her shirt over her head, then braided her hair quickly in one long plait down her back. Time enough to do the many small braids she preferred later, when she was back on board ship.

Her boots were tucked under the bed. She picked them up, turned them upside down, and banged them together, before pulling them on and standing. Her hat was exactly where she'd left it, hanging with her sword belt on a loose nail near the window. She glanced outside as she retrieved them.

The Cup o' Gold was one of the more popular inns on Eldraga; being situated as it was between two single-floored buildings, the lucky patrons could have a view to go along with their uncomfortable beds. Not a beautiful view, considering the salt-fogged glass of the window, but a view nonetheless.

The sky was a bright, almost painful blue, with a few fluffy white clouds hanging heavily out over the ocean, remnants of the weather they'd survived only a day ago. She could just make out the harbor from here, billowing sails moving slowly as ships navigated their way out into the open seas. She sighed. Soon, she'd be back out there, too. For her taste, it couldn't happen soon enough.

Slapping the hat against her hand to knock loose any stowaways that might have crawled in during the night, she jammed it on her head. She slipped her sword belt around her hips, latched it tight, and made her way down the stairs.

The inn's common room was almost empty. The serving wench was casually wiping the bar with a rag, glancing now and then at the customers. Two men in dark cloaks sat whispering together at a table beside the unlit hearth, mugs before them. A step creaked under Kestrel's foot, and one of the men glanced at her suspiciously, leaning his head a little closer to his companion, as if to keep her from overhearing their conversation. She turned her face away, as if she hadn't noticed them in the first place, although the irritated man had looked slightly familiar, but not enough to risk starting an altercation by staring.

Binns sat alone at a table near the stairs, with his back to her, his shoulders hunched, and his elbows moving. Apparently breakfast had already been served, and he wasn't waiting. Not that she was overly hungry—the combination of being on land and worrying herself to sleep had effectively destroyed her appetite.

She lowered herself onto the bench next to her captain, moving her sword back out of her way but not quite managing to stifle a groan as her body settled.

"Good mornin', lass!" Binns boomed. He raised a hand as if to slap her in greeting, but stopped short, laughing at the look of alarm she flashed him. "Sleep well?"

"I see you did."

Binns had apparently wakened with a fierce appetite. On the wooden trencher before him, a huge block of yellow cheese was surrounded by piles of salted fish, slices of beef, and some small green fruit she'd never seen before, smooth-skinned and dotted with drops of water. Half of a freshly baked loaf lay on the table next to a bowl of thick broth, and a mug of ale was in his hand.

"Nothing like sleepin' on land to liven your belly," he said. "Unless, perhaps, it's sleepin' on land after you've managed to make the best deal of your career." He picked up one of the green fruits and offered it to her. "It's a beryl. Very sweet, very tender. Grown only on the north coast of Bix, imported especially for our fine innkeeper."

She shook her head. "I'll be having bread and cheese, thanks."

"A bit of bread and cheese it is. Ahoy, wench!" Binns called out, snapping his fingers importantly. "A mug of the dark to help my quarter here face the day!" He popped the tiny beryl into his mouth and pushed the plate toward Kestrel. "Help yourself. There's plenty."

Kestrel shuddered. Just looking at the mound of food in front of him made her queasy. Thank the gods she hadn't become drunk last night—seeing such a meal with an ale headache would have sent her scurrying toward the first open window.

Not that she could have become drunk if she'd tried—her distrust of the McAvery fellow had tightened her nerves to nearly the breaking point, and no amount of drink could have made its way past. The fact that the deal seemed perfect was the most worrying aspect. Perfect never was.

The serving wench arrived with a brimming mug. Kestrel thanked her. Reaching over, she claimed the half-eaten loaf and began tearing bite-sized pieces off it. "Have you seen him yet?" She tried to make the question sound casual, staring pointedly at her plate.

"McAvery? No." Binns broke the gigantic cheese block in half, placing one part in front of her. "We're meetin' at the dock this morning. Weren't you listenin' last night?"

"Course I was. I wondered if he'd been down to breakfast, is all."

Binns shoved a whole salted fish in his mouth, and began chewing. "He wasn't stayin' here," he commented, his words muffled by the mouthful of food. "Nearly out of cash, poor lad." He washed the fish down with a swig of ale. "Stayed out on the *Thanos*, getting his affairs in order." He raised an eyebrow and pointed a finger at her growing pile of torn bread. "You plannin' to punish the cheese, too?"

She took a bite off the heel of the mutilated loaf still in her hand. "Sorry, Artie. I'm not going to feel good about this deal until we're well away from your poor lad McAvery. There's something about him I don't like."

"You want to know what the problem is, my girl?" Binns chuckled. "He's by far the best-lookin' fellow you've come across in a long time. Good, strong body, that fine, shiny hair . . . under any other circumstance, you'd have been a flirtin' and a cooin' like any other sweet lass. Trouble is, he got the better of you. Made a bit of fun of you before you even met proper, and you're mad."

Kestrel ground her teeth together. "I think I'm smart enough to see past a handsome face, Artemus Binns," she growled. "His looks have nothing to do with it. He's a magus and a rogue and until I see his sails fade over the horizon in the opposite direction from the one I'm headed, I'll have my hand resting close to my sword hilt." She shoved the rest of the loaf in her mouth and chewed angrily.

"That's a girl. Try some of your cheese, too." Binns rolled a fish into a slice of beef and took a bite, sighing happily. "I'd suggest a bit of this beef to put some color in your cheeks, but you look like you've got enough there already."

"What do you mean?"

"Oh, it's nothin', I'm sure," he said, not meeting her eyes. "You started blushin' the second I mentioned his name."

She placed a hand on her cheek; her skin was warmer, as if she was flushed. "Over that idiot McAvery? You couldn't be farther off course." She picked a morsel of cheese free from the chunk, wrapped it in a bite of bread, and chewed.

"Be angry then. Better than worried," he said. "At least now you're eating." He leaned back from the table, sighing, and patted his belly. "I've reached my limit, I think. You want this last beryl? Good for you. Keeps the scurvy away."

Damned old sea dog, she thought. *You always do know just how to take the wind out of my sails.* As much as she wanted to stay cross with him, she could feel a smile twitching at the corners of her mouth. Finally she sighed, and held out a hand. Binns plopped the little green beryl into her open palm. "You'll like it. Very sweet, it is."

The sleek skin of the fruit was a brilliant green that would put a parrot to shame, and tight with ripeness. It was almost too pretty to think of eating. She raised it to her mouth, then stopped.

"Pop it in, all at once," Binns urged.

"Artie," she said, "if you're sure this deal with McAvery is balanced in your favor, then I'm right behind you, like always. But promise me you won't turn your back on him until everything's done. Maybe he's not a magus. He could be a royal treasurer's agent, laying in wait to charge you for the taxes on the *Thanos* the second you put your mark to paper. You'll keep your eyes on every move he makes, your ears tuned to every word he says, and your nose close to smell a rat. And let me read whatever he might ask you to sign, just so you don't accidentally sign away your eternal soul or somesuch."

"As if my eternal soul is worth more than the cost of this meal." Binns patted Kestrel's shoulder. "If I could have chosen a daughter, she'd have been you, lass. No father could have a more loyal child than you've always been to me. For your sake, I promise. I'll stand on my tiptoes until the deal is signed and done and no turnin' back. Now eat your beryl."

She grinned, tossing the green jewel of a fruit into her mouth. It burst into summery sweetness, and her eyes widened. "By the gods, these are incredible!"

"I told you. Next time maybe you'll try them before they're all gone." Binns rose from the table, patting his belly with a contented smile. "If you've eaten all you're goin' to, let's get movin'. We have an exchange to settle." He frowned suddenly. "D'you have the log?"

No self-respecting sea captain, military, merchant, or pirate, ever made a move without his ship's log, and Binns was no exception. Each evening around sunset, while Kestrel called the changes of the watch, he would scribe the day's report on the pages of the leather-bound book. Every time a cargo was taken, a sailor was injured, or a new course was charted, it was written in the log. As soon as the ink dried, he'd tuck the book away under the thin mattress of his bed.

Once a year, when high summer was upon the Islands, the *Wolfshead* made its way north to wait out the spinstorm season. Binns made a stop on Eldraga, not only to release any of the men who chose not to remain in his crew, but also to replace the log for the coming year. It was a trip he made alone, walking away with the salt-dulled book tucked under his arm, then returning to the ship a few hours later with a gleaming new one, a handful of fresh-cut quills, and half a dozen pots of ink. Where he hid the old ones, Kestrel never knew. The only time she ever asked, Binns answered with a grave shake of the head. "Never you mind about that, lass. The information in even one of those old logs would be enough to see us all hanged, so it's best you don't know where I stashed 'em." She hadn't bothered to remind him that the courts wouldn't need an old leather book to hang a bunch of pirates. Let him have his secrets, if they made him happy.

"Last I saw, you were tucking it into your pack. Which I also don't see anywhere about." She tilted her head upward. "Did you leave it in the room?"

"Pickle my heart in brine, so I must have done," he sighed, glancing sadly at the ceiling as if he could see into the room above. "All the way up the stairs, and me so full of victuals I can hardly walk on the flat. My knees are creaking at the very thought of the climb."

If Binns had put his energies into being an actor instead of being a pirate, he'd be playing before the king's court today. Might as well join the game. She clasped her hands before her in an imploring gesture. "Captain, I insist you let me, your lowly servant, fetch your bag for you."

Under the woeful expression he was wearing, she saw the twinkling hint of a grin. "Would you, lass? You're so kind. Surely the gods will reward you for it." He sank dramatically back down to the bench, releasing a heavy breath and leaning back against the table.

Rolling her eyes, Kestrel strode to the stairs at the back of the common room, and took them two at a time. Her back had started easing since she'd risen, and she was feeling more like herself. Or maybe it was the anticipation of being near the water again, even if they were only going as far as the dockmaster's office.

Binns's room was a mess—sheets pulled loose from the moorings of the mattress, the thin blanket in a crumpled heap on the floor. On first glance, she couldn't see his pack, so she dropped to her hands and knees to peer under the bed. Sure enough, there it was. Must have been kicked under without him realizing when he stumbled into bed. She reached under and pulled it out, crossing her legs and settling the pack into her lap. She untied the knotted cords holding it closed, and dug around inside. Buried under an extra pair of breeches, she found the logbook, right where it was supposed to be. Lifting it out from the pack, she retied the cords and hung the pack on her shoulder, slid the book under one arm, and returned to the stairs.

A crowd seemed to have gathered in the few minutes she'd been gone. The beams of sunlight she'd seen the first time she descended the stairs were now shadowed. The whole room wasn't visible, but from up here she could see several pairs of feet standing close together where none had been moments before. *It's a mite early for the drinkers*, she mused, *must be a crew just in from the docks*. One never knew in a harbor town. She'd descended a few steps when a loud voice caught her attention, its words sending ice running through her veins.

"My name is Laquebus," an imperious voice announced. "Artemus Binns, you are hereby remanded to the custody of His Majesty's Navy. You'll be incarcerated until such time as transport to the Royal Tribunal on Pecheta can be arranged. There you will face trial for the crime of piracy on the high seas. And may the gods have mercy on your soul."

Kestrel crouched down to peek like an errant child from between the slats on the banister. The common room, empty when she'd trotted up the stairs only moments ago, was not just crowded—every inch of floor space was held by men uniformed in the blue and gold appointments of the Royal Navy. One man, sumptuously dressed in a blue velvet doublet and white satin slops, was rolling up a scroll and smiling, a tight, evil smile full of contempt for the prisoner. Next to him stood another man, fidgety and sharp-faced, wearing crimson merchant's vestments. Unlike his companion, his brow seemed permanently furrowed and he continually glanced left and right as if afraid of someone creeping up and grabbing him. But it was the figure behind the two of them that made her breath catch in her throat.

He (or possibly she? There was no way to tell) was covered completely in a robe of rusty black, wide sleeves covering the hands and hood pulled forward far enough that the face was the merest shadow in its depths. The only decoration was a length of blue ribbon stitched to the outside of the left sleeve. They'd brought along a Danisoban. Kestrel's head swam, and she fought the panic that rose in her chest.

Binns was standing by the table, his hands bound behind him in chains, his face almost as gray as his hair. As if he could feel her gaze, he turned his head slightly, and caught her eye. A lump caught in her throat and she swallowed hard—no time for feelings, not when Binns needed her help. She laid her hand on her sword's hilt and began to rise. Someone must have located his old logs, after all this time. Or else whoever kept them for him finally decided to claim their bounty. *The only way out of this now*, she thought, *will be by spilling blood. I never wanted to live forever. By damn, maybe the gods'll be kind, let me take the magus with me*, she promised herself.

Before she could move, Binns suddenly shook his head, tossing his ponytail over his shoulder and back in her direction. She let her gaze stray to the back of the room. The two men whose conversation she'd interrupted were standing against the wall, arms crossed and satisfied looks on their faces. Now that they'd come out from under their cloaks, she knew them. The two who'd been dicing last night. What could they have to do with this? And why did Binns want her to notice them?

"I fear you've got me confused with some criminal, Master Lickboots," Binns said, mispronouncing the man's name just a bit more loudly than necessary. "My name's Nesbit. I'm a humble trader in spices, captain of the sloop *Fancy*. We put in just yesterday for repairs. Check with the dockmaster if you won't take my word."

The man holding the scroll scowled. His face had darkened with the insult Binns casually threw his way, but he drew a deep breath and smiled again. "You waste your breath with protestations of innocence and mistaken identity, Master Binns. We have indeed spoken to the dockmaster." He turned to the ominous black-robed magus. "Brother?" he asked.

The Danisoban raised his arms. The sleeves fell back, exposing slender white hands and a bright silver cuff around one wrist. He twisted his hands in a complicated pattern, and suddenly an image appeared in the air before him. A wizened, sour-faced old man, sitting behind a cramped desk in a dark room, and he was talking. "His name is Binns. Couldn't stop crowing about how tricky he was to get his hands on that fine big ship. I always told him pirating would be the death of him."

The image disappeared with another wave of the hands, and the magus stepped back again. Laquebus smiled evilly. "As you see, that gentleman tells us you sailed into Eldraga harbor yesterday on the stolen merchant ship *Thanos*. With his testimony, we have you dead to rights."

The *Thanos*! Of course! Damn that McAvery! She wasn't sure if it wouldn't have been better if he'd just cast some spell on them. If only Binns had listened to her. Not that she'd suspected this particular turn of events. Who would have guessed McAvery would use the Navy itself to further his own ends?

Laquebus was still speaking. "You will be transported to Pecheta to stand trial. No extraordinary circumstance, whether forces of nature or powerful associates, will save you from your rightful destiny."

Binns dropped his head and turned his chin up toward her, as if he were merely stretching a stiff neck. While his head was turned, he caught her eye once more, and tipped her a slow wink.

Of course. He wanted her to go back upstairs. So far as she knew, her name hadn't been mentioned in the arrest scroll. As things stood, she was his only hope.

If what she'd overheard was true, the popinjay with the nasty smile and official scroll planned to put Binns on a ship for Pecheta, a good four-day journey at best. If she didn't go back up and hide until the soldiers took him away, they'd both be arrested. There'd be no one left to come after them until it was too late. But if she stayed free, she could round up the crew, set sail tonight, and waylay the Navy ship before it reached port. They'd rescue the captain and skip away, staying low until the furor died down. Most of the crew would have to be released elsewhere to avoid anyone giving Binns up. The crew was all good sailors, that was never in dispute, but outlaws were outlaws. If it came down to a choice between Binns's life or his own, any one of the pirates currently under his command would hand him over without a backward glance.

The few remaining—she, Shadd, the handful of others she knew to be faithful to Binns—would likely have to hide in an out-of-the-way town with only a fraction of their usual take to tide them over until the storm season passed and they could go back to sea again. It might send Binns into retirement earlier than he'd expected, and he'd certainly be disappointed about never getting his hands on that fine big gunship, but at least he'd not be hanging from some dockside gibbet, with black birds pecking out his eyes.

She stepped backward, feeling for the next stair with her heel. No one was looking at her, and with any luck no one would notice her moving. She took another step. Just as she let her weight settle on the board, it creaked. She froze.

"Hey! Didn't you have a girl with you, mate?" someone asked.

"Aye, he did!" came another cry. "And that's her up on the steps!"

Kestrel didn't wait. Spinning on the step, she charged the rest of the way up, running down the hall to the room she'd slept in the night before. She slipped in the door, closing it gently against the footsteps she heard now pounding up the stairs. *I've only got a minute,* she thought raggedly. She grabbed the chair and shoved it under the doorknob. That wouldn't be enough, though. The bed . . . she seized the heavy frame, and yanked hard, dragging it across the few feet between it and the door, and shoved it tight against the restraining chair. It wasn't much of a barricade, but it could buy her another few seconds.

Crossing to the window, she slid her fingers into the small handholds at the bottom of the sash. More than likely the wood had long ago warped, permanently closing the window. But she had to try. *Please, Grace, and all you gods who might be listening,* she prayed, *I'll bring you a tithe of every cargo we take from this day forward, if you'll let this window open.* She took a deep breath, then let it out and strained with all her might. The window refused to move.

Thumping footsteps were coming closer, their owners beating on doors and yelling out. Kestrel let go of the sash, wiggling her fingers and taking another breath. Its panes were small squares, not one by itself big enough for her to crawl through. If it came to that, she'd have to break out all the panes and the dividing wood slats as well. Best to try and open it one more time. *Come on, you gods,* she begged, *if Binns was right about you rewarding me, now would be the perfect time.* She slid her fingers back into the sash, and pulled.

"Open up, in the name of the king!" The voice bellowed from the other side of her door, close enough to send a frisson of fear down her back. Her time was up. Hands battered at the door. "It's blocked with something, sir," someone reported.

"Fetch the magus to spell this door open," said another voice.

"Nonsense," said the first voice. "Break it down."

Spell the door open . . . could it be so simple? Kestrel rubbed her tortured hands. She'd never tried something like this, but now was as good a time as any. She started tapping her fingers on the sash, beating out the rhythm of a song she vaguely recalled. The familiar tingling sent gooseflesh along her spine. She didn't know if it was working the way she wanted, but something was happening.

"Get this door open!" someone barked outside.

No more time. Closing her eyes, she slipped her fingers into the sash again, and heaved, the skin of her hands blanching, her shoulders stinging with her effort. The window flew up, smooth as butter, nearly banging into the top of the sill.

Her head was spinning, but there wasn't time to let the dizziness ease off. Kestrel climbed on the sill, sitting long enough to gauge the distance to the roof below. A good ten or twelve feet, she reckoned, and she'd likely plunge straight through the roof onto the astonished merchant's floor, breaking her legs and making her an easy catch.

Behind her, the thin wood of the door was cracking under the onslaught. Time to go. Kestrel shrugged off Binns's pack, but tightened her arm against the logbook she still held under one arm. Binns would need that back when they rescued him. She planted her feet flat against the wall behind her, and launched herself into the air.

$\mathcal{S}$even

And what if all-avenging Providence
Strong and retributive, should make us know
The meaning of our words, force us to fear
The desolation and the agony of our fierce doings?

—SAMUEL TAYLOR COLERIDGE

Bloody damn!" she howled.

She didn't know whether to be grateful to the merchant below for building such a sturdy structure that it didn't break under her weight, or angry that the same sturdiness had been so hard under her leading shoulder. When she'd pushed off against the inn wall, she'd forgotten the sword dangling at her side. Her foot caught on it, and she jerked in midair, twisting her body into the wrong angle to land safely. She'd taken her whole body's weight on her right shoulder, which was now, by turns, tingling and throbbing. Binns's voice crept into her thoughts. "Tuck and roll, lass! That way, nothin' gets broken." How many times had he made her climb riggings and then let go, just to teach her the proper way to fall? She flexed her arm. Sharp pain stabbed her, and she winced.

"There, on the roof!" The cry came from the window she'd just leaped out of. Kestrel chanced a quick look back. Two men were framed in the opening, pointing her way. Broken arm or not, she wasn't free and clear yet. "At least it isn't my legs," she muttered, scrambling to her feet and running across the wooden roof.

It wouldn't do to climb down the front—by the sound of it, they'd be swarming any second into the building on which she stood. The back alley was her only option. She'd learned to run the alleys as a street urchin; unless the Eldraga Council had suddenly developed an interest in the condition of the back alleys in the few short years since she'd been on the street, all her old ways should still be open to her. Using them she could easily elude the soldiers.

She sat down on the edge of the building, swinging her legs over. The cramped alley was narrower than she remembered. Brackish puddles dotted the filthy ground, in between heaps of discarded rubbish and food scraps rotting against the muddy walls, the domain of street children and stray animals. Looking up and down, she saw the passage was empty except for a mongrel dog sniffing at a refuse pile a few yards away. It was only about nine feet to the ground; not an impossible jump, but she wished for a second that she had the use of both arms. *It would be a lot easier if I could let myself down a foot or two,* she thought, *but if wishes were wings I'd be flying.* Holding the logbook flat in front of her with her healthy arm, she dropped it. The loud slap it made frightened the dog, sending him scampering up the alley. With her left hand, she wiggled the sword free of its sheath. This treatment couldn't be good for the blade, but hurting herself again would be far worse. Pointing the tip toward the dirt floor of the alley, she threw it. It flew clean. The tip buried itself some inches into the dirt, and the swept hilt waved back and forth merrily.

Kestrel took a deep breath and wrapped her right hand over her left hip, holding the injured arm tightly against her side. *Just like he taught you,* she reminded herself, then hopped her hips forward. She hit the ground with both feet and rolled onto her good side, letting the momentum carry her through the roll and back onto her feet. It was a good landing, but her head swam as her wounded shoulder protested this new shock. She crouched in the shadowed alley. There weren't any windows in the building's back wall, only a skinny wooden door that looked as if it hadn't been opened in a decade or more. Indistinct shouts echoed from the street. The dog had disappeared, and she seemed to be alone. So far, so good. Kestrel got to her feet. She'd retrieve her sword and the logbook and be gone before the bluecoats arrived. The book lay next to the building right where she'd dropped it. But where her sword had been was only a shallow hole in the dirt.

"Good thing you ate your breakfast, like you were told," a voice drawled from behind her. A short, stocky man in a charcoal-black cloak emerged from the shadows, strolling in a calculatedly casual manner toward her. He had a round face, ash-colored hair, and a sparse beard that gave him the look of a boy trying his best to appear manly. She hadn't taken such a good look when she'd seen him the first time, whispering with the other man in the inn's common room, but she recognized him just the same. The dice player.

"Lose something?" He grinned, raising his left hand from the folds of fabric. Her sword was dangling off his thumb.

Kestrel took a step backward, trying to stay out of blade reach. "You shouldn't be playing with that," she said. "You could put out your eye."

"I'm not the one playing the dangerous games, am I?" he said. He twisted his hand suddenly, palming the hilt, then drove the sword's point into the mud and stepped between the weapon and its owner. The hilt swayed behind him like a metronome, now visible, now not. "We don't have to be enemies, you and I."

He'd had a companion when she saw him earlier. So where was the other one now? Kestrel stepped back again, feeling as tightly strung as a bard's harp and twice as closely held. "Indeed not. I have all the enemies I can use right now."

His grin faded from his broad face. Flinging open his cloak, he drew his own sword and brandished it at her. "Then I suggest you tell me where your meeting place is."

Meeting place? She'd figured him for a royal agent, come to take her into custody along with her captain. Obviously he was no such thing. Maybe he was an assassin, frustrated after having lost the target. Whatever he was, he must have mistaken her for someone else. She didn't have time to stand around arguing with him, whoever he might be.

"The meeting place?" she asked brightly. "I was just on my way there. We're all gathering in an hour at . . ." She paused, wracking her brain for a location at the other end of the city from where she was heading. "The shipyard. But I have an errand, so I'll just take my sword and run along. Wouldn't want to be late, would I?"

He shook his head sadly, keeping himself between her and her weapon. "We were doing so well," he said. "Don't ruin it now by playing stupid." He took another step, putting himself just past the merchant's door.

She swallowed, the lump of nervousness hard and painful in her throat. Hand-to-hand fighting wasn't her strongest skill, even when she wasn't hurt. Not that she'd have a chance to land a blow on the man. He'd probably slice her open if she tried. She had to get her hands back on her sword to stand a chance. "Tell me who you're looking for and we can settle this right now."

As she moved out of his blade's reach again, she felt a sharp prick against her backbone, and froze.

"Maybe she isn't playing stupid, Burk," said another voice. Kestrel tilted her head to the side, reaching her gaze as far as she could. All she could see was a figure, also in dark clothing, taller than she was. So there he was. They'd herded her like a wayward sheep. She bit her lip to keep from cursing out loud.

Burk was grinning again. "She's not an idiot," he said. "I think she doesn't understand the gravity of her situation, that's all." He trained the sword's point between her eyes. "We could turn you in, to the proper authorities. Let you accompany your fancy man to Pecheta for the Hempen Ball. Wouldn't you two look fine hanging next to each other?" He let his sword point drop, aiming now at her belly. "Or I could let Volga kill you right here. Open your gut and spill your intestines all over the ground. You'd never make your meeting then, would you? They wouldn't find you until you started to stink."

Kestrel held herself as still as possible. Her hands were freezing, as if all the warm blood inside her had already flowed away. She wiggled her toes inside her boots, trying to keep her feet from cramping. If the opportunity to run showed itself, the last thing she wanted to do was stumble on her first step.

There wasn't time for this nonsense, not when it seemed the

entire Royal Army was after her. Maybe these two were betting house strong-arms, dispatched to collect a gambling debt from a member of the crew. Or a quicklender, tired of waiting for his repayment, had hired them. But why would they assume she knew who they meant?

Burk was still rambling. "Those are just some of my options. But I'm a gentleman, you see. So if you'll just tell us where he's hiding, sweetness, perhaps I won't kill you right away." He slid his tongue out, licking his already-wet lips. "I'll bet there are uses you're better suited for than sailoring, eh?"

Were there any men in the whole Nine Islands who didn't keep their brains in their pants? Her gorge rose at the thought of his blubbery lips coming near hers. As if he'd even be what she'd choose if she did want to play. A hundred vicious comments rose to the surface of her mind, but out of nowhere, she remembered something Olympia had once told her. *Treat a man like he's the handsomest, finest thing you've ever laid eyes on, and he'll let you get away with damn near anything.* Kestrel had never been much of a flirt, but she didn't see a choice. Between being weaponless and wounded, Olympia's way was at least worth a try.

Kestrel forced a sickly smile. "A fine-looking fellow such as yourself? I'm sure I'd enjoy telling you whatever you wanted to know." She poked her lower lip into a pout she hoped was charming, and dropped her head, looking up at him through her lashes the way she'd seen the wenches do a thousand times. "I'm just a silly woman, not very good with names. Who did you say you were looking for?"

The man behind her yanked suddenly on her braid, pulling her head back and pressing his blade more sharply into her spine. "Your partner, bitch," he hissed, his breath hot and foul against her cheek. "That double-dealing, two-faced bastard who thought he could rob us and get away with it."

Kestrel's breath was coming fast and shallow, and she was nearly having to stand on her toes, he was pulling her hair so hard. So much for the flirting. Thoughts whirled through her mind as she desperately tried to come up with an answer that might assuage these idiots. "Double-dealing," he'd said and "two-faced." No member of Binns's crew fit that description—whether it was cheating at cards or bearing false witness, the culprit was always put ashore the instant his misdeed became known.

There was only one man she knew that she might call "two-faced." And it was the one man she'd happily watch dance from a gibbet. *Damn you, McAvery,* she thought, *is there anyone that isn't ready to slice your throat?*

If only she could get her hand on her sword. She glanced at it, reflected darkly in a muddy puddle. Maybe there was a way. "Fine," she said. "I'll take you to my partner. But would you mind if I call my dog back? I'd hate him to end up in someone's soup pot."

Burk frowned. Before he could argue, Kestrel blew a hard two-toned whistle, staring at the filthy water at Burk's feet. It geysered up, spraying into Burk's open eyes. He flung his head back with a roar.

"Burk!" Volga cried. He lurched forward, as if trying to move past his captive, and released his death-grip on Kestrel's hair. Crooking her left elbow, she drove it into Volga's midsection. He bent, clutching his abdomen. She spun free.

He was younger than she'd thought, nineteen or twenty at most, with a shaven head and a long, skinny beard hanging from his pointed chin. The blade he held was a dagger only, not even six inches long, but still enough to kill. He straightened, swept his blade at her. She hopped out of his way, then turned sideways and kicked, landing her foot squarely into his belly. He gasped and staggered back, fighting for breath.

Burk grabbed for Kestrel. She skidded around him, and pulled her sword free of its muddy sheath. Swinging the point up, she jabbed at Burk. Pain shot down through her shoulder. She hissed with the shock of it.

He twisted to avoid the sword point, and sidestepped awkwardly. His foot slipped from under him. He fell, landing on his back. His eyes widened, then rolled out of sight, and he lay still. Kestrel turned back to Volga.

Volga's face was blue now. He tried to straighten, hitting himself in the chest with one hand as if to loosen his crippled breathing. It didn't help. With one last squeaking gasp, he toppled onto his face.

She stood for an endless moment, her heartbeat pounding like surf in her ears. Neither man moved. She reached out a toe toward Burk's head, and tipped it away from her. Redness stained the puddle below it, but just below the water, she saw the rock he'd hit. He was still breathing; both of them were. Volga would probably wake up in a few minutes. Burk's head wound was bleeding profusely, as head wounds did, but she didn't have the time or interest to bother patching him up. He'd have to hope his own gods were looking out for him.

In the meantime, she couldn't wait another second. She'd used her power twice in the same location—the Brethren might already be coming for her. Her shoulder was on fire. As well as she'd managed opening a window and splashing a little water, there was no way she'd be strong enough to fight a Danisoban. Binns's logbook was on the ground where she'd dropped it. She knelt to retrieve it, tucking it under her left arm, and rose.

"Well, hello."

Pain exploded against her right temple, followed by merciful blackness.

Eight

As if through a dungeon-grate he peered
With broad and burning face.

—SAMUEL TAYLOR COLERIDGE

H er head . . . someone had pounded a huge iron stake through her head. They must have. Nothing else could hurt this much. She groaned, and immediately regretted it. Even the small sound rattled her teeth in their sockets. Kestrel inched her lids up, wincing. Vicious blades of light stabbed her, and a fierce rumbling thundered in the vast emptiness behind her forehead. She pressed the heel of her hand against her eyes, trying to stop the stampede.

"Sorry I had to do that. I knew you wouldn't come along without a fight, and I didn't want to kill you."

The stampede inside her head changed into an angry bull slamming the walls of her skull. "I'd prefer death to this headache," she murmured.

The voice laughed, as if she'd made a charming joke. "You're only worth a thief's bounty dead."

Kestrel struggled to sit up. Her back was stiff, and cold. Wet. She pushed herself into a sitting position, and slitted her eyes open. Her sword belt was gone, as was the log. She was sitting in a small, square cell. The floor under her hands was damp dirt, and the walls gray stone. The ceiling was barely higher than her head. At the top of one wall was a barred opening, about a foot wide, through which sunlight beamed.

"How long—" she began, and stopped. She was alone in the tiny room. Had she imagined the voice? Dreamed it?

"How long what?"

Now that she was paying attention, she realized the speaker must be outside the bars. Kestrel rolled onto one hip, tucked her leg under, and rose, her knees shaking. Her head swam, but she managed to stay on her feet. She shuffled to the opening, her eyes adjusting slowly.

"How long what?" the voice repeated.

"How long have I been unconscious?" she asked.

"An hour, maybe a bit more. I didn't hit you all that hard."

An hour. Thank the gods for their minuscule favors. Kestrel raised a hand to shield herself from the light, and chanced a look outside.

A green meadow stretched before her, ending some yards away in a thicket of fruit trees. Jaeger was sitting, cross-legged, on the ground next to the barred opening. He smiled. The friendly farmer became a predator in an instant. "Feeling better?"

"What in blazes are you up to?" she snapped.

"Does seem ungrateful, after all your kind assistance to an innocent merchant," he said. "I'm a bastard."

"You're a bounty hunter. Working with the other two, I reckon. Fine, you caught me. What've you done with my captain?"

"Not a thing." He reached into a leather pouch lying next to him, and withdrew the battered logbook. "Soldiers took him. He's in jail by now. I was more interested in you."

Kestrel frowned. She'd assumed she was in a prison cell, and that Binns was in another nearby. "This isn't the jail?"

Jaeger flipped open the cover of the log, and shook his head. "I'm sure they want you, too, but no. You're worth much more to the Danisobans."

Damn. She'd been watching for the dark robes and silver wrists, but she never thought they might use an ordinary hunter. Nor that he'd catch her so easily.

"I used to take on any commission I could find, until the Danisobans approached me. They offered four times as much as a normal bounty. Since then, I've hunted for the Brotherhood. The last eighteen seasons." He grinned. "Businessman, you see. Always watching for the best deal."

"How'd you know about me?"

"Lucky chance, that. You blowing up that little windstorm in the market just when I was strolling by. Wasn't like you were being subtle. Hell, a child could've guessed it!"

Bloody Grace, she thought desperately. *All these years running, and I'm caught with a breeze and a knock on the head.* "So where am I?"

"Danisoban safe house. It's where they put their own. Teach them a lesson, keep them from misbehaving, whatever. All that water."

"What water?" Kestrel asked.

"Just wait. Tide's turning."

A breeze ruffled the loose hairs of her braids, tickling her cheek and bringing with it the smell of the sea. She'd noticed the floor was damp when she woke up, but now it seemed to glisten. Kestrel lifted one foot and listened to the mud drip from her boot heel. The sea was making its way in, slowly as always. She hated her feet being wet inside her boots.

But what he'd said sparked a thought. She was a Promise, a mage in the raw. According to the pattern, she should have been just as weak and powerless in proximity to the water. Yet her magic had been perfectly strong when she was at sea. It was a quirk that would serve her excellently now, when she was soon to be up to her knees in seawater. Why didn't the water limit her as it did others of her kind?

"Soon as you're good and soggy, I'll head for the School." He turned another page, and sighed. "Why were you so attached to this book? It's dull reading."

She rolled her shoulders, testing. A sharp pain lanced through the right, making her grit her teeth. She reached up, gripped the bars of the window with her uninjured left arm, and planted her feet against the stone wall. The bars held.

"No point in tiring yourself," Jaeger said. "You can't break out that way. Not without a cannon to blow open the roof." He leaned close to the opening, peering in at her. "Hungry?"

Her stomach tightened at the word. She'd eaten almost nothing in the inn. The memory of the beryl's sweetness was sour in her mouth.

Jaeger sat back, digging in the leather pouch again. He pulled out a round, red cremefruit and held it out to her. "Are you sure?"

"I take no gifts from Danisobans," she snapped.

"Danisoban? Me?" He laughed. "I'd hardly say that."

"What would you say? That you just work for them?" She snorted. "That makes me feel so much better. You can keep the fruit. I'd rather be hungry."

"I don't think you mean that." A crunch followed—the breaking of a ripe skin, as if someone took a generous bite from it. Its aroma wafted to her, making her stomach growl more loudly than before. Kestrel swallowed hard and ground her back teeth, trying to stem the desire for food.

His hand slid through the bars, holding half of the fruit, sliced apart. "Eat. I swear to you I've done nothing to it."

Her toes were cold. She looked down. The mud had been replaced with water, enough to begin seeping through the laces of her boots. She sighed. Cold water, hunger, and now a guard to taunt her with food that could be poisoned, for all she knew. "It just gets better and better," she grumbled.

"So if it ain't food you're wanting, what could it be? I'll venture a guess," he continued. "I guess you want out of this hole you're in."

"What gave me away?" she asked, her voice dripping poison.

He chuckled. "I'm just smart like that." He tossed the cremefruit section toward her, and in spite of her suspicion, she caught it. It smelled so wonderful, sweet and fresh as springtime. She sighed, and turned her hand, letting the cremefruit plop into the dark water below her.

"Suit yourself." He took another bite of his half, chewing loudly.

"Go away," she said.

"I plan to. Just as soon as your feet are covered."

"If this cell is so unbreakable, why bother waiting?"

"Standard practice. Just because you made a little wind blow doesn't tell me how powerful you are. If I leave too soon, you could escape. I wouldn't be paid."

Kestrel stomped one foot, splashing muddy water onto her breeches. "I'll pay you double your fee if you'll let me out of this blasted hole."

"Splashing now? Sounds like time for me to go." He rose, looping the pouch strap over his shoulder. The logbook was still on the ground at his feet, but he picked it up and tucked it under his arm. "Can't be leaving this behind."

"Why not?" Kestrel asked. "If it's so boring . . ."

"I have a feeling others might find it more entertaining. And since you want it enough to jump out a window with it, it must be worth keeping." He touched two fingers to his forehead, in mock salute. "Be seeing you."

She watched him walk away, as casual as if he'd been on a morning's ramble. She had to find a way out of the hole before he got far, or Binns's book would be lost to her. Binns's book, in the hands of . . . She shook her head at her own idiocy. Jaeger was fetching the Danisobans. The book was a minor worry now.

Water swirled around her boots. The tide was rising quickly, more quickly than she hoped. At least Jaeger didn't know about her difference. What was she going to do? Binns would be hanged, she'd be enslaved by the Danisobans, and nothing would ever be right again unless she freed herself. Fighting tears, she laid her head on the edge of the barred opening. Bits of plaster stuck to her sweat-damp face.

Plaster. Could it be? She'd assumed the bars were set straight into the stone. She raised her head, and looked closely. The bars were sunk in drilled holes, filled in with plaster. Plaster could break. Kestrel leaned her elbows on the ridge of the barred opening. There had to be something she could use outside. Maybe a stone to break the bars. The grass was too high. She couldn't see so much as a heavy stick.

Sitting down in the water, Kestrel dragged one boot off. The heel was wood, but seasoned by life aboard a ship, it had become hard as a rock. Maybe it would do. She stood. Turning the boot backward, she struck at the plaster casings. Tiny slivers worked free, and cracks appeared, but it wasn't enough. At this rate, she'd be pounding until the end of time. She needed something stronger.

What had Jaeger said? He couldn't gauge her ability just from what he'd seen. What if she was stronger than even she knew? She'd always hidden from the magic, never tried to see how far she could take it. Here was a perfect opportunity. If she failed, no one would be hurt except perhaps herself. And if she succeeded . . .

Taking a deep breath, she whistled. Gentle fingers of tingling power crept along her skin, teasing, swirling, and finally coming together in the breath of her whistling. She imagined what it would look like if she could see it—hundreds of tiny diamond twinkles, perhaps. Or a flow of white silken flame.

She reached out, toward the bars, and wrapped her power around one of them. She drew in more air, then sent out a lively trill.

The steel bar shuddered violently and began to vibrate. Plaster shards exploded in every direction. Kestrel shielded her eyes, ducking occasionally. She kept up the trilling. The bar shook harder as more plaster, in larger and larger pieces, flew free.

She stopped when she ran out of breath. Her head was woozy. *I'd better take it easier next time, or I'll pass out*, she thought. She reached up to the bar. It was hot under her hand, hanging loose in its placement. Kestrel raised her boot again, and slammed the casing once more. The casing shattered, and the bar slipped to the ground, splashing into the water.

"Yes!" she cried. With one bar gone, there still wasn't room for her to slide out. Two more should do it. Kestrel set about whistling the plaster free, focusing on the cracks she'd already made. When she ran out of breath, she pounded with her boot heel until her head was steady again. It seemed to take hours. Eventually, the other bars slipped out, leaving her room to wriggle through to freedom. She slid her muddy foot back into her boot.

Jaeger was a tiny speck on the path through the trees. Her talisman for rescuing her captain was walking away with him. If she didn't get out soon, she'd never catch him. She gripped the remaining bar with her left hand, and pulled, bracing her feet against the wall. Her sodden boots slid down the wall. Between the water below and the smooth stone walls, there was no purchase. A thought crossed her mind,

She changed her grip on the bar, took a deep breath, and whistled. She sent the sound low, slipping like fingers under her feet. It lifted her, gently. Her heart was thumping from the effort. She dragged herself up, and with the last bit of breath, wedged her shoulders through the opening. The tingling power under her feet eased away. She grinned. As much as she hated the Danisobans, she had to admit magic was awfully handy.

She hung there for a moment, regaining her breath. Reaching out, she dug her fingers into the long grass and pulled her body forward, working her hips through the tight space. Finally, she was out. She rolled onto her back, drawing in great gulps of sweet air and letting her heart slow from its wild gallop.

Have to get up, have to catch him. Kestrel sat up, and looked at the prison she'd escaped. It resembled a stone box, big enough for six men to lie shoulder to shoulder but only hip-high. No wonder the water had been rising so fast. She'd have been neck-deep in cold water in a few hours. Such treatment would have sickened the average magus so much he could have drowned from his weakness. How many had died in that hole? And why was she immune? No time for such musings now. She stood, water oozing from her waterlogged boots, and ran in the direction she'd seen Jaeger walking.

IN minutes, she'd caught sight of him, strolling down the shady path through the trees. He was wearing two sword belts, one of them hers. As soon as she was in range, she put on a burst of speed, and launched herself through the air at his undefended back.

They collided, falling to the ground together with a bone-jarring thud. Before he could slip away, Kestrel wrapped her left arm around his neck. She yanked him back against her, flinging her legs around his waist to hold him still.

"Can't . . . breathe . . ." he wheezed.

"Shut up," she muttered in his ear. "You're going to give me my book and my sword belt, or I'll just hold on until you die."

He nodded, scrabbling at the strap across his chest. It snapped from the pouch, and fell free of him. His hands fell to the sword belt, and soon it, too, was on the ground.

Kestrel let go and planted her feet on his back. She pushed hard, and he rolled away from her, gasping. She grabbed the pouch, turned it up, and dumped the contents. An assortment of objects had fallen with the book, among them a dagger, some coins, and a bronze badge on a chain.

Jaeger was back on his feet, coughing, fire in his eyes. Kestrel lifted the dagger and pointed it at him. "Keep your distance. It's a dangerous place for a woman, this island. I might hurt you." Never changing her gaze, she retrieved her sword belt.

"I've never lost a commission yet," he growled.

"Sorry to ruin your reputation." She tucked the dagger into her waistband, and with her book under her arm, latched her belt around her waist. "Maybe you should call me the one that got away."

"You're hurt, and already tired. The minute you run from me, I'll catch you again. How long do you think you can run, in your condition?"

He was right about that. She had the energy to get back to town, but not enough for a fight, too. She glanced up at the low-hanging branches. "I'll have to slow you down." She licked her lips, and blew.

The tingle swept out, away from her, and enveloped Jaeger. He struggled as Kestrel lifted him high enough to snag his shirt on a branch a few feet above the forest floor. As soon as she was certain he was stuck, she let the whistle fade.

"You shouldn't have been able to work . . . you were knee-deep in water!" he cried. His eyes widened. "Wait! Don't go!"

Kestrel waved a hand at him as she turned to run for town. "Be seeing you."

"But I need to talk to you!"

She didn't look back.

O'ercome with sufferings strange and wild
I wept as I had been a child . . .

—SAMUEL TAYLOR COLERIDGE

Her arm was throbbing and her chest was heaving with exertion by the time she reached the market intersection. Camberlin's stood like a shining haven, just across the street. Any other time, she'd have said she could dash from where she stood to the swinging doors of the pub in a few seconds flat.

But this wasn't any other day. She hadn't been far from town, she'd soon discovered, but it had taken her longer than she'd hoped to navigate all the way down here through the alleys and passages she knew from childhood. Secret hidey-holes she'd used when she was young were now too small for her, and she'd had to invent new ones. Twice she thought she heard official shouts, and she'd pressed herself inside whatever nook or cranny was available to hide. Her breeches were sopping wet from slipping and splashing through the muck, and her silk tunic was mud-spattered and torn. Wherever she looked, she seemed to see an enemy standing ready to get his hands on her. She'd never paid such close attention before—was that flash of blue a soldier, or a lady's cloak flapping in the ocean breeze? The clink she heard from somewhere in the street could be a horse's bridle jangling, but it sounded like chains, ready to bind her. *Stop it,* she ordered herself. *It's your imagination.*

How do you know? Another voice chimed in, shouting down the reasonable side of her with its suspicious whispers. *Binns said you were imagining things about McAvery, too, and look where it's got him. Maybe you should listen to your imagination more.*

While she stood there, frozen with self-doubt and acting like an idiot, her captain and closest friend was being carted off to a prison ship. Across the way was safety and help. What right did she have to think of herself at a time like this? The voices inside her fell silent. Tensing her jaw, she looked straight ahead. She'd come this far, she could make it the rest of the way. But she wouldn't run. Less noticeable if she strolled across the street, a sailor like any other, heading for some fun at the pub. She stepped out into the sunlight, blinking, and held her breath.

No one cried out. No one shouted at her to halt. She joined the flow of walking traffic, making her casual way across the wide intersection. *Almost there*, she thought, *a few more steps.*

Sabas stepped from between the swinging doors as she neared. Catching sight of her, his eyes widened. Her heart thudded, fearing what his look meant. Were there soldiers behind her, ready to pounce? Or worse, had they beaten her here, and were they waiting inside to arrest her? She tightened her grip on the log under her left arm.

Sabas trotted out to meet her halfway. "What happened to you?" Sliding one arm around her shoulders, he squeezed gently as if trying to hold her up. She yelped, the still-tender shoulder flashing in a lightning of pain. He released her, his face a mask of worry. "Where's your boots?"

"I'm in trouble," she breathed. "Soldiers took Artie. They're after me. Got a Danisoban on my tail." She sagged against him suddenly. He bent, placing one arm at her back and the other behind her knees.

"No, I'm fine," she protested. He didn't listen. Without a word, he swept her into his arms and carried her into the quiet of the public house. It was still early. Here and there a customer slept, head pillowed on crossed arms, having passed out from too much drink the night before. Since Camberlin's never truly closed, no one saw the point in throwing the poor wretches out.

The wenches in their wraps were gathered at the big table in the middle of the room, eating their morning meal and gossiping together. Silence fell at the sight of Sabas and his complaining burden.

"If you don't put me down I'll pound you on the soft top of your head!" Kestrel declared.

"What, with that arm that hurts just to be squeezed?" he asked dryly. He'd pinned her uninjured side against his body when he lifted her.

"If I have to," she snapped.

Sabas raised both eyebrows. "So that's how it is, ask for help and then yell at the one who gives it? Act like that and see if I rescue you again."

"Rescue?" she shouted. "Where were you when Artie needed rescuing? I made the whole long trip across town by myself, and all you did was cart me in the door like an invalid?"

She regretted her words as soon as they left her mouth. Sabas said nothing, but the stricken look in his eyes spoke volumes. None of this was his fault—he didn't deserve angry words. He'd acted like a friend. The least she could do was accept the gesture.

"I'm sorry," she finally said, her voice humble. "Please put me down?"

He complied, setting her on a bench and yelling at the wenches to bring him water. Kestrel laid the logbook on the bench beside her, and relaxed against the table. She hadn't known how tense she was.

"Kestrel! Oh, my darling, what have they done to my baby?" Olympia wailed, careening down the stairs with her chemise hanging dangerously low off one shoulder and her hair tousled. She rushed to her friend, throwing herself to her knees and touching Kestrel on her face, hair, and hands. "Get her some rum, can't you see she's dying?"

"Stop fussing. It's not so bad as that," she said, pushing Olympia's hands away firmly. Most times, Kestrel found her friend's dramatic behavior amusing. At this moment, it grated on her nerves like the keel of an overloaded ship in a shallow passage. "I hurt my shoulder is all."

Tears rose in Olympia's eyes. She sat back on her heels, her lower lip poked out. "But your face, there's blood on it and your shirt, oh my gracious, your nice shirt is all torn up and filthy." She squinted suddenly, her mouth tightening into a scowl. "Did someone beat you? Should I send Sabas to teach him a lesson about raising a hand to a woman?"

"I was in a fight." Kestrel tried to smile, giving up when the pain in her arm and the worry in her heart forced her lips back down again. She'd been facing death regularly for five years, but Olympia still treated her like a helpless wench. "I left two of them sleeping in the dirt, but the third one tried to sell me to the Danisobans. I'm all torn up from escaping him and sneaking through the alleys. They're not as wide as I remember them."

"It ain't the alleys that shrunk, it's you that growed." Sabas threw a leg over the bench next to Kestrel, motioning toward a wench holding a wide wooden bowl. She set it on the table; it was full of clean water, some white cloths floating within.

"Let's see that arm now." He pinched the ruined silk of her sleeve in his fingers. "Care if I tear this off? That way you won't have to strip down to skin here in front of me and everyone else."

Kestrel glanced at her shirt ruefully. The silk had felt so nice compared to the sturdy broadcloth tunics she usually wore while she worked. "It's naught but rags, now."

Sabas gripped the neck of the shirt in his other hand, then gave the sleeve a sharp tug. It came away easily. Her bared shoulder looked normal, a little puffy perhaps, but the constant throbbing remained. She winced as Sabas pressed a cold, wet cloth from the bowl against her joint. Why did the cure always have to hurt worse than the injury?

Olympia cleared her throat. "Who were you running from?"

"Soldiers." Kestrel snorted. "And bounty hunters, and possibly a magus or two. They showed up at the inn, scroll in hand. They arrested Artie."

"What for? Surely not for piracy, after all these years?"

One of the girls approached, offering a bottle of rum and a full glass. Kestrel took the glass and downed half of it in a smooth swallow. "That man I told you about, the one with the ghost ship. It's all because of him."

"The good-looking one?"

"A good-looking face that hides a demon's black soul," Kestrel snapped. "If it's the last thing I do, I'll find Philip McAvery. By all the gods who care to be listening"—she drained the glass, and glared at it, her eyes dark with fury—"if so much as a hair on Artie's head is missing, I'll whip every inch of skin from McAvery's back." She sucked in a quick breath—Sabas had lifted her elbow to get a better angle for binding her shoulder. The stab of pain brought a tear to her eye. "Olympia, I need you to roust Shadd from bed."

"All in good time," Olympia said. "You're not doing anything until Sabas finishes tending to you. Then we'll clean you up and put you in better clothes."

As if in answer to Olympia's words, Kestrel's shoulder throbbed, and she winced. "They're taking Artie to Pecheta for trial."

"On what ship? When do they plan to leave?"

"I don't know. I assume today, on the next tide." The ache in her shoulder was slowly subsiding, now that Sabas was nearly finished, and she was feeling more like herself. "What's the damage?"

"You're lucky, it wasn't yanked loose of the socket. Looks like you got a nasty whack, is all. Should be back in fightin' mettle in a week, maybe less."

"A week?" she asked, shocked. "I don't have a week."

Sabas shrugged, turning away to clean up the spilled water on the table. Olympia positioned herself in front of Kestrel again, before she could get up from the bench. "Don't you think it might be a good idea to find out what's really happening, instead of sailing off half-cocked and under the wrong wind?"

"What are you going on about?"

"He won't leave today. I guarantee it."

"And how can you be so sure?"

Olympia tossed a lock of hair back over her bared shoulder. "I've lived on this island a long time, darling, and if there's one thing I know, it's that the government never does anything quickly. They have to prepare a ship, an official naval transport. Of the two in port right now, one is still on its side being careened. The other has nearly all its complement on a shore leave. Take at least a full day to put out the call to duty." She smiled mischievously. "I happen to know that three of the Navy's finest are upstairs this minute, sleeping the sleep of the well-drunk."

"Yes!" Finally, something was going her way. "Turn 'em over to me, let me ransom Binns for them."

Olympia held up a silencing hand. "Hush, child. You're misunderstanding me. Kidnapping sailors is a deal more serious than waylaying the ship en route to Pecheta, like you wanted to do. But you can't go haring off into the sunset. You need to know when they're leaving, and on what ship, the route they intend, and what marina they plan to put into once they reach the island. You see? The details are key. Otherwise you'll be attacking every naval vessel for miles, drawing far too much attention, wasting your time and guaranteeing that Binns is not the only one to die."

As much as every muscle in her body was screaming at her to move, fight, do something—she needed to get herself to sea as soon as possible, for safety from Jaeger and whoever he might bring with him next time—she knew Olympia was right. It would take a little while, but a good plan, a solid plan, could mean all the difference. "You have a suggestion?" she asked reluctantly.

"I have a special relationship"—Olympia winked—"with the guards in the Courthouse."

Kestrel lifted her eyebrows questioningly.

"Not that kind of relationship, darling. They're some of my best customers. I give them a special rate, and they accidentally look the other way when I visit the jail."

Hope had flared in Kestrel's heart, along with an odd sense of disappointment, an opportunity missed. She'd been spoiling for a fight, and now she was having to engage in more subterfuge. It rankled on her. A straightforward battle was so much simpler. "You can bribe the guards to let Binns escape?"

Olympia's well-manicured fingers shot to her mouth. "Oh, good gracious, no. I've taken years to cultivate these friendships carefully. If I tried something so heavy-handed, I'd be arrested in the blink of an eye. Besides, I don't have the sort of cash it would take."

"You're making no sense." Kestrel leaped to her feet, pacing across the room in thudding, irritated steps.

"Sit down." Olympia's voice was low, controlled. "We'll go together, down to the Courthouse. You'll have to dress as one of my girls, of course. You'll talk to your captain, settle your heart that he's unharmed. I, meanwhile, will help myself to the charts on the watch master's desk. Information, Kes. It's the path to his freedom."

Ten

Deeds to be hid which were not hid
Which all confused I could not know
Whether I suffered, or I did;
For all seemed guilt, remorse or woe.

—SAMUEL TAYLOR COLERIDGE

W hat was I thinking, listening to you?" Kestrel fumed.
"They aren't going to believe this. I'll be lucky to get out
with my head attached."

"Hush. All is well, and all will be well if you do as I told you. Just
follow my lead, and don't worry so." Olympia resettled the huge
basket on her hip, lifted the hem of her skirts just enough to still
be modest, and strode up the wide, majestic marble steps of the
Eldraga Maritime Courthouse.

Kestrel sighed. The idea had seemed so simple back at Camberlin's, with Sabas and Shadd and half a dozen sleepy-eyed wenches
gathered around nodding their approval. Relatively harmless, with
a useful payoff if she didn't ruin it. Olympia would play her part to
perfection, of course. So long as Kestrel kept her head down and
avoided tripping on the vast skirts, she could manage. Or so it had
seemed at the time.

Now, standing on the steps and looking up into the shadowy
depths of the most forbidding building on Eldraga, she wasn't so
certain. The huge bronze double doors, tinged green with exposure, stood open, the darkness beyond an ominous cave, the secret
lair of unspeakable justice, a pirate's worst enemy. *No,* she told herself, *I'm not uncertain. I'm terrified.* Let a ship come close, and
she'd be leading the charge, teeth bared and blade flashing. She'd
never backed down from a hand-to-hand brawl, no matter how

fearsome the opponent. So why should a minor mission like this make her gut twist into knots?

It had to be the skirts. According to Olympia, in the filmy chemise and flowing skirts, with her hair brushed into shining locks falling over her shoulders, Kestrel would blend in, just one of Olympia's girls. The tightly laced bodice made it hard for her to breathe. By far the worst were the skirts. Thick, heavy layers of swirling fabric that had a mind of its own, slipping between her feet and threatening to upset her with every step she took. Life was so much easier in breeches and boots. Having to watch every step filled her with apprehension. Or maybe it was the fact that being recognized in this place was enough to get her thrown into a cell right next to Binns. Just stroll through those doors on Olympia's heels, and in minutes she'd be able to see her friend.

She climbed the shining marble steps, holding her skirts up the way Olympia had done. For one irrational second, she envisioned how nasty a spill she could suffer were she to slip on steps as smooth, hard, and cold as these. Was that why they built courthouses out of such material? So that accused criminals could be put to death without the inconvenience of an actual trial? She missed the wood of her deck beneath her feet.

Olympia halted on the top step. She crooked her finger. "Come along, child," she ordered. "I'm not getting any younger." She turned, a queen without her crown, and marched into the Courthouse. Kestrel followed close on her heels.

She'd grown up running the streets of Eldraga, and thought she knew every inch of the island. But penniless orphans weren't the sort to seek justice in the Courthouse, so she'd never set foot inside before. The air inside was cool, as if the breezes of winter continuously blew through its hallways. The ceiling was dizzyingly high. Immense walls were covered in richly colored tapestries depicting ancient battles and coronations of kings whose names were long-forgotten. In the center of the gigantic room stood a pulpit of dark red wood, taller than she was. A man sat within, dressed in the blue robes of an Eldragan official, pale and pinched, with a quill in his hand. He glanced up at the *tap-tap-tap* of Olympia's shoes on the marble floor. A smile split his face like the sun coming out on a rainy day.

"Why, Mistress Camberlin! What a pleasant surprise!" He beamed. "To what do I owe this visit?"

"I would say I had missed your handsome self, but we both know where you were three nights ago," she simpered. "Truly I'm here on an errand. In the prison."

He nodded, the smile never wavering. "What sort of business are you up to, with that basket on your hip?" he asked. "I'll have to inspect it. Can't have you sneaking a lockpick or a dagger in to one of the prisoners."

"Silly man! As if I'd even want one of those desperate outlaws free to roam our streets," she replied. "This basket is for you and the other gentlemen, of course." She peeled back the linen covering, revealing the golden brown tops of freshly baked muffins, each one the size of a small melon. The delicious aroma wafting from the opened basket made Kestrel's mouth water.

It apparently had the same effect on the bureaucrat. His eyes widened, and he licked his lips. "Those look fine, indeed. I don't see any reason you can't run your errand while I eat my morning snack, eh?"

Olympia lifted out an enormous muffin, and placed it in his waiting hands. "Enjoy that. We won't take long." She replaced the covering and *tap-tap*ped past the pulpit to a wide wooden door at the rear of the room. It opened into a long windowless corridor, lit by flickering torches every few feet. The door fell closed behind them with a gentle thud.

"Food?" Kestrel finally asked. "You bribe them with muffins?"

"Muffins, cookies, a lovely meat tart. It's a better enticement than money," Olympia whispered while they walked. "Start giving cash for small favors, and they eventually want more. They get nervous, think they need to hedge their bets in case they get caught out and lose their livelihood."

"On the ocean, it's never so tricky."

"On the ocean, you rarely have to see the same people twice."

They arrived at another door. Olympia rapped on it, and a peak-hole slid open. A suspicious pair of blue eyes looked out.

"Olympia Camberlin!" The hole slammed closed. In an instant, Kestrel heard the dull, metallic sound of a lock being thrown open, and the door creaked wide.

"Bless my sin-blackened soul!" The guard was short and stocky, with a pasty complexion and a uniform that hadn't been properly laundered in far too long. If Kestrel had seen him on the street, the pallor of his skin would have convinced her he suffered from some dreadful disease. "It's been too long since you came by to see me."

"But not since you came to see me," she said, sweeping into the main guardroom. "Elspeth says she hopes you'll visit us the next night you have off duty."

"Does she now?" He grinned, pink rising high on his fair cheeks. Kestrel swallowed a grimace at the thought of being close to a man like this. The smell of his clothing alone was enough to make her faint. This Elspeth had to be a woman of strong constitution. "What are you doing here today?"

"Alas, I have a bit of business with one of your unfortunates."

"Which one?" he asked. "We're nearly in possession of a full house."

"Pirate. Name of Binns." She waved a hand in Kestrel's direction. "Bastard wheeled and dealed the heart right out of my girl, here, and the poor thing's just distraught." Kestrel dropped her head in response to Olympia's words, and covered her face with her hands. Olympia patted her back. "Wants to wish him farewell before he sails off to be—" She drew a hand across her throat with a gagging sound.

The guard chuckled. "That old coot? I wouldn't have thought he had it in him." He leaned forward and chucked Kestrel under the chin. "You sure you wouldn't have yourself a real man? I could make you forget the sea dog. Probably pay you better, too."

Kestrel bit her tongue, keeping the angry words that bubbled up from her throat from spilling out. Binns was worth twenty of this foul little man—hell, any of the men on her ship were better than him. But because he had a uniform, he thought himself admirable.

He smiled, displaying brownish teeth. "Don't get yourself worked up, lass. Time enough to get to know each other later, after your buccaneer has met his reward. We'll get you your sweet good-bye." He frowned suddenly, squinting his pale blue eyes at Kestrel. "Wait a second. There was a girl with him, one of his crew they said. This ain't her, is it?"

He was leaning in close, trying to get a clearer look at her face. Kestrel sobbed suddenly, hoping she sounded less like a tortured kitten than she feared she did. She wasn't the actor Olympia was. She dropped her head and let her hair fall. What if this soldier had been along with the arresting force? How was she supposed to rescue Binns from the inside of a jail cell?

Olympia insinuated her curvaceous body between the suspicious guard and Kestrel. "How long have we known each other, hmmm? Would I be so stupid as to try something like that? Next you'll be saying I have a weapon hidden somewhere on my person." She stepped backward, nearly catching Kestrel's toe and forcing Kestrel to move farther away from the inquisitive man. "You can search me, if you like," she simpered, spreading her arms wide and giving her chest a little jiggle.

His eyes switched back and forth from Olympia's cleavage to the basket she still held. He licked his lips, and Kestrel had to fight off a grin. Flirt and tease she might, but in the end she remained mistress of the house, inviolate. The fellow had to know what sort of treats he could expect from Olympia, yet he still held out hope.

"What's in the basket?" he asked after a spell, tearing his eyes free.

"Lunch," Olympia answered. "I thought you and I could share a nibble together."

What attention the guard had left, he was no longer wasting on Kestrel. "Off you go," he said to her, waving a careless hand toward the cell area. "Next to last on the right." He snaked an arm around Olympia's pale shoulders.

Olympia glanced back at Kestrel, and gave her a mischievous wink before she allowed herself to be led away toward the paper-strewn desk.

Kestrel turned, quick-stepping into the slender corridor that ran several yards into the shadowy depths. No lighted torches flickered along the way—apparently prisoners didn't deserve to see their surroundings.

Not that there was much worth seeing. The floor and walls were made of stone, broken every three feet by sets of iron bars. The cells were small and windowless, each one housing a miserable creature, some hunched in the corners, moaning and bewailing their situations. Others snored on the filthy floors, sleeping the sleep of men with nothing left to lose. The rushes covering the floors looked as if they'd been fresh way back in her grandfather's day. The air reeked of unwashed bodies and stale urine. She wondered how long it had been since the cells had been swept out. The idea of being locked away in here, with no access to air and sunlight, filled her with revulsion. For the first time, she understood what Binns had been saying during their talk on board the *Wolfshead*. Any life, even one outside the law, would be preferable to being in a foul place like this.

"Binns?" she called. "Artie?"

"Here, sweetkins, I'll be yer Artie," came a voice from a nearby cell. She ignored it, and all the other catcalls that erupted after. Next to last on the right, the guard had said. She peered into the dimness, the frail illumination from the guard's station just barely enough to let her see all the way in.

If the guard hadn't told her where he was, she doubted she'd have recognized the tired, old wreck inside. He was sitting on the moldy rushes in the far corner, arms crossed over his knees and head resting down. The fine clothes he'd been wearing at breakfast were dingy and stained. The right sleeve was torn at the shoulder, as if he'd struggled. He bore little resemblance to the proud man with whom she'd sailed the oceans.

"Artie," she whispered. He didn't move. He'd only been in custody for a few hours. The bastards must have beaten him within inches of his life, trying to get him to admit to a crime of which he wasn't guilty. Wasn't that how it worked? She kicked at the bars, wishing she could break iron with her feet. She still had her boots on—Olympia had tried to convince her to wear slippers, but Kestrel wouldn't budge.

Good thing. Her toes were stinging from kicking the bars, and Artie still hadn't moved. A finger of doubt tweaked her mind. He was filthy, and torn, but he didn't look wounded. No blood on his clothing, for one thing. And he was sitting up. If he'd been beaten, shouldn't he be sprawled across the floor senseless? Blood . . . it was too dark to see much, but she was pretty sure there wasn't any bleeding. Any drubbing he'd received hadn't been serious enough to incapacitate him. But if they weren't using physical pain, then how could they have broken him so quickly?

The thought popped to the forefront of her mind, as readily as if it had been waiting there for her to get around to noticing. Danisobans. Disgusting magic workers. Over the stench of the ancient rushes and unwashed bodies in here, she should've smelled the stink of their foul presence on the situation. They'd pried his mind open like a ripe coconut, scraped around hunting for a confession that didn't exist, then left him to rot in this cell, shattered.

"Captain Binns, look at me this minute!" she hissed. He didn't even take a deep breath. Had they stolen his memories as well? Maybe there was nothing left but a broken husk. "Don't you know me? Artemus?"

As if his given name were a charm to break the spell he'd been lost in, Binns finally raised his head, peering out toward her with watery eyes. He sighed, seeming not to recognize her, and laid his head back down on his crossed arms.

Anger flashed through her suddenly, dancing like lightning in the rigging of a ship. "So this is how a captain behaves? One little scrape and you give up without even the least kind of struggle? If I didn't know better, I'd think you wanted to die. Too tired. Or maybe you're just too old. Maybe it'd be easier to let them hang you." She couldn't believe she was talking to Binns this way. The words spilled from her mouth on their own, sharp-bladed whispers designed to pierce and injure. She squinted angrily. "Is that it? Couldn't stand the thought of retiring. Everyone knowing that old Binns used to be a pirate. Is it easier to go out in a blaze of glory? You'd be dead, but they'd sing about you. So much better than fighting for your life."

He looked up again, lifting his head like it was an oversize anchor on a low-gauge rope. "Get out of here, my girl," he muttered. His voice was low and gravelly. "For the sake of the love I bear you, take the ship and sail away. If they ask you, say you don't know me."

Her breath caught in her throat at his words. He'd spoken. Hopeless words, certainly, but it was a start. "Artie, was it the Danisobans? Did they do something to you?" First her own parents died at their hands, now they'd gotten a grasp on the only family she still had. If she ever got the opportunity, she swore to all the gods in all their temples that her revenge would be cold and vicious and oh, so sweet.

"Danisobans?" His voice was muffled from the cradle of his arms. "No, this is the work of ordinary men." He peered through the shadows, seeming to focus truly on her for the first time. "You're in skirts."

She smiled weakly. "Olympia's idea. Only way I could get in to see you before . . ." She gulped. *Before you die? Before they sail you away to hang from a rope by your neck? For pity's sake, woman, get hold of yourself. You're acting like a child.* She squared her shoulders, and blinked hard to clear her eyes of the wetness that had welled up. "Artie, listen to me. We're going to get you out."

"Stupid," he said. "Waste of time. I'm an old man. Let me go to my just reward." He struggled to his feet, and hobbled over to the door of the cell. He wrapped his fingers around the heavy bars. His knuckles were scarred and dirty. Kestrel reached up, laying her own hand gently over his. His work-calloused skin was so cold under her touch, she felt like her own hands were burning him with their heat.

"Artie, I can't. I have to help you."

He was staring at her hand on his, as if mesmerized. "How do you plan to save me, then? Chase down the entire Navy? In our little eight-gun sloop?"

"Yes, if we have to. Soon as we find out what ship you're to be on, we're sailing right behind you."

"Damn foolish notion. That little sloop's good enough to pirate from, but it can't stand up to a warship. Especially not now. You'd be blown so hard out of the water there wouldn't even be flotsam to mark where you'd been." He spoke offhandedly, as if discussing the weather, but a spark appeared in his eye.

"I'm working on a plan, Captain. We can do this. Shadd believes. So do I." She tightened her grip around his fingers. "We won't let them hang you, Artie. I won't let them."

"There ain't a thing you can say about it. Not with my log in his possession."

"Your log? In whose possession? McAvery's?" Kestrel scowled, her hand dropping to the empty space at her belt where her sword usually hung. It gave her an unpleasant sense, anxious and incomplete, to notice it wasn't there. As if she had just lost an arm. "I should have known he was behind this. Don't worry, Artie! As soon as we get you clear of the Navy, I'll hunt him down, gut him, and serve you up his head on a platter."

But Binns was shaking his head emphatically. " 'T wasn't McAvery had me arrested. Trust me, if he'd stayed in the same inn we did, he'd likely be in here as well. He's a lucky sod. You'd have done well to fall in with him. He isn't what he seems." He stopped. "No matter. I was doin' my duty. I knew the risks."

Duty? She frowned at him. He was a pirate, free as any bird, coming and going as he wished and answerable to no man save himself. What duty? She'd been nervous when he started his ramblings about retirement. But this was utterly unexpected, and frightening. Binns had been a pirate for years before he hired her on; she accepted that there were pieces of his life about which she knew nothing. All this talk of duty and risk coming from the man who'd taught her how to be free could only mean he'd been keeping secrets from her, the kind that led unwary pirates into deadly situations. She'd trusted him, and it was turning her world inside out.

She shook her head, trying to clear the confused fog that threatened to take her over. "Don't worry about the log, Artie. Don't you remember?" She stopped, catching herself as her voice began to rise. "You sent me upstairs to fetch it from your pack, just before they arrested you?"

The spark she'd noticed before flared into blazing life behind his eyes. "You're not humorin' an old man? You really have it?"

"Of course. I'd already retrieved it when they chased me out the window. It's safe. But what's in it that's so important?"

Binns gripped the bars and lowered his voice to a whisper. "Don't try to rescue me, lass. Take the book to Pecheta. Don't read it. Don't add any entries."

"What have you written in there that's so important?" Cold was washing through her gut, making it hard for her to breathe. All the sense she'd managed to make of the world and her place in it was melting away. Who gave a tinker's damn about books? Nobody but magi and nobles, both of whom she made a point of steering clear away from. And now Binns wanted her to put herself right in their midst? Like hell she wouldn't read it. Reading his log had become the first thing she planned to do, once they got this all sorted out.

"There's information in there could get you killed, Kes. Trust me. Gather up the men you can, and leave on the late tide. Once you arrive, find a way to see a man called Lig. He's an advisor to the king."

Her eyes widened. He's snapped, she thought. The king of the Nine Islands was rumored to be immortal. Older citizens would swear he'd been king when they were children, yet he never looked a day over fifty. Kestrel had never put much stock in the tales, since she never expected to meet the man. And now Binns was trying to tell her he had some clout with him? The torture had broken his mind, it had to be.

Binns was grinning. More like the man she knew, that dangerous glint that always told her they were about to fall into trouble twinkling in his eye. "How am I supposed to get past the palace gate?"

"You're a resourceful lass, you'll think of something. It's vital my book reaches the king. Lig's the man can accomplish that. Not the porter, nor the steward, not even Prince Jeremie. Especially not the prince. Do you follow me?"

"I follow." *Even if I get myself thrown into a dungeon on Pecheta,* she thought.

"One other thing, my girl." His voice dropped to a barely perceptible whisper. "Don't trust your first impressions about anyone. Treachery can rise from the least likely of sources, but so can help. Accept what fortune offers you, no matter how you feel about the package it comes wrapped in. Do you understand me?"

She frowned. "Not a word. You're starting to sound like that beggar and his secret messages. But I'll do my damnedest to keep your counsel."

"I know you will," he said. "You always were a stubborn one."

"Had to be, to work with you," she snapped, "otherwise you'd be forever steering us into one scrape after another."

He spread his fingers, letting Kestrel's smaller ones slide in between and squeezing them gently. "I wouldn't ask this for myself. I couldn't go to my grave knowing you'd died for my sorry carcass. But that book, it's more important than I can tell you."

"Time's up!" The announcement rolled down the corridor, sooner than she wanted.

Kestrel reached up to her left ear and slid open the clasp on her earring. It was a small silver hoop, plain and delicate. Binns had given it to her after her first battle, as a symbol of her new life. She'd never taken it out. Until now.

Palming the tiny circlet of silver, she slid it onto the first joint of Binns's little finger. "Take this," she whispered. "Keep it safe for me."

He nodded, pulling his hand back and wrapping his other hand around it. "Fair winds, lass," he murmured. "Here's hopin' I'll be givin' it back soon."

THE warm air of the street outside the Courthouse was as welcoming as a lover's embrace. Kestrel stood still for a moment at the top of the marble stairs, letting her eyes adjust to the bright sunlight. Throngs of shoppers and businessfolk surged past, all intent on their very important tasks and errands. How could the world look so normal when everything was so very wrong?

"And one for you!" Olympia blew a kiss to the last of her gentleman friends and joined Kestrel. "Well, I'm exhausted. What would you say to a drink, darling?"

"Only if there's talk to go with it," Kestrel said. Now that she'd seen Binns, spoken with him, her task seemed doubly urgent. If there weren't guards searching the streets for her, she'd have thrown off Olympia's silly disguise and run at top speed for the docks.

Olympia patted her arm. "Patience, sweeting. All in good time."

The two women descended the steps and joined the river of humanity, jostling and bumping their way into the approximate middle of the wide street and letting the current guide them in the direction of Camberlin's. Kestrel glanced around. Seeing no blue uniforms, she decided to chance a word. "Well?"

"Well what?"

"Did you get it?"

Olympia patted Kestrel's hand. "Relax, love. We'll talk when we get home."

"I can't wait!" She startled herself with her own vehemence.

"Such an impatient woman you are. Keep flinging about like this and one day you'll run into a brick wall."

"I think I'm running into one right now," she grumbled, and Olympia chuckled.

"Pouting, too? I never suspected so many talents."

Kestrel stopped in her tracks, causing the human flow to part and slide around her as if she were a rock in the river. "Just tell me the name. Please."

Olympia slid her hand into the crook of Kestrel's elbow, drawing her close enough for a whisper but continuing to walk along the busy street, the now-empty basket swinging lightly from one wrist. "You may know every inch of a ship from bow to stern and back again, but you haven't any idea how this game is really played. Do you truly think," she murmured, her eyes flashing fire, "there aren't as many ears here on the street as there are in yonder Courthouse?"

Was that true? Kestrel glanced around. No blue uniforms nearby, but that didn't mean much. That woman, moving awfully slowly—was she attempting to listen to them? Or the ragged boy, slipping in between the taller members of the crowd, completely unnoticed by most? What could he have heard, and how much might someone pay for what he knew?

She rubbed the space between her eyebrows, where a nagging pain seemed to have taken permanent residence. "It was so bad, seeing him like that."

Olympia rolled her eyes heavenward. "Ye gods, save me from pirates," she moaned dramatically, "ten times more emotional than all my wenches put together." She let her head bump against Kestrel's, so close the younger woman could smell her hair. She'd dressed it that morning, with sandalwood oil. It was a soothing scent. "Don't fear, dear," she whispered, "victory is within your grasp." She let go of Kestrel's arm and swept away down the street.

The pirate stared after her friend, incredulous. Until it hit her what Olympia had said. What she'd told her. In a roundabout way that fit the strange landlubber's game of politics and strategy that Kestrel feared she'd never understand.

The *Victory*. She knew the ship. A fast little brigantine, twelve guns. Carried a minimum complement, which meant that she might even stand a decent chance of taking the ship without losing too many of her own men.

She fell into step behind Olympia, holding the softly whispered name in her heart like a priceless gem. Hope was springing within her, and she almost felt she could fly. They had a name.

Binns had charged her with a different strategy, but she couldn't let go of the original plan. After all, who was she? An outlaw, a pirate, nobody worth the notice of a king's advisor. If the royal guards didn't kill her on the spot, she'd find herself languishing in a Pechetan dungeon.

No, it was better all around if they kept to their first plan. If they could waylay the *Victory*, she wouldn't have to bother going all the way to Pecheta and rousting out this man Lig. Binns could deliver his bloody book himself.

Eleven

Day after day, day after day
We stuck, nor breath nor motion,
As idle as a painted ship
Upon a painted ocean.

—SAMUEL TAYLOR COLERIDGE

As soon as she and Olympia returned to the inn, they'd been met by Shadd, Red Tom, and Jaques. The three of them were dressed, angry, and more than ready to charge off to Binns's rescue. Kestrel calmed them down long enough to let Olympia share her information.

"The *Victory* sails with this afternoon's tide."

"I thought you said there was no way he'd be moved for at least a day," Kestrel said.

"That I did. The process is moving unusually fast, this time. The fellows I told you about, sleeping a drunk off upstairs? Rousted out while we were gone on our errand this morning." Olympia shook her head. "This is more than a mere piracy charge. Somebody wants your captain. Somebody important."

"All right, that settles it." Kestrel felt a tiny flicker of relief. She'd hoped to be off this island before the Danisobans sent out more than bounty hunters looking for her. She thumped the table with her fist. "Tom, Jaques, you men hit the street. Find and alert as many of the others as you can put your hands on. Shadd, you're coming with me to ready the *Wolfshead*. I'm sailing with the afternoon tide," she warned, "no matter who's on board. Any man gets left behind, it's his own fault for not moving quicker."

"Aye, Quarter." The two of them practically ran out the door. Kestrel didn't try to fool herself that their enthusiasm was for her.

Artemus Binns had sailed the Nine Islands for longer than some of them had been alive—being along on the adventure to rescue him might be dangerous, but success would guarantee their names going down in folktales for generations.

"Olympia, can you find me some breeches and a shirt? I need to change out of this frippery."

"That's a bad idea. They're on watch for a female pirate, especially now," she tsked, waving her hand up and down. "You go marching through the streets in breeches, you'll be in chains before you can smell the pastries in the market."

She had a point. Not only would the authorities have a description of her, but her shirt was ruined, and her breeches were stiffening from the mud that had soaked them. It would have taken too long for them to be laundered and returned to her.

"Fine. But only until I get back aboard my ship." Kestrel tapped the logbook. "How do I carry this without anyone noticing?"

"Why don't you leave it with me?" Olympia asked. "You can come back for it after you've rescued Artie."

"No. If I can't catch up to that ship, it's the only currency I have to buy Artie's freedom."

"Who d'you think will want it so badly?"

Kestrel leaned closer to her friend. "Artie says it's to be taken to the king."

"That can't be right. A book?" Olympia reached out to lift the cover. "What's in there that's so valuable to the Ageless King?"

Kestrel slapped the cover closed. "Artie said not to read it."

Olympia poked her lip out in a childish pout. "Keep your secrets, then. I had a marvelous way for you to carry the bloody thing unnoticed, but perhaps I'll keep my mouth shut. It's not as if you need my help." She sat back in her chair and stared off into space.

Kestrel sighed. "I'm sorry, Olympia. Artie made me promise. He said whatever's inside was too dangerous for anyone to read. And I couldn't forgive myself if I let anything happen to you."

She tipped her chin a little higher and huffed out a long breath.

"I suppose if you laced a bodice nice and tight, with the book between it and your back, it might go unnoticed."

Bloody Grace, not the bodice again. Even if the lump on her back showed, her hair, falling in waves of black to her hips, would hide it from casual notice. She hated the way her hair slid across her vision and stuck to her lips whenever she took a deep breath, but if it was hiding the book on her back, she hadn't much choice.

Once she was laced, she handed her sword to Shadd. "Carry this for me, lad?"

He nodded, unbuckled his own belt, and slid her sword frog next to his. Kestrel felt naked without her sword. It hadn't looked right hanging among the skirts, which twisted and swirled around her legs, catching on her boots and threatening to pull her down with every other step.

Kestrel turned to Olympia. "Thank you for everything. Remember, the Danisobans may call on you, looking for me. If I don't come back—"

"Hush, girl." Olympia's eyes were brimming. "I'm not afraid of those wrinkled old men. Go and rescue Artie. I expect to hear all about it when you're finished." She threw her arms around Kestrel. "Be careful, sweetness."

Sabas shook Shadd's hand, then hugged Kestrel, too. "Easy on that shoulder, lass."

She smiled at him. "Thanks, Sabas."

They left the inn without looking back. Meandering toward the docks, stumbling every now and then to fall against each other, she and Shadd did their best to look like a pair of drunkards headed for a rendezvous on board a ship, a common enough sight on Eldraga and one that would attract almost no attention.

"Come here, wench, and give us a kiss!" Shadd bellowed suddenly. Tightening the arm he'd snaked around her waist, he swung her up against his broad chest and pressed his cheek against hers.

"Put your mouth on me and by all the gods, I'll tear your stones off with my bare hands," she hissed.

"I ain't that stupid," he muttered against her ear, "bluebacks, across the way."

She inclined her head. Two guards were leaning against the wall of a dockside warehouse. Their attitude was relaxed, two fellows doing their job with as little effort as possible. Their eyes were alert, watching everyone who passed by. Maybe they weren't looking for her. Certainly there were other criminals more important than she was.

"Slip into that alley," Kestrel directed, flicking a finger toward the shadowed break between two buildings behind Shadd. In three steps, they reached the vague protection the alley had to offer. Shadd put Kestrel on her feet, and backed her against the wall, placing his meaty hands on either side of her head and effectively blocking her with his body.

"So, are they following?" he whispered, dipping his head as if trying for another kiss. Kestrel glanced under his arm, taking a quick look back the way they'd come. The soldiers were still reclining against the wooden wall, staring up the street.

"Nope. We're good." Shadd straightened and the two of them made their way down the narrow side street. This close to the sea, the strangely comforting smell of dead fish and tar rolled over them. Slimy, purple-green fungus grew from the slowly rotting walls of the warehouses. Reaching the other end, the big gunner stepped out first, glancing left and right, then waved Kestrel forward.

"Our lads are waitin'," he murmured, "down that way." The docks were busy as always, men loading and unloading crates and barrels from small rowboats. A band of soldiers, in the blue coats of the Royal Army, walked casually down the dock, in the opposite direction. Kestrel was surprised that such a small contingent had been left to cover the entire dockside, but she didn't waste time wondering about it. At the rate the bluebacks were moving, they wouldn't be back to this end until she and her men were long gone.

She turned her gaze toward the water. The *Victory* rocked gently at anchor on the opposite side of the harbor from where she'd left the *Wolfshead*. She was a tight little vessel, paint bright and sails clean, with six gunports on each side. Blue-coated men scurried over her decks, making ready to get under way. A hackney boat was rowing out to her, crowded with more bluebacks. Kestrel wondered if it was carrying supplies or captives. Binns could be sitting there, surrounded by soldiers, chains around his hands and feet. She turned away. It was too far to make out who any of the figures might be, but Kestrel suddenly feared her resolve would break if she saw a shackled man in that boat.

She steeled her chin, peering in the other direction for her own sloop, hoping most of the crew were already aboard, making ready. The *Wolfshead*, being both small and empty of hold, hadn't drawn much water. She'd dropped anchor close in, where the bigger, heavier vessels couldn't go for fear of running aground. Kestrel squinted against the brightness of the sunlight glinting off the water, and moved a lock of hair from her eyes. Nothing changed. She didn't want to believe what she wasn't seeing. Where the *Wolfshead* had been anchored was now an empty expanse of shimmering water.

"No," she whispered. She grabbed a handful of Shadd's shirt and pulled his head down to hers. "Where's the damned ship?"

The gunner scanned the busy harbor. "Scuttle me!" he growled.

Kestrel planted an elbow on Shadd's massive chest and rested her forehead on her hand. *This isn't happening*, she said to herself. *I'm going to count to three and when I look back up the ship'll be sitting right there, right where we left her. Right where I left her. One . . . two . . .*

"Kes, what are ye doin'?" Shadd sounded mystified. She finished her count silently, and looked back over the water. The *Wolfshead*, despite her hopes, was still missing.

"Ye think the soldiers took her into custody, as evidence or suchlike?" Shadd asked. Kestrel shook her head. As far as she could tell from what the emissary had read off his scroll, they thought Binns had come in on the *Thanos*. In the few minutes she'd had with him, before he knew she had the log and had become so excited, he'd tried to get her to take the sloop and run. Sure evidence that he'd never said a word about it to his captors. No reason they'd have even known about the *Wolfshead*. So where had it gone?

"Not likely," she said. "Even if they did, they wouldn't have moved her. They'd just put a contingent aboard."

Shadd paled, making a protective gesture. "Ye don't think . . ." he began, his voice sounding oddly muffled. "After all, that ghost ship disappeared, too. Mayhap the ghosts got on the *Wolfshead* while we were in town, and vanished her into wherever it is ghosts go when the sun rises."

She should have known the crew was still spooked. She and Binns were the only ones who had heard the whole story. "Trust me. The *Wolfshead* hasn't been cursed by ghosts. But it's obvious someone stole her."

"Well, if it weren't ghosts what took her . . ." Shadd squinted suddenly, rage replacing superstition in the space of a breath. "Them rats I left aboard! When I catch up with 'em . . ." He pounded his fist into his palm angrily.

Kestrel straightened. "Not our boys," she said, a slow burn awakening inside her. Pirates weren't known for their honor. At least once every season a crew went rogue. The lucky captains were marooned or set adrift in a longboat unharmed. Far too many were tortured and mutilated by their former underlings. This was no mutiny, she'd swear to it. There'd been only three men left aboard, for one thing, too few to sail even a small vessel like the sloop easily.

"Kes!" Shadd jerked his head toward the *Victory*. Her anchor was slowly rising, sparkling drops blinking from her dark points. The sails belled, and she began to move. Kestrel watched in growing horror as the prison ship navigated its careful way toward the open ocean. With her captain in its hold. And here she stood, marooned as surely as of she'd been dropped on a deserted island alone. After all their plans—sneaking into the Courthouse, wearing these godforsaken skirts all damned day—and she couldn't do anything but watch as her hopes sailed away.

What cruel deity would do this to her? A sickening flash of understanding crept into her thoughts. It wasn't an act of some capricious god. Nor had the soldiers known about the *Wolfshead*. But there was one man who did. The same man who'd set in motion Binns's arrest for stealing a ship he'd never even set foot on.

McAvery. The name hung like a half-chewed bit of gristle in her throat. Like Binns, she'd been wrong about him. He wasn't a magus at all. Nor was he to be trusted, as Binns had tried to make her believe. He was a thief, and a skilled one. That's why Burk and Volga were hunting him. Bounty hunters, they had to be. McAvery must have stolen the *Thanos*, intending to refit and repaint her, only the authorities and the stalking horses were too close to his tail. He'd played Binns from the minute he saw him on the water, titillated the pirate's greed with that fine ship and farm-boy act, and hung him out like yesterday's washing. She still didn't know how McAvery'd managed to disappear during the storm, but that no longer mattered.

He isn't a magus. The words echoed in her mind, sharpened by the clarity of hindsight. As Olympia had insisted, so McAvery turned out to be. A magus would have been able to take what he wanted, instead of running confidence games. He'd played her, too, but now she saw through the illusion he tried to create. His heart pumped, his lungs worked, same as hers. Philip McAvery was an enemy she could defeat. No supernatural advantage to turn the tide in his favor. Merely a flesh-and-blood man who'd used his charm and skill to put her best friend's life at risk and stolen her ship. And being a man, balls to bones, he could die like any other. The fear she'd wrestled over the last day faded like so much morning fog. She ground her teeth together, dropping the drunken-wench act, hiking up the skirts, and striding in her usual way toward the waiting crew. Let the soldiers notice her now; she'd as soon run them through, just to keep herself in practice until she could lay hands on the bastard McAvery.

They reached the gathered throng of men. "Talk to me," Kestrel demanded, keeping her voice low and twisting her mussed hair out of her face and into a queue over one shoulder.

The small gathering of men had stopped their low conversation

at her approach, and were now staring at her in wonder. She furrowed her brow. "What, have you all had your tongues cut out?
What's the matter with you?"

Some of them blushed, looking away nervously. Others were
grinning, and one man whistled suggestively. Shadd slid closer to
Kestrel and tightened his fists. "Belay them thoughts now, you
dogs. We got us a situation to handle."

"Sorry, Kes," one fellow offered. "It's just that we ain't seen you
like that afore. I mean, in a skirt, and looking like . . ." He trailed
off, turning his red face toward the sparkling harbor.

Uncomfortable laughter rippled over the group. She glanced
down, only then noticing the cleavage created by the tight bodice.
She blew out an angry huff. *Damn these clothes!* she thought. *I
knew they'd be trouble.* What was the problem with men? She'd
held her own alongside them for months, slept in the hold like they
did, cursed and fought and drank with the best of them, but put
her in a skirt and what happens? They start thinking with the least
important of their body parts. "Listen up, men," she barked, "I
don't have time for your romantic notions. Binns is out of commission, and that means I'm in charge." She glared, trying to catch as
many of them by the eye as she could. "Any man jack of you wants
to have a go at me, now that you're thinking like that, try it. But
don't be too fond of your innards, 'cause you'll be leaving them on
the deck."

The smiles disappeared. Several of them dropped their heads,
and muttered apologies that she could hardly even make out. *I'll
have to watch my step the next few days*, she thought. *One of these
might not be so penitent as he's pretending right now.* "Who can tell
me what happened to the *Wolfshead*?" she demanded, changing
the subject.

Bardo stepped forward. He'd been with Binns long before
Kestrel came aboard, serving as cook and surgeon. Rumor had it
that he'd been a mighty fighter once, until the day he tried to stop a
sword with his arm. He'd kept his hand but it was twisted now, and
useless for holding a weapon. He was a short man, barrel-chested.

His hair was dull brown mixed with white, his face so sharp-pointed and his manner so fidgety that he reminded Kestrel of a bilge rat. "I come out here a mite early. I figgered on rowin' out and relievin' the fellows what stood guard duty last night. Exceptin' the ship ain't there. And none of us has seen hide nor hair of them as was left on board." He ducked his head nervously. "Ye don't think it was ghosts took 'em, do ye?"

"No!" Kestrel barked, before remembering herself and dropping her tone again. "There's no ghost. Regardless of what we saw, your ghost ship lies anchored yonder, real as you are. And so's her captain. I saw him myself, yesterday, on Market Street under the midday sun. Cast off that ghost nonsense right now."

Several of the men grinned at each other, nodding and muttering. Kestrel snapped her fingers to regain their attention. "Anyone spoken to the dockmaster?"

"Ain't got the chance yet," Bardo said, looking even more frightened. "When I saw the *Wolfshead* missin', I wanted to ask after her, but when I got up close to the dockmaster's office, well, what did I see but a crowd of bluebacks all 'round it, so I kept walking." He stopped wringing his hands, shoving them under his arms and beginning to rock forward and back on his heels. "Kes, I been from one end of this harborside to the other. I prit'near decided the captain sailed off without me, until Jaques showed up, yammerin' about how Binns was taken by the soldiers, and we was leaving on the afternoon tide whether every man was aboard or not." He shrugged. "I knew ye'd be needin' us all, so I stayed here and kept the others from leavin'."

Kestrel stared at the little man. She'd always thought he was a bit slow, the way he grinned and nodded and almost never spoke. Obviously Binns had recognized something in him that she had missed. It was a skill she needed to build in herself, this knack for recognizing the value in a plain package. If not for Bardo, the men who answered her summons might very well have seen the *Wolfshead* gone and assumed they were left behind. She'd have been sunk before she started. She clapped her hand on Bardo's skinny shoulder. "I owe you a debt. Rest assured I'll tell the captain, when we get him back."

He bobbed his head and stepped back, shrinking into the shadows of the other, bigger men surrounding him, but with a tiny hint of a smile on his face. Kestrel felt a twinge of relief.

"First thing we do, we'll have a friendly chat with Lord Dockmaster. Find out why he saw fit to betray our captain."

Men snarled and cursed, exactly the reaction she'd expected. The dockmaster, grasping and foul-tempered though he might have been, had always been trustworthy at least. If it got out that he'd played the pirates false, Eldraga would suffer.

Bardo piped up. "What'd he do?"

"Word is he testified to Captain Binns havin' arrived on the *Thanos.*"

"What's the *Thanos*?" a sailor asked.

Kestrel jerked a thumb in its direction. "The one you all said was a ghost ship. Real I said she was, and real she truly is, but she's also stolen. Just not by us." She shot a glance toward the dockmaster's office. "Shadd, you're with me—keep your blade ready. Angus, Jaques, you'll block the door, keep the nosy types out. The rest of you, stay here, and look casual. This may be our only chance to get in there and make him admit to lying." *As well as find out who put him up to it,* she thought bitterly, *as if I needed any proof of that.*

Twelve

And I had done a hellish thing
And it would work 'em woe . . .
—SAMUEL TAYLOR COLERIDGE

The dockmaster's office was a tiny, cramped place, just big enough for him, his desk, and a set of shelves that reached from floor to ceiling across the rear wall. According to rumor, he had turned down an offer of money from the Eldraga Merchants' Council to enlarge his office, saying that as long as it stayed the size it was, he never had to deal with more than one visitor at a time. As soon as the current customer left, Kestrel and Shadd slipped inside the shadowed doorway.

The old man was hunched over his books, scratching notations with a feather quill. He glanced at the newcomers for only the briefest second. "What do you want?"

"I need to speak to you about a ship you logged in yesterday," Kestrel said.

Slowly, he lifted his head. Wrinkles crisscrossed his sagging cheeks, making him look as if someone had beaten him with a fishing net every day of his life. His eyes burned out from the mass of wrinkles with vicious glee. He looked her up and down, and snorted.

"Run along back to your brothel, whore," he said. "If some sailor's up and left without paying you, it isn't my business."

The dockmaster's foul attitude was legendary, but this was going too far. Kestrel cocked her eyes to Shadd. Sabas had bound her shoulder securely, but it still ached. There'd be no swordplay for at

least a day, and she was determined she wouldn't let the men realize it. Hard enough to lead them as things stood. She'd entrusted
Shadd with her secret, and he'd agreed to be her strong-arm until
she could do for herself.

He nodded. Drawing his dagger he slid behind the wizened
dockmaster, yanked him to his feet, and pressed the point against
the loose skin of the old man's neck.

"You won't get away with this, thief," he croaked. "The guards
patrol these docks and they stop in to check on me . . ."

"First whore, now thief?" Kestrel interrupted him. "You'd do
well to find out who your visitors are before calling them names.
I'm quartermaster on the *Wolfshead*." She placed her left hand flat
on the pages of his books and leaned forward until she and he were
nearly nose to nose. "You recall the *Wolfshead*? Twelve guns, empty
hold, but you still charged us four octavos for anchorage. Or perhaps you'll remember my captain's name. Binns. Artemus Binns.
You bore false witness to him today. You told the bluebacks he stole
yonder warship. When you turned in my captain, you should have
expected his crew to come a'running."

"I don't know what you're . . ." he began. Shadd squeezed his
shoulder, increasing the pressure on the dagger's tip held against
his throat, and the old man squeaked into silence.

"Now." Kestrel pushed the heavy account book backward onto
the floor, and propped herself on the empty spot. "As I see it, you
have a choice to make. You can tell us why you accused our captain
of a crime he never committed. Or my man here'll cut you a new
breathing hole." She tsked. "Make a terrible mess on your nice
books, all that blood."

"It wasn't my fault!" he squawked. "Said he'd gut me for fish
bait if I didn't do what he wanted."

"Who?"

"The young fellow."

"Which young fellow?" Kestrel asked through gritted teeth.

"The one who bought the *Wolfshead*."

Bought? With what currency, his winning smile? According to

Binns, they'd come to an agreement but no money had changed hands. "What made you think he'd bought our ship?"

He swallowed, the gulp loud in the tense closeness of the office. "He had papers. Signed and witnessed. He told me he'd bought the *Wolfshead* but I should tell whoever asked that your captain came in on the *Thanos*, that big gunship out yonder. Or else he'd come back and get me." His watery, old eyes switched nervously from Kestrel to his desk and back again.

McAvery. Just as she'd suspected. Every trail she followed led straight to him. But something didn't smell right. He was a conniving backstabber who'd twisted everyone around his little finger to get what he wanted. Only trouble was that he hadn't actually threatened anyone, up until now. The heavy-handed thug method didn't fit. She'd known him barely a day, but he seemed to put great stock in style and appearance. If he was going to throw vicious threats around, wouldn't he have come up with something more poetic than "fish bait"?

The dockmaster was shaking visibly under Shadd's grip. How many years had this old man been in his current job? If he treated everyone the way he usually did Binns, overblown promises of hideous death would have to be part of the package. He'd been accused of being hateful, foul-mouthed, and rude beyond imagining, but never frightened of anyone. Yet, he stood there, acting as if he was scared to death of a man who wasn't even in port anymore. She could have understood his apprehension if McAvery really was a magus. But a real magus wouldn't have needed threats of bodily harm—he'd just spell his victim into forgetting they'd seen each other. If he didn't turn him into a toad instead. She scowled at the dockmaster.

"It'd be right hard to gut you if he's out to sea. You could've alerted the guards, had him chased down and arrested." A thought struck her, and she smiled, cocking one eyebrow. "Unless that wasn't a part of the bargain?"

His gaze dropped suddenly, toward his desk. Kestrel lifted her feet, swinging them over the desktop and back down on the other side. "Move," she ordered. Shadd dragged the old man around the open space between desk and wall. Sliding off the desk, Kestrel began rummaging through the drawers one-handed.

"Stop that! You're standing on my book!" the dockmaster hissed, his voice no longer quavery. "I'll call for the guards!"

"No you won't," she taunted, continuing her search, "especially not if I'm right." She crouched down. The lowest drawer on the left held only a handful of papers. She riffled through them, then tossed them on the floor to inspect the drawer more carefully. It was deeper on the outside than it appeared on the inside. A false bottom. Pulling the drawer all the way out with her good hand, she hefted it up onto her thigh, then heaved it onto the desk.

"That's a mite heavy for an empty drawer," she said.

"Put that back!" he roared. Any pretense at fear was gone now—the dockmaster's face was red with anger, and despite the dagger still held to his throat, his fists were clenched.

"What have you hidden in here?" Kestrel turned the drawer on its side to see the bottom closely, then checked the back end. All the joints seemed well made, no warps or splits. Odd, being so close to the water, that the wood hadn't succumbed to nature. She checked inside again.

The desk and its drawers were constructed of some tight-grained wood, stained nearly black. Yet the inside bottom of this drawer had a much rounder grain. As if it had been added later.

"There's nothing in there that should concern you!" he insisted. "This is your last chance. Let me go or I'll call the guards."

Kestrel cocked her head curiously. "So you keep saying." She pushed the drawer forward, off the edge. It fell heavily, but with the cracking of wood was another sound. The muffled jingle of coin.

"Well, well. So there was more than paper in the drawer, eh?" She leaned over the desk. The false bottom had split, and a bit of woven cloth hung halfway out.

Kestrel slid back over the desk. "Care to change your story?" she asked, not waiting for him to answer. She drew back her foot, kicking the broken panel and revealing the cloth to be a drawstring bag. She hefted the bag in her left hand. It was fat with coins. By the look of it, more than some of her crew would see at the end of season. And therein lay the dockmaster's dilemma.

There'd be no screaming for the bluebacks. Arrest the pirates they surely would, but then they'd take the money in as "evidence," and he'd never see it again. Worse than that, with the proof of his bribe-taking, they'd keep a closer eye on him. And while muffins worked for Olympia, the bluebacks would want harder treats from the old man. They'd be in his office daily, demanding their own cut until he had nothing left. No, he wouldn't be calling for help from that quarter. He had too much to lose if the authorities walked in.

The dockmaster's jaw twitched. "Fine. Yes, he paid me. A tidy sum, to overlook the inconsistencies in his sale papers."

"And to sell my captain out?"

He shrugged. "No, that was my doing. Your stingy captain argued me down to half the usual mooring rate when you docked, and I figured it'd do him good to be humbled a bit."

"Taking bribes is illegal." Kestrel set the bag on the desk and studied the knotted string keeping it closed.

"So is piracy," he countered.

It was a good knot, too tightly tied for her to undo. But knots could be undone by more than deft fingers. She drew her own dagger, and sliced through the string, pulling the bag open. She gazed inside and began to chuckle.

"What's so funny?" the dockmaster demanded. Kestrel didn't answer. Turning the bag upside down, she poured its contents onto the desk. Shadd laughed out loud. The dockmaster paled.

Dull bits of metal lay in a heap on the desk, different sizes and shapes but all flecked with the telltale black soot of a smith's furnace. "Quite a tidy sum indeed," Kestrel said. "I'll bet poor McAvery got his hands terribly dirty picking these out of some garbage bin."

The dockmaster's eyes widened. "Where's my gold?"

"That'll teach you to take a bribe sight unseen," Kestrel scolded.

"But I didn't," the old man moaned. "I saw the gold. Two hundred gold, all shiny and yellow and mine . . ."

It was an old grifter's trick—show the victim something valuable to convince him to do what you want, then switch the item with something worthless. Just proved what a good thief McAvery was. Kestrel leaned one hip against the desk, and began cleaning under her fingernails with her dagger. "Shadd, I think you can let go of our friend now. Last thing he wants to do is admit to a bribe in front of guards." She fingered the metal bits, sweeping up a handful and letting them drop again. "Especially a bribe as lucrative as this one."

Shadd grinned, and withdrew his blade. The dockmaster leaped toward the pile, as if he needed to touch them to believe the truth. "He cheated me!"

"You'll forgive me if I'm unsympathetic," Kestrel said. "Now that we're in the same longboat, why don't you tell me everything he said to you?"

The dockmaster sank into his chair, resting his white-haired head in his wrinkled hands. "He showed me the gold. So warm and heavy. Enough gold to keep me in brandy and beef for the next four years. All I had to do was stamp the sale papers and throw anyone who came asking off his track."

She stared at him in disbelief. "So to throw them off your friend's trail you condemned a man to hang?"

"I thought your captain would have an alibi. I was supposed to guess they'd take him without an investigation?"

Kestrel bit her lip. His words were painful in their truth—there hadn't been time for an honest investigation. Binns had been targeted, arrested, and sentenced all in the space of a night. Outlaws had few rights, but they did have some. What had made Binns different? She was suddenly aware of the log, still belted under her bodice, heavy and sticky where the leather rested against her thin chemise. "When did the *Wolfshead* set sail?"

"Before sunrise."

"Was he alone? Did he have a crew?"

He shrugged. "A few men. Enough to sail the ship, no more. They helped him transfer some cargo."

"From the *Thanos*?" she asked. "What kind of cargo?"

"Biscuit, couple barrels of water. And a crate." He ran the tip of one despairing finger through the slag on his desk. "Loaded their boxes and left."

"Against the tide?"

"He had to get a tow out to the lanes. Paid extra." He dropped his head onto the mound of scrap. "It was gold last night."

"Did he say where he was headed?" Kestrel persisted.

"Not in so many words." He didn't raise his head to answer her. "Said something about an appointment with the king."

Kestrel exchanged looks with Shadd, who nodded slowly in understanding. If McAvery was going to see the king, he could only have headed in one direction. The same as theirs.

THEY left the dockmaster pounding his forehead onto the pile of metal that had broken his heart, and hurried back to their crew. Shadd bent his head close to Kestrel's. "So what's the plan, Quarter?"

"I'm still working on it," she answered. It had seemed so clear only an hour ago. Get to the docks, set sail, rescue the captain. But now they were a shipless crew, and the man responsible for all their hardships had sailed away, safely out of their reach. If she could have gotten her hands on McAvery, forced him to confess. Wishing wouldn't help her. The image of Binns's dead and sun-bloated body hanging by a rope flashed before her, and she shuddered.

"Damn that McAvery," she muttered.

"Too bad we can't take his ship the way he took ours," Shadd commented.

"With half our men still drunk and abed somewhere?" she snarled. "The *Thanos* must be crawling with armed men right now."

"No, it ain't." Shadd touched her shoulder, making her stop. He pointed. "I been watchin'. There's never more'n three or four."

Kestrel looked out over the busy harbor. The *Thanos* sat quietly, sails furled, her decks empty of the usual activity one saw on deck.

Without her glass she couldn't be certain, but it seemed as if Shadd was right. Big as the ship was, she'd come to rest in the deepest part of the harbor, just a heel and a ho from the open seas. Catch the tide right, and Kestrel could be gone before anyone knew she'd raised anchor.

Her heart began beating faster. With a vessel like the *Thanos,* they could catch up to Binns's captors faster than she'd hoped, and maybe even intimidate them enough to gain an extra advantage. She grinned up at her master gunner. "It'll put a higher price on all our heads."

He winked. "You think that'll bother any of them lads, to be advanced from 'pirate' to 'famous pirate'?"

More of Binns's men had arrived while she was gone. There were nearly thirty standing around, enough to crew the *Thanos,* if they all stood double watches and no storms struck. Some of them were wearing the dull, still-drunk-next-morning glaze, as if they'd been rolled out of bed and forced to their feet. She didn't care about the reason they'd come. All that was important was that they had.

She waved them all close. "Listen up, now, all you lot. The captain is taken, and apparently our ship as well. Lucky for us they're sailing him to Pecheta," she sneered, "for trial."

"How is that lucky?" one of the men asked. "Trial's just another word for hemp fever."

A few of them grumbled in agreement, but Kestrel raised her palm. "It's lucky because we know he's got at least four more days to stay alive. Plenty of time to chase down that ship and rob the hangman of his prize."

"Chase him down? You plannin' on swimmin'?" another called out. "We got no vessel."

Kestrel smiled. "We will by sundown."

Thirteen

All in a hot and copper sky
The bloody sun at noon,
Right up above the mast did stand
No bigger than the Moon.

—SAMUEL TAYLOR COLERIDGE

B est we don't talk out here," she said, pointing down the docks.
Some yards away was a warehouse, its wide doorway boarded
up and marked with a royal seal. The owner had likely neglected to
pay his taxes, so the place would be empty. She sent one of the men
to check for any other doors. He returned with the happy news that
not only was there a side door, but it was neither sealed nor locked.
They broke into smaller groups, and made their separate ways
down to the empty warehouse. Once everyone was inside, they
gathered around Kestrel.

"It's become obvious," she whispered, "that the man responsible for all our woes isn't the dockmaster, but a foul and devious
vagabond going by the name of McAvery. 'Twas he stole the big
ship in the first place, set the dogs on our captain for it, and made
off with our sloop." The men growled, and a few pounded their
fists into their hands. "So here's what I'm thinking. We'll steal a
couple of rowboats, row out to the *Thanos*, and sneak aboard.
Shouldn't be hard to take the guards out, seeing as there's only
three of them."

"You sure that's all there is?" Bardo asked, his thin lips twitching
nervously at the corners. He'd planted himself near one of the salt-
fogged windows. "What if there's a whole company belowdecks,
waiting to jump us the minute we set foot on her?"

"Shadd's been keeping an eye. Far as we can tell, there's only three. Even if there is a whole squad lurking on board somewhere, there's still thirty of us. More than enough to roust a few lazy, overfed bluebacks."

Laughter rippled softly through the group. "We'll tie them up, drop them in the rowboats, and raise anchor. The tide'll be turning in our favor within the hour. We catch it right, we can be on our way before much of anyone notices we're moving."

This would be the tricky part, convincing the men to go along with her new plan. At first, chasing down the royal ship and retrieving Binns had seemed enough. That was before McAvery had stolen their ship. Kestrel wanted to see the man swing in Binns's place, if for no other reason than to laugh at the look on his face when he understood he'd been bested.

"To my mind, we need to lay hands on the real villain. Hear me out," she said hurriedly. Better to say her piece before they all got their questions formed. "McAvery isn't but a few hours ahead of us, and I know which way he's headed. Can we let him get away with nicking the *Wolfshead* out from under our noses?"

She glanced around. No one was protesting yet. They all seemed to be thinking her proposition over. "We catch up to him, retake our sloop, and sail to Pecheta. We show up with the stolen ship, and the real thief in chains, not only do we get our captain back hale and healthy, but maybe a reward as well." Not to mention whatever Binns hoped would happen if she managed to gain audience with the king's man and turn over the log. What could be in there? Once they'd caught McAvery and recaptured the sloop, she'd have to take an evening to read it. Couldn't hurt to be ahead of the game. "Think about it, lads," she offered, "we pull this off, every one of you'll be famous throughout the Nine Islands. If nothing else, the stories alone will get you free ale and food for the rest of this season and long into next."

By the looks of happy greed on their faces, she thought they'd probably be cheering if they could. Luckily they made do with clapping her on the back. She kept her smile even when some of the blows hit her wounded shoulder, biting the inside of her mouth to keep from crying out. She had them in hand now. If they knew she was unable to draw steel, their confidence might waver. That secret would stay between herself and Shadd.

She let them go on a moment longer, then raised a hand to quiet them. "There's a set of rungs amidships, and I'm willing to bet there's an identical set on her other side. We'll row out to the vessel beyond her, then swing 'round and come up on her from seaward. I'll climb up first. Shadd, you choose the next lot to board, and follow me. Soon as we give the all-clear, the rest of you'll make your way aboard after us. Those of you that can come up the rungs, the rest of you use ropes and grapples." She pointed. "Jack, and Red Tom, go now and lay hands on some grappling hooks. Jarvis, see to fetching us some rope. And Bardo—"

He'd been looking left and right fearfully, almost as if he was expecting to see someone, and didn't. "Aye?" he asked, stepping forward and dry-washing his hands over and over.

"I want you to find us a likely boat. Best if it's one that can carry us all, but two smaller ones'll do. Check first where the ship's boats are tied up. If we steal a ferryman's dinghy, we'll be caught before we're two strokes out."

His eyes were wide, and his lips were twitching faster than they had before. He looked even more like a mouse than he ever had, and for an instant, Kestrel thought he was going to refuse the order, if he didn't faint outright. But he nodded instead. "Aye, I'll do it."

"That's a lad," she said, smiling encouragement. "Off you go then, meet back here as soon as you're able. The tide won't wait."

Within a quarter hour, the men she sent for rope and hooks had returned, their arms full. Bardo hadn't been long behind them. "There's a harvester's boat," he'd reported. "Broken shells still in the bottom, but there's plenty of room for all of us, and by the looks, it's been sitting tied up for a couple of days."

Leaving the warehouse in small groups, they followed Bardo down to the tie-ups. Busy as the docks always were, no one had paid them any attention. They loaded themselves into the big boat, cast off the lines, and put their oars to the water. Kestrel sat backward, unwilling to take her eyes off the shore. A squad of bluebacks rambled past, but never even glanced toward the boat.

Just as she was ready to turn and face her destination, something caught her eye. A movement, purposeful and quick—someone running to the dockside. Jaeger. His pouch was tied in a clumsy knot around his waist. At the distance, it was hard to tell, but he looked much the worse for wear. He stopped at the edge, his hands clenched in fists. He glared across the water at her. Soldiers were close enough for him to call, but he remained still. She stared at him, wondering why he wasn't betraying her. What kind of bounty had the Danisobans offered that was so huge he couldn't risk involving the soldiers? She kept her gaze on him until he was too small to clearly make out. She had an unsettling feeling she'd cross paths with him again. And when that happened, he'd be holding a grudge.

NOW they sat, in the shadow of a Bixian galley, staring at their goal rocking gently in the deep water of the harbor. It had almost been too easy, as if the gods, or the fates, or whoever might be paying attention, had wanted Kestrel to succeed. Not that she was relaxing—if there was one thing she'd learned about the powers that be, it was that the minute she thought they were on her side, the boat she was riding in would spring a leak or a storm would spin up. Best to keep her edge sharp. There'd be time for relaxing when she was old and gray.

Now that she was so close, the *Thanos* was more imposing than Kestrel had at first realized, her black-painted sides rising from the slow-rolling water at least the length of four men standing on each other's shoulders, and maybe farther. All the gunports were tightly closed, their edges so flush they could have been watertight. As she'd gambled, a set of rungs rose from the waterline to the rail amidships on this side as well—no rope ladders for the *Thanos*. She was ten times the ship the *Wolfshead* had been, a fine vessel indeed. Binns could have made quite a name for himself with a ship as big and fast as this.

Thoughts of her captain flooded her mind. Images of him in chains, being beaten, him walking slowly up those final steps toward a rope that swung lazily in the ocean breeze . . . Kestrel clenched her fist until the nails bit into the skin of her palm. *We'll get him back. He's not dead yet,* she rebuked herself. *He will not be hanged. I won't let them.*

"Any further along on that plan o' yours, Quarter?" Shadd whispered. "Seein' as we're here now, and the tide'll be turnin' shortly."

She pointed at the rungs. "We'll climb up, real quiet, take the soldiers by surprise."

Shadd frowned, and leaned forward, his mouth close to her ear. "It's the climbin' concerns me, Kes. What about yer bad arm?"

She tensed her shoulder, feeling a throb in answer. Climbing up was nowhere near an easy task, but it wouldn't be impossible. She snuck a peak at the men sitting behind her in the longboat.

Gone were the drink-dulled gazes, the squints against the bright sun, the slumped backs. During the long, slow row out to the *Thanos*, they'd had time to get their heads wrapped around the coming enterprise. It was the sort of thing pirates dreamed of, when they weren't having visions of head-high piles of gold and jewels, an adventure that would be forever enshrined in the history books.

They were watching her expectantly, the fire of battle glinting in each and every eye. She was their leader now, until they got their captain back safe and sound. She couldn't back down, show any weakness, or the whole thing would fall apart. For the first time she thought she understood why Binns worked so hard, pushing himself to be twice the pirate any man of his crew was. A captain had to be larger than life, an example. If she was going to pull this off, she was going to have to be merciless in battle, last to eat and sleep . . . she sighed. And first up that accursed ladder.

"Not like I've got much choice, is there?" She glanced down at her lap. "But there is something I need from you."

"Anything," he said, nodding.

"My sword belt." She lifted a handful of skirts in her fists, letting them drop again with a contemptuous snort. "I've no mind to trip myself on the way up."

Shadd grinned. "Ladder climbin' ain't usually a wenchly duty, I warrant." He unbuckled her sword belt from around his waist, and offered it to her. "Ye'll be wantin' to leave that book here as well."

She'd nearly forgotten it was there on her back. She didn't want to risk it getting ruined if her right arm suddenly gave way on the climb up, and she fell into the water. But it was too important to place in anyone else's hands, even Shadd's. She shook her head. "I'll have to take the chance. It'll make me more cautious, knowing it's there."

Kestrel bent, pulling the backside of the skirts forward between her legs, tucked the hem under the front waistband, then buckled her belt as tightly as she could stand to hold the fabric in place. The legs of her makeshift breeches were billowy, reminding her of pictures she'd seen once of mythical desert folk who went continually barefoot and rode on giant four-legged beasts, but the familiar weight of her sword on her hip reassured her.

"First thing I do, once we're under way, I'm scavenging that ship for a decent pair of pants." She rolled her shoulder slowly, trying to loosen the aching muscles for the climb ahead.

"Orders?" Shadd asked.

She hoped she looked more confident than she felt. "Row us up close. I'll climb the rungs, and the rest of you follow, quiet as you can manage. We'll slip up on those card-playing laggards before they can blink." She looked around, then nodded once, hard. "Let's get to it. Row us up to yonder ship. The tide won't wait."

Oars dropped with gentle splashes into the water, and they began to move. Kestrel directed the oarmen to come alongside the *Thanos*'s seaward hull from an angle, as if they were only meaning to skirt around it. Not that she really thought anyone would pay attention to their route—the harbor was bustling with dinghies and longboats ferrying people to and fro, and her lot stood out no more than any other boatload as far as she could see.

Shadd was holding the spyglass, snatching quick glances every minute or two as their boat neared. He lowered the glass when they entered the ship's shadow, and grinned at Kestrel. "Must be a fine game of cards they're at," he reported, his voice low as a cat's purr. "Not a man of the three's even looking around the deck, much less down toward us."

"Let's hope it stays that way," she murmured. "We'll need every advantage." She held out a hand toward her oarmen. "Easy now, lads. Get me close as you can, but try not to bump up against her hull too hard."

The men nearest the black hull secured their oars, while the outer rowers used theirs as guides, pulling against each other's strokes to slow and steady the longboat. Kestrel shivered; it had to be her imagination, but since they'd entered the shadow, the breeze had become chilly, raising gooseflesh on her skin. Now that they were right on it, the ship seemed like a monstrous black whale. Would it throw her off when she touched the rungs, bucking and writhing in protest? She shook her head. *Cast off those fancies,* she told herself. *It's a ship, a construction of wood and fabric. Keep your mind on your job.*

Shadd had stood, trading places with one of the inward oarmen. He reached out and grabbed the lowest rung, pulling the longboat close against the *Thanos's* black hull. It thumped gently, and everyone froze, looking up to the rail above. But no face appeared to investigate.

Kestrel rose. Touching a finger to her lips, she pointed, first at herself, then at the ladder. Shadd nodded, pointing at himself, then two others. The rest held still. They'd all follow as the turn presented itself. She drew a deep breath, rolled her injured shoulder once more, and reached out to the waiting rungs. Gripping as far up as she could reach with her good left hand, she stepped onto the lower ones, and began to climb.

She'd known the ascent would be a dicey proposition—nowhere near as hard as climbing a rope ladder, but tricky nevertheless. The gentle rocking of the ship put her balance off, making her take each rung twice as carefully as she would have. She used her left arm as much as she could, releasing and moving that hand up to the next rung quickly, keeping her right bent at the elbow as she grasped for the second or two it took to move her stronger hand. Her hands were slick with sweat and her right shoulder was aching before she'd climbed five feet, but there was no help for it. Going back down would be no easier. The only way to save her captain lay up, over the rail above her head. She gritted her teeth, and drove herself to take another rung.

The pain was a white-hot knife by the time her head drew level with the bottom of the railing. Several water barrels stood just beyond it. Perfect cover for her to slip on board. Flashes of light were dancing at the edges of her sweat-stung vision, but she squinted, peering between the barrels, and made out the three guards, seated on bales of straw next to the anchor winch. All three were thoroughly engrossed in their game. They didn't appear to be talking much, but the betting was fast and furious, glinting coins flashing in the afternoon sunshine.

Kestrel grabbed the nearest spindle and moved her feet up the rungs as high as she dared. *The hard part's almost through. Just have to pull yourself up and over.* Her right hand seemed to be losing strength, but she wrapped her fingers around another spindle and threw her left over the railing, biting her lip against the scream she wanted to let loose as her wounded arm took the full weight of her body. Despite its fatigue, her left arm held firm. She pulled herself up, sliding one leg over the railing. Grabbing down to the spindle again on the inward side, she tried to brace and pull herself the rest of the way over. But her hand was too slick, and her grip slipped. She shifted her hips toward the deck, letting herself fall with a gentle thump, and lay on her back, as still as death.

CHAPTER

Fourteen

Alone, alone, all, all alone,
Alone on a wide, wide sea!
And never a saint took pity on
My soul in agony.
—SAMUEL TAYLOR COLERIDGE

Had they heard? She didn't move, didn't dare to breathe. Pain was pounding through her body, matching the wild beating of her heart. She imagined for one frenzied second that the card-players had heard the thudding in her chest, and were slowly creeping up on her hiding place, ready to pounce. The silence was deafening. Would they kill her before they tossed her overboard?

She waited for what seemed forever, but when nothing happened, she chanced another look between the barrels. Cards and coins still changed hands—not a one of the soldiers had risen from his seat. They weren't even chatting between each other. In spite of the situation, she wanted to laugh out loud. Supposedly the royal guard were the best soldiers the king's money could buy. If these were the kind of men her crew would have to face when they caught up to the ship Binns was on, she stood a far better chance than she'd assumed of getting him back without injury to any of her own men.

She extended her left hand past the railing's edge and crooked her finger, signaling Shadd to begin his climb, then sat up and pushed herself away from the edge, keeping low behind the barrels but making room for Shadd and her other men to join her. Not a sound carried from the game—they must have run out of conversational topics hours ago, and relaxed into the companionable stillness that men often preferred. There was no way that she could see outright to get the drop on the soldiers, especially as quiet as they were, other than their own lack of attention to anything but their entertainment. That would have to be enough.

Shadd's head appeared below the railing. He raised his eyebrows in question. She put a finger to her lips, quirking her head for him to join her behind the barrels. Grasping the smooth wood, he pulled his body up and over the edge, letting himself down without even a thump. For such a big man, he was surprisingly graceful, and she found herself feeling glad that he hadn't seen her own awkward fall to the deck.

She leaned close, raising her eyebrows and inclining her head. Shadd pointed two fingers toward the railing. As if he'd been waiting for a signal, Red Tom poked his fiery head above the edge of the deck. Kestrel nodded to him to come aboard. Jarvis was a few rungs below him, climbing hand over hand up the side of the ship, a dagger clenched in his teeth. She nodded in satisfaction and leaned close to Shadd again. Swinging her hand in a circle that included herself and her men, she made a fist and jabbed it in the direction of the card-playing soldiers. Shadd frowned, laying one meaty hand on her injured shoulder and shaking his head.

While it was nice to know there would always be someone watching out for her, Kestrel sometimes hated the way Shadd turned into a mother hen where she was concerned. She was well aware of her limitations. She intended to lead the charge only, dropping back at the first threat of a real fight breaking out. She patted the scabbard hanging from her left hip and half drew the blade with her left hand, baring her teeth and snarling silently.

He didn't look convinced, but finally he sighed. Jarvis had come aboard, his short blade still held tightly between his grinning teeth. His enthusiasm was contagious—she had to force herself not to grin back at him. After the job was done, then they'd have time to laugh again. Not to mention reasons.

She pointed at Shadd and Red Tom, then waved for them to move off to the right. Gesturing toward Jarvis to accompany her, she duck-walked to her left, stopping behind the final barrel in the row. She crouched down, worked her sword free from its scabbard with her left hand, and gripped it tightly. She knew how to fight double-handed, but it had always been a dagger in the left before—the extra length of blade pulled oddly at her forearm. Lifting her right hand, she held up three fingers, then two, and finally one.

"Yaaaaahhhhhh!" As her last finger dropped, she leaped to her feet, howling like a wild cat. As a man, the four pirates exploded from behind the barrels, yelling and capering with steel drawn, running toward their victims as if they meant to slice them to ribbons. Kestrel brandished her own sword, wrong-handed, above her head, waiting for the guards to react.

But nothing happened. Instead of leaping to their feet and grabbing their own weapons, the three men continued their silent game.

This wasn't at all the way she'd pictured the battle. In her mind's eye, she'd imagined cards flying everywhere as the three startled men fell over themselves trying to defend the ship. Or the three of them flying to battle against the pirates, steel flashing and blood spraying on the black deck. Anything except being completely ignored. Not only didn't it sit right—it smelled rotten.

"Yer game's over, lads," Shadd announced. "On yer feet, and over the side with ye. This ship's now taken."

The three men didn't look up, seemingly engrossed in a thrilling round of betting. Shadd lurched forward, swinging his cutlass broadside at the nearest guard's back. His shining blade swept toward the blue-coated man nearest him, but instead of connecting and knocking him over, it seemed to slide through his body, emerging at his opposite shoulder bloodless. Shadd staggered as his own momentum carried him into a tight spin. Regaining his balance, he turned toward Kestrel, his face paling.

"They ain't real," he said. "It is a ghost ship!"

"Belay that!" she hissed, too late. Jarvis was crossing himself, his sword hanging forgotten from his hand. Red Tom was muttering something under his breath, his lips moving and his eyes wide as saucers.

"It's a trick, is all," she said, her voice betraying her own sudden nervousness. No way were these spectral visitors from worlds beyond, but there was definitely something strange going on. She raised her sword, and stepped forward, poked at the man nearest her. Just as had happened with Shadd, the point of her sword slid past his blue coat, drawing no blood and meeting no more resistance than if she'd poked at the empty air. Ghosts were supposed to be transparent, while these fellows looked as solid as the rest of the ship. Now that she was close to them, she could detect a faint shimmering around the edges of the men and their cards.

Her belly twisted in fear-cramps. She was beginning to recognize what smelled so rotten about the situation. Ghosts didn't shimmer, or appear in the daylight, but illusions did. And the only people capable of casting illusions were capable of much more dangerous behavior. The hackles on her neck prickled, and for one panicked second she envisioned a black-robed Danisoban behind her, reaching out with gnarled hands to drag her away.

"Retreat!" she yelled, spinning on her heel. The hell with climbing down—she'd just as soon jump and hope the impact of hitting the water didn't kill her. Still a better death than she'd get at the hands of a Danisoban.

She stopped, her eyes widening in shock. Six soldiers were lined along the railing, armed with crossbows pointing down toward the water. Another three advanced on Kestrel, swords drawn. Behind them stood a tall man, half again as tall as she was, broad-bodied and grinning, dressed in the blue and gold uniform of the Royal Navy, fairly dripping with ribbons and medals.

"But you've only just arrived," he drawled, his deep voice sounding welcoming and threatening at the same time. "Surely you can stay a little while."

"We're late for another engagement," she said.

"That's right," the leader said, taking another huge step toward her. "You've got an invitation to meet Mistress Hemp, isn't that right?" He chuckled at his own joke, and his men joined in.

Kestrel backed away, trying to keep a distance, and shot a fast glance over her shoulder. Between her and the opposite railing was the capstan and a number of boxes and barrels, as well as the three men still tossing cards at each other. *Not men,* she cautioned herself. *Merely fancies, nothing to fear.* She wondered, for one wild instant, how strange it would feel to run right through them, then returned her gaze to the real man who was still advancing on her. Likely she'd find out any minute.

Shadd had regained his color, the angry red rising in his cheeks. He brandished his cutlass. "Keep yer hands off me captain, ye blackguard!"

The closest swordsman sprang to action, blades clanging as he connected with Shadd's cutlass. Jarvis and Red Tom, no longer frozen by fear, drew their own weapons and joined the fight.

Kestrel ached to be by their sides. Battle was something she understood. None of those mumbo-jumbo incantations the Danisobans used to keep people living in fear. Not even her own meager tricks, such as they were. Steel was the only thing she believed in. Fighting for her life, back against the mast and a good sturdy rapier in her hand, that was something none of those magi could ever comprehend. Her heart thumped in anticipation. *Sore shoulder be damned,* she told herself, *your place is in the thick of it. Left hand or right, fighting's still fighting.* She hefted the rapier and took a step toward the mêlée.

Suddenly a length of steel dropped in front of her. Wide and curved, the blade sported nicks along its edge and scratches on the flat, all stained with the brownish red of long-dried blood. She turned her head slowly. The leader was still grinning, and Kestrel promised herself fervently that before this was all over, she would slap that smile off his face.

"Captain? You?" he commented, as casual as if they were discussing the weather. He lifted his sword and moved in front of her, turning the vicious point toward her belly. "Who would have guessed we'd find a band of vicious cutthroats being led around by a woman?"

"Who better? Certainly no man." She raised her chin in defiance.

Just because he was bigger than she didn't mean he'd automatically won. Big men often fell hard, especially when a smaller someone got under his feet to help him along.

"What do you use to keep them in line, your pretty smile?"

"That, and my wicked blade," she answered.

He leered, letting his gaze roam down her body and back up again. "I'll bet I've got just the right blade for you. Why don't we go into the captain's cabin and talk about it?"

I swear, if I ever meet a man who doesn't see me as a bedwarmer, I might marry him on the spot. She managed a cold smile. "Men to the left and right of me, and you assume I'd pick an overfed ape like you?"

Despite his bulk, the man moved as gracefully as a dancer, forcing her to circle, matching his steps, a bizarre tuneless waltz at blade's range. She squinted against the redness of the afternoon sun. Smart man—he'd moved her into the blind side.

"Since you don't want to talk." He dropped back, swinging his sword toward her with a swift and singing chop. She parried, just managing to block his strike, then pushed off to spin away and gain a measure of space, before thrusting her sword's point at his ample belly. He knocked her blade easily—it shuddered in her hand, and she nearly lost her grip.

Not good, not good, she thought frantically, skipping backward to regain control of her sword. Her left arm just wasn't strong enough for this. If she'd only had time to go back to Jack's and get her new *sinistre* . . . but there was no time for musing. He was charging at her again.

She brought her sword down, connecting with her opponent's swing and wincing at the squeal of metal on metal. Their pommels came together with a clang, and for a moment she was nearly nose to nose with the big man.

"Belly-crawling wharf rat," she growled.

"If you're of a mind to curse me, get it right," he whispered, his breath hot against her cheek. "The name's Cragfarus."

"That's a name?" she snorted, pushing away from him and freeing her blade. He began pacing in the familiar circle again, his eyes burning as he stared at her.

"It's the name that'll see you dead," he bellowed. He jabbed toward her, missing as Kestrel hopped backward, an inch out of reach. Both hands clenching his hilt, he swung his blade in a wide arc. Kestrel flung her sword up to parry, but at the last instant, he pulled his blade closer, slipping under her awkward attempt to block. Faster than she realized, he whirled, the flat of his blade slamming broadside into her bad shoulder.

White-hot bolts of pain roared into her. The deck beneath her feet became soft as dry sand—was the world spinning? She staggered and dropped to her knees, panting.

Cragfarus lumbered toward her, his sword point dancing before her eyes. "Wicked blade, did you say? Not so wicked as far as I can see." He swung his sword in a figure eight, over and over, close enough for her to feel the breeze of its passage. "Give my best to the UnderLord when you get there."

I can't die like this, she thought wildly. *Artie needs me.* She heaved her rapier up, over her head, hoping to block his killing blow.

It never fell. Just as the big soldier swung the blade down, a giant blur flashed between them. Shadd, his bright yellow shirt torn and bloody, howled like a banshee and swiped his sword toward Cragfarus. He caught the blow meant for Kestrel, deflecting it harmlessly away. Keeping his gaze on Cragfarus, Shadd spoke over his shoulder.

"Get up, Kes," he yelled. "I've got this one." He feinted forward, but the soldier didn't flinch, instead jabbing his own sword at Shadd's chest.

Kestrel rocked back on her heels and stood. Shadd and Cragfarus were circling each other, both gripping their weapons two-handed. Shadd was breathing hard, and favoring one leg as if he had a wound she couldn't see yet. He threw a quick glance her way, grinning when he caught sight of her standing on her own.

It was the mistake Cragfarus had been waiting for. Before Kestrel could open her mouth to shout a warning, the big soldier lunged forward, the sharp point of his blade sliding neatly into Shadd's ribs.

He froze, staring in dumb horror down at the steel spitting him. Cragfarus barked out a laugh, pushing against Shadd's chest as he pulled his blade free. Blood gouted from the wound, spattering on the deck.

"No, Shadd!" Kestrel cried. He turned his shaggy head toward her. His face was graying, and he had to fight to keep his eyes from rolling back.

Cragfarus turned away from the bleeding man, all his attention on Kestrel once more. He tossed his bloodied sword back and forth from his right hand to his left and back again. "No need to cry, woman, you'll be joining your lover in hell."

Blood was soaking Shadd's shirt and breeches. He was rocking slowly, as if he'd fall any second, but he tipped her a wink. Dragging a deep breath into his tortured body, he flung himself at the grinning Cragfarus, letting his bulk knock the big guard off his feet. Both men toppled heavily to the deck and the soldier's curved blade skittered across the deck.

Fury pounded through her, the pain in her shoulder overpowered by the worse pain in her heart. Her ship stolen, one friend destined to hang, another bleeding to death at her feet, and the man responsible getting farther away with every minute she wasted here.

Enough was enough. The dizziness that had plagued her a moment ago was replaced by the diamond focus of vengeance. Shadd had bought her an advantage with his own blood. She would not waste it.

Gritting her teeth, she hefted her rapier into her right hand. Had there been pain before? She no longer felt anything but icy certainty. Her hand wrapped around the hilt, familiar and sure, and she stalked forward.

A soldier lay wounded and gasping on the deck a few feet away, being tended by one of the crossbowmen. Pirates and bluebacks had all stopped their battles, watching their leaders with shared bloodthirsty interest. Cragfarus had struggled out from under Shadd's unconscious bulk and gotten to his knees, crawling toward his sword, cursing. His sword still lay on the deck a foot or two away from his reaching hand. Kestrel got there first, placing one foot under the flat blade and flipping it into a shining spin. Catching the hilt easily, Cragfarus snatched it out of the air. He lumbered to his feet, his lip curled into a wolfish snarl.

"Honorable fighting? From a pirate?" he said, crouching and beginning his now-familiar pacing. "The boys and I'll be laughing about this for years to come."

She stepped back, trying to angle the coming fight away from Shadd, then smiled. "Honor has nothing to do with this," she said, sweeping her rapier into the en garde position. "They can't claim it's murder if you're holding a weapon when I kill you."

Fifteen

For the sky and the sea, the sea and the sky
Lay like a load on my weary eye
And the dead were at my feet.
—SAMUEL TAYLOR COLERIDGE

Cragfarus rushed forward, yelling, and swiped his thick blade at her. Kestrel skipped aside and spun, extending her sword to nick the big soldier on the back of his neck. He stopped short, roaring as he turned. Droplets of blood fanned out in midair from the cut she'd bestowed on him.

"Flash-packet bitch!" he yelled, color rising in his face. He attacked again, jabbing at her midsection. She swept her own sword into a downward parry, then slipped under his guard to thrust toward his ample gut. Before she could connect, he'd recovered from her parry, slamming his sword against hers hard enough that she felt the impact down to her heels. She shuffled backward, buying herself a little breathing room.

"You can't win, little girl," he taunted, waggling his blade at her.

She gritted her teeth against the desire to answer him. He was trying to distract her, get her to concentrate on his chatter instead of his weapon. Better to use her energy for fighting.

He charged at her again, slamming his blade around as if it were an ax. He aimed a pass at her head. She ducked, letting the sword pass over with room to spare. The strike had been intended as a death blow—the carry-through buried Cragfarus's thick blade in a nearby crate.

It was well stuck. Cragfarus cursed, yanking on the hilt to get it free. Kestrel leaped forward. His face was exposed, and with luck she could end this fight with one clean stab. She extended her blade, angling up toward the soldier's eye. He threw up his meaty arm, knocking her sword away, then turned to face her again with his freed weapon.

"Is that the best you can do?" he growled. "Your clumsy lover was more of a match for me. I'm almost sorry I cut him into shark food."

She shot a quick glance toward Shadd. While the soldiers were placing bets on her fight, Jarvis had made his way to the fallen gunner and seemed to be pressing his hands against the bloody hole in Shadd's side. Nothing she could do for him Jarvis wasn't already doing. And she had a fight to finish.

The mountainous man was rocking on the balls of his feet, his face red with exertion but merriment dancing in his eyes. She could almost read his mind—he'd play with the pirate wench until she grew tired and made a mistake, then either kill her straight off or drag her to a quiet place for a tumble. His blatant self-confidence was radiating off him in waves. In the blink of an eye, new anger washed over her. How dare this foul, sweating toad assume he had her by the short hairs? She raised her chin and her sword, dropping back into the en garde position. "It isn't my friend who'll end up being the shark food. Say your prayers, and hope your gods are listening."

With a growl, Cragfarus was on her, jabbing and cutting almost faster than she could parry him. She cursed herself, stinging sweat dripping into her eyes as she bent under his onslaught. He'd played on her feelings, forcing her attention away from the fight. The big oaf could have had her head clean off in the second she squandered staring at her injured friend. She lunged at Cragfarus, her rapier point striking one of his brass buttons and sliding harmlessly away.

He swiped toward her, and Kestrel skipped backward, out of his sword's range. She was a fine swordsman, but he had far too long a reach—he'd slice her arm off at the elbow before she could get far enough inside his defenses. Assuming she could even put enough power behind the blow, fighting wrong-handed as she was.

Plainly he wasn't having any of the same doubts she was. Almost as if he was bored, he launched at her again, not letting her have an inch of extra space. His blade sang past her ear as she ducked sideways again. This common back-and-forth style wasn't going to work against an opponent so much larger than she. She had to come up with something better, and quickly, before she tired too much for it to matter anymore.

"Come now, my pretty," Cragfarus cooed, tossing his blade from one hand to the other and back again. "Give up before I have to cut off your best features." He lunged forward, and she swung her sword in a downward parry, sending his strike clanging off to the right. With his sword arm knocked away, his midsection was exposed. Kestrel brought her rapier up, trying for a belly thrust, but not fast enough. He scooted backward easily, laughing.

Her pulse was pounding in her ears, and the air seemed thick, too thick to breathe. Her arm was aching, unused to fighting this way. Gloom began to darken her mind. It was a noble mission she was on, trying to save an innocent man. She'd managed to escape capture, collect and convince the crew and board the ship she'd need. Before she could even raise anchor, she'd run against a brick wall in a soldier's uniform. And here she was—fighting a duel with her weak left arm to spare her injured right, against an opponent who never seemed to tire. How was she supposed to win? *Damn your eyes, you gods above, a turn of fortune would be nice right now*, she railed silently. *I'm trying to be the hero.*

Cragfarus was staring at her, his forehead creased in a frown. She brandished her rapier at him, but he didn't react. He wasn't staring at her, but at a spot behind her. Several of his soldiers were pointing and muttering together, and fully half of the crossbowmen had turned their weapons in the opposite direction, pointed toward their commander. She didn't want to take her eyes off Cragfarus, but her curiosity got the better of her.

Six dripping men straddled the railing on the unguarded side of the ship, some holding swords and others with daggers clenched in their teeth. Her men. Last she'd seen them, they'd been sitting in the longboat. They must have slipped out when the soldiers' attention was drawn by the sword battle, swum around the *Thanos*, and clambered up the other side. It had been a good idea. If they all survived this, she promised herself she'd find out whose thought it had been and reward him.

"Well, look at that," Cragfarus drawled, his composure apparently returning. "Your friends have come to watch the show. Come aboard, men!" he cried, waving with his broad blade.

The pirates looked at each other, then at Kestrel. She nodded once. The six slid onto the deck, stepping away from the railing as more men appeared. About a dozen and a half in all. It was still up to her, but if she died, at least the ensuing battle would be a more even match.

They moved forward, but the commander shook his head. "That's far enough." Cragfarus twisted his chin at the guards nearest him. "Watch them while I finish with their little bitch."

"Not bloody likely!" The shout came from the crowd of wet pirates. She didn't know who said it, but as a man they all began nodding and agreeing. "Not our Kes!" "She's like a bolt o' lightnin' with a sword!" "You'll be lucky to walk away with your ears still attached!"

In spite of her tension and fear, her heart swelled at the show of support. Kestrel blinked to clear her vision. He was coming toward her again, spinning his blade in the mesmerizing figure eight pattern he seemed so proud to be able to perform. His face contorted in rage; he'd probably been expecting the praise for Kestrel even less than she had herself. Spare lines dangling behind him moved in the light breeze like a huge web, with Cragfarus a huge hairy spider, scuttling to collect his cornered prey. "Give up, girl. While you still breathe."

"Never," she muttered. The lines shuddered in the light afternoon breeze, almost as if they were waving at her. Before he'd ever taught her swordcraft, Binns had made her learn sailoring from the bottom up. Including how to work the rigging. She could climb the lines as skillfully as a monkey, and she had a wild vision of a game they used to play in quiet coves when the day's work was finished.

Please let this work, she breathed. She ran at Cragfarus, waving her rapier wildly. He raised his blade in a quick parry, but instead of striking him, she skidded past on one side. Tossing her sword up, she caught it in her right hand and leaped up, grabbing a length of line in her left. The power of her leap carried her in a swinging arc behind the soldier.

Strong he might be, but not quick. He was still facing the other direction when the momentum of her swing carried her around. With a wild cry of victory, her sword's point slid neatly into his undefended back.

Cragfarus stood where he'd been, her rapier sheathed in the muscle of his back. His head dropped forward, as if he were staring with rapt attention at the pointed steel standing out from between his ribs.

Kestrel released her hold on rope and rapier, landing on the deck with both feet flat. Her breath labored in and out of tortured lungs. The pain in her shoulder had returned, now that her fury had passed, a white-hot scream from within her body that almost made her wish the man had killed her when he had the chance. She stepped forward, grasped her hilt, and pulled her weapon free of the big soldier. Blood gushed from the wound; as if it had been the only thing holding him upright, he wavered, then tipped slowly forward onto his face, redness pooling under his still body.

Soldiers and pirates alike were stock-still, all eyes wide and wary. An eerie silence blanketed the ship, broken only by the occasional slap of water against the hull far below and Kestrel's own panting. She'd done it. Shoulder in flaming pain, her men outnumbered, but somehow she'd won. A slow grin spread over her lips. It was a good omen for the rest of the mission—it had to be.

Jarvis was kneeling next to Shadd. He glanced up from his patient and cleared his throat before speaking. "I got his bleedin' stopped for now. You want I should see to that other fella, Cap'n?"

He was looking at her expectantly; she realized with a start that when he said "cap'n" he referred to her. The situation was still too sticky—she'd wait and correct him later. Even if they didn't get the

Wolfshead back, until she saw him dead beyond saving, Binns was still the captain.

She shook her head, turning instead toward the soldiers lined up against the rail. A few of them were holding their positions, not that it mattered anymore, now that her dripping crew had arrived. Others had turned to watch the fight, and Kestrel caught the eye of one of them.

"One of you, get over here," she ordered. A fair-haired young man turned, a guarded expression on his face and his cocked cross-bow cradled on his arm.

She jerked her head, indicating he should join her. The man hesitated, half raising his crossbow. She scowled. "Don't make me spill your blood, too. I already have enough to scrub off my deck now."

Kestrel hoped she looked and sounded as dangerous as she felt. The soldier blanched, set his weapon gently on the deck, and stepped forward.

Now that he was close to her, she noticed that his chin wasn't shaved, but sported a downy fuzz that hadn't darkened into a man's beard yet. Sixteen at the most, barely old enough to leave his mother's knee. He was carefully avoiding looking at the bloody car-cass of his commander, instead keeping his eyes straight ahead as he'd been trained to do. Possible this was the first killing he'd ever witnessed, or at least the first killing of someone he knew. *We all have to grow up sometime,* she thought. *Today appears to be your day.* She crouched next to Cragfarus and wiped her rapier blade clean on the back of his breeches. She grinned up at the uncomfortable young soldier.

"What's your name, boy?"

He squared his shoulders a little tighter. "Guardsman First Level Axel, miss. I mean, ma'am. That is"—he threw a nervous sideward glance down at her—"Captain?"

There it was again. The name she couldn't accept, that kept be-ing thrown at her. It had been bad enough when Jarvis called her "captain," as if he and all the others didn't really believe Binns would be rescued. But to hear the soldier use the word was just too final, too permanent. She couldn't be captain, not yet, not under these circumstances.

She could, however, pretend. *It's just a word*, she told herself, *with no more meaning than what I allow it to have.* If she let this pup of a soldier call her captain, the other soldiers would hear. Letting these uniformed buffoons believe she commanded a pirate crew could work to her advantage. Binns wouldn't begrudge her that. Especially if it helped her to save his life.

"Captain will do fine," she said. She rose to her feet and sheathed her blade. The movement sent fire licking down her arm, but she kept her face deadpan. *Show no sign of weakness, or you're ruined.* She stepped close. "Your commander is dead. You're outnumbered. And I don't have the time to waste killing you."

He stiffened. "I'm sorry, ma . . . uh, Captain. I do not have the authority to negotiate terms of surrender with you." His voice quavered.

"Surrender?" She laughed. "I don't want your surrender. I want you off this ship. Lucky for you I'm a pirate, not a barbarian. You and the rest of your squad behave yourselves and you'll survive the day."

"I'm a sworn officer in His Majesty's Navy." He frowned, his boyish face suddenly mature. "It's my duty to stop criminals like you."

"By my count," she said, pointing her finger at each soldier, one by one, "I've got three men to your one. Look at my crew." She inclined her head toward the horde of men behind her, their clothes soaked and their faces determined. "If I so much as whistle, there'll be nothing left of you but the memory."

He wasn't used to making the big decisions, that much was obvious. A single bead of sweat slipped from the line of his baby-fine hair, sliding down his tensed and twitching jaw. His face had gone deadly pale, and he was standing so tightly at attention he didn't even seem to be breathing. She laid a hand on his shoulder, and he started violently. Better talk quick before he passed out. "Take your squad, dead and alive, and get the bloody blazes off my ship."

He looked miserable, and his shoulders sagged. "I'll be whipped for this."

The tide had turned—she could feel the *Thanos* pulling under her feet, a mighty beast trying to get free of its leash. She'd been patient with this boy, but time was not going to wait. She had to raise anchor now, before the villain McAvery could get any farther away. She slapped his back. "Whippings heal. Get your men moving."

Axel's mouth dropped open, making him look like a hooked fish. She glared at him, refusing to break the stare. Finally, he looked down, then turned toward the waiting soldiers. "Squad, we're moving. Someone get the commander's body."

Kestrel allowed herself a breath. For a second she hadn't been sure this wouldn't end without another fight. Maybe the gods were smiling on her after all.

"We need to move him," Jarvis murmured. He'd cut away Shadd's ruined shirt, using whatever pieces were big enough to stanch the bleeding. Kestrel crouched down beside Shadd. His chest rose and fell regularly, but his color was still pasty.

"Put him in the captain's quarters."

Jarvis shot her a startled glance. "Where'll you sleep?"

She rolled her eyes and sighed. "I'll hang my hammock in there. Someone will need to stay near him at night, in case he starts to bleed again. Besides, with a wound as bad as this, Shadd needs to be lying flat, not swinging to and fro all night."

She rose. Her men were wandering the deck, as excited as children. The gunners had apparently already slipped belowdecks; Kestrel could hear their muffled voices calling to each other under her feet. She glanced out at the harbor. Hackney boats still moved back and forth from ships to shore. There didn't look to be any patrols swinging by. So far, so good.

"All right, men, that's enough relaxing. Aloft you go, and let's look lively." They responded to her command, and in moments sails were belling out, fat and full of the afternoon breeze.

Axel was nearly through loading his men. Cragfarus's corpse had already disappeared, and the last few bluecoats were waiting their turn to climb down into the boat below. Kestrel crossed the deck and elbowed the young man. "Don't forget to take your magus with you. I find him, I'll toss him to the sharks."

Axel looked confused. "What magus?"

"Whoever's responsible for this." She swept a hand toward the hay bale, and the perpetual card game.

Axel nodded sagely. Striding across the deck, he bent and picked up a card, and thumped it with his finger three times. Instantly, the three men vanished. He held the card out toward Kestrel with a half smile.

"They call it an abiding illusion. Cast the spell on a solid object, like this card." He shrugged. "We use them all the time, to lay traps and confuse enemy armies into thinking we have more men than we do. Cheaper than having a Danisoban on the payroll."

Gingerly, she took the card from his hand. She wasn't sure what she'd been expecting—tingling, perhaps, or heat. It felt no different from any other playing card. She turned it over. The Ace of Spades. She flipped it around and held it up to Axel, quirking an eyebrow.

"The death card?" she asked.

The young soldier spread his hands out. "The commander always had a taste for the dramatic."

Kestrel walked to the railing and looked down. The tidal current was stronger, creating eddies around the waterline of the big ship, and drawing it out to the length of the anchor line. Without turning around, she said, "Time for you to go, Axel. Sorry about the whipping."

He didn't say anything. A moment later she heard footsteps. Slow, reluctant footsteps, but definitely moving away from her. She held the card, turning it over and over again, and thumped it between her fingers. Just a card. But not a card at all. A bit of glossy paper, with the power to fool any number of men into believing what they saw. A heavy shudder ran down her back.

The rhythmic splash of oars drew her attention. The squad of soldiers was rowing away in the whaling boats she'd used to get out here. The alarm would be raised any minute.

"Should we raise anchor, then?" Red Tom called, as if he'd read her mind.

"Aye, raise anchor. We've already wasted too much time on this venture." She listened to the creaking of the anchor winch being turned. The *Thanos* bucked under her feet, responding to the fast-moving water and wind tugging against the sails above her head, as ready to go as Kestrel herself.

The waves were tinted red-gold with the coming sunset. Her stomach growled, and she wished again she'd eaten more at break-fast. Had it only been one day? The sweet taste of the green beryl Artie had given her sprang into her mouth. He was a pirate and an outlaw, but a kinder, gentler man was never born. If anyone deserved to hang, it was the black-hearted snake who'd swindled Artie out of his ship. The only question in her mind was how she'd keep herself from tearing McAvery to pieces before she could deliver him up to the courts.

She glanced at the card in her hand again. What could it hurt to use the card if the opportunity presented itself? It wasn't as if anyone had been murdered to make the spell. Suddenly, the faces of long-lost children moved past her mind's eye, their sorrowful eyes as fresh as they'd been when she was a child herself. No one had been murdered to make this spell, but enough had died for the Danisobans that it was all the same to her. She'd have nothing to do with it. Cocking her hand sideways, she flipped the card into the air, watching it flutter down toward the shining water below just as the anchor cleared the surface, then turned away.

"I'll be damned!" someone cried. "Would ye look at that!"

Several of the men were gathered against the railing, and Kestrel looked curiously. Sitting on the water, bobbing with the motion of the waves, were the three card-playing soldiers. As the ship moved farther away, one of them threw down his cards with a smile and leaned forward to scrape up his imaginary gold.

Sixteen

The Sun's rim dips; the stars rush out;
At one stride comes the dark;
With far-heard whisper, o'er the sea
Off shot the specter bark.

—SAMUEL TAYLOR COLERIDGE

While the rest of the crew had been piloting the *Thanos* out of the harbor, Jarvis and Bardo had moved Shadd to the captain's quarters. It was spacious and warm, bookcases full of volumes lining one wall, and various framed charts hung on the other. Near the door stood an armoire, carved in weird and intricate patterns that reminded Kestrel of Olympia's bar. It had a gold handle and keyhole, but no key was evident. She tried the door anyway. It slipped open easily, revealing velvet coats and breeches, and silk shirts. Kestrel took a minute to shuffle through them, relishing the exotic nap of the velvets, the slithery smoothness of the silk. To her delight, there was one red shirt hanging there. It looked a little large for her, but she decided to take it as a good omen. She took it and a smallish pair of velvet breeches behind a nearby screen, and changed out of the uncomfortable skirts.

Unlacing the bodice was a delightful relief, and she drew a deep breath once her ribs were free again. The log slipped loose and thudded to the floor. Kestrel left the women's clothing hung over the screen once she'd changed, but she picked up the book and carried it to the armoire. She slid it onto the floor under the hanging clothes. Time to find a better hiding place later.

A mirror-backed sideboard hunkered next to the armoire, stocked with crystal decanters of rum and gin, and a number of sealed wines. In the middle of the floor stood a shining round table with four chairs. It had been carved from some dark wood, but it bore an ashy gold circular stain in the dead center, as if a pitcher of beer had spilled and never been cleaned up. In a room as well kept as this, the furniture so polished it shone, the stain was glaring.

The stern window at the rear of the cabin was made of panes of beveled glass, throwing light over the wide, well-appointed bed positioned beneath it. It was big enough for three people to sleep comfortably. Shadd was resting—whether comfortably or not, she couldn't say. They'd settled him in the bed, tucking the soft linen sheets securely around him. His bandages leaked scarlet while they struggled with his unconscious bulk, but he hadn't wakened. Kestrel retrieved a hammock from below, and hung it from the dark wooden beams crossing the ceiling. She'd intended to stay near, in case Shadd woke. Or took a turn for the worse.

But sleep had proved elusive. Thoughts of Binns on the prison ship, chained in a dank and miserable hold, puddles of brackish water leaking into his boots and his stomach rumbling with hunger, kept her mind swirling and restless. Besides, her shoulder was throbbing, not as badly as when she'd first injured it, but enough to keep her from ever reaching a comfortable enough position to sleep. She'd finally tipped herself out of the hammock and returned to the deck to pace and prowl and worry.

The sea was a shifting mirror of black, distant swells glittering in reflected light from the half-moon. Except for the occasional moan of the wind in the rigging, the big warship was running nearly silent, nary even a creak of the wood below Kestrel's feet. The men were uncharacteristically somber. Instead of breaking open a rum cask and toasting their success, most of them staked claims to hammocks below and turned in to sleep. The few remaining on deck for the night's running worked without anything but the most rudimentary conversation. A steady breeze had arisen just at sunset, keeping her sails filled long after the dark fell. If she'd been a superstitious woman, Kestrel would have liked to believe nature itself was on her side. Except that any wind she was using was also pushing McAvery that much farther as well. She peered through the spyglass, hoping for a glimpse of the little sloop she knew so well.

Now that she was free to move and breathe, the unpleasant images of Binns in chains had faded from her imagination. They were replaced by a handsome, smiling face, the face that threatened to send her and all she cared about into a doomed future. She cursed herself for letting McAvery get within fifty yards of her captain. She hadn't spoken out against him hard enough—she'd let her fear of magic show too well, and had ended up sounding like an hysterical girl instead of the street-wise woman she was. If she'd only chosen her words more carefully. If only she'd made Binns understand the danger. She sighed, crossing her arms over her chest. For that matter, if only she'd run McAvery through when she glimpsed him in the market. The what-ifs raced through her mind, making her feel as if she were spinning in violent circles.

Stop it, she told herself. *What's done is done. It's no different from sailing into a spinstorm. Batten down and ride it out, then repair the damage after.* The best way she could see to fix what was broken was to clap McAvery in chains in the hold of this fine ship they'd both had their turns at stealing, and sail at top wind for Pecheta. He had the advantage of hours on her, but she had the better ship, especially knowing where he was headed.

Of course, what if McAvery hadn't been headed for Pecheta? He was a confidence player after all, practiced in the wily arts of covering his tracks and disappearing without a trace. He'd been two steps ahead since he first saw them sailing into Eldraga. Once he managed to snatch her sloop, he must have assumed she'd question the dockmaster once she discovered the theft. His passing comment could have been another red herring, carefully contrived to lead her in the opposite direction from him. "An appointment with the king," he'd said. If it had been the accidental truth or a carefully planted red herring, his comment remained the only lead she had to go on. She scanned the horizon again, hoping for the glitter of an aft lantern or the gleam of moonlight on white sails to tell her she was on the right track. If she couldn't find and capture McAvery, she wasn't sure what course would be left to her.

The crew wasn't hers. She refused to deceive herself that they were along out of any loyalty to her. Call her "captain" they might, but it was Binns they still followed, Binns who kept them inspired. In their eyes, he was the promise of gold and rum, blood and battle. That, and the fact that this stolen vessel was far bigger and better gunned than the sloop. It looked like an easy capture, standing up here. They would never agree to attack a well-armed Pechetan military ship, not with their numbers depleted and not without a seasoned captain leading the charge.

A memory of their last boarding floated into her mind's eye. It had been a rather small caravel, transporting a duke's ransom in salt and other spices from the Continent and not especially well armed for all the riches they carried. Excitement had pulsed over the sloop in waves, every member of the crew taut with attention. They'd raised their false Pechetan flag, luring the caravel into a dangerous feeling of security.

The caravel hadn't realized the danger until too late. Half of the sailors on the merchant vessel were scampering to stations, while the remaining were disappearing belowdecks. Binns was dangling in the rigging, wearing the dark red linen shirt he always donned before battle, his face smudged with gunpowder and sweat, bellowing orders to his ropemen as they flung grapples over to catch and keep the merchant ship. Within minutes, the caravel was taken. They hadn't lost a single man. Later that night, during the drunken celebration that always followed a successful capture, Binns had confided in Kestrel. "Y'ever wonder why I always put the red shirt on before a fight?" he'd asked, his words slurring a little from the rum coursing through his blood. "It's a bit o' fraud, y'see. If I'm cut, the bleedin' won't show on the red shirt. Long as the men think I ain't hurt, they'll keep fighting 'til the battle's won."

She'd tried to follow his example earlier, fighting left-handed. She raised her hand and pressed carefully against the wounded shoulder, wincing at the answering throb. Only Shadd had known about her wound, and as far as she could tell, he hadn't told anyone. Had it made any sort of difference in the way the crew saw her? How could it if they didn't know she was fighting injured? She stared across the black water, wondering for the hundredth time how he managed to make command seem so effortless.

She'd been proud to serve under Binns. He was brave and strong, cunning and clever. She would happily have died for him. If only he'd been the one to escape, and she the one clapped in irons. He'd have known just what to do. He would have sailed in to rescue her and likely captured the cargo as well. What a page in his log that would have been.

The log. Binns could have left some clue, a morsel of guidance in the log's pages. Maybe it was time for some reading. She certainly wasn't getting any sleep.

A tear rose in her eye, blurring her vision. She wiped it away angrily, even though the only men on deck were on the quarterdeck, one steering and the other navigating, and neither close enough to have noticed. She drew a deep, shuddering breath, letting the salty air fill her lungs. It wasn't over yet. She would read the log, gain whatever wisdom Binns left within. But she would also trust that McAvery had meant what he said, and that she was right behind him.

"Yo, Kes!" Red Tom called, one hand still gripping the massive wheel and his face eerily lit by the half-closed bull's-eye lantern hanging from the spar over his head. He was pointing into the inky darkness. "Cast your glass 'at way—I caught a flash o' summat."

She swung the glass up to her eye, searching the direction he'd pointed, her breath catching in her throat. Could it be? So soon? White glimmered against the midnight edge where the sea met the sky. Definitely a sail. Too far away to make out what kind of ship, or who might have been aboard, but she grinned, her heart thumping with excitement. It was him. It had to be. A niggling thought fought to the surface, trying to remind her that it was a big ocean, and other ships had the right to be in her path besides the one she sought. She pushed the doubt away, unwilling to entertain it for even a moment. She let the glass fall to her side and turned toward Red Tom.

"Well, lads, our quarry's at hand." She quirked an eyebrow. "Who's ready for a bit of a chase?"

Red Tom, his hands still wrapped around the wheel, stared down at Kestrel from the high quarterdeck, an uncertain grimace tugging at the corner of his mouth. "Are ye sure, Kes? It be dark and all. What if yonder's only a fishin' boat?"

Her stomach twisted into a knot of frustration. He was questioning her order. She'd been expecting it to happen. Hell, the fact that they'd done as she said up until now should have been more than enough miracle for her. Maybe she'd gotten too used to the feeling, enjoyed the control that had fallen into her lap upon Binns's arrest. Now that the reality was upon her, she felt the hand of panic closing, tightening. The air, fresh and cleansing only a moment before, had thickened, and Kestrel struggled to breathe.

Because, whether she wanted to admit it or not, he was right. She was leading them across the ocean, chasing a flash of white in the dead of the night, on a hunch. What if they caught up to the ship, only to discover it wasn't the *Wolfshead*? Gods only knew how far ahead of them McAvery would be by then. Any control she had over this crew would fly like a gull before a gale. If she was lucky, she'd only find herself set adrift in a longboat with a compass and a jug of water. But if it was the sloop, and they didn't give chase, McAvery would escape scot-free and Binns would hang. It wasn't a risk she was willing to take.

The image of Binns in his red shirt popped back into her head, along with the words he'd shared. And in a flash she understood the lesson he'd been trying, in his gruff way, to pass on to her. It didn't matter whether the men had known she was hurt when she fought Cragfarus, no more than it mattered for them to know their captain bled through his red shirt. The important thing wasn't what the men saw, but what she could convince them to believe they saw. "A bit o' fraud," he'd called it. Maybe it was time for her own.

"Look closer." She held the spyglass up to the frowning pirate, urging him to put it to his eye. "Do you see her? Watch the way her topsail flutters just so. And the little shudder when she drops out of the swells? It's doubtless the *Wolfshead*, and no other."

She watched his face as he stared over the dark water. Was he buying the nonsense? She hadn't been able to see the ship any better than he had, it being so far away as to be only a glimmer across the ocean from them. It could be any vessel at all. Something inside her was telling her she was right. The *Wolfshead* lay ahead, and she couldn't let it get away.

He dropped the glass, and to her great relief, a grin broke across his face. "Aye," he said, "there ain't no doubt that's our Wolfie." He handed the glass back down to Kestrel. "So what's yer orders, Cap'n?"

The roiling in her stomach eased, replaced by a giddy light-headedness. She'd done it. She wanted to dance across the deck, shout her victory across the waves to Binns, locked in his chains in a dank hold somewhere out there, but she fought the urge, keeping her face calm and her feet still. "What's our position?"

"Southwest of Cre'esh. We'll pass the Teeth after sunup."

Kestrel clenched her jaw. The submerged shoals and jagged rocks known as the Teeth of Cre'esh had sunk better ships than either of theirs before. Most mariners avoided sailing anywhere near the Teeth. If the submerged shoals didn't rip the hulls out from under the ship, the vicious currents could easily drag less powerful vessels into the Mouth, a monstrous whirlpool that spun where the land used to be. Good thing they wouldn't be passing close by until it was light.

"Bring her about and give chase. Ride him close, but not too close. Mind the reefs." She yawned, the weight of what she'd done suddenly settling on her shoulders, as heavy and ungainly as a load of damp flour. It occurred to her that she hadn't slept since the night before Binns was taken—she'd been running on worry alone. There wouldn't be a better opportunity, especially not with a fight on the way. She'd be no good to the crew if she was exhausted to the point of collapse. Binns had slept regularly. She could, too. "I'm grabbing a few winks. Wake me before dawn."

A young crewman with flaming hair and a face covered in freckles touched her arm. "What do you want me to do, Cap'n?"

Kestrel searched her memory for the boy's name . . . Hudee, that was it. Middle child of a peasant family, no prospects and nothing much to lose by flouting the law. Binns had taken him on only a few weeks before. Good fellow, he'd turned out to have a thefty hand with the lines. Could be a fine bosun someday, if he lived long enough. She waved a hand toward the deck hatch.

"I'll need the gunners rousted before dawn. Roll them out of their hammocks if you have to, but make sure they're up when I need them."

Hudee grinned, bobbing his head. "Aye, Captain, I'm yer man."

She looked down at the makeshift breeches she still wore and grimaced. "One more thing, my lad. I've been through his cabin, but the last captain this ship had was a wider fellow than I am. Search below and see if you can't find me a decent pair of pants."

He nodded and scampered off toward the hatch. Another huge yawn fought its way to the surface. Kestrel turned away, striding toward the door of the captain's cabin, toward the hammock that now promised comfort and rest. Her shoulder had stopped hurting altogether, and she noticed that, for the first time, the word "captain" hadn't irritated her.

Seventeen

The boat came close beneath the ship
And straight a sound was heard.

—SAMUEL TAYLOR COLERIDGE

Kes? Captain?"
Kestrel swung an aimless fist in the general direction of the annoying fly buzzing her name, connecting with a suspiciously fleshy smack. How would a bug know her name anyway? She popped open one curious eye.

No insect at all, but a giant rat was standing next to her hammock, dressed in shirt and breeches and rubbing its cheek. She shook her head. No, not a rat but little, pointy-faced Bardo. His pale hand was against his cheek, but she could see a red mark on the skin he hid. "Ye din't need to hit me. Hudee told me ye wanted to be waked afore dawn. Go hit him, why don't ye?"

Kestrel blinked and sat up, rubbing the sleep-sand out of her eyes, and let the memory of her mission return to her. She was aboard the *Thanos*. They were chasing a low-down, thieving liar who'd stolen their sloop, wrongly accused their captain, and put all their lives in jeopardy. "Sorry, Bardo."

With a distinctly childlike pout, he turned and stalked toward the door of the cabin. "By the way," he announced, pointing, "there's clothes for ye."

A neat, folded pile of fabric lay on the table. Before she could thank him, Bardo had disappeared. Kestrel swung her bare feet over the side of the hammock, slipping to the floor. Unfolding the clothes, she was pleased to see a smallish pair of brown wool breeches and a darker brown linen tunic.

Stepping behind the wooden screen, Kestrel tugged off the silk shirt she'd slept in and slipped the clean linen over her head. The tunic was a little long for her, the hem falling halfway down her thigh. She unclasped the skirt latch, letting the makeshift breeches fall to the floor, then pulled on the new pants. She sighed, relishing the pleasant feel of the new clothes. They would have felt better if she could have bathed beforehand, but clean was still clean.

She reached for her sword belt. Her right shoulder twinged. Not nearly as bad as it had been. Thank the gods for small favors— she'd been afraid that the fight yesterday morning, and her foolish decision to use her right hand, might have damaged her even more. But the injury was no more painful than a bruise would be. She could easily get her job done in spite of it.

Her nap—she couldn't rightly call it a night's sleep, since it couldn't have lasted more than two hours—seemed to have done a world of good. Her skin tingled, and her stomach rumbled with . . . was it hunger? The last thing she'd eaten had been breakfast with Binns two mornings ago. What she wouldn't do for a handful of those green beryls now. She still didn't know the extent of the stores aboard the *Thanos*, but if the supplies were anything like as high quality as the captain's sleeping place, a fine meal would soon be shared by all. Once they'd locked McAvery in chains, that is.

She spared a glance through the fancy beveled glass of the windows. Tom had managed some fine sailing during the night. The ship was still a distance away, but not so far they couldn't catch her easily. A minuscule line of purple split the sky from the sea; sunrise was just beginning.

Shadd groaned softly, from the depths of the snowy linens surrounding him. His color had settled out during the night, the usual ruddiness returning to his cheeks. Despite his groan, he seemed to be breathing more normally. Kestrel pulled back the top sheet carefully. His bandages were still clean. No seeping blood had made its way through to the outside. A very good sign.

"If I'd had the notion that a belly stick would be the thing to make you pull me covers back, lass, I'd've got myself stabbed long ago." Shadd's eyes were open, though still at half-mast with fatigue, and his voice was raspy, but his grin was wide and infectious.

Leave it to Shadd to wake up with a joke on his lips. Relief flooded through her; if he'd died, it would have been her fault. She didn't think she could have lived with herself if she'd gotten him killed. "So this was all a ploy?" she retorted, letting the sheet fall back over him. "It'll take more'n a deadly wound to get me into your clutches, you big beast."

"Where the blazes am I?"

Kestrel couldn't resist the note of pride that crept into her voice. "You're on the *Thanos*."

"You took her?" With a strained chuckle, he tried to rise. "In that case, I think I'll have me a stroll along the decks."

Kestrel pushed him back down firmly. "You are as stupid as you look. No getting up for you."

"I can't stay in here."

"This is the best place for you. Until you get your guts knitted back together, you don't want to be swinging in a hammock."

"These'd be the captain's rooms. And I ain't no captain."

"You'll stay in here until I say you can leave." She planted her hands on her hips and glared. "You're a lucky piece of flotsam. You might even live the day, if you do as I say. None of us wants to see you walking around with your intestines hanging from your belly."

"Hell and damnation, stop threatening me." He relaxed against the pillows again, the grimace on his face easing. "So what's happened while I've been sleepin'?"

She glanced out the windows again. The purple line had softened to a midnight-blue, sending barely perceptible fingers of light across the waves. The white sails of the ship they pursued were even easier to see. She pointed toward it.

"Yonder's the *Wolfshead*."

"I thought we was goin' after the *Victory*."

"Changed the plan while you were having your beauty sleep. The man who caused all this, he's got the sloop. If we catch him, not only do we get our ship back, but we can use him to barter for Binns."

Concern flashed into his eyes. "Help me up, Kes. You need me." He struggled to sit up, groaning with the effort. She placed both hands on his shoulders.

"I've got it well in hand. The gunners are waking their ladies, the men are ready for battle, and we're passing the Teeth. McAvery will have no place to run to. He'll have to give in or sink."

He lay back again, the smile returning to his lips, along with another emotion she couldn't quite put a name to. "You'd sink the *Wolfshead*?"

"Not if I can help it . . . ." She shrugged. "I mean to do what I must, Shadd. I have to get my hands on McAvery. If it means scuttling the sloop, that's what'll happen."

"Aye. You've always been the determined type. That's why Binns picked you, I reckon." He reached up to her hand still pressing against his shoulder, and patted it gently. "Just don't rock me around too much, aye? Damn, I'm feelin' sleepy again." He yawned and settled down into the bedding. He closed his eyes with a contented sigh.

She walked slowly out of the cabin and closed the door behind her. The horizon line was growing lighter by the second. Red Tom was still at the wheel. Up all night, but he didn't look the slightest bit tired. She rubbed her face again, hoping she'd managed to rid her eyes of all the sleep-sand, and climbed the quarterdeck ladder. "Morning, Tom. What's our position?"

"We're no more'n a half hour from the Teeth."

"Fine, good." She slapped her hands together, enjoying the freshness of the dawn air. There was always something exciting about being up before the sun, even when she wasn't getting ready for a skirmish. A number of the crew were emerging from belowdecks, stretching and buckling on weapons belts as they came. They gathered below the railing of the higher deck on which she stood, some talking quietly together but all watching her.

The young fellow from the night before—what was his name?—was struggling up the ladder, one-handed because of a box in his other one. He approached her, holding the box forward.

"Hungry, Captain?" She glanced into the box. Dozens of hardtack biscuits—her belly grumbled at the sight. Hardtack was usually tasteless and dull, the last thing anyone would choose for breakfast. Unless she hadn't eaten properly in days. She took a handful and smiled at the boy.

"Have you slept, lad?" she asked.

"I been up and down every inch of this ship, Captain, and she's a fine one. Whoever had her before us musta been getting' ready for a long voyage—there's fresh fruit and barrels of clean water, smoked meat, jars of pickled vegetables, a wheel of sharp cheese, and biscuit. Lots of biscuit. And I found some clothes below, but I just guessed at whether they'd fit ye."

Hudee, that was it. She'd sent him off to have a look around, but she'd thought he would just find a cozy corner and fall asleep. The boy must have stayed up all night, exploring the ship. She'd have to let him give her a tour of the nooks and crannies after the coming battle was over; he probably knew the ship better than anyone else already. "Thanks, lad. You did fine."

He glanced over his shoulder and dropped his voice. "There's one other thing, Captain. Something I heard while I was scuttling around in the dark." He leaned in closer, and Kestrel had to strain to hear him. "Some of the men were complaining. Said we'd all end up dead from this. One fella even said you was going crazy and ought to be locked away!"

She patted the boy's back. "I'm not surprised, Hudee. If there's something pirates are good at besides drinking and fighting, it's fussing. I'll tell you what. You keep that sharp ear open, and let me know if the talk gets more serious."

"Aye, Kes!"

"Good lad. Now go and see if anyone else wants a bite."

He nodded and walked away, offering his meager biscuits to anyone else who looked hungry.

Nibbling at the crisp bread, she rejoined Red Tom at the wheel. The sun was rising, pinkish red against the dark blue of the water at the horizon. A light, cool breeze, redolent with the scent of tropical flowers, fluttered the loose hairs at Kestrel's temple. The deck under her feet rolled in long, smooth dips over the pleasantly tossing waves. It was the kind of morning she relished. She drew a long breath. "So, Tom, are you ready for some excitement?"

"Aye, Captain. I been ready since yesterday, when I saw the empty spot in Eldraga harbor."

"As have I, Tom. You're not too tired? You've been awake a mighty long time."

He gritted his teeth, making the skin at jaw and temple tight and pale. His expression hadn't changed but the fury he nursed was shining all around him like a halo. "There'll be time enough to sleep when I'm dead."

For a brief instant she hesitated. She'd been kicking herself angrily, determined to keep the blame for all that had happened. Until this moment, she hadn't understood how badly Binns's capture had affected the crew. They would probably tear McAvery to pieces like a pack of rabid dogs, if she didn't play this right.

Tom cleared his throat. "I got a question for you." He shifted his eyes toward her. "Last night, when you ordered me to follow yonder ship, you didn't know if it really was ours or not, did you?"

She hesitated, drawing a deep breath before answering. "Does it matter now?"

"No." He tipped the wheel an inch, catching the changeable breeze into the sails more deftly. "It was a fine gamble." He grinned. "Captain."

"Thank you, Tom," she said at last. He'd known, all along, but he'd done as she said. Maybe this was all going to turn out well.

She stepped forward and leaned over the smooth railing. Faces turned up toward her, some yawning and still wiping sleep-sand from their eyes, others munching on hardtack, but all of them expectant, excited. Poor lads had been idle too long—they were spoiling for a decent fight. Her belly fluttered. If it was a fight they wanted, a fight she would give them. "Listen up, all of you. The foul fiend who put our good captain in chains lies yonder, my hearties. In the sloop he stole from us. Are we going to let him sail away?"

"No!" The cry went up suddenly, loud enough to shiver the deck beneath her feet. Her chest tightened, her heart swelling with pride. They could do this. They would do it. *Artie,* she thought, *hang on. I'm bringing your boys to you.*

"Tom," she ordered, "it's time. Match course with the *Wolfshead*."

He frowned. "Match course?"

"You heard me. As we get closer to the Teeth, I want you to close in tight." She scanned the crowd below, until she found the man she wanted. "Searlas, I want all the gunports open on the starboard side."

"And the deck guns, Captain?" Shadd's second gunner asked, the lilting rise in his voice betraying him as a Bixian.

"Not today. I want all the men below, just in case our quarry decides to fire on us. We don't have enough men to run a proper battle as it is, and if we play this right, you won't need more. But I'd feel better if the ones I do have are behind the *Thanos's* sturdy hull." She winked at Searlas. "Indulge me?"

He nodded once, a bright smile his only answer.

"Kes." Tom's voice was low, so only she could hear. "I ain't meanin' to question you, but if we only match course and don't have enough gunners to man the ladies, how are you intendin' to defeat the fella?"

Off in the distance, rising from white-capped waves, were the Teeth. Sharp edges of wet stone gleamed in the morning sun. None of them were the same size; some were taller than her masts, menacing rocky giants. Others barely showed above the water, but those were the most deadly. Let an unsuspecting hull run up against one of the submerged Teeth, and it could tear a big enough hole to sink a ship in minutes.

She gestured toward them. "I'll just catch him between a rock and a hard place."

Eighteen

Like one, that on a lonesome road
Doth walk in fear and dread,
And having once turned round, walks on,
And turns no more his head;
Because he knows a frightful fiend
Doth close behind him tread.

—SAMUEL TAYLOR COLERIDGE

L egend had it that the island of Cre'esh had once been the largest of all the Nine, until Mohon Dro lost his temper. According to the story, the mighty Danisoban had been trying to enslave a water demon. Before he could finish the incantation, his young apprentice sneezed. The spell had gone horribly wrong, turning the boy's bones to water. As the hapless assistant writhed on the floor, a bag of skin and fluid, Dro cursed out loud.

Unfortunately, the spell wasn't complete, the magic hanging unfinished in the air. Dro's one angry word, on the heels of the spell, increased its intensity. Fishermen, plying their trade off shore, later reported a violent earthquake that rocked the island, followed by a raging fountain of water shooting high into the skies above the Danisoban's stone castle. Within hours, Cre'esh had been reduced to a slender curve of beach and mountain, guarded along one coast by the jagged Teeth, and its inner shore surrounding a raging whirlpool.

The event passed down through history as the Great Cataclysm. Whether the story was true or not didn't make much difference to Kestrel, but the whirlpool was real enough. Not to mention the rip currents it spawned. When Cre'esh was still a dark shadow on the horizon, the roar of the Mouth was easily heard, forcing everyone to talk louder just to be understood.

They'd slipped in close to the little sloop and matched her

course just tight enough to keep McAvery from tacking back into the open waters. The *Thanos* was big enough to hold her own against the currents at this distance, but the *Wolfshead* was much lighter. It would take some skillful sailing on his part to keep control of his helm and stay clear of the Teeth. She hadn't believed the farm-boy story he'd fed her back on Eldraga, but she also didn't think he was much of a sailor. Didn't have the walk, for one thing.

Now that the sun was up, Kestrel watched the man, moving quickly from one end of the *Wolfshead's* deck to the other. None of the gunports were open—had he no gunners at all? He was running with barely enough crew to man a skiff. What few men he did have seemed to be all deckhands, and all performing double duty just to keep the sloop afloat. She squinted suddenly, at one familiar figure. Was that Dreso? He'd been on the *Wolfshead* the night Binns was taken into custody. She'd left him on watch, him and his incessant worrying about ghosts, and the little charms he made to ward them off. She'd assumed he was dead after McAvery stole their sloop, but there he was, working the lines fast and furious.

Or perhaps Dreso had been in league with him all along, awaiting the right opportunity. It would explain so much, McAvery having a confederate in their midst. Appearing out of the storm like a ghost, and Dreso fashioning his protective charms and kindling the fires of superstition and worry. Kestrel dropped the glass. She'd know soon enough whether her former crewmate was a traitor or a helpless captive.

"Closer," she ordered. Tom obliged, easing the wheel over just enough to tighten their course. The sloop was still running from her, not turning to fight. McAvery had to have realized who was chasing him, but he never looked her way, as if by not looking, she'd perhaps vanish as he had done. Those of her own crew not actively involved in sailing the *Thanos* were dangling from the rigging, some hooting and shouting taunts, others blowing discordant wails on brass bugles, hollowed-out shells, anything they could find to amplify their voices. The cacophony rattled her teeth.

Searlas appeared suddenly, popping up from the quarterdeck ladder. "The belowdecks ladies is all loaded and ready, and each man be standin' by to hop to your command, Captain," he said, in his lilting accent. "Ain't got enough men to fire all at once, but it shouldn't be a problem. We'll double up, if we have to."

Red Tom gripped the wheel against the currents that pulled at the big ship, even at such a distance. "So, Cap'n, what's the plan?"

"We're going to pull ahead, and fire a few yards ahead of his bow. Shake him up. Force him to make a mistake. If I can bump him against a Tooth or two, he'll probably surrender without too much argument." She smiled tightly. "I don't want to hit the *Wolfshead*. I only want to break McAvery's nerve. Can you give me that, Searlas?" He nodded once. "Get yourself below, then, and keep an ear perked for my signal."

"McAvery's nerve'll be a sight harder to hit than the side of that sloop, you know," Tom said. "You sure it's worth the risk?"

Kestrel opened her mouth, intending to defend her plan, then stopped. They were calling her "captain" these days. When Binns was standing in this spot, facing battle, his orders were written in stone. She hoped there was room to write her words on that same stone.

"I'm sure," she said finally. Tom nodded, silent, and turned the wheel again, bringing the *Thanos* a few yards closer to the *Wolfshead*. A helpful breeze sprang up, pushed against the *Thanos*'s huge sails, causing her to leap forward like an unbroken horse. The distance was about right. She couldn't ask for better.

She strode to the ladder's edge and leaned out over the main deck. "Fire starboard guns!"

She heard the order echoed below, followed seconds later by the heavy *thump* of the cannons belching smoke and fire. The deck trembled under her feet. Kestrel swallowed back the laugh that threatened to explode from her. She'd felt the pounding of cannon under her before, but never with such velvety quiet. It hadn't been at all like the bone-shaking that the sloop suffered. More like the heart of a gigantic beast, beating slow and hard. The *Thanos* was strong enough to fire several guns at once and still not disturb the tea in the captain's cup.

She peered across the water at their target. McAvery was running for the hatch amidships, yelling something, his cloak sweeping behind him. Probably trying to teach his deckhands how to manage the guns. He looked frantic, waving his arms like that. Good. Cursed ship-stealing bastard. About time he experienced how it felt to run for his life, to have his plans dashed on the rocks. She smiled, her mouth tight with unspent fury. Another volley from the belowdeck guns should do it. One more time and maybe this would all end as it was supposed to.

Her shout was more casual the second time. "Again, lads, fire starboard guns."

She shivered, once again enjoying the exciting new sensation of a warship in battle. *I could get used to this so fast,* she thought hungrily. *But it's only for a while. You can't keep the* Thanos, *so don't grow attached.*

Kestrel focused her gaze on the sloop, trying to dispel the unwelcome thoughts. McAvery should have been opening the gunports, trying to fire, but they remained closed. A huddle of men were pulling something heavy from below. A box, or a crate, she couldn't quite tell what it was. McAvery had a smaller box tucked in the crook of his arm, but was gesturing wildly with the free hand.

The sailor at the wheel was having trouble controlling the sloop. Even from the distance, Kestrel saw the strain in his arms, the worry lacing his face. He braced his feet and struggled to keep the *Wolfshead* on a steady line, but the little sloop wasn't tough enough to handle the currents. The sloop's side scraped against the sharp granite of a nearby Tooth. A crackling squeal bounced through the air, and Kestrel winced. What sort of idiots did McAvery have sailing her sloop? And why wasn't he ordering the helmsman to steer away?

Another of the Teeth was standing dead ahead. McAvery's helmsman would have to turn sharply, or risk running smack into the huge rock. He yanked at the wheel, but not hard enough. Instead of taking a sharp turn around it, the little sloop bounced against the huge jutting rock, like a ball hitting a stone wall. The *Wolfshead* hadn't been built for this kind of punishment. Kestrel half expected to see it fly apart at the seams, with the pounding it was taking.

She stepped to the railing and drew a deep breath. "Ahoy, the ship!" she bellowed. "Do you surrender?" But the men on board the sloop didn't seem to hear. The morning wind coupled with the rushing and splashing of the waves around the rocks and the roar of the Mouth drowned her voice.

McAvery had finally noticed his helmsman's troubles. He ran to the man's side, pushed him aside, and took the wheel himself. He pulled at the wheel handles, trying to turn the little ship better into the wind and away from the vicious rocks, but his effort was too late. With a groan that fluttered over the water like a dying swan's call, the sloop heeled over, spilling two men into the water. The sickening shriek of wood being split tore at Kestrel's ears, and she watched in horror as the sloop stopped dead. She hung in the ocean, eerily motionless, waves of white foam cresting around her bow. Bubbles bobbed up from below the waterline on her hull.

"No!" Kestrel yelled, hitting the rail with a clenched fist. "My ship!" She thought she'd been prepared to sink the *Wolfshead*, but seeing the poor thing like this, holed on an unseen rock, had pierced her heart. As if this were a harbinger for the remainder of the mission, a crier of doom on their hopes. Her sloop was dying. Binns had trusted her with the care of the ship. And she'd as surely killed it as if she'd cut the hole in it herself.

"Bring us about!" she ordered, and Tom complied. The *Thanos* dropped into a wide circle, slowing down and getting a little farther from the worst of the currents.

"Hudee." The boy sprang to attention. "Drop rescue lines over the side, for any of them as manages to reach us through these waters."

"Aye, Captain," he agreed.

Kestrel pointed to the longboats suspended above the railing on the main deck. "Jaques. I want you to cable two longboats to the railing, and lower them down. Jarvis!"

"Aye, Kes!"

"You take the first boat. Fetch up whatever stragglers you can. Jaques and I'll bring back her captain."

"What if he drowns before you get to him?" Red Tom muttered from behind her, for her ears alone. She gritted her teeth and flashed him a tight smile.

"I'll drag his carcass to land, pay a Danisoban to return him to life, and beat the breath out of him myself."

Tom laughed out loud. "In that case, I'll throw in a coin or two. For the cause, and all." Reaching the end of the slow turn, Tom straightened the wheel, letting the big ship slide close enough to the stranded sloop for their rescue boat to help. Kestrel, Jaques, and four oarsmen boarded and rowed, fighting the strong currents, out to the scuttled ship.

The *Wolfshead* looked far worse up close. Her sides were scarred and torn from running against the Teeth and she was listing dangerously. The riptides weren't as bad as she'd feared now that they were up close. She wondered if it was the sloop that protected them, while it remained above the surface. Some of McAvery's crew had abandoned ship, fighting the currents to swim toward the *Thanos's* longboat. Her men busied themselves by tossing lengths of rope out to pull dripping, angry sailors out of the sea.

A hand slid over the gunwale of her longboat, followed by a familiar face. "Well, Dreso," she said, giving him an arms-up. "Not quite drowned yet?"

"Good to see you, Quarter," he sputtered.

I find out you were working with him all along, I'll throw you overboard with my own hands. Out loud, she said, "Glad you're no ghost, Dreso."

Wiping one hand over his sopping hair, he glanced around curiously. "Captain back on the ship?"

"Oh, the captain's along, never fear." If he wasn't a traitorous dog, the news coming later wouldn't do him any further ill. It wasn't as if she were lying, anyway—just withholding the information that the captain wasn't who Dreso thought.

McAvery himself was standing on the deck next to a wooden crate, one foot propped on the sloop's railing. Now that he'd lost, he'd abandoned his histrionics, choosing instead to strike a pose, probably for her benefit. His cloak was billowing behind him, and in his left elbow he was holding a wooden box. The sloop was obviously sinking fast. Time to rescue her bargaining chip. "Philip McAvery, do you surrender?" Kestrel called.

"Kestrel, as I live and breathe," he replied. "I was wondering when you'd get here."

She crooked a finger at him. "Unless you're of a mind to go down with the ship, you'd better step lively."

"I'll be needing to bring my luggage," he called, patting the huge crate next to him on the deck. It was nearly as tall as he himself, and half as wide as it was tall. The boards were stained dark with exposure to the salt air, and whatever was written on it was too obscured to decipher.

With a heavy creak, the floundering *Wolfshead* shifted. McAvery grabbed the crate to balance himself. "I'm ready to leave whenever you give the word," he said.

Kestrel studied the box. Big enough to hide an assassin, who'd sneak out in the gloom of night to slice all their throats. If not a hired blade . . . she swallowed hard. If the box was big enough to hold a killer, it was big enough to conceal a Danisoban, too. And what had Olympia told her? Something about Danisobans sleeping on their own soil, wasn't it? She shook her head. "Tell me what's in your box that's so important."

"What's in my crate is not any of your business."

Kestrel shrugged. "My ship, my business."

He raised a shocked eyebrow. "Your ship is currently sinking under my feet."

Curses bubbled under the surface, but she ground her teeth together to keep them in. Rising to his bait would only serve his purposes, not hers. "Show me your wrists."

"Now that's a fine flattery, my dear. You think me a Danisoban?" He shoved both sleeves up to his elbows, and held his arms high.

Sun-browned skin, but no trace of silver at his wrists. And no scarring to imply he'd once had the silver bracers there. It was a small comfort. Her other suspicions remained firmly possible.

"Tell me what's in the box or you go down with the *Wolfshead*. No matter who it belongs to."

"You need me," he threw back defiantly, "and I don't leave without this crate." He set the smaller box on top of the wooden crate and crossed his arms, his face stormy.

She sighed. Stubborn bastard, he'd probably stay in that position until the *Wolfshead* keeled over in the water, just to spite her. It was a tempting image—watching the foam subside as he let himself drown instead of giving in. He had her over a barrel. He was only valuable to her while he remained, unfortunately, alive. Hell, if he wanted the crate and its contents enough to drown for it, it could be worth something to her, too. If nothing else, she could find a way to control him with it. Threaten to toss it over if he didn't do as she said, maybe.

Jaques was standing in the bow of the longboat, watching her and waiting for her orders. She flicked her hand toward McAvery.

"Move in closer. If the cable allows it, bring us alongside the *Wolfshead*. Be certain to tie us up tight. Once we're secure, go fetch Binns's sea chest from his quarters. He'll want it when we get him back. If you can reach them safely, get your own and any others, but don't risk drowning for them." She sighed. "And while you're about it, have someone load yonder thrice-damned box." She turned away, but not before she caught a glimpse of McAvery's satisfied grin. Let the bastard think he won, as long as it got him onto her ship and under her control. *My ship. It is mine. I stole it fair and square*, she thought, the idea of mastering her own ship at the same time startling and comfortable.

The *Wolfshead*, its hull torn open on the Teeth, was shifting slowly to the side as it took on water. The wind whipped through its rigging with eerie wails, and a painful lump rose in her throat. She found she couldn't look at the sloop anymore. When she did, she seemed to see an image of Binns, hanging by his neck from the yardarms, his eyes open in death, accusing her.

She turned her back to the derelict, and stared over the water toward the *Thanos*. The huge ship rocked, in complete denial of the tragedy that was the sinking sloop, calm as a shadow, with the sun still rising behind her. She'd tasted Kestrel's blood but hadn't swallowed her up. Kestrel's heart thudded in her chest. Never had she felt this way about the sloop, nor any ship she'd ever set foot on. The *Wolfshead* had been a refuge, but the *Thanos* felt like home.

Her reverie was broken with a thump from behind her. Jaques had Binns's sea chest propped securely on one shoulder, and another under his arm. Hers. She glanced away before he could see the sudden shining in her eyes. She hadn't given her own sea chest a thought.

Two of McAvery's men had loaded his crate in the wide midsection of the longboat. Now that she could see it close, the writing on the wood was faded and smudged, still impossible to read. Clods of dirt had eased from between the slats, falling to the bottom of the boat in soft plops. If there was a Danisoban hiding in there, he'd have to dig his way out first. She'd be waiting with a ready blade.

#

Without thee were but a becalmed bark
Whose Helmsman on an ocean waste and wide
Sits mute and pale his mouldering hulk beside.

—SAMUEL TAYLOR COLERIDGE

McAvery walked across the deck of the *Thanos*, strutting like a visiting potentate, his box tucked in his left elbow as he nodded agreeably to the sailors gawking at him. Some didn't spare him a second glance, a few stared, and the rest snickered after he'd passed by.

"Take my crate belowdecks, lads," he said.

"Belay that." Kestrel laid a hand on the crate, scowling. "You'll not be handing out orders while I'm breathing." She patted the discolored wood. "I'm feeling powerful curious. I want to see for myself what's inside this trunk of yours."

He raised both eyebrows in an expression of innocent surprise. "I thought we had an agreement."

"I agreed to bring your box along. Not to let you keep it secret." She crossed her arms. "Now you're on my ship. If you want to remain here, you'll do as I say."

"No."

He stood before her, placid as a bowl of milk, but steadfast about his crate. Not that it seemed to bother anyone else. Jaques had wandered over to chat with his shipmates, who were patting him on the back for managing to bring back nearly all their sea chests. McAvery's own men didn't seem to be paying too much attention, busy wringing the water out of their clothes. He must not have paid them very well. She could probably run him through without them caring overmuch.

There was only one reason he would defy her, her and over thirty armed men, here in the middle of the ocean where his drowned body would never be discovered were she to dispose of him. He was hiding a Danisoban in the box. He had to be.

She'd give him one last chance. "What if I say it's the box or your life?"

"You'd kill me over a crate?" He seemed honestly amused. "There's no treasure inside."

"Do I look like so much of a fool? You insist on saving the box from a sinking ship, yet there's nothing of value inside? Mayhap it's not filled with gold or jewels, but whatever is within is worth at least your life."

"Nothing of value to you," he emphasized.

"Excellent. If I won't be tempted to steal it from you, then you can't be afraid to tell me what's in it."

"I'm not afraid," he said, smiling brightly. "I could offer more than the contents of a box to please you." He leaned forward, his words stroking her cheek like a warm breeze. "In the dead of the night, Kestrel, when the stars are twinkling and the ship is quiet, when your hammock suddenly seems far too empty with only yourself lying in it . . ."

She snapped her head back, breaking the connection. McAvery was grinning, a lascivious curve of the lip that could have been desire or triumph. She didn't know which, but suddenly she didn't care. He was playing with her, as if she were some innocent puppet there for his diversion. She tightened her jaw. Talking wasn't working. But she knew what would.

Striding over to the crate, Kestrel ran a hand along its uneven edges. The boards weren't flush—each one had a minuscule break between itself and the next. It smelled of fresh-dug dirt and salt-warped timber. She stepped around it, making sure the heavy box was between McAvery and herself.

"Jaques, Tom, to me," she ordered. The two men glanced at each other, but stepped to her side. "Draw your blades, if you'd be so kind."

Without hesitation, both men did as she asked, their blades shining in the morning sun. Kestrel cocked her head playfully, glaring over the edge of the weathered box at its owner. "Men, I want you to stab your swords through the cracks in this crate. No matter what happens, keep stabbing. Until I say stop."

McAvery looked confused, but not at all worried. Was he so confident in his Danisoban's chances? Perhaps he didn't truly care. If he'd been hired as escort, and paid in advance, Kestrel could easily believe McAvery would let the Danisoban die, spitted on the pirates' steel. He'd even find a way to shift the blame onto her and the crew, she'd bet. But it didn't matter. The only good mage was a dead one. She'd deal with the consequences later. Kestrel nodded to her men.

Tom and Jaques raised their blades, stabbing them into the spaces between the boards. Kestrel watched the swords as they came out. Both were marked with dirt, but no blood. They stabbed the crate again. And again. They moved to various spots, high and low, top and sides. Anyone remotely human-sized would have been struck by at least a few of their blows, but when they withdrew their blades, the only marks left behind were dirt.

She finally allowed them to stop, not satisfied but convinced that no one was hiding inside. Tom and Jaques wiped their swords off on their breeches and sheathed them, then stood back. Her men were watching curiously, but not a one of them had said a word. McAvery was leaning against the railing, inspecting his fingernails.

Drawing her own blade, she strode up and laid her sword against his neck. Steel against skin, sharp pushing into softness. It would be so easy to cut, bleed him out and be done with it. She pressed the edge against his flesh, filled with a burning desire to see what his innards might look like. But she didn't have that luxury.

"If you wanted a kiss, girl, you didn't need the dagger."

Muttering a curse under her breath, she withdrew her blade and pushed him away. "What's in it?" she demanded.

"You're finished killing my crate?" He waved a hand toward the dirty swipes on Tom's leg. "Soil. Dirt, sod, loam, earth, mud, clay, dust of the road." He quirked his lip ever so slightly. "Soil."

"You were willing to risk your life for a box of dirt? You expect me to believe that?"

"Haven't you proved it to your own satisfaction? In fact, I applaud your tenacity. Most pirate captains would have killed me and opened the crate."

"I don't want your praise." She spat on the deck at his feet. "What I want is your head, but I'll make do with having you in shackles. Jarvis." The pirate ran to do her bidding. Within seconds, McAvery was securely restrained.

"Store the crate below, lads." She favored her captive with an icy smile. "And please see to Master McAvery's comfort. After all, it's his fault we're here."

Her men snickered. "Aye, Captain," said Jarvis. "I think there's a cabin available, with some sturdy bars to keep him all safelike."

McAvery leaned forward and dropped his voice to a conspiratorial murmur. "I see now he didn't tell you everything. Did he?"

"Who?" The sudden lump in her throat ached.

"Binns. Kept things from you. Probably thinking to keep you safe. A soft heart, that one. Strange he'd have been chosen for the job."

"He's a fine captain. Earned himself far more loyalty than you did from your men," she said.

He shrugged. "True enough. It'd probably matter to me more if they were actually my men. Tell me"—he gave her a strange half smile—"have you read the log yet? Or do you follow him so very blindly?"

She balled her left fist and hooked McAvery's jaw. He rocked back, his eyes wide with surprise. "Thank your gods I'm feeling generous enough to keep you breathing."

He said nothing, his cheek reddened from her blow. Kestrel jerked her head toward the hatch. "Get rid of him."

Jarvis hustled McAvery away.

"Tom. Set course for Pecheta, then get yourself below and rest. Jaques, you take over for him."

"Aye, Captain," they both answered.

All she'd been able to think about for the last few days was catching this man. Now that McAvery was in her custody, she'd have to keep the closest of eyes on him. For his own safety as well as hers. He wasn't worth anything to her dead, but the men might not see it as she did. The idea of spending the next few days with him without killing him would be almost unbearable.

Hudee came forward and cleared his throat.

"What?" she asked irritably.

"It's the crate." He shrugged. "We can't fit it through the hatch, and we don't have the proper winch to open the bigger cargo panel."

The crate was sitting in the middle of her deck, a dark enigma. McAvery's small box was on the deck next to it. Kestrel picked it up. It was as long as a bottle of wine, and half again as wide, made of slender wood slats. The lid appeared to fit down into the tops of the side slats, but there were no nails apparent. Heavier than she'd expected—whatever was inside slid to the side with a gentle clunk.

"Captain?" Hudee asked. "The crate?"

"Secure it here on deck. And make sure everyone knows to keep one eye on it at all times." Kestrel picked at the lid of the wooden box. It slid up a bit. Seemed like it would be very easy to open. "I'm taking this to my cabin."

She walked to the cabin, and let herself in quietly. But it didn't matter. Shadd was sitting up in the bed, all the fluffy pillows shoved under his back to raise his head up.

"What are you doing!" Kestrel snapped.

He glanced over his shoulder at her. "Living in the lap of luxury. Besides, my belly won't heal up right with me lyin' flat." His normally shaggy hair was flat from lying in bed, and his eyes were bright.

"No fever?" Kestrel laid a hand against his brow. "Have you eaten anything today?"

"I'm fine. Jaques brought me a mug of broth and some bread. And some crushed-up leaves, tasted bitter as old dust, s'posed to make me sleep. Fussed over me like a woman, but he said I'd be able to get up tomorrow." He raised an eyebrow. "Did ye bring me a present?"

She set the box on the polished table. "McAvery was carrying it when we caught up to him. Thought it might be important." She drew her dagger, slid the point into the space between lid and box, and pried it up. It popped open with a squeak.

"What's in there? More of that slag he used to pay the dock-master?"

Kestrel started laughing. Reaching into the box, she removed a plant in a china pot. Its broad, dark leaves were gleaming. From a central stalk, two smaller branches extended. In between the two, there was a roundish mass bulging from under the surface of the stalk.

"Got a goiter, does it?" Shadd commented.

She touched it with the tip of one finger. It was solid, and ever so slightly warm. "Bloody Grace!" she said. "Take a look at this." She picked up the plant and positioned it over the stain on the table. The china pot fit perfectly within the boundaries of the stain.

"Of all things . . . he stole our ship from under us, but took a soddin' plant as a memento of this one?" The big gunner shifted in the bed with a gentle groan. "What's the plan now, then?"

"Changing course for Pecheta. We'll waylay the *Victory*, trade our captive for Binns."

"Ye think they'll believe us? Just give us the captain and send us on our way with a pat on the back and their hearty thanks?"

Kestrel sat down, propping her elbows on the table. The plant seemed like an ordinary shrub, except for the bulge in the middle. It didn't look diseased. Just wrong somehow. Not that she was familiar enough with plants to know.

"No," she said, "I'm sure they'll put up a fight. That's where this ship comes in handy. *Victory*'ll stand down in the face of our guns." She leaned back in the chair and pulled a lock of hair forward over her shoulder. Dividing it into three sections, she started braiding. "Even if they don't, we've still got enough firepower to force them."

"And what happens when we accidentally kill our own captain?"

Kestrel let go of her hair, letting the half-completed braid unravel. "We won't."

"Ye can't be sure o' that. Knowin' them bluebacks, they'll fight 'til their ship's sinkin' under 'em, and then we're no better off than we were." Shadd's eyes were dark, and he stretched his mouth open in a huge yawn.

"Mayhap." What he'd said bothered her more than she wanted to let him know. Standing up, she crossed to the sideboard. A dozen crystal glasses were lined up against the mirrored back, next to the decanter of rum. She pulled the stopper out, taking a deep, appreciative sniff of the fine rum within. "Want a drink?"

"Thank ye, but I think them herbs is workin' on me, Kes. I'm feelin' right foggy." In seconds, he was snoring gently.

Kestrel poured herself a glassful and took a sip. Fine stuff, indeed. The last captain had excellent taste. Not that she couldn't have guessed from the accommodations. It really was a wonderful room, now that she had time to look at it. Light streamed from the wide, many-paned window across the back wall. The bookshelves were loaded with leather-bound tomes of various thicknesses and heights. She ran a finger along the edges, reading the intriguing titles. Once upon a time, her mother had read to her, and Kestrel had kept that fondness for books. These had been well cared for, and each one looked as fresh as the next. Very different from the battered and water-stained spine of Binns's log.

She'd promised not to read it. But she couldn't help wondering how McAvery had even known it existed. Granted, at the time, he'd been doing his best to avoid being shackled, so he'd have said anything. There had to be a reason he mentioned the book. So much happened that she knew nothing about. She needed to know what secrets Binns was keeping. Dangerous or not, it seemed high time for her to learn.

Taking another swallow, she set her glass down on the table, opened the armoire, and retrieved the hidden book. Might as well just start reading and figure it out on her own. She carried the heavy book over to the table. The plant looked healthy, its dark green leaves gleaming in the stray beams of sunshine from the beveled windows. Maybe it would bloom soon. She stuck a curious finger in the soil. Damp. How much water did a plant like this need?

Kestrel sat down in the chair, the heavy leather book across her knees. She ran her hand over it, appreciating the well-worn smoothness. Binns had warned her not to read it, not to even open it. That would have been well and good if she didn't have bounty hunters and soldiers chasing her, and Binns's very life in the balance. He'd only cautioned her to protect her. What she didn't know she couldn't accidentally let slip. The situation was far more complicated than he'd known. With a deep sigh, she opened the book.

The pages crackled, parchment never having been meant for a life at sea. No fancy page for the title. The first page began with the date, the first day after spinstorm season was over. Usual stuff— initial course heading, cargo manifest, crew listing, all scrawled out in Binns's unmistakable hand. Below that was a brief paragraph detailing his plans for the coming season, including several specific ships along with their owner's names and the cargo they intended to carry. Spices, precious metals, and other goods that would be easily taken and sold on the dark market. How had he gotten his hands on such carefully guarded information? He must have had a source in the legitimate markets, a well-paid one, certainly. With foreknowledge like this, it was no wonder he came through so many battles with his skin intact.

At the bottom of the page were a few lines of strange squiggles, as if he'd been practicing with his new quills. They were all uniform in size, with breaks between sets. Like written words, but in a language she'd never seen before and could not begin to decipher. She frowned, and turned the page.

The date at the top was a day later. Binns had written a glowing account of the first night at sea, paying particular attention to the excellent meal they'd eaten. The first few days at sea were always favored with fresh meat, good wine, and merry fellowship. Kestrel recalled the meal. Whole roast tusker, the meat grilled over coals until it was tender enough to fall off the bones. Naranas and sweet velvets, luscious with the sunshine they soaked up, and rich butter-melons plucked from inland fields of MelaDoana. Fresh-baked loaves of dark brown bread, and bottle after bottle of rich, blood-red wine to wash it all down. She sighed, the dry feel of the morning's hardtack still coating her mouth.

Below the account of the meal was another set of the squiggles. Longer this time. The symbols were unsettling, as if in some other place and time, she would have recognized them and been able to read what they said. Binns had never claimed to know any language but the shared tongue of the Islands. They certainly didn't look like any language she'd ever seen. Which meant that either these were merely doodles, or someone else was writing in Binns's book after he was finished with his day's entries.

There was a third option—he'd lied to her.

She tried to ignore the twisting in her gut. The idea that Binns would have deliberately lied to her, would have used her loyalty to him to further some unknown ends of his own, was too much to consider. She turned pages quicker, searching for a word or phrase to leap out at her, begging the gods for something to prove her mistaken about her suspicions.

The words flashed by. The curlicues low on the pages writhed and squirmed, like tiny creatures dancing across the parchment. Kestrel stopped.

What did the patterns stand for? They must be a language. When would Binns have learned to write it? As far as she knew, he was barely literate in the shared tongue. She bit her lip, drawing a tiny bead of blood that she licked away quickly. As each day passed, she realized she knew less and less.

She picked up the open log and slammed it hard on the table. "Damn you, Artie, why didn't you tell me anything?" she growled. The sound of her voice shocked her in the quiet of the cabin. Shadd mumbled, and turned sideways, but remained asleep.

Kestrel looked back to the book. The strange etchings at the bottom of each page seemed to be moving, reshaping themselves. Into letters she recognized. Into words. Scribed in the very recognizable hand of her captain. She shivered. The rum was still at hand, so she threw back the last swallow, then returned to the sideboard for a refill.

Magic. Just like when she'd thumped the illusion card, and made the men reappear, slamming the book made the letters form. Why was Binns using magic? How could he? He was just a former bartender forced into a life on the sea. Wasn't he?

Taking her glass back to the table, she sat down to read.

Twenty

... *and till my ghastly tale is told,*
This heart within me burns.
—SAMUEL TAYLOR COLERIDGE

The message I'd hoped not to hear was delivered today, he wrote. *The plan is coming apart. The blasted dogs are on the hunt. Still seems to be an ounce of luck on my side, though. The storm made me late, but I managed to lay hands on the Knave tonight on Eldraga. Younger than I thought he'd be, but he gave me the signal. Fine-looking, too. Didn't surprise me Kes doesn't trust him.*

"Damn right I didn't," she muttered. That wasn't going to change. Just because he was working with her captain didn't make him innocent.

She's an excellent quarter, but it took a good sight longer to arrange our business with her paying close attention. I should have told her before, when we had the chance. When this is all finished, and the sanguina is in the right hands. If we all live through it.

Told her what? It was hard enough for her to believe he'd had business with McAvery, but what was he wishing he'd told her? And what was a sanguina? Kestrel turned the page.

After transferring the sanguina to the Wolfshead *as planned, we'll trade ships, and he'll make the delivery. Jeremie's dogs are looking for us both, but as far as we can determine, they only know about the* Thanos. *Jeremie doesn't pay well enough to hire smart fellows.*

Ice shot through Kestrel's veins, and she gripped the table with both hands for fear of sliding to the floor. The bounty hunters. She'd assumed they were hunting McAvery for some unpaid debt or stolen trinket. And here Binns was telling her they'd be coming after the *Thanos*. What about Jaeger? Was he with the first two, as she'd thought? Or was he something more? Another complication.

An ache was growing behind her eyes. She dropped her head into her hands, and rubbed at her temples. Four years she'd sailed under the man, and she felt as if she'd never known him. Why hadn't he confided in her? It had to be more than just some protective impulse. He'd never kept her from a fight in all the years she'd been under his command.

She turned the page, but there wasn't another entry. He must have made the entry the night before he was arrested. Kestrel pushed the book away, and let her head fall back. The ceiling was as smooth and rich as the rest of the cabin. She could almost see her face reflected in the wood.

The way it appeared, she could sit here and read all afternoon, or she could get quicker answers. Assuming he was cooperative. She'd have to make it clear to him that his own head was on the line. Not from the king, though. If Binns's log was correct, McAvery was an ally. But she'd happily dangle him from the yardarms if he proved to be an obstruction.

She rose, and opened the door. "Jarvis!" She looked back at Shadd, then sighed heavily. Too bad he was asleep, and likely to stay that way, with the herbs he'd been fed. She could use his ear about now. But she needed him fit. "Bring our prisoner up here. I need to talk to him."

LOOKING into McAvery's mocking face, she knew anything she said would be instantly twisted and transformed, and she'd be made to look a fool. She was no stranger to games, having spent many nights at cards or chess with Binns. The kind of games McAvery engaged in were beyond her ken.

It wasn't easy, with him staring at her the way he was. His eyes were intense, as if there was a light shining out from behind their blue depths. And when had they turned blue? When she saw him up close that night in the pub, she could have sworn they were brown. Magic, it had to be, though for the life of her, she couldn't see any point to it. A tense shudder forced its way down her back.

"May I sit?" McAvery shuffled his feet, shackles jangling. "My new wardrobe is a little weighty."

"Sit," Kestrel said. She'd positioned herself with her back to the armoire, arms crossed. Shadd was snoring lightly.

McAvery used his knee to pull a chair out from the table, then sat. "What do you have around here to drink?"

"Why should I waste my rum on a blackguard like you?"

He shrugged. "Best way to seal the deal. Unless you're afraid to drink with me?" He cocked his head to one side, a vaguely intimate motion, as if by turning his head just so, he could see deep into her soul. It was strange, alluring. The tiny hairs rose on her arms, coldly prickling, her midsection felt oddly hollow, and she was at once aware of every thud of her heart.

"Fear you?" she asked. "I was weaned on rum—you couldn't outdrink me if I had two to your one."

"Care to make a wager on that?"

Kestrel barked a laugh. "Risk my good coin on a cheating scoundrel?"

"Your good coin?" he asked. "That's rich, coming from you."

"What do you mean?"

"There's not a penny in your purse that's truly yours."

He's a trickster, she reminded herself. *He's talking in circles, trying to make you upset.* He saw everything as a means to his ends, thief and liar that he was. Maybe it would be smarter to run him through and present his dead carcass to the king. *Sorry, Your Majesty, he didn't make it.* She'd still have the log, after all, and it would certainly be quieter. "Let me get down to business. They're going to hang Binns."

"I'm no bargaining chip."

"I know that already."

He grinned. "A little light reading, was it? Good. I'll be having these chains off, please."

She shook her head. "Sorry, but I'm a long way from being convinced. Just because Binns believed you were trustworthy doesn't do a thing for me, under the circumstances. I can't quite accept you didn't hand him off to the bluebacks."

"I wasn't there."

"No, you weren't." She leaned forward, resting her hands on the table and glaring into his face. "According to the dockmaster, you were busy bribing him with slag magicked to look like gold."

"Certainly looks that way." He glanced at the plant. "Be sure and water the sanguina, would you? It's somewhat delicate."

The plant was the sanguina. "Your plant is the last thing I'm concerned about."

"Ought to be the first."

Loud pounding erupted on the door. "Kestrel?" Bardo called from outside. "There's somethin' ye'll want to see."

McAvery had leaned forward over the table, his chains dragging against the finish. He was leisurely rubbing the dark green leaves of his plant with his thumb. As much as she wanted to be away from his company, she couldn't leave him here, to his own devices. "Let's go."

"Why? You're the captain."

"You're coming with me."

He stood up and swept a hand toward the door. "As you command, madam."

She started to move toward the door, then thought better of it. "You first. I don't trust you at my back."

"What do you think I could do to you with these shackles on?" McAvery quirked his lip mischievously. "Besides, the view's so much better from behind."

Kestrel laid a warning hand on the pommel of her sword. "I imagine I could make a good enough case to free my captain with just your dead carcass as evidence." Meeting his gaze, she stared, unblinking.

He sighed and nodded. Kestrel yanked open the door and waved him through. Bardo was waiting outside the door. He glanced nervously from McAvery to Kestrel, looking like a frightened mouse. "Thinks he still owns this ship, that one does," she said, rolling her eyes. "Pay him no mind. What is it you wanted me to see?"

"Ship, Kes. A Pechetan spitster, still a good ways off."

"Matching our course or crossing paths?" she asked, pulling the cabin door closed.

"Good ways off, on an intersecting course," he said, nodding. "But they're closing fast."

She clapped him on the shoulder. "Good man. Go alert the gunners."

"Aye, Kes," Bardo said as he scampered off.

Jarvis was a few feet away. "Want me to put him back in his cell?" he asked, pointing at McAvery.

"No," she said. "I still need to get some answers out of him. Chain him to the mainmast, and then get to your post."

McAvery frowned. "I'll have trouble telling you anything if I'm crushed under a broken mast."

"You'd better pray it doesn't come to that."

Kestrel crossed the deck to the quarterdeck ladder, and scrambled up. Red Tom had one hand on the wheel. In the other he held the spyglass, through which he was staring intently.

"Thought I told you to rest." He shrugged, and she decided not to press him. "Talk to me, Tom."

"Pechetan spitster, coming toward us from the west. She's a little 'un, eight guns, I'm guessin', though at this distance, I could be mistaken."

"Is she pursuing us?"

He handed her the glass. "Hard to say. Could as easily be sailin' in the same direction, is all."

Kestrel raised the glass to her eye. Under the glare of the midday sun, the approaching ship's details were hard to make out, except for the flag flying atop its center mast; black edged scarlet, with an empty black noose in the center. A bounty hunter's flag.

"Damn. They've sent hunters after us already. Bloody Axel must have avoided his whipping." She sighed. "Looks like it might be time for a real fight."

"You want me to give the order?" Tom asked.

The order to make ready for battle was always the quartermaster's job on Binns's ship. Kestrel hesitated. She'd given the order many times before, without a second thought. Somehow it felt wrong to let another do her job, as if she was promoting Tom to quartermaster without having left the job herself yet, but there was no way around it.

"Aye, Tom, do that. Let's make Binns proud of us," she declared. "I want that ship to regret ever passing our way."

Red Tom nodded again. Securing the wheel, he turned toward the main deck of the ship. "All hands on deck!" he bellowed, descending the ladder and heading for the main hatch. "On deck, you bastards!"

Within seconds, the deck was covered with men running to their posts. Binns had chosen well, each and every one of them, and trained them just as thoroughly. She watched as they skidded across damp wood to their positions. Even if she'd had time to round up the entire complement of the *Wolfshead*, there still wouldn't have been nearly enough men to properly crew a ship the size of the *Thanos* in a battle. And there hadn't been time enough for the ones she did have aboard to learn the warship, explore, and discover her secrets and strengths. On the silver side, though, the *Thanos* had the advantage of size and guns. She let out a heavy breath. No bad thoughts. They could do this.

McAvery was leaning against the center mast, the chains he wore doing nothing to protect his rich clothes from the tar that coated the mast. Noticing her gaze on him, he waved two fingers.

"I'm too busy to play word games with you."

"It wasn't a word game I had in mind," he called. "More of a numbers problem." He looked up at her. "Do you know how unfavorable the odds are that you'll live through this?"

"Are you taking bets?"

"That would certainly be a diversion. If I were in a pub and not on the open sea."

"I'm not worried." She waved a hand. "We've got the advantage of size and guns."

"I merely offer another suggestion for our current predicament."

She took another look through the glass. The vessel was a little closer, and she could just make out figures on the deck. Were they even now loading their guns to try and blow her fine, stolen ship out of the sea? She had a few minutes before she showed them what she could do. "Open the larboard gunports," she yelled.

"I can make it so they don't even see you."

Kestrel imagined how good it would feel to kick his handsome face and send him sprawling on the deck. "We're not cowards. We don't run from fights."

"But what purpose would a fight serve?" he asked, rising another step. "You and this ship are still on your wedding journey. You don't know her rhythms, her quirks. Sail your ship into a battle none of you are ready for, everybody dies and your captain stays in prison. Until the authorities get around to hanging him, that is."

"Thank you for the suggestion. Shut up."

He raised his eyebrows, then sighed and leaned back again.

"I'll bet yonder ship carries some friends of yours, doesn't it? Burk and Volga, that was their names, right? You're afraid I'll run up the white flag and hand you over to their tender mercies."

He spared a look across the water, and chuckled. "You've met the boys, have you?"

"And their friend Jaeger, too."

"Who?" McAvery tilted his head. "I don't know this Jaeger, but I can guarantee the other two want the ship even more than they want to catch me. Offer those two a deal and you'll find yourself rowing back to Eldraga. Assuming they bother to give you a longboat at all."

"I won't run. This ship can handle the likes of them."

"But why waste ammunition, when there's another way?" Standing on his tiptoes, he reached up. Kestrel followed his hand. Sticking out of the mast was something that looked like a badly designed fork, a thick handle with two blunt tines extending from the midpoint. Pressing the nail of his middle finger against the pad of his thumb, he thumped the fork.

Kestrel instantly tensed. "What the hell are you doing?" she growled, and started down the ladder toward him.

McAvery grinned at her. "You work too hard, girl."

A low, reverberating tone filled the air. But not only the air was shivering—the lines were undulating in time to the sound. Wrinkles moved through the sails like ripples of water in a windblown lake. The pirates stopped what they were doing, some grabbing their midsections, some dancing from one foot to the other. Kestrel's own feet were tickling, the low sound moving up through the deck into her booted feet. She fought an urge to yank off her boots and scratch her soles, and turned blazing eyes on McAvery. "What have you done?" she demanded, her voice vibrating slightly.

He pointed overhead. A curtain of sparkling white mist, originating somewhere above the crow's nest, fell in shimmering waves on either side of the *Thanos*. For a moment, it glistened, thick and snowy, marring visibility. But only for a moment. Before she could demand further explanation from McAvery, Kestrel noticed that the crystalline drops were thinning, and a few seconds later, they'd stopped falling completely. In their place was a gentle, glowing light through which she could see the bounty hunter's vessel still approaching.

McAvery raised an eyebrow toward the startled pirate. "Pretty, isn't it?" He stretched his arms in front of him, and yawned dramatically. "Well, I'm exhausted. Saving the entire ship and crew takes a lot out of a man. Time for a nap." He leaned his head against the mast and closed his eyes.

The pirates were staring, stunned. Kestrel stalked to her captive and grabbed his shirt. "I didn't need your help. Release your magic right now, or I'll cut off something you do value."

"Can't. But don't worry. It isn't permanent." He waved a hand in the direction of the pursuing ship. "It's a shield. Lasts about an hour, plenty of time for us to change course and let our friends pass us by." His eyes held her as surely as a shackle. They were golden brown again. How did he manage to change their color so often, and why did he even bother? It couldn't be for her benefit, could it? Had he realized that she noticed? She suddenly became aware of the heat radiating between his body and her hand, and snatched her arm back before it could be burned.

"What do you mean, a shield?" she asked uncomfortably.

He sighed dramatically. "It's a magic shield. Once it's activated, no one on the outside can see us in here. We won't even cast a shadow. It's rather fascinating, based on a series of tones designed to . . ."

"I don't care what makes it work." The bounty hunter's ship was passing by them, close enough for her to see the helmsman gripping the mighty wheel, the navigator standing beside him with a glass to his eye. He was swinging it right and left and back again, searching fruitlessly for the ship that he could no longer see.

Her crew seemed to have realized their good fortune, and began laughing and calling gibes to each other.

"I'd recommend changing course. It's only a matter of time before they try looking where they saw you last." McAvery jerked his head toward the deck. "You'd best get your crew quiet—the tone shield blocks sight, not sound."

Kestrel clapped her hands once, hard. When the men glanced toward her, she cut her hand across her throat. Silence quickly fell. Gaining Tom's eye, she jerked her head sharply to the southwest. He nodded, and turned the wheel, catching the breeze and moving easily away. The pirates stood together, watching their former pursuers sail past them as if they weren't even there.

"Pretty good, wouldn't you say?" McAvery asked. "Much easier than trying to make a getaway."

Kestrel grabbed his wrist and shoved his ornate sleeve up. His arm was tanned, with a scattering of golden hairs. She checked the other arm, but it was the same. No silver bracelet, and no paleness or scarring to indicate that one had ever been there. Although he wore no Danisoban bracelet, McAvery was using magic. Something that should have been unheard of. The Danisobans had controlled all magic for over a century. How had he managed to get his hands on such a powerful object as the tone fork? More importantly, how could she expect to keep him under her control?

"Oh, don't worry," he said, as if he was reading her mind. "That's all I have." At Kestrel's raised eyebrows, he said, "The fork. It's the only magic I own. Got it from a merchant who hired me and couldn't pay. Comes in handy, don't you think?"

"Very handy. Trouble is, the Danisobans watch for this sort of thing. They could be targeting us this minute."

"You're afraid of the Brethren?" he said with a laugh. "Out here?"

"Even if they aren't a threat to us," she said, talking over his chuckling, "don't assume I didn't realize why you used your little gadget just now. The bounty hunters were after you."

He tilted his head, staring at her in a way that made her extraordinarily uncomfortable. "You still don't understand, do you? It's not about me. Or you, or Binns."

"Jarvis!" she snapped. When he ran to her side, she said, "Put this man back in his cell." *And don't let him out again, even if I ask you to.*

SHE cornered Dreso shortly after they were back under way. He'd kept his head down, once he was told about the change in command. He seemed to be avoiding her, so as to not answer questions. But she couldn't wait long—if he was guilty of any sort of treachery, she had to find out before he could endanger her chances of saving Binns.

She came across him coiling rope, all alone with nowhere to escape to. No time would be better. Approaching him on quiet cat's feet, she laid a hand on his shoulder, enjoying his deep shudder of surprise.

"Sorry, Quarter, you startled me." He dropped the rope, laying a hand over his chest.

"I find myself in need of a little information, Dreso."

His eyes shifted uncomfortably. "Well, I'm awful busy. Angus has a list of duties for me a mile long, and I don't—"

"Angus answers to me now, and if I stop you for questions, he'll bloody well grant me the time. Sit your ass down." Dreso drew back as if she'd slapped him, bending slowly to seat himself on the coil of rope he'd been making.

"Better." She planted her feet solidly and crossed her arms. "I left you on board the *Wolfshead*. I trusted you and the other two to keep watch. I come back and find my sloop stolen and all three of you vanished. I'm ready for you to tell me what happened. How you managed to be the only survivor."

He swallowed hard, not meeting her eyes. "Isn't much to tell."

Fury rose in her chest, the heat of it half blinding her. She blinked to clear her vision, but the anger remained like a boiling pot just under her skin. "Did I give you the impression I was asking?"

"Hell, Kes, couldn't you just go ahead and flog me?" He glanced up, his face plastered with misery.

She frowned. He certainly wasn't acting like a traitor. More along the lines of a man who's been humiliated beyond all measure. But McAvery had played himself off as a farm boy.

"Talk or swim."

He sighed. Dropping his head into his hands, he mumbled something.

"Didn't quite catch that, my lad."

He raised his face. "I said, it's all my fault. Will and Steven, they was itching to go into town. Kept badgering me to cover for 'em. Promised me they'd pay me their share if I kept watch by me lonesome. I was right afeared of the ghosts comin' aboard, but I had my charms with me, and I really wanted the extra money." He shrugged, his cheeks red with embarrassment. "I told 'em to go along, I'd be fine. We was in Eldraga harbor, after all."

"So you were by yourself," she commented. "Stupid. Dangerous. I assume the other two are still on Eldraga somewhere, wondering what happened to us?"

"Guess so," he said, "I ain't seen 'em since. Figured they was with the rest of you."

"What happened later?"

He hung his head. "I fell asleep. Curled up behind the main deck water barrel and snatched forty winks. How many times have we been anchored in Eldraga harbor, or dozens of other places, and nothing happened? Not one damned thing. Who knew I'd be playing the odds this once? When I waked up, the sun was peeking over the water and we was being towed out of the harbor. Three sailors I didn't know snatched me up by the scruff of my neck. Dragged me in front of that McAvery fellow."

"And he offered you what for your loyalty?"

"Pretty much the same thing you did just now. He said I could work or swim. I worked." He turned his face toward the railing. "I didn't know if I'd ever see any of you lot again. For all I knew you was dead and drowned. A man's got to keep going."

His story sounded legitimate, but her short experience with McAvery had taught her not to believe a pretty tale. She assured Dreso that his story was between them, and let him go back to his duties. Later that afternoon, when she found a spare moment, she went to Shadd.

"Funny ye should ask. He dropped down t' see me jes' a little bit ago. He kept talkin' about how that fella McAvery didn't know nothin' about sailin', givin' orders that was contradictory. Said he can't believe the sloop didn't sink on her own, out of frustration."

"So what does he think about our plan to get Binns back?" she asked. If it was betrayal he had in mind, she hoped she'd be able to detect it before he convinced others of the crew to go along with him. But Shadd insisted there was none.

"Well, he ain't stupid. He knows I'm yer man, lass, so I don't know as he'd tell me straight up if he was planning anythin' against ye. But he claims he's behind ye 'til the ends of the earth. Says he'd been prayin' every night for summat to happen, hoped it would be McAvery fallin' overboard. Can't stop thankin' Great Pantheus fer ye comin' along when ye did."

Exactly what I would say if I wanted to throw the suspicion somewhere besides on myself. Shadd might be convinced of Dreso's innocence, but she wasn't. Without evidence, all she could do was wait and watch.

Twenty-one

How long in that same fit I lay
I have not to declare
But ere my living life returned
I heard and in my soul discerned
Two voices on the air.

—SAMUEL TAYLOR COLERIDGE

Tendrils of gray fog swirled and eddied around her as she moved, obscuring her vision. She reached out, questing ahead with her fingertips, hoping for the snake of a loose bit of rope, the slick smoothness of the railing, anything that might orient her, keep her from slipping overboard. Weather as thick as this muffled sound as well as sight. No one would even hear her splash.

The mists parted, curtainlike, revealing a figure in black robes. Hooded, unmoving, and genderless. It stood with its arms hanging limply by its sides. It didn't seem to notice her—it didn't seem to be a living thing, so still it was. But Kestrel shuddered, and laid a hand on the hilt of her sword.

"Who are you?" she tried to ask. In the instant she opened her lips to speak, the fog rushed in, filling her mouth, clogging her throat like thick cotton, silencing her voice. She scrabbled at her neck, as if she could tear open her skin and release the cry that bubbled inside her.

The figure lifted its arm slowly. The overlong black sleeve fell back, exposing a deathly white, claw-tipped hand, with a silver bracer encircling the wrist. The skeletal fingers beckoned to her, urging her without words to follow, follow. And suddenly Kestrel knew, with a certainty that tore at her very soul, that to follow the figure, the Danisoban, would only mean endings. Of her freedom, her identity, her life.

She tried to step back, move away from the dangerous hand, but her feet were frozen, rock-solid, to the deck. She could not run away. But she could still fight. She tightened her grip on the sword, pulling it free of its sheath. She swung the glittering steel forward and up, holding it in both hands, trying to convey without words her readiness to kill. But the Danisoban stood, still as death, its arm upraised toward her, as if her challenge was no more fearsome than a child's fists would be.

With a soundless bellow, Kestrel brought the sword down, slicing through the wrist, and the silver bracer, the symbol of the dreaded office. Where her blade passed, it should have left blood and shattered bone and broken silver in its wake. Instead, the hand remained, outstretched, waiting. It would never go away, not until she placed her hand within, accepted the dreadful offer it brought.

Despair filled her, stealing the strength from her hands and from her soul. Her sword slipped from her nerveless fingers. Did it clatter to the deck? She couldn't hear it. Her senses were dull, as if she'd had too much ale the night before and was waking up drunk.

"Kestrel . . . sweetheart . . . come to Mama . . ."

She swung her head left, right. The gentle, soothing voice had seemed so near, but everywhere she saw only mist. Mist, and the cloaked figure.

"Back away, Kestrel . . . don't let it touch you . . ."

The voice seemed to come from every direction. She turned in a slow circle, searching. "Mama, where are you? I can't find you."

The fog parted. A woman, clad in a garment as gray and ragged as the clouds from which she emerged, stepped forward and held open her arms. Her hair was black as night, falling loose over her back, and her brown eyes were bright with love. "Come to Mama."

Kestrel gulped back a sob, and started forward. "I didn't want to believe . . . you were dead . . ." Something moved in the corner of her eye, and she cocked her head to look. The cloaked figure had raised both hands to its face. It was whispering, not in words she knew but in some other speech, one sibilant and threatening. Suddenly the hands sprang outward, sending a bolt of energy over her shoulder and straight into the gray woman's belly. She gasped, doubling over before collapsing to the ground.

"*Mama!*" Kestrel shrieked. She ran forward, but the woman's body seemed to move away from her, becoming more distant with every step Kestrel took, receding finally into the mists. Leaving her alone.

But not alone. She'd run so far, yet the cloaked figure was still right behind her, waiting. Nothing left to do. With the barest energy, she lifted her arm, letting her own hand sink into the bony embrace of the Danisoban's . . .

"Kestrel."

Her eyes sprang open. Dark, shadows covering everything. And the world was moving, rocking back and forth. Where was she now? Was this some exclusive hell reserved for the victims of Danisoban demons?

Something touched her. She struggled out of her hammock. The deck was cold enough to curl her bare toes, but she ignored it. She drew the dagger she wore when sleeping and brandished the blade. "Face me, beast."

"Ain't necessary. I give up." Shadd was staring at her, concern in his eyes.

Now that her eyes were adjusted to the darkness, she recognized the expansive cabin of the *Thanos*. The bed was behind her, most of the luxurious bedding piled on the floor at its foot. She was neither in hell nor lost in a fog. She'd been dreaming again. She was on board the *Thanos,* safe and healthy. In pursuit of the men who'd arrested her captain. And her mother was still . . .

She sheathed the dagger. Shadd reached up to flip open the dampening door on the lantern hanging from the ceiling, flooding the cabin with a warm glow and dispelling the last vestiges of Kestrel's nightmare.

"Kes? Are ye all right?"

Her heart was still thudding painfully. She raised a finger and shook it at her friend. "Why are you out of bed?"

"Yer moanin' woke me."

"Sorry." She sat down in her hammock, but she could already tell she wouldn't be going back to sleep easily. Never could, after dreaming that dream. Her nerves were too jangled to relax. Outside the window was darkness, with no hint of a sunrise. "Lay back down, lad." She rose and took hold of the door catch.

"Where're ye goin'?"

"Figured I'd take a walk around the deck, see what's what."

Outside the door, the sky was black velvet, and waves splashed softly far below. Tom had finally given in and taken to his hammock, leaving Charlie and Bardo at the wheel. They were talking, heads close together, although she couldn't hear what they said. Bardo caught sight of her and raised a hand. She moved to the railing, running a hand along the polished wood. The gentle sounds of the night's running were soothing, but it would be a long time before she relaxed completely.

After sending McAvery back to his cell, Kestrel had stayed on deck until the bounty hunters' ship was no longer in range. Once she was sure it was gone, and they were back on course for Pecheta, she returned to the captain's cabin. It was clear McAvery wouldn't offer up a straight answer to anything. She'd spent the afternoon reading Binns's log, and if everything she'd learned was true, it was a hard meal to swallow.

A tear welled in her eye, trickled down her cheek and off her jaw. "Artie, why didn't you trust me?" she whispered. The night breeze brought her no answer.

McAVERY was stretched out on the meager bench opposite the barred door of his cell. At first, she thought he was asleep, but he turned his head at her approach. "What brings you by to see me at this hour?" His long hair was unbound, and his feet were bare. A cream-white tunic hung loose over tight black breeches. The lacing was undone and the tunic gapped open, revealing sun-browned skin. His Adam's apple bobbed, and she caught herself staring, suddenly wanting to press her lips against it.

"I couldn't sleep."

"Bad dreams? Want to talk about them?"

"How . . ." she began, catching the words in her throat before they could betray her further. He hadn't known. It was just a guess.

She'd never told a soul about her dream, not even Binns or Olympia. She remembered almost nothing about the day her parents died, except for the reason why. The reason she'd had to live with every day of her life, the reason that had driven her to a life on the water but that kept her always looking over her shoulder.

A chill shrouded her, as if a cold fog had descended. She wrapped her arms around herself, the coldness of her fingers stinging like a frozen branding iron through the thin fabric of her shirt. McAvery had no idea what he was asking with his nonchalant offer to listen to her nightmares. But he was nodding sympathetically.

"So you assumed I'd also be lying awake? Pining for a visit from you, perhaps?"

"I hoped I'd have to throw something at you to wake you. Something sharp preferably." She scowled. "I finished reading the book."

He sat up, leaning his elbows on his knees. His tunic fell open. She had a sudden memory of how hard his body had felt under her hand that afternoon. Kestrel looked pointedly at his face, afraid to let her eyes settle anywhere else. She rested her hand against the hilt of her dagger, not only so the cool metal would quell the sudden racing of her pulse.

"I want to hear your version. You have to admit it's a far-fetched story."

His eyes were dark brown now—perhaps it was just the darkness that made them seem to change color this time—and he was staring at her, unblinking. This wasn't his ship anymore. She'd captured it fair and square. Yet he was sitting in the tiny cell as if he belonged in the captain's cabin.

"It's late. You must be tired. Wouldn't you prefer to do this in the morning? Over breakfast, perhaps?"

She eyed him suspiciously. She'd ordered Jarvis to search the man once he was returned to the cell. Nothing of interest had turned up. He claimed the silver fork was the only magic object he owned, but he was a master of deception. For all she knew, he could have an arsenal of magic at his disposal, tucked away all over the ship. He could even be using some trinket on her now, to alter her perception of him, even to make her desire him. She'd only be happy when he was gone, and no more threat to her. "Enough with the trifling. We're running short on time."

"Let me out of here, and I'm sure I can help you sleep."

"I can imagine what your definition of comfort might be."

"Would that be so bad?" His eyes burned into her.

"Yes." She shivered.

"What do you want, Kestrel?" He hadn't moved, but his voice was silken, sliding over her and sending gooseflesh prickling up on her arms. The air was suddenly close and thick. She found herself watching his mouth as he spoke. So fascinating, the way lips moved, shaped words. Smoothly sensuous, their dark pink softness was so inviting. She felt her own lips puckering, in response.

"To understand," she managed finally, jerking her gaze away. "And nothing else."

McAvery leaned back on the bench and crossed his arms behind his head. "Very well. Ask your questions."

She snorted. "Oh, I'm sure you'll answer whatever question I put to you. How am I supposed to guess which parts are true, if any? You'll weave a pretty tapestry that you think will soften my heart and possibly uncross my legs as well. What did you have in mind? You've already used the 'poor farm boy' tale, so we can cross that one off the list. 'I was unloved as a child' or perhaps 'I was stolen from my noble parents as an infant and raised by wolves'? Or is there a special story you've been composing just for me?"

"You've unmasked me, Captain. I can hide nothing from your discerning eye." He snapped his fingers. "What if I give you a guarantee of my honesty?"

"I can't think of any way you could do that."

He rose slowly, lifting his tunic and sliding his hand carefully into the waist of his breeches. Before she could protest, he pulled out a tiny cloth drawstring pouch. He opened the pouch and up-ended it. A blue stone fell out into his palm.

He tossed it into the air and caught it between thumb and fore-finger. "My name is Philip McAvery," he said.

"I knew that already . . ." Kestrel began, stopping in midsen-tence. Her knees went wobbly, and she stepped backward, pressing her spine against the damp wall.

The tiny, blue stone was glowing. Magic.

"It's a surety stone," McAvery was saying, as casually as if he were ordering up a mug of ale. He glanced at her, furrowing his brow. "Is something wrong?"

Part of her desire to go to sea had been to keep a barrier be-tween her and the Danisobans. She'd been in contact with more magic in the last three days than in the prior eighteen years. Spending all those years running and hiding seemed to have done her no good—the magic found her anyway. Just like in her dream.

"Jarvis said you didn't have any more," she said.

"Any more?" he asked.

"Magic." She pointed an accusing finger at the tiny rock. "You told him the fork was the only thing you had."

"Did I?" He tossed the stone, catching it again. She flinched, in spite of herself, half fearing he was throwing it at her. "Sorry. I sup-pose I forgot about this little precious. Very handy in negotiations and trials of all sorts. It glows blue if the holder says a true state-ment. No glow means no truth."

"I won't touch it." Her voice sounded small to her ears.

"You don't have to."

In response to his words, the gem flared. She winced. "And what else does it do?" she asked wryly. "Hypnotize me into being your willing slave?"

He laughed, a genuine dark brown laugh that would have drawn her in as well, if she hadn't been so agitated. "Of course not. Slaves, even willing, are added weight. I travel light." When she didn't join his laughter, he sobered. "I swear, it does nothing else." Blue light flashed in his palm. He held it up to show her, but she frowned. "You're unconvinced. Ask me a question to which you know the true answer."

She ground her teeth, then said, "Are you called the Knave?"

He looked into her eyes. "Yes," he eventually answered. The stone brightened in his hand. "You see, I can be an open book if you wish it."

Just a minor magic object, she told herself. Possibly even useful. Nothing to fear. Not from the blue stone, at any rate. She sat down, grateful for the bars between herself and McAvery. "Fine, let's do this," she said. "Why did you steal the *Wolfshead*?"

"Because I was hired to." The stone remained dark, and Kestrel raised an eyebrow. McAvery chuckled. "I suppose that's not entirely accurate. I didn't steal her. Binns and I had an arrangement."

Blue flash. Truth. And it meshed with the account in the book. "You haven't told me why."

"The dogs were barking. Found out what I was up to, and were hot on my heels. We thought it might be better if we traded ships, so that's what we did."

Again, truth. "What were you up to?"

He stared at the little stone in his hand, a tiny grin playing at the corner of his lips. "We were hired to deliver the sanguina to its rightful owner."

"All this . . . for a plant?" It seemed like a fool's errand, but men were in danger over it.

"It does look humble, but my little green friend is more valuable than you might assume. Have you been watering it?"

"What makes this thing so important?"

"The sanguina." He raised his eyebrows at her lack of reaction. "You've never heard of it?"

"Can't say as I have."

"Most people think it's a myth. Which is lucky, or it would have become one long ago. The sanguina grows only on the back side of Cre'esh, near the top of the mountain. Fruits once every fifty years, give or take a few days. And the fruit only stays on the branch a few hours."

"Why does this matter to me?"

He leaned close to the bars. "Because eating the fruit while it's still on the branch grants health and life for the next fifty years. Perpetual life."

Immortality. She had to admit such a thing would be tempting. To know for certain you'd come out of battle still breathing, that was a prize. "But the two of you couldn't both eat the fruit."

"No, it's all or nothing." He shrugged. "Besides, who wants to live forever? We were tasked to aquire it for the king."

The stone flashed blue again. It was a soothing color, the blue of warm, shallow seas and bright summer mornings. She could understand the appeal of such an object. So the king wanted this life-giving plant. She could also understand that. Kings and generals, men of power . . . they always wanted to keep what they had forever.

"You're an agent of the king?"

He nodded. "The Knave acts as the king's left hand. I accomplish certain tasks he couldn't publicly acknowledge."

"Seems a little strange for you. You struck me as a man with no loyalties."

"Pays well."

That made sense. He probably enjoyed a great deal of freedom along with the pay. After all, McAvery knew things about the king that could get him dethroned and beheaded. But mention of the king had brought her attention back to the question she'd feared asking. Time to ask it, and be done.

"How is my captain connected to the Ageless King?"

"You haven't figured that out?"

She had. She just hoped he'd say something different. Something that would allow her a sigh of relief as the blue stone flashed its truth. Her heart thudded like a stone.

"Your friend is a king's man. The Privateer."

"No," Kestrel whispered. The Privateer was a myth, one of those tales sailors told each other when deep in their cups. All her life, she'd heard stories of the man who hid in plain sight, the outlaw who had the king's ear. She'd never believed in him, yet now it was all true. Artemus Binns had spent the last twenty years collecting revenue for the crown from the independent merchants of the Nine Islands. "If he's"—she couldn't bring herself to say the word—"a king's man, why was he arrested? Why are they going to hang him?"

"Because he's not the prince's man. Jeremie's a dissolute waste of skin. His father the king recognized it long ago. He tried to steer the boy in a more responsible direction, but he just isn't one suited to power. If Jeremie became king, he'd have run through the money in a season's time." McAvery stretched his torso languidly, then sighed. "Children can be a burden."

"But the king's immortal."

"It would appear so, because he's eaten the plant once before. His first wife was barren, and the second wife produced only Jeremie. His Majesty wants to stay healthy another fifty years, keep his son from inheriting, and with any luck, get another princeling on this latest wife. One that will turn out better suited to rule, one who'll protect the family name's honor for the history books."

"People have noticed. Doesn't he worry the nobles will rebel?"

"He's let rumors get out that the Danisobans are keeping him this way. The nobility is terrified enough of the Brethren to keep their distance. And the Brethren recognize the value of that terror for them, so they haven't exposed the secret either."

"What's to stop him doing it again, now that you're wanting to replant the sanguina in his own garden?"

"I don't know, but since I doubt I'll be alive at the time, I'm not inclined to worry about it."

He had a point. And she had more urgent problems to handle. "So the prince has my captain?" she asked.

"That he does."

"And you're on my side."

"Such as it is." He stood, smiling. "Let me out, now?"

She glanced up at him and shook her head. "Can't. Jarvis has the key."

He sank back onto the bench and tossed the surety stone at her.

She put up a hand to catch it, remembering only then she hadn't wanted to touch it. It was warm from his skin, smooth as a river rock.

"Fine. I'll stay here, then. But let me ask you something."

What harm could it do? He was locked up tight, and if he really was on her side, which his little stone seemed to back up, she'd want his goodwill later, when things became complicated. "Ask."

"Why do you fear magic?"

Kestrel stiffened. She'd expected him to demand the details of her nightmare again. She'd already constructed a false one, all about slavering weretigers chasing her through a desolate wasteland. In five simple words, he had blindsided her. He asked of her the one question no one ever had.

As long as she could remember, her mother had always warned her away from singing or whistling. Most parents tried to hush their children, but this had been different. Days in the little shop her parents owned were filled with music—the rhythmic thumping of Mother's loom as she worked, Father's gentle humming while he carved the delicate fishing floaters that had become terribly popular with the Eldraga linefishers. But Kestrel wasn't allowed to sing a note, not even to tap out a beat on the wooden floor with her fingers.

Whenever she made music, things happened. Usually minor events—the wind would rise up, or dust devils would spin at her feet. Once she'd made one of Mother's afghans flutter and drift as if it were a ship's flag caught in a breeze. None of it was exceptional. Nothing anyone would have blamed on a little girl's whistle.

Mother knew. Kestrel didn't know how she'd guessed. Maybe she had the gift herself. Or possibly she'd heard enough tales to recognize the danger her child was in if anyone else should figure out their secret.

But in the end it hadn't mattered. The Danisobans had come, knocking on the door one evening after sunset, in their black robes and whispery voices. The law demanded that all children who showed potential for magical ability be taken into the custody of the Brotherhood to be trained. Kestrel had only been four years old, but she'd already garnered their attention. It was best, they said, if she come with them now, before her power became strong and uncontrollable.

Father had barred the Danisobans from coming into the shop, planting himself in the doorway and refusing to move. Mother had gathered Kestrel up in her arms. She'd run to the back of the shop, into their cramped living quarters. Setting the child down, Mother had shoved the table aside and lifted the old woven rug. A loop of thin rope lay on the dingy floorboards. Mother grabbed it and pulled. To Kestrel's amazement, the floor opened up, revealing darkness underneath. Mother gestured for her to climb in.

"I'll be right behind you, darling."

That was her last clear recollection. She knew she had dropped down into the hole, but afterward was only a vague, confused image of screams and fire, the glint of silver on a hand grabbing for her from within a thick wall of smoke, and then running. Running, as fast as her little-girl legs would carry her, through the musty, muddy alleys of Eldraga.

It wasn't a story she'd ever told anyone. Who could she trust with such knowledge? Her closest friends would never betray such a confidence, but any magus worth his salt could pry the information from an undefended mind, likely killing the unlucky soul in the process. If anyone she loved died because of her—anyone else, she reminded herself bitterly—she didn't know if she could stand living.

McAvery was staring at her, waiting for her response. The intense look on his face brought the blood rushing back into her body, and the sudden warmth made her dizzy. Gods, he was beautiful enough to make her breath halt in her chest. She'd been around the harbor long enough to know what was going on. The heat he was stirring inside her was powerful and attractive, but it wasn't real. Their game had gone on long enough. Getting to her feet, she marched to the door and opened it. Steeling her jaw, she dropped the stone into the pocket of her breeches, tilted her head regally, and stared back at him.

"Denying the truth only keeps you from enjoying a good night's sleep." He stretched out on the bench, propping his head on his hand. "You owe me an answer. I will get it."

"You owe me a ship."

"We appear to stand in check," he said. "I'll give you an option. You're not loyal to the king. Your choice, and none of my concern. That plant is more valuable than anything on this ship. You want your captain back? That's the best currency to buy him."

Kestrel's knees were as wobbly as an overripe plum. But leaning against the door, looking as if she were watching McAvery, wouldn't do at all. Standing straight, she closed the door, then headed for her cabin. Bardo waved at her again, but this time, she didn't return his gesture. She let herself into her cabin as quietly as she could, and rolled into her hammock. Shadd was sleeping soundly.

"Oh, Artie," she murmured into the darkness, "is this man going to get the better of me?"

Just as she closed her eyes, she was startled by a tiny flash of light. Was that blue? She looked down, but the stone in her pocket was dark.

Twenty-two

. . . some fair bark, perhaps, whose sails light up
the slip of smooth, clear blue betwixt two isles
of purple shadows . . .

—SAMUEL TAYLOR COLERIDGE

For the next two days, Kestrel busied herself with running the ship. From the first fingers of dawn until the black of full night, she pushed herself to the limits of her strength, doing everything she could to avoid thinking about McAvery and his magic. Not an easy thing to do, with his surety stone still on her table next to his plant. It wasn't that she was afraid to touch either, but returning them to him would result in talking to him, and she wasn't the slightest bit interested in beginning a conversation with their roguish refugee. No matter how she imagined the encounter, she knew that he wouldn't let her get away without another complicated debate that would leave her head aching. By leaving both objects where they were, she could at least be certain they couldn't be used against her.

By the end of the second day at sea, she knew every inch of rigging, and had explored the cargo hold from bow to stern. Bardo had shadowed her, keeping notes as she inspected the crates that were still secured below. No sparkling treasure hoard had yielded itself to her search, but what she did find was far more useful.

Bags of root vegetables and two sides of smoked beef hung from the crossbeams. Cartons of fresh oranges and melons sat waiting like gold for a king, alongside bottles of dark red wine, thick and inviting. Dried fruits in every color of the rainbow and kegs of black rum made Kestrel's mouth water with the promise of their sweetness. Boxes of carefully packed hard biscuit exuded a sharp, spicy fragrance from the burlap sacks of smoked jerked meat stacked under them. It was a feast fit for a pirate king, and one less weight on her tired shoulders. The threat of starvation was always a gray ghost over the sails of a ship, waiting to claim its victims. Other dangers still loomed ominously near, but at least her crew would die well fed.

She assigned a contingent of men to clear out the former crew's possessions. The hold was crowded with the kind of equipment one always found on a working ship. Hammocks swung from pegs, blankets folded inside them, and sea chests of every size were stacked carefully underneath, each one full of tools, changes of clothing, and small personal treasures. Whoever owned the *Thanos* before McAvery made off with her definitely hadn't expected to lose her. Everything still in usable condition was piled on the main deck amidships and offered to any man who might have a need.

True to his word, Shadd had dragged himself out of his enforced rest days ago, insisting he needed the fresh air and sunshine more than sleep. He moved slowly and carefully, sometimes holding a hand over the wound in his belly as if to keep his intestines from spilling out, but the color was swiftly returning to his cheeks and his hearty bellowing could be heard ringing across the deck. He sounded healthy and happy. Kestrel knew he'd only be truly content when he was back on the gundecks again, but if he felt well enough to hobble around, that could only be a good sign.

She was aware of McAvery always, the way a hunted animal senses the predator it can't see. Not that he wasn't nearly always in her sights, whenever she turned around. Now that she'd ordered him chained to the railing at the foot of the quarterdeck ladder. The chain was long enough to let him crawl under the ladder if weather turned inclement, and to reach the railing when he needed to relieve himself, but not long enough to let him get in anyone's way. It had been more convenient when he was locked in the hold. Certainly quieter. But now that she knew who he was, she knew he was also in more danger from the crew. Not to discount the increased chance for him to plan a mutiny against her if she couldn't watch him. There were a total of three men aboard she thoroughly trusted, and none of them could be spared to keep a guarding eye on the scoundrel. Until they got to where they were going, she wanted him under her thumb.

He'd taken his incarceration cheerfully, and faced each morning with a smile. He sat on the deck, enjoying the sunshine or peering out over the shining blue water with a battered spyglass he'd produced from the gods knew where. None of her men said more to him than what was necessary, steering clear of him if they could. He didn't seem bothered by their treatment, instead forcing conversation on whichever unfortunate happened to meet his eye.

Sorry as she felt for the pirates who had to endure his chatter, she continually thanked the gods it was them and not her. The effect McAvery always had on her was too much to handle. She wasn't an innocent; growing up on the streets, she'd taken love where it was offered. Back then it hadn't meant anything more than warmth and comfort, as much a children's game as it was anything else. Even working in the brothel, where she'd been off-limits to the customers due to her barmaid status, she'd still had opportunities aplenty. She'd never felt like this.

Pure heat radiated from him, of a sort she'd never felt before. Other lovers had been bright candle flames in a life full of cold and loneliness. This man, this McAvery, was a damned open bonfire, threatening to burn her up if she let him lay so much as a finger on her skin. He was pursuing her, though to what end she could only guess. Things would be so simple if she could be sure he wanted a frolic, a few nights of passion and nothing else. She couldn't accept that as his only motivation. Comely as he was, he could have any woman he wanted—pursuit was never a necessity for men like him. Whatever he wanted, his desire for her was only a means to an end.

Trouble was, every time she tried to consider what he really wanted from her, her thoughts quickly degenerated into speculations for which there were no words. Ideas that made her skin tight and tingly, her throat dry, and her knees weak. Remembering his handsome face so near to hers, the sensuous way his mouth moved, and the fascination of those ever-changing eyes, she shivered. It would have been so easy to give in to him, close her eyes and let him kiss away the stress and pain until the sun came up. If only that were where it all finished. The next morning that inevitably followed would be too much to bear. She might like it too much, and McAvery wasn't the type to stay around. Better to keep him chained to the ship. She had to keep her mind focused on her mission. Besides, she still didn't trust him any farther than she could throw him with both hands cut off. Neither him nor Dreso.

THE third day out dawned clear, bright, and promising. They'd been lucky enough to hold on to a good breeze filling their sails the entire time, and hadn't encountered any other ships since the hunting vessel. No sign of the *Victory* at all.

Red Tom thought they'd pass by Bix somewhere near sunset, which put them a day away from Pecheta. Barring storms or as-yet-unknown enemies, she'd be tacking into port by the morning after next. Her plan to waylay the ship and rescue Binns was coming apart, and she didn't know what to do in its place.

"Good morning, Kestrel!"

She turned around reluctantly, rolling her eyes. Suddenly the day seemed a bit less bright, the ordeal a bit less over. McAvery was grinning. He'd removed his shirt, revealing a well-developed chest, the skin surprisingly sun-browned. She wouldn't have guessed him to be the sort who ever took off his shirt long enough to let a tan take hold. Sometime during the night he'd combed out his long hair, and it lay gleaming across his bare back like a silken mantle. He threw her a jaunty salute, his chains jingling with the movement.

I will not stare at his body. I will not let him goad me. I can have him tossed over the side whenever I feel like it. She drew a deep, calming breath. "What do you want?"

He shrugged. "What does anyone want? Money, a roof over my head, concubines to feed me peeled beryls with their toes . . ."

"I'm busy, McAvery."

"Suit yourself," he said, leaning back against the banister. "I thought you might want to know what's going on under your nose. Or perhaps I should say under your feet."

"And what would you know about it, Lord Chained-to-the-Railing?"

"I hear things. I see things. I've made a life out of noticing the minor subtleties that most people ignore, the nuances that tell me whether a man is trustworthy or not, whether he's planning treachery."

She grasped the ladder rails and placed a foot on the lowest rung, but he put a hand on her ankle to stop her. She kicked toward his head, and he ducked easily out of the way.

"Captain, I meant only to warn you."

"Of what?"

"Of the possibility that all your wildly impulsive lack of planning will be for naught."

"You shouldn't be throwing insults, McAvery." She smiled humorlessly. "But I imagine that's all you can throw, in your current position."

He shrugged. "If you'd rather not hear my thoughts . . ."

Damn him. She didn't want to hear him, unless what she heard was his cries for mercy as he was sucked into the whirling nightmare of the Mouth of Cre'esh. Either the information he had to share was vital, life-threatening and immediate, or else it was part of one of his endless confidence games. She had no way to know for sure, but the unease he inspired was enough to force her to listen. Whether she wanted to or not.

In front of the crew, she worked hard to show only the tough face, the strong, determined attitude of a woman on a mission. No fear, no weakness. Tears and worries waited until nightfall, released only then into the muffled safety of a soft pillow. Somehow, McAvery had figured it out, recognized the mask she wore. He seemed to revel in her secret, continually pushing her toward mistakes. He hoped she'd fail, probably in order to enjoy the spectacle of her dreams and desires spinning off into a maelstrom of defeat. At a time like this, when she needed to keep her mind clear, he was hinting at mutiny. Was he doing it to rattle her, or was there actually a problem? The only way to really know was to let him talk, as much as that irritated her.

"All right, McAvery, let's have it."

He didn't speak, staring over the water as if she wasn't there.

"McAvery?"

Still nothing. He gazed away from her as if they'd never met. What was wrong with the man? She'd opened the door that he was pushing so hard against, but now he wouldn't walk through. Was she supposed to beg? She'd throw herself into the sea before she'd beg him for anything. So he'd changed his mind about what he wanted to tell her. Fine. One less headache for her to suffer. Let him keep his secrets. She started to climb the ladder again.

"There's grumbling." His voice was soft, almost a whisper. "A definite faction developing in the lower decks."

She hesitated. The lower decks. Where the men slept, and ate, and diced for coins. From the second they'd arrived on this huge monster of a ship, she'd separated herself from them. Time was her enemy. She'd careened forward without a look behind at the men following her. Standard procedure was for a crew to vote for their captain. Should she have laid the mission on the table and let the men choose who would lead them?

Stepping off the ladder, she crouched close to McAvery. "Very well. Who's doing this talking?" she murmured.

"I don't know."

That was a surprise. She'd figured he was going to say Dreso, even though she couldn't think of a smart reason for McAvery to give up his man yet. If not his own man, why wouldn't he finger some other member of the crew, someone who wouldn't have enough of an alibi to argue?

"Well, well. You don't know who. Try for what. Is your unknown whisperer planning to set me adrift?"

"Not that I've heard."

"There's a mutiny brewing, but you don't know who's starting things or even what those things might be. Remind me, please, why I'm having this conversation with you?"

"I've heard complaints."

"Complaints?" She shook her head. "Half of what spills from every sailor's mouth each day is complaint. That proves nothing."

"These are different. Secretive, whispered over rum cups in the hold."

"Were you born this infuriating?"

A smile stretched slowly across his face. "It's taken me years of practice."

She backhanded his shoulder with a quiet slap. McAvery turned his head, concentrating on the spot she'd touched.

"Stop that," Kestrel growled. "I don't have time to play with you. Either you've heard something or you haven't. Talk to me, or let me get to work."

McAvery sighed dramatically, and turned to look out over the water again. "I haven't been told but I have heard the complaints. Vicious words, offensive and bruising."

"Like what?" she asked. Damn him, he was talking in circles, and they were right where they had begun. If he answered with something vague again, she was determined to kick him. And this time she wouldn't miss.

"It started shortly after I came aboard. Seems you've been stingy with the treasures in sweet *Thanos*'s belly."

"What treasure? Granted there's enough food down there to fatten my crew like calves for slaughter, but I haven't located anything else. If someone is angry about not getting a share of gold or jewels, I hope he'll move over and make a little room for me."

He nodded. "Understandable. But there's also the matter of your, uh . . ."

"My what?" She wanted to scream the word, but she kept her jaw tight, her voice low.

He looked at her with a face oddly devoid of expression. "The usual rhetoric revolves around your lack of ability due to being a woman."

Kestrel laughed. "I've been quartermaster on this crew for the last year and a bit. I spent a year before that fighting every male on board, just to convince them to keep their paws off my nether regions. Sorry, McAvery. You lose this hand."

He turned to face her, his eyes glazing over. In a heavily accented, higher-pitched voice than his usual, he said, "That's likely how she got the job, flat on her back. Whoever heard of a woman in command, anyhow? Only a madwoman would go to sea. Did ye see 'em after he shot at the ghost ship? Prancing off to Binns's cabin for a drink and a snuggle, I'd lay ye odds. I didn't join up with Binns to be led around on his bitch's leash."

His words chilled her to the bone. There was no way McAvery could know about that. Even if he'd been watching from wherever he was, assuming he could manage a clear view through the smoke, the darkness, and the driving rain, Binns's cabin had been belowdecks. Either he'd just made an extremely lucky guess . . . or he really did know something.

"How did you do that?" she whispered.

His eyes regained their focus, shifting to gaze at her once more. They were bright blue, matching the sky above them. "The accent? I'm a good mimic. But the words . . ." he quirked his lip. "They don't care what a prisoner hears."

The voice he'd mimicked had sounded familiar, but he could have chosen anyone on board to pretend on. Still, besides the accent, the words McAvery'd said were alarming. The kind of details small enough that only a disgruntled fellow would have paid any attention. Bounty hunters and royal ships chasing them, Binns getting closer to a rope each day, and now a mutiny building among her crew. Unless he was making it all up to distract her.

She shivered, tiny beetles of apprehension crawling down her backbone. Pirates were moving from one end of the deck to the other, all hard at work, but the nearer ones glanced her way now and again. If what he said was real, she wondered which ones were listening to the sedition, agreeing with it. They'd thrown in with her plan heartily enough. They needn't have followed her from the start, but they had. It wasn't as if she'd stolen the ship from their captain. She was trying to save him. Couldn't they recognize that she'd give every bit of the power back to Binns the minute she could? Which one was now trying to sink her? She snorted, trying to keep the rush of righteous anger from fading into nervous trepidation. "Can't do the job because I'm female, is that it? I'm more man than three of them put together."

McAvery cocked an eyebrow, running his eyes up and down the length of her slowly, the touch of them as physical as hands would have been, reminding her more clearly than words could have of the power and danger of her gender. He was chained to the ship, couldn't reach her if she stepped away.

"I'm not afraid of lily-livered boys trying to impress each other with talk." The words, meant to be brave, sounded hollow in her own ears.

"Many's the dethroned king who wished he'd paid heed to the grousing of his common folk while they were still harmless."

"True enough," she admitted.

"Pay attention. See what they hide from you. Peel away the layer of loyalty and find the serpent that hides underneath. Listen to the whispers floating on the wind."

Whispers on the wind, hiding serpents, indeed. He was full of tricks, this one. Pulling bits of magical flotsam out of the air, weaving tapestries with his words when the trinkets didn't suffice. He wouldn't drag her into his web this time.

"Keep your ears open, McAvery. The talk gets more serious, you'll tell me immediately."

He stared at her for a moment, as if trying to fathom some difficult mathematical problem. For an instant, she gazed back at him, clear-eyed and guileless, then turned toward the ladder. Act like he didn't matter, and he'd crack.

"So what's in this bargain for me? Seeing as you intend to toss me to the wolves as soon as we reach Pecheta?"

She stopped, but didn't turn around. "I'll ask the king to let my face be the last thing you see before you hang. How's that for a reason?"

"Tempting, indeed. I'll have to work harder for the rest of the trip."

"You, work?" Kestrel barked a laugh. "I've seen how hard you work, sir. That's why you're chained in place."

"Oh, yes. I forgot the chains." He jingled them for emphasis. "I meant that I'd have to work harder on you."

She fought to keep her tone light, uninterested. "I find myself quite immune to you."

"Of course, you do, dear lady." His sardonic tone floated through the air as she climbed the ladder to where Red Tom waited.

Twenty-three

I looked to heaven, and tried to pray
But or ever a prayer had gushed
A wicked whisper came, and made
My heart as dry as dust.

—SAMUEL TAYLOR COLERIDGE

H er navigator wasn't alone. Shadd had risen early, his blond mop floating in the morning breeze as he stood next to Tom. He raised a meaty hand in greeting at the sight of her.

"It's a rare morning," he bellowed. "And here's a rare captain to grace it!"

She cleared the top of the ladder, swung her leg up and over, and stood, breathing deep the fresh air. Only a few steps below her, men were busy at their duties, but the weight of worry had lifted off her back. It was as if the short climb had taken her to a new world, where the tensions and fears didn't plague her. Up here, there was no suspicion, no secrets. And no McAvery.

Kestrel strode across the deck and slapped her master gunner on his shoulder. "How are you feeling today, you big lummox?" She knew better than to fret over his injury, especially since he'd suffered it on her behalf, but she couldn't resist the asking. He'd stopped holding his side so often, but he still caught his breath now and again when he climbed the ladders.

The grin that split his face was full of his usual good spirits. "Fit and whole, like I never got carved up at all." He patted his gut. "All the innards still in where they belong, and runnin' like aces." Tilting his head back, he gazed up into the rigging and nodded sagely. "So, ye're learnin' her ropes, are ye?"

"Aye, we've managed. Made good time, too. We'll be in sight of Pecheta tomorrow."

"No sight of the *Victory*?"

"Not yet."

Shadd nodded, his shaggy blond locks bouncing with the movement. He squinted into the distance. "I been meanin' to talk wi' ye about that." He glanced at Tom, then back to Kestrel. "Can ye spare me a bit o' time?"

At that moment, Tom yawned hugely and stretched his arms. Kestrel winced at the crackles from his joints. He'd been taking the dark watch since the loss of the *Wolfshead,* and she knew it was telling on him. "Tom," she called, "you're relieved."

His normally taciturn face cracked into a tiny smile. Without a word, he secured the wheel and left. Kestrel took the wheel herself, releasing the noose that held it steady and wrapping her fingers around the handles. She relished the feel of the ship under her hands. The pull of water against the rudder so far below her was like the rush of blood through her veins. "Shadd," she said, suddenly inspired, "do you ever wonder if a person can be born for the sea? Born to live on water always?"

"Ah, not me, lass. I love it, that's a sure fact. But I wager I'd be as happy firin' cannon off the walls of a fortress in the Continental Mountains. It's the roar o' the guns, the stink o' powder, keeps me feelin' alive." He leaned against the railing and considered her oddly. "You, though. If I believed in that sort o' thing, which I ain't admittin' I do, I'd swear ye be the one with the sea in yer blood. But I didn't come up here to chat about destiny. I find m'self powerful curious as to this mission."

"Curious how?"

"How it's to be carried out, for one thing. Do ye have a plan, or are ye intendin' to make it up as ye go?"

She studied his face curiously. "I thought we understood what had to happen. Don't you trust me?"

"I trust ye, Kes. I also noticed we ain't seen hide nor hair of yon ship we was chasin'."

The wheel creaked softly, as if in agreement with what he'd said.

"Tomorrow we'll anchor off the Pechetan coast. I'll take McAvery and two of the fellows in a longboat. We'll stroll up to the palace and demand an audience with the king."

"The king?" His eyebrows shot upward in surprise. "What makes ye think ye'll get in to see him? Might as well ask for a meetin' with Great Pantheus hisself."

She wondered how he'd take it, if she told him about what she'd read, who McAvery was, who Binns truly was. Would it weaken Binns in Shadd's estimation, knowing that he was connected to the law? Would McAvery's life be forfeit? She couldn't take the chance by telling him. Binns hadn't trusted her with his deepest secret, even when his life was on the line. Shadd was a good man, and she couldn't share what wasn't hers to give. Not yet.

"Likely they won't let me see His Royal Marvelousness in the flesh, but I figure I can get someone important enough to hear my grievance. Binns gave me a name to ask for. I've got the log and I could offer up the *Thanos* in exchange as well."

"Ye'd give up the ship?" He shook his head in dismay. "The *Wolfshead* sunk, and the *Thanos* given away . . . what'll we use to make our livin'?"

"I didn't say I'd give them the *Thanos*. Just that I'd make the offer." She turned the wheel a degree, letting the ship move into the center of the breeze. The sails belled, and the *Thanos* leaped under her hands like a live thing. "The ship will be hidden, for as long as I need it to be. Once I have Binns back, I can sail her to somewhere quiet, careen her, repaint her, and change out the sails and rigging. No one will be able to prove what ship she used to be."

"Ye don't think her very size'll give her away?"

"Likely raise suspicions, but without proof that's all they'd be." She stroked the smooth wood. "And who'd be able to take us with the *Thanos* under our feet?"

"Sounds reasonable. There's just one thing ye left out."

Kestrel raised her eyebrows in question.

"I know I've been in sad condition these last few days, but my belly's healed up tight. I'm fit."

"Are you asking to come along when we go ashore?" He nodded vigorously. "No, lad, you're recovering yet. I'd never forgive myself if you opened that wound again on my account. Besides, this'll be a simple exchange. No need for bringing forth the big guns." She smiled. "Nor my big gunner."

"Don't tease me about this!" he said suddenly, harshly.

"I didn't mean it to sound like I was teasing, Shadd," she said. The pleasant expression had gone from his face, and she felt a tightening of apprehension in her belly. Whatever was bothering Shadd, it was too serious to ignore.

"You don't want me to endanger myself. But what about yer own safety?"

"Me?"

"Ye think ye can stroll up to the royal shack without runnin' into an armed man or two? And that's assumin' ye make it all the way to yer destination."

"It's not some lawless place, Shadd. It's Pecheta. Peace and order, calm and quiet. What do you think is going to happen?"

"Is he"—the gunner inclined his head toward the bottom of the quarterdeck ladder—"included in your plans?"

"McAvery?"

"Aye." He shrugged, looking shamefaced. "McAvery."

She glanced down. The rogue had moved into the shade, only his legs sticking out from the shadow. His feet were bare now, too. At the rate he was removing his clothes, he might end up stark naked by tomorrow. She shivered at the image that flew past her mind's eye, and yanked her attention back to a safer topic. "I told you he's going along," she said. "That's why we've come, after all. I suppose I could attempt to gain a royal audience without my evidence in tow. But if I hand him over, the offer to give up the *Thanos* will come across as far more convincing. Besides, I'd rather take him with me and get him off my hands first thing."

"Off yer hands. Sensible." Shadd wouldn't look at her, his eyes downcast. She'd never seen him act so strangely. The usual bellowing gunner had been mysteriously replaced with a man she didn't recognize.

"Spit it out, Shadd. What's bothering you? Do you know something about him that I don't?"

"I jes' don't like it that ye'll be alone with him."

Shadd was many things—bold, brash, and noisy—but never had she ever seen him like this. Hesitant, nervous, never meeting her eyes. Not concerned about how her plan would work, but who would be with her. He was almost acting . . . jealous.

Kestrel's shoulders tensed, and she gripped the wheel tightly enough to whiten her knuckles. The weight she thought she'd left behind on the main deck returned to lie on her shoulders like a giant albatross. Out of all the men on board, Shadd was one of the very few she trusted. He'd always been friend, brother, keeper of her secrets. If he'd been looking at her with romance in mind, she'd never once realized it. And he certainly had picked the least perfect time to make his feelings apparent. "Shadd," she said, as gently as she could manage, "I appreciate you wanting to protect me. You've always been so good to me. You watched my back, trained me until I could defend myself. You'll make some woman very happy one day, and I'll be there to cheer for you."

"What're ye goin' on about?" His forehead wrinkled in confusion. "What woman? Did someone else come aboard while I was out?"

"No, no one else. I'm just . . ." She stopped, not sure what to say next. "I don't want you to worry about me."

"Too late for that, lass." He stepped to the railing, staring out over the water instead of at her. "I can't help worryin' when ye get ideas like this in yer head."

"But you know I can take care of myself. If your feelings are distracting you," she said, "you need to put them aside."

"What feelin's?" He turned to face her, his eyes wide with surprise. "Ye thought I was confessin' . . . that I was . . ." His face reddened, and he dropped his head.

The pulse point on her temple was pounding, and she raised a hand to rub the pain that suddenly sprang to life there. As if merely misunderstanding wasn't complicated enough, she had to go and jump to humiliating conclusions. "Shadd, it's been a long three days. What are we talking about?"

He didn't look at her, but she saw the redness fading from his cheeks. "I don't know what ye're talkin' about, but I was referrin' to him."

"Him who?"

"Yer fine fellow what ye got chained to the ship. Yer McAvery."

"He isn't my anything." This conversation was beginning to grate on her. If it wasn't jealousy eating at her master gunner, she was at a loss. As far as she knew, Shadd hadn't even spoken to McAvery, so there was nothing he'd know that she herself hadn't discovered. A thought struck her.

"You haven't been talking to Dreso about him, have you?"

He struck the railing with his open hand, a meaty slap. "Dreso again? Ye're fixated on poor Dreso, but ye're missin' the point. It ain't Dreso what's out to hurt ye, and all of us in the process. It's yonder pretty boy."

"I'm not at all afraid of him."

"I know ye're not. But ye should be."

Twice in one day someone was telling her what she should be doing. She felt as if she were being whirled in circles. Who was she supposed to believe? And what could she do with the information once she decided?

"He's no danger to me. I'll be fine."

He swung toward her. His fists were clenched and his arm muscles bunched tightly under the linen shirt. His lip lifted in a snarl, and he bellowed, "No, ye won't! He'll twist ye 'til ye don't know which way ye're goin', then leave ye danglin' from a gallows right next to Binns!"

Several of the men looked up from the main deck, their attention drawn by the yelling. Kestrel stared at him in shock. "Keep your voice down."

"Why?" he snapped. "So ye can pretend ye know what ye're doin'? So ye can claim ye didn't have no warnin'?" He planted himself next to her, one hand on the mighty wheel, and squinted at her. "McAvery stinks of lies. Did ye notice how none o' the crew'll get anywhere near him? Ye told them yerself how he put our captain in the hands of the jailer. And if that tone fork o' his is any indication, he's got magic. Magic, Kes, remember? Ye hate it, with a bleedin' passion. Ye thought ye kept it to yerself, but there ain't a fella aboard doesn't know! And what about yer midnight visit? Ain't a man hasn't heard already. What were the two o' ye doin' in there, discussin' the best route to take on our trip?"

Kestrel's mouth was hanging partway open, and she snapped her lips closed before something could fly in. The gossip had spread like wildfire throughout the small community aboard ship. Poor Shadd was jealous, but not the way she'd assumed. He'd been her only confidant and supporter. Maybe if she'd told him everything the morning after, they wouldn't be having this conversation. How was she supposed to tell him his captain wasn't a pirate, that he'd been working for the law he despised so? In his eyes, she was betraying him.

"None of this is what it seems," she said slowly, choosing her words with care. "Yes, I visited McAvery in his cell. I talked to him, is all. I needed to know why he'd done what he'd done."

Shadd lifted one eyebrow. "And now ye know? But won't tell me. Ain't that charmin'."

"You don't believe me?"

"I'm wonderin' whether ye've forgotten what we're on about, yer mind gettin' so filled with a handsome face there's no room for anyone else."

"Like you?" she spat at him, a flash of defensive anger rising to the surface. He shook his head.

"Like Binns."

The words hit her hard, a verbal slap across the tender feelings she'd been wearing on her sleeve for days. "How dare you?" she growled. "Everything I've done has been for Binns. I'm the only person on this ship that cares about his life. All the rest of you want is someone to take the blame if the next raid goes wrong."

"Hell, Kes, I took a sword in my gut, damn near killed me! Ye think I did that for the chance of gold down the line?"

She shoved at his hand on the wheel, her jaw clenched. "I haven't forgotten what you did. I'm grateful, more than I can tell you. But don't tell me I can't run this my own way just because you couldn't get clear of a man with a sword fast enough!"

He grabbed her by the shoulders. In an instant, without thinking, she lashed out, punching him in the belly. He released her, doubling over and staggering backward, retching wetly.

"Shadd!" Grabbing his elbow, she helped him to a sitting position. He was breathing hard and cursing, holding his wounded midsection. Under his fingers, blood began to seep, staining his tunic.

Kestrel ran to the edge of the high deck. "Get Jaques!" she yelled, pointing at the two men nearest. "Now!" She returned to Shadd's side. He was stretched out on the wood, but his eyes were open and he was smiling again. She crouched beside him.

"I'm an idiot. I shoulda known what'd happen if I grabbed at ye. Good to see yer trainin' still holds, even against yer own teacher." He groaned, trying to lean forward to get a look at his reopened wound. Kestrel pushed him back.

"It doesn't look much different. Same as it was before, except without any steel in it this time."

He shuddered, his breath coming a little raggedly, and lay his head back on the deck. His eyes slid closed, as if he was passing out.

"Oh, no, you don't." She shook his arm, but gently, just enough to get his attention. "Stay awake."

"What for?" he grumbled. "So's ye can beat on me some more?"

"Don't be ridiculous. Shadd, I need you here. There's no one else I can trust. Who am I supposed to put in charge of the ship while I'm off making the trade for McAvery? Bardo?"

"Couldn't do a worse job than me, could he?" He chuckled, screwing his face up at the twinges of pain the effort brought on. "Fine quarter I'll be now ye've torn open my gut again."

Jaques arrived, carrying a fabric bag. He eyed the big man lying on the wooden planks of the deck. "Damn it, didn't I tell you to take it slow? I should yank your intestines out for you, and be done with it."

"My fault," Kestrel said, before Shadd could frame a reply. "I pushed him to do too much."

Jaques shrugged. Setting it down on the deck, he pulled out rolls of gauze and a small bottle. Kestrel stood up, not only giving him room to work but putting space between herself and her friend. Her heart hung, stone hard, in her chest as she gazed at Shadd with new eyes. In two years, they'd had their spats and disagreements, but he'd never looked at her so coldly. What had he been hoping for? Taking the blade meant for her had been too much. There was no way she could ever live up to what he'd done. Shadd had given her the greatest gift anyone could give another, and he was sorry he'd done it. He resented saving her. She swallowed the lump that had formed in her throat with the sudden understanding.

Shadd wished she'd died. Everything would have been easier. With the *Wolfshead* gone, and their quartermaster spitted on Cragfarus's blade, the men would have scattered, taken ship with other captains, gone on with the lives they knew. Binns would have died, too, but that was the risk they all took, and none of them would have grieved for long. Within a few months, the story would have become a tale told late at night in the taverns, embellished to an unrecognizable state. Within a few years, it would have been completely forgotten.

Drawing his knife from his belt, Jaques slit open the old wrappings. Kestrel winced. The skin was red and raw around the long, uneven cut, the stitches ragged but holding. Jarvis splashed some liquid from the bottle onto Shadd's belly, ignoring the gunner's grunt of protest, finished rewrapping the bandage, and helped his patient to sit up.

Kestrel hunkered down, putting herself face-to-face with Shadd. "I'm not going to try and sway you with talk. You're going to have to trust I know what I'm about."

His eyes were slits, his mouth equally tight. "I want to, Kes. I want to believe ye're doin' the right thing. Y'ain't makin' it easy on me, carryin' on with that blackheart. I'll stand by ye as long as I can. But if ye let me down, don't be surprised when I'm at the head of the mob that comes for ye."

Without another word, he let Jaques help him to his feet and down the ladder. She watched them walk away. She felt dwarfed by the huge ship under her feet and the tricky mission ahead of her. The wind around her grew chilly, teasing goose bumps up on the exposed skin of her arms. She shivered. No one left. She had no one left to trust on board. She'd never felt so alone in all her life, not even when she was living in the alleys.

The water ahead tossed and flashed, tiny whitecaps peeking under the onslaught of the steady breeze. Sky as blue as a sapphire stretched over her head. Maybe she was born with the ocean in her blood. The loneliest sort of life a body could choose. So her last friend was on the verge of abandoning her. It shouldn't have come as a real surprise. Years of depending only on her own abilities should have taught her that lesson. She'd deluded herself thinking there could be any such things as lifelong companions for a woman like her.

It didn't matter—she was determined not to let any of it matter. The only important thing was her captain. She would save Binns. By herself, if necessary. She would show every man aboard what kind of sailor, what kind of fighter, she was. Let them go their own ways after that. The story they would tell in the pubs at midnight would have a much different ending. Kestrel turned to grab the wheel she'd forgotten, only then noticing the bloody handprint Shadd had left, like a brand, on her white linen shirt.

Twenty-four

Fear at my heart, as at a cup,
My lifeblood seemed to sip . . .
—SAMUEL TAYLOR COLERIDGE

K estrel stared at the bloody handprint, transfixed. If she was superstitious, she'd take it for an omen, and not a good one. She'd never been one to believe in the tall tales sailors made up to entertain themselves, but for a long moment, she almost thought she'd changed her mind.

No, she told herself, *it's naught but a stain. But I don't need to be sporting blood on a calm day like this. There's enough rumor flying around this ship without me adding to it. I'll go to my cabin and change, so as not to frighten the men.*

She secured the wheel, stepped to the edge, and scanned the main deck, breathing a sigh of relief. Jarvis was sitting on a barrel, tying knots in a length of rope. Just the man she could use right now. "Ho there, Jarvis. Take her wheel for me, there's a good lad."

He glanced up at the sound of his name, and his eyes grew wide. Slowly he stood, and made his way across the deck to the ladder. He stopped at the bottom and threw a look at McAvery's legs sticking out from underneath.

"Come on, man, the day'll be half over by the time you get here!" Her impatience was born of nervousness, but she'd do herself a disservice if she didn't keep up the demanding role of captain just the way she'd watched Binns play it. Jarvis started at the bellow in her tone and quickstepped up the ladder to her side.

"That's better." Taking his shoulders in her hands, she pushed him in front of the wheel. "We're on course for Pecheta, should be off her shores by evening. Take care of her for me. If you need me, I'll be in my quarters."

He nodded. "Aye, Captain." He made to release the wheel, then turned toward her. "Are you injured?"

She held out the arm with the bloodied sleeve. It seemed to swim in her vision, receding from her, until it was no longer her arm, but someone else's, seen from across a distance. The blood was so much less alarming from over there. As if it were rust from bumping too close to a deck gun. Just an ordinary stain. Not blood from a trusted friend she'd nearly killed twice now.

"Captain?"

Jarvis's face was as uncertain as his tone. She shook her head, trying to dispel the ominous shadows that threatened to overtake her, and dropped the bloodied arm down to her side, out of her direct sight.

"I'm fine. You just keep us on course. I'll be in the cabin for a time." Kestrel hopped down the ladder before he could come up with any more questions. She neither hesitated nor looked McAvery's way, striding instead to the door of her cabin.

Inside, all was cool and shadowy. She sighed, enjoying the brief respite of solitude, and pulled the ruined shirt off over her head. Tossing it into the corner, she slipped on a fresh shirt and sat down on the edge of the bed, resting her face in her hands.

She'd hit Shadd. Punched him, hard, right in the belly. He'd only been trying to help her, to make her see what a mistake she was making trusting McAvery. He'd taken a sword to the gut, nearly died, all for her. And she paid him back by hitting him, tearing open the wound. He could have bled to death on the deck above them and it would have been no one's fault but hers.

Rum. Walking to the sideboard, she popped the top from the rum decanter and poured herself a cupful, then sank into the chair at the table. The plant stood, right where she'd put it days before. It mocked her with its silence. She squinted at it; the swelling at its center point seemed to have increased. Had it been watered lately?

She tipped her cup at the edge of the pot, letting rum stream into the soil.

"You're more than you appear, it would seem," she whispered. "I wonder what you can do."

She reached out and stroked the shiny green leaf. It felt like every other plant she'd ever touched. It couldn't be magic.

If only there was a way to tell. Her own ability was such a small thing. She'd kept it so close to the vest all her life, for fear of being sold out to the Brethren by someone more money-hungry than crew loyal. There were stories of magi who could transform people into animals or fly through the skies. Surely there must be a way to use the skill to detect real magic. Maybe the plant would react some way, if Kestrel whistled it a little tune.

She bit her lip and looked over her shoulder. The door was closed, and she'd thrown the bar. No one would know.

Kestrel licked her lips, moistening them just enough, then pursed them together and blew gently. A soft tone issued from between her lips, high and thin but audible. Licking her lips again, she tried to change the tone, to whistle a simple tune.

Slender ripples of energy tickled along her skin, unseeable sparks dancing around her and forming into fingers that reached out away from her. The curtains over the window began to flutter, and even the bedclothes shivered.

The plant trembled, its leaves shaking with the breeze she was creating. The pot shook, tiny clumps of dirt hopping out to land on the table. She stared at the crotch of the little plant, the thickened place between its two major stems, and as she watched it, the swelling surged. A tiny bit, to be sure, but it definitely changed, grew.

She ran out of breath and slapped a hand over her mouth, cold filling her body with the panic of what she'd done. McAvery had said that time was a factor, that the fruit was only good while it remained on the branch. Was the swelling a bloom forming? In playing games with it, just out of curiosity, she might have hurried along whatever was destined to happen, and doomed them all. If it wasn't in either the king's or the prince's hands by the time it fruited, her only bargaining chip would be gone.

Sitting back, she groaned. There was someone aboard who knew what would happen. Chained outside, patiently waiting for her to need him. Damn his eyes. He'd known from the start that she would eventually have to turn to him. It gnawed at her soul to even think of turning to him for help, but he was the only one with the answers she needed. He'd already named his price. She no longer had the luxury of choosing whether or not to pay.

Twenty-five

The moving Moon went up the sky
And nowhere did abide
Softly she was going up
And a star or two beside . . .
—SAMUEL TAYLOR COLERIDGE

The opportunity was long in coming. She left the cabin, having donned a fresh linen shirt, with every intention of making McAvery confess all. Before she could even get to him, Angus snared her attention. Two men had gotten themselves tangled in the rigging, and a sail was torn from their thrashing around. Throwing herself into the job at hand, it didn't take long to get the men free and back on deck. Hot on the work's heels came another task, and soon she found that the day flashed past the way they had used to do. Suddenly it was afternoon, the sky darkening to gold and flame as the sun neared the sea.

"Yonder land!" came the cry from aloft. Sure enough, as Tom had predicted, the straight line of horizon was broken by the black hump of an island—Pecheta. Kestrel stretched her arms and shoulders, enjoying the warm achiness of a hard day's work well done. She'd missed being just a sailor. For a few hours, her mind had been full of nothing except the working of the ship—no magic, no hangman's noose, and no McAvery. She felt renewed, and very glad she hadn't gotten to McAvery earlier. She was in far better shape to interrogate him now than she had been this morning.

"Dark watch up!" she called out. "Day watch below. See to your supper." A few of the men sent up a cheer, and the rest smiled and made their way to the hatch, where the night crew were struggling up onto deck, Bardo among them. He shuffled across the deck toward her.

"Evenin', Captain," he said. "Red Tom ain't feelin' all that well, so I assigned another man to helm. That is, if it's acceptable to you?"

"What's wrong?" she asked. "Should I send Jaques along to see to him?"

He shook his head. "Already seen to. I think he maybe got a bad bit of meat or the like. He'll be fine tomorrow."

"You're a good fellow, Bardo," she said, clapping him on the shoulder. "You've been a great help to me during this whole trip. Be assured I plan to tell Binns when we retrieve him."

He ducked his weaselly head, and began dry-washing his hands over and over. "Thank you, you're most kind to say such things."

"Not at all, Bardo." She yawned, and stretched again. "Looks like I'd better go see to my supper, too, eh?"

"Actually, I already had something sent to your cabin."

"What would I do without you, Bardo? You straighten up after me, send me food." She grinned at him. "You're a godsend."

An odd look passed over his face for an instant, replaced by his usual ingratiating smile. "Happy to be of service. Have a good evening."

She strolled across the deck toward her cabin. McAvery had come out from under the ladder once the sun had moved off. He was nibbling at a heel of bread and a cup was in his hand. He raised it in her direction.

"Did you enjoy your day? Climbing around the ship like a mere deckhand again?"

"Tomorrow we anchor in Pecheta. Happy?"

He tore loose another bite of bread, and chewed it slowly. "Why should that make me feel any way at all?"

"To get the answer to that question, you'll need to dress. You're joining me for supper."

He quirked an eyebrow. Placing his cup and his heel of dry bread on the deck at his feet, he stood. She'd forgotten how much taller he was than she. He was still shirtless and barefooted. His eyes . . . they'd lightened, to a blue that was nearly silver, and more startling than any color they'd been so far. Standing this close, she caught the smell of warm male skin, a heady scent that gave her gooseflesh.

Living among men for the last two years, she was used to seeing half-naked bodies. It was this body that caused the problems. Seeing him in such an intriguing state of undress brought too many thoughts to the forefront. Distracting thoughts. She slid the key into its lock on the shackle around his waist. It fell free, and he stretched suddenly, arms at their full length over his head, pulling his muscles into sharp focus under the golden overlay of his skin. She turned away.

"Are you sure you want me to dress? Waste of time later, wouldn't you agree?"

She spun to him and slapped his face, hard. He didn't even try to move out of her way. His cheek reddened with the force of her blow, but he was still grinning.

She steeled her jaw. "I said, put on your shirt."

"As you wish, Captain." He picked it up, sliding it over his head with a practiced motion and padding after her barefooted. She stopped when they reached the door to her cabin and took a surreptitious glance around. As she'd thought, she'd drawn attention. She poked a finger into McAvery's chest.

"Keep one thing in mind, McAvery. You're not here as my guest. You'll stay long enough to tell me everything you know, and then it's back to the ladder for you. Try anything and I'll flog you myself."

He tilted his head, then nodded once. Out of the corner of her eye, she saw the men who'd been watching turn away, returning to their tasks. Kestrel let out the breath she'd been holding and opened her door, ushering McAvery inside.

Plates of food sat on the table, the plant in the middle like a centerpiece. Salted fish slices, dried fruits, hunks of hard cheese, dark brown bread, a bowl of honey. She hadn't known there was honey on board. And next to it all a pitcher of ale. Her stomach rumbled.

"Shall we eat, Captain?" McAvery pulled out a chair for her. She scowled and crossed her arms, standing firm until he finally let go of the chair and seated himself in the other one.

She sat, reaching for the pitcher and pouring herself a cup of dark ale. Creamy foam billowed from the top of the cup, spilling over onto her fingers. She stuck them in her mouth to lick clean and froze. McAvery was watching her hand with unnerving fascination.

"All you're getting from me is supper. So you might as well save yourself the effort."

"As you command. You wanted answers. So why don't we get started?"

"Good idea. The faster I have you back on deck, the better." She put some cheese and bread on her plate, abandoning the salted fish. Binns might love it but it was low on her list.

He helped himself to a few dried fruits, popping one into his mouth. "Mmm," he hummed. "Much better than what I had last night."

Reaching into her pocket, she pulled out the surety stone and rolled it toward McAvery. "Pick up the stone before you answer."

He reached out, lifting the little pebble and tossing it in his hand. "Ask what you will."

"I know you were delivering the sanguina to the king. I also know you claim the prince is the one who has my captain."

"I can't be sure," he said, "but Jeremie's dogs are a good indication." The stone flashed blue.

She grabbed a chunk of bread and began tearing it into bits. "Fine. Since I've missed the *Victory*, I'm left with two options. I can do as Binns asked me, deliver his book to the palace and hope this fellow Lig can help."

McAvery chuckled and took a swallow of his ale.

"You think that's funny?"

"Absolutely not." The blue stone remained dark. Kestrel raised an eyebrow, but McAvery's face was a mask of seriousness. "What's your other option?"

"I find this prince of yours and trade him the plant."

"Bad idea." McAvery bit into a sausage. "He'd use it to take over the crown."

"What care I what kings and princes do to each other?"

"You still won't get your captain back. He's too important. Jeremie'd promise his release, then kill him and you. Problem solved."

Just as she'd feared. She needed McAvery, but not as a tool. He was the only one who could help her.

"It wasn't easy harvesting this thing." He stroked one of the plant's thick, green leaves. "Only grows on the highest cliffs of Cre'esh. As far as I know, there's only the one tree." He slipped another cerise into his mouth, speaking around it. "Digging up the tree wasn't easy. We had to be extraordinarily careful not to cut any of the roots. But the real torture was—"

"The dirt!" she exclaimed, startled by the sudden insight. "Sanguina has to rest in its native soil, yes?"

"Very good, if a bit poetic. If it's to be transplanted, it required a good deal of the dirt it came from to thrive."

"And there was never a Danisoban on board with you?" She was almost disappointed.

"No. There was no need for their particular skills on this trip. And I make it a habit never to work with them. But speaking of the Brotherhood," he said, laying the stone down on the table, rotating it gently with one finger, "draws us back to a place I think we've been before. There's a question you haven't answered for me yet."

So there it was. He hadn't forgotten, nor had she assumed he would. There was more they had to talk about, in order to make a workable plan. She'd never told anyone, but no one had ever demanded the tale, either. Until this man.

"The Danisobans killed my parents, when I was a child." Not the whole truth, but close enough. She hoped.

McAvery was idly shredding a fish, sometimes eating one of the bits, but never looking her way. "Why?"

"That's not your business. It's my turn now." Kestrel shoved a piece of cheese in her mouth.

"You're not much of a negotiator, are you? Probably pay full price in the market, too."

Under his breath, he began humming a little tune, nothing she recognized, but it sent a thrill charging down her spine. Did he already know? Was this his way of hinting? She had to change the direction before he hit too close.

"About your little sanguina"—she frowned at it, turning the pot a half turn—"is that thickening in the middle the bloom?"

"Yes. It's getting bigger. Probably be in fruiting in a matter of days." He smiled, a coldly calculating expression. "My turn," he murmured. Kestrel felt a sinking feeling in her stomach. She'd used up her leeway. And her turn. With two words he'd made it clear that the game was over until she admitted why the Danisobans had murdered her parents.

She rose from her chair, hands wrapped around the ale cup. Outside the window, the sun was halfway below the water, staining everything a lovely gold. Like every day. How many sunsets had she watched this way, and how few would be left to her once she told him her secret? But it appeared to be the only way. She had to know what he knew. Binns's life was all that mattered. If she ended up with the Danisobans . . . at least she'd have her memories.

"When I was four, they came," she murmured. "As tall as trees to me, all scratchy voices and long black robes. Papa wouldn't let them in. Mama tried to hide me, told me to run. When I looked back, the house was on fire."

"Not very smart. Didn't they know what would happen if they defied the Brethren?"

She spun and faced him, fury like a wildfire sparking in every inch of her, at the Danisobans for what they'd done, and at McAvery for making her admit it. "Of course they knew! But those hideous old men were after me. My parents died. For me." She strode back to the table and slammed her ale cup down, sloshing the last swallows onto the shining wood. "I'm a Promise, damn your eyes. I should've been trained into the Brotherhood, but my parents let themselves be burned to death instead." She planted both hands flat on the table in front of him and glared into his eyes. They were green now, but she no longer cared how he did it, nor why. "Does that answer your question, Master McAvery?"

He hadn't flinched at all during her outburst, but his face had softened, let go of the infuriating smile. His green eyes searched hers, holding her gaze without touching, but a sure grip nonetheless. He tilted his head to the side, in that way he had that made her so uneasy, his golden hair slithering aside like a wave of satin. She was abruptly aware of her own heart beating, hard and painful under the bones of her chest, her breath coming fast and shallow at the nearness of his mouth to hers. Anger shifting into something else, flowing like silk through her veins. So close . . . it would be so easy to lean into him, press her mouth against his warm skin. Heat surged within her. It had been so long since she surrendered herself to such temptation.

His kiss was sweet, his lips warm and supple under hers. She sighed, relaxing as his arms came up and around her, pulling her down to sit on his lap. She wrapped her own arms around his neck, and let her head fall back. He nuzzled her exposed neck, teasing the tender skin with his teeth, sending shudders down her spine. His hands rose to her waist, tugging the hem of her shirt free of her breeches, and slid under. His fingers were hot against her bare skin. Working her feet loose from her boots, she kicked them off and turned to straddle McAvery. He grasped her hips and pulled her hard to his body.

The niggling part of her conscience that she'd been steadfastly ignoring flared into focus. She jerked back, onto her feet, and drew her sword, its point inches from his green eyes. He sat back in the chair, his face flushed and questioning.

"Wait." His voice was low, soothing.

"You're one of them," she spat, keeping her blade raised between them. "You're spelling me now. I can feel it."

"No, Kestrel. I couldn't if I wanted to." He got to his feet and took a step toward her. She backed up farther, until the backs of her knees bumped the edge of the bed. Her hand was shaking, the tip of the sword wavering between his chest and throat.

"Not a step closer, or I'll kill you."

He stopped, showing his palms in surrender. "You've told me your story. I won't betray the confidence."

She laughed harshly. "Of course you won't. You'll just spell me into obedience and into your bed!"

McAvery sat back down in the chair and placed both hands flat on the table. "I'm no Danisoban." The sleeves of his shirt were pulled up, high enough for her to see his wrists. His perfectly shaped wrists, with no silver bracelets. And no marks of ones having been there. "Don't you remember? You checked me when I came aboard."

Joining the Brotherhood was a lifetime commitment. The bracelets worn by every magus were spelled to explode if the wearer made a successful attempt to remove them. Most died. A few were lucky enough to only lose an arm, although the mutilation ended their magical careers. If McAvery had ever been claimed by the magi, it would show.

She sank to the bed, sword still firmly in hand, her gaze not moving from him. The panic was sliding away, along with any hint of the desire she'd almost given in to, but her apprehension remained. "Fine. Assume I believe you're not one of them. How did you get your hands on magic? How did you even learn to use it?"

"A man who understands the delicate art of negotiation can learn much, and gain more."

"You mean you cheated some poor soul out of his magical baubles, after tricking him into teaching you the secrets?"

"Never a poor soul, and certainly not just one." He winked at her. "But yes, I suppose you could describe it that way."

She let the sword point drop to the floor. He was exactly what she thought he was. Thief, charlatan, and liar. But not a magus. Not a real one.

"You can come back to the table, now, Captain." He pushed the plate of fruit closer to her side of the table.

Kestrel stood, sheathing her sword and tucking her shirt back into her breeches. The fruit did look tasty, and she was plagued with hunger pangs from the hard day of work. She sat down and took a dried cerise from the offered plate, her fingers shaking. It was sweet and tangy, and melted on her tongue.

"If I ask you another question, will you promise not to decapitate me?" He'd leaned back in the chair, stretching his legs before him, his head pillowed in his hands behind him.

"Possibly. Do I get another chance, too?"

"As I told you once before, my life is an open book to you."

She rolled her eyes. "Ask your question."

"You're a Promise. As I've heard it, there are five different skills in the Danisoban canon. Do you know which one you are?"

"I don't know how to do magic," she said hurriedly.

"I didn't mean to imply that you did. Did your parents catch you changing the water in your cup into juice, or having lengthy conversations with the house cat?"

She stared at the man across from her. He already knew what she was. What difference would it make now if she told him? Or better yet, she could show him. Licking her lips, she pursed them carefully and blew.

The honey-gold mane of his hair began floating and fluttering, twisting above his head into a false braid before falling down again. McAvery's eyebrow popped up in surprise.

"How handy for you!"

"Are you out of your skull?"

He shook his head. "No, but think of it. You can whistle up the kind of winds you'll need, whenever you need it. Everyone else is stranded in the harbor, but not you. You go floating by, sails full and gaining speed."

"No, I can't. I won't." She crossed her arms and frowned at his enthusiasm. "Too dangerous. Do you know how much a slaver would pay for me, if one of my crewmates decided to sell me out?"

"But, Kestrel," he began. His argument was interrupted by a loud rapping on her door. "Should I answer that for you, Captain?"

She glared at him. "You sit." She rose and opened the door.

Bardo was standing there, with several men behind him. "Sorry to disturb your supper, Captain, but we got a little problem."

"You're not disturbing me, Bardo." She stepped out of her cabin onto the main deck. The few men of the dark watch were standing around, watching her. She glanced up at the quarterdeck. Red Tom was at the wheel. He must have recovered from whatever ailment bothered him before. He wasn't alone—another deckhand, Charlie, was standing next to him, so close there was no space visible between the two. Tom squinted at her, the expression on his face a combination of dread and warning.

Kestrel spun to face Bardo again. The little man was grinning, his discolored teeth and pointy chin making him look even more like a rat than usual. "What's going on, Bardo? Is there a ship near?"

"No, Kes." Bardo jerked his head. Two men grabbed her arms, holding her tight between them. "The problem's you."

Twenty-six

An orphan's curse would drag to hell
A spirit from on high,
But oh! More horrible than that
Is the curse in a dead man's eye!

—SAMUEL TAYLOR COLERIDGE

Kestrel struggled against the two men, pulling against their grips and stomping at their feet. If only she hadn't taken her boots off. "What in blazes do you think you're doing?"

Over Bardo's skinny shoulder, Kestrel saw two more men leading McAvery from her cabin. He wasn't fighting them. Cold swept through her like a sudden blast of winter. Oh, gods, he wasn't struggling at all. Son of a flash-packet whore, but she'd been right about him. And she'd told him everything. Her gorge rose, threatening to spill out onto the decks. Binns's life, the ship, her own freedom, it was all gone, thrown overboard by her carelessness.

She looked up at Red Tom again. The man next to him had moved back a bit, enough for her to see the sharp blade poised to pierce Tom's kidney should he make a sudden move. McAvery was standing quietly between the two fellows who'd led him from the cabin, as if waiting for something.

She jerked against the restraining hands on her arms, not succeeding in loosing herself. "You slimy bilge rat. Binns trusted you. I trusted you!"

"Aye, Kes, you did." He chuckled, obviously enjoying himself. "That's what made this so easy. I can't tell you how funny it was, watching you looking over your shoulder all the time, suspecting every man but me. Don't blame yourself, though. You're only a lass, after all. Whoever heard of a woman in command?"

Those words, said in just the same way . . . it was so familiar. Not just the usual blather she'd heard for years about women being unlucky. Closer than that, more threatening. In a flash, it hit her where she'd heard the words before. McAvery was staring at her, his eyes intent. He seemed to recognize the instant she understood, tilting his head once in confirmation.

The voice he'd mimicked, the words he'd said . . . Bardo's. Of all the men on board, Bardo was surely one of the last she'd have ever thought would be the culprit. He'd worn such a good mask, kept his head down and his actions hidden. Deep in the nights, in the darkness of the lower decks, he must have been whispering his sedition to any man who'd listen. How long had he been waiting for this opportunity? Since long before they'd crossed paths with McAvery, apparently. The two of them could have made contact anytime, in any port. She reached for a thread, some connection between the two men, but it was too hard. Conspiracy had become an easy thing to blame, but this time it didn't make sense. Bardo had been with Binns for years before she came aboard. If he'd harbored resentment, it could have been festering for longer than she knew. Trouble was, she couldn't find an advantage for McAvery in Bardo's plan. He already had custody of the *Thanos*. The idea to chase him had been hers, not Bardo's. Neither ship had treasure aboard worth running off with. And she couldn't fathom McAvery doing anything that offered no profit for him.

"Damn you to the seven hells, Bardo. You and your friend McAvery."

Bardo's eyebrows flashed up. "He's no friend of mine. Just the lucky circumstance I needed. I figured on making my move after Binns retired at the end of this season, but this way it works out so much easier. He was a neat distraction for you. I get the ship and a tidy reward in the bargain."

"What reward?" she asked.

"For him, and for you." Bardo swept a melodramatic bow toward McAvery. "You, my fine fellow, are worth quite a pretty penny to certain interested gentlemen. And you, lass, are worth a king's ransom to a fellow I met back on Eldraga."

Kestrel's head spun. One minute she knew where she stood, what she was doing, whom she could trust. The next, friends were enemies and enemies friends. McAvery was still watching her, unsmiling. Bardo's threat to turn him over to the bounty hunters must have struck a sensitive nerve. Whatever she might have hoped, the mutiny was Bardo's alone. "You expect me to believe you?" she asked, knowing what his answer would be.

"I don't much care what you believe, Kestrel." Her name sounded small the way he said it. Had it only been a few days since she hadn't wanted to be called "captain"? Already she missed the word next to her name.

She glanced over the small crowd gathered around them. Ten or twelve in all, some grinning, some grave. Shadd wasn't among them, but she wasn't sure whether to be relieved or frightened at his absence. He'd been so angry before. He could be in his hammock, letting Bardo do the job he couldn't manage with his injuries. Or he could be bleeding his life out below.

The mutineers appeared to be all dark watch. Not a day man in sight. Except one, the one she'd expected to see. Dreso was amidships with another man, moving a water barrel across the deck. Unless she was mistaken, he was standing it on the hatch door that led below, blocking it. If anyone wanted to come up, the barrel would make it impossible.

"What have you done with Shadd, and the rest?" she asked, curious to hear what his explanation might be.

Bardo backhanded her. Not hard enough to knock her out, but enough to make a good show. The tender skin of the inside of her mouth split under the blow, and she tasted blood.

"You're in no position to ask questions." His high-pitched voice sounded so out of place spouting such tough talk. Kestrel glared at him, and he stared right back.

So not all the men aboard were in league with Bardo and his

bunch. Otherwise they wouldn't feel the need to imprison the day watch. If she could get free of these two fellows and move that barrel, maybe she could get out of this. It wasn't much to hold on to, but it was all she had.

Bardo pointed at her. "Tie her up, good and securelike. Him, too. Mind your knots, so Master Fancy-Face doesn't loose himself and rescue Captain Bedwarmer, eh?"

Boisterous laughter belled out from the gathered crowd. The two holding Kestrel began dragging her toward the mainsail mast. She kicked out at her captor's legs, connecting but not succeeding in tripping them.

"You might as well relax, Kestrel. It'll go easier. And you'll fetch a higher price if you ain't got no wounds on you."

She spat toward Bardo, but he was standing just out of her range. He glanced down at the dollop of shining spittle on the deck. "I should make you clean that up off my ship, bitch."

"Play your little game while it pleases you, Bardo," she growled. "But this will never be your ship."

Bardo snapped his fingers. The two sailors holding Kestrel's arms yanked her off her feet, slamming her against the tarred mainmast. Kestrel turned her face to the side a second before striking the wood. One man plastered himself over her back, holding her still with his body. The other grabbed her hands and pulled them around to hug the mighty wooden pole, tying her wrists viciously tight with a length of rope.

Hands slid in between her hips and the mast, fumbling with the latch on her sword belt. It came free, belt and sword clattering to the deck. She couldn't have reached her sword if she'd tried, in this position, but knowing it was out of reach made things seem somehow more hopeless. She struggled briefly with the knots around her hands, but they'd been well tied. The rough rope scraped her skin, threatening to shred it from her bones if she worked it too hard. The shoulder she'd injured days before protested the unnatural position, flaring with renewed agony. She choked back a groan and glanced left.

Dreso was pulling the knot tight on McAvery's hands. Leading him like a slave to market, the pirate threw the free end of rope up and over the lowest yard. He grabbed it on its return flight, pulled it taut, drawing McAvery's arms up and over his head and forcing him onto his tiptoes. Dreso tied off the free end and stepped away to join the small crowd of mutineers.

McAvery twitched his lips, seeing Kestrel still looking his way, and slowly, imperceptibly, let his feet drop flat to the deck. His arms pulled tighter above his head, but it seemed far less painful than being on his toes. Kestrel frowned. Something wasn't right about this. Even if McAvery had lifted high on his toes to buy himself some room to move, the usual practice was to pull until the captive was completely off the deck, swinging in midair. Why had Dreso stopped short?

"Tom," Bardo yelled, his whiny voice ill-suited to barking orders. "Bring us around on a new heading. I have an appointment on the north coast of Pecheta. And mind you, don't try anything, or Charlie's ready to bleed you where you stand." Kestrel felt the ship come about, her course changing. It wasn't Tom's fault—he had no more choice than she herself at this moment.

Bardo strolled close to Kestrel. Safe enough, she guessed, now that she was bound and helpless. He patted her back, and she winced from the light pressure.

"Did I hurt you?" He patted again, higher and harder. Sharp darts of pain shot through her muscles, but she bit her lip to avoid letting him see her react.

"Bardo," she said, using every ounce of control she had to keep her voice steady. "You have no love for me. That's your right. But what about Artie? If we change course now, we won't be in time to rescue him."

"True enough."

It was becoming difficult for her to breathe, pressed so tightly as she was against the mast. The stink of tar was burning her nose and mouth. "He doesn't deserve hanging. Not when you can prevent it."

Bardo's face reddened. "And what does Bardo deserve? I gave

Binns four years of service, stuck by his side through raids and storms, spilled blood and damn near starved one season. But what happens?" He slapped her rear, more familiar with her now that she was bound and weaponless. His tone knifed through the air between them. "You. Little barmaid spills a beer and suddenly it's farewell Bardo, hello my new quartermaster." He slammed the heel of his hand suddenly into the wood next to her face and leaned close. His breath stank of decay and old rum. "I should have been captain after him. And now, I will be."

She stared at him, her cheek beginning to ache where it kissed the tarred wood. He wasn't in league with McAvery. Jaeger hadn't told him why he was hunting her, only that she was worth money to him. Bardo didn't know what she was, beyond pirate and victim. Her secret was still hers.

Vengeful and angry Bardo might be, but his scheme went no deeper than that. He wanted to be in charge. Poor Bardo hadn't paid attention to anything else around him, being so focused on achieving the captaincy. He hadn't seen beyond the nose on his face. In his haste to take the ship from her, he hadn't bothered to sway the majority of the crew, and he hadn't dug deep enough to find the information that could have strengthened his hold on the *Thanos*. He must have assumed Burk and Volga would help him take care of any resisters. From what she'd seen of those two, they would likely have thrown Bardo over the side and sailed the *Thanos* away. But Bardo didn't seem to suspect that. She'd asked the gods for favors. Maybe this was their way of answering her prayers. Wasn't much, but it would have to suffice. The rest would be up to her to accomplish. If she survived this action, she promised herself a long, earnest chat with the gods about their ways, and her opinion of them.

McAvery was uncharacteristically silent. The muscles of his chest strained, pulling with every breath, but he managed to look perfectly at ease in his captivity. The situation was almost funny, in a demented way. The thief dangling by his hands, she hugging the mast like a lover. And Bardo, little rat-faced Bardo, the perfect ship's steward, harboring dreams of being a mighty pirate captain. If she weren't lashed nearly immobile, she might have laughed.

Bardo turned away from her, strutting across the deck to the ladder. She twisted her head around to watch him. He climbed up to stand next to Tom at the wheel, planting his hands on his hips and striking a pose that she thought must have been meant as jaunty but only looked ridiculous on his diminutive body. He wasn't quite as tall as the wheel itself. Kestrel found herself wishing he'd take a step closer and let the spokes whack him as they spun.

"Hssssttt."

She glanced back at McAvery. He'd finally stopped staring at her and was squinting over the darkening horizon.

"What?" she whispered.

He turned toward her, his face questioning.

"Any good ideas?" she persisted.

"You're the captain."

She rolled her eyes. "If you have nothing to say, why did you hiss at me?"

"I didn't." He flicked his gaze forward. "He did."

Dreso leaned against the rum cask a few feet away, picking at his fingernails with the end of a table knife. He appeared intent on the task before him, but suddenly he reached down and patted the barrel underneath him, then rattled the cup hanging on its side. As if he was signaling her.

She didn't want to trust him. He'd worked for McAvery without protest, and now he was in Bardo's group. Likely he wanted an excuse to ridicule her, but nothing had been as it seemed since they began this voyage. A little abuse from Dreso wouldn't make her situation any worse, and if he did intend assistance . . .

"Hey, Bardo!" she called, her voice hoarse with the proximity to the stinking tar on the mast. "I'm thirsty."

He stepped forward and leaned over the rail. "I don't serve you, girl."

"I won't fetch any price at all if I die of thirst."

Bardo sighed heavily, loud enough to be heard belowdecks. "If it'll shut you up. Dreso!"

The pirate sat up, as if startled by the shouting of his name. "Aye, Captain?"

"Give the captive a swallow of rum. Only a swallow, mind you."

He hopped to his feet and pried the lid off the small barrel. Dipping the cup, he brought it up dripping and stepped across to Kestrel.

"Drink, and listen to me," he whispered, putting the cup to her lips. She gulped gratefully, the rum burning a sweet path down her dry throat.

"He's got the day watch secured by yonder barrel. I s'pose they'll eventually chop their way through the ceiling, but it'll take a while. 'Specially since, far as I can tell, they ain't even noticed they're cooped up yet." With his free hand, he pulled gently on the ropes binding her wrists. "Who knows what state you'll be in by then? I figure I can move the barrel if you can keep Bardo's attention. Get this all taken into hand before morning."

"How am I to do anything in this position?"

"What kind of bosun's mate would I be if I couldn't work a knot one-handed?" He grinned. "Should be loose enough to get yer hands free."

She wiggled her wrists. Dreso was as good as his word—the rope was fairly falling away. Freedom was hers when she chose; a very good thing. But it meant nothing if she couldn't fight to keep it. "Where's my weapon?"

"Foot of the quarterdeck ladder. Still in its scabbard. You'll have to see to retrieving it yourself." He shot a look toward the quarterdeck. "I best be walking away now, afore Bardo notices."

"Dreso," she said urgently, "why are you doing this?"

"Binns is my captain. You're his second. If you're after saving him, I'm your man."

He stepped away, leaving her more confused than she'd been before. So Dreso was on her side. Or claimed to be. She refused to think too hard about her dilemma. Her hands were free. If she could get to her sword, she could take Bardo down. Anything more than that, she'd deal with when the time came.

He'd said her sword was next to the quarterdeck ladder. She struggled to turn her head far enough for a look. It was still in its sheath, belt hanging loose, and not guarded by anyone. Fifteen, maybe twenty steps. An easy run, if it weren't for the deckhands in between her and that ladder. Dreso needed a diversion to move that barrel, but who would make one for her?

A creak of rope close by caught her attention. McAvery had turned around to watch the activity on the quarterdeck. He inclined his head in her direction. "Retaking the ship, are you?"

"Be silent." Bad enough that she couldn't reach her weapon. If he kept talking to her, he'd draw the kind of attention she hoped to avoid. Instead of defeating the mutineers, she'd end up flogged. Or worse.

"I know a way you can get your hands on your sword."

"There's ten men know it, too, and stand ready to stop me."

"What an utter lack of imagination." He swung toward her, pivoting on the ball of his bare foot. "Anyone can make a suicide rush across the deck. But you . . ." Pursing his lips, he blew a low whistle and wiggled his eyebrows.

"I can't." No matter how bad the situation, it could only be made worse with the addition of magic to the mix. Especially magic wielded in untrained hands. Whistle a tune off-key, and the lines would tangle themselves, the sails flog themselves free of their yardarms. She shuddered at the thought. "Even if I wanted to."

"How do you know until you try?"

One of the men strolled close, a black leather cat-o'-nine-tails in one hand. Its tails were thick and ugly with dark rust-brown stains. It had been used before. "Shut yer gobs, or I'll have the skin off'n yer backs."

Kestrel turned her face away, McAvery's words echoing in her brain. Damn his black heart, why did he have to be right so much? One little whistle, a bit of luck, and she could have her sword. No Danisobans for miles. Only the mutineers to bear witness. If she won the day, no one would pay heed to the outlandish stories the defeated sailors would tell, of the pirate whose sword came to her with a whistle. If she wasn't successful, let the Danisobans come. None of it would matter.

She laid her head against the sticky mast, closing her eyes. *Mama,* she thought, *I did what you said. For twenty years, I've kept my head down and I've run. I've run so hard, so far. But I don't have any other way left. I can't run anymore. I have to save my ship.*

The sun was almost completely gone. Someone had lit lanterns; they swayed with the ship's rolling, casting eerie shadows. Up on the quarterdeck, Bardo was sitting on the railing, his stumpy legs swinging and making him look like a naughty child. He was singing some dreadful pub song in every key but the correct one, at the tops of his lungs. Dreso was busy at the rum cask, handing over cupfuls of liquor. Kestrel wondered if she could just wait out the night, let Bardo's fellows get so drunk they couldn't stand, then make her move.

"Well, hello, Kes, me darlin'," a drunken voice slithered out of the darkness next to her ear, so close she could feel the rum-warmed breath. A hand slid around her waist, teasing at the drawstring knot of her breeches. "I've had dreams of you in a position like this'n. Lucky me."

She couldn't see who was behind her, but Bardo had apparently noticed. His face split in a delighted grin. "Aye, Henry, why didn't I think o' that? We'll try her out." Climbing off the rail, he scurried to the ladder and stopped at the top. "He didn't say nothing about her condition. Long as we deliver her alive, I don't think the buyer'll mind us having a bit of fun."

Kestrel shot a glance toward McAvery. With Bardo's announcement, he'd suddenly started doing his best to tear the knots on his wrists loose, but unless he had something better than his nails, he wouldn't be able to do it. Just one more piece of the puzzle. He let them take him and truss him without a fight, but now that she was being threatened, he was determined to be the hero. Or so it appeared.

The man behind her pulled a length of her shirt out of her breeches and snaked his hand under, rising to cup her breast. He squeezed hard, and she gasped.

From the edges of her vision, she saw McAvery bend his elbows and jackknife his body backward, swinging in a wide arc. On the forward swing, he kicked, connecting with the man behind Kestrel. With a surprised grunt, the groping hands were gone. She heard the thud of a body hitting the deck.

Men began shouting and running. Bardo hurried down the ladder, screaming for someone to grab McAvery. He was kicking, trying his best, but he couldn't elude the grasping pirates. They dragged him to a stop, holding him still. Bardo marched to face him, grabbing the black cat from his crewman and bouncing it in his hands.

"Admirable, trying to save her virtue. Not that it's worth anything." The whip's tails cracked against McAvery's chest. He cried out, his eyes flashing fire. Bardo stepped behind him and let fly the cat again. McAvery arched his back under the blow.

They were going to kill him. Up until that moment, she hadn't feared for her life, nor anyone else's. Certainly not McAvery's. Then again, yesterday Kestrel wouldn't have guessed Bardo would even have the balls to wield a weapon himself. Or lead a group of men into mutiny. Yesterday there were so many things she wouldn't have believed possible.

"Take a last look." Bardo drew back his arm, and paused. "I'll bet I can make him even prettier with the kiss of my cat." He swung the whip in a slow circle over his head, lining up for a strike to McAvery's unprotected face.

She'd run out of time. Scoundrel and thief he might be, but if McAvery died, so did Binns. Flexing her biceps, Kestrel jerked her hands down and back, clear of the ropes. Her muscles protested at the sudden activity, twinging nearly into cramps. Shaking her arms out, she spun to face the quarterdeck.

Her sword had fallen over, lying half out of its sheath, tantalizingly far away. If she dashed to it, McAvery could lose his eyes. Or worse. *No other answer. It's the only way, Kes. Just try.* Reaching her hand out toward her sword, she pressed her lips together, and blew hard through them.

The tone was shrill, like a rusted nail being dragged out of old, warped wood. Her sword shook, working itself free of the sheath. She drew another breath, and blew again. This time the sword slid across the deck and lifted into the air. It was flying! She'd done it! She held out her hand to catch it, mightily pleased with herself.

Something hit her elbow a second before she noticed the cries echoing around her. A dagger clattered to the deck, followed by several more swords from every direction. She looked up, her eyes wide in surprise. Swords and daggers were working their way clear of their sheaths all over the main deck, to the amazement of the pirates. What had she done? She'd only meant for one sword to come, just one. Not the entire ship's complement. One man was gallantly trying to hold on to the blade of his sword, blood dripping down his arm as the weapon fought to get away.

Her own weapon slammed into her right hand with stinging force. A dagger zinged past her head. She ducked back and grabbed it out of the air, letting her momentum spin her around.

Henry was coming for her, breeches untied and hands outstretched. Put his hands on her, he had. Never again. Raising her blade, she skipped sideways and brought the sword down with all her strength, slashing both his arms as if they were butter. He fell back, shrieking, flailing and spraying blood.

Despite the confusion of blades flying loose and men shouting, Bardo still had hold of the cat. He threw his hand back and tensed for the downstroke. Kestrel strode the few steps forward brandishing her blade. The newly disarmed men holding McAvery's legs yelped at the sight of her, scrabbling away. Kestrel ignored them. She had to stop Bardo.

Slipping between the two men, she bent her left arm and blocked the whip. Bardo growled. She drew her sword back, shoving the point against Bardo's skinny belly.

"Drop it," she snarled. "Or my sword finds itself a new home."

Twenty-seven

With sloping masts and dipping prow
As who pursued with yell and bow
Still treads the shadow of his foe . . .

—SAMUEL TAYLOR COLERIDGE

Bardo hesitated, anger suffusing his face. There was no way he could win, not with her steel poised to slice him open, but for one endless second, Kestrel thought he might try to fight on principle.

Finally, he released the cat-o'-nine-tails. It tumbled from his hand and thudded to the deck. "Good. Lay down on your belly, with your hands behind your back."

He did as she ordered, dropping first to his knees and then stretching his body out, scrawny hands twisted behind him. Kestrel planted one foot on the small of his back and aimed her sword at the base of his neck. She glanced around.

The mutineers had all stopped, staring instead at Kestrel. She imagined she looked fearsome; hair half loose from her customary braids, blades in both hands and black slashes of tar decorating her face and clothing. Swords and daggers were littered over the deck in a rough circle at her feet. Dreso had crossed to the water barrel, shoving with all his might to get it clear of the hatch. Shouts and pounding from below were shaking the deck under her feet.

Up on the quarterdeck, Red Tom was turning the wheel, heaving the *Thanos* back onto her original course. Charlie was draped over the quarterdeck railing; dead or unconscious she had no idea. Tom must have had enough, taken care of the problem when all the fighting began. Kestrel waved at him.

"Tom, secure that wheel and come help Dreso."

He nodded. Slipping the becket over one of the wheel spokes, he hopped down the stairs and joined Dreso. Together they hoisted the barrel up onto one edge, rolling it away from the hatch.

The square door slammed open. Men surged through the opening, weapons drawn and yelling curses. And behind them, moving slow but sure, was a familiar blond head of shaggy hair. Shadd lumbered over to where Kestrel stood.

"What's going on, Captain?"

Kestrel nodded toward Bardo, lying quietly under her foot. "Nothing I couldn't handle. Bind his hands and secure him in the brig."

Shadd looked down at Bardo, swallowing back a chuckle. "Him?" He didn't wait for an answer. He reached up to the neck of his tunic and unlaced his lanyard. Bending down carefully, he lashed Bardo's hands tight with it, then yanked the small man to his feet. Kestrel sheathed her sword, but kept the dagger at the ready in her left, making sure Bardo could see it. She gripped his shoulder and squeezed. "Before I decide what to do with you, you're going to talk, little man."

He spat at her, but she jerked back in time to avoid being hit. Shadd thumped the back of Bardo's head with a meaty hand.

"Captain wants you to talk, boyo, then by the gods, you give her what she wants."

"I have nothing to say to her."

Kestrel tossed her dagger in midair, watching it spin. She caught it deftly and swung it down to Bardo's eye, waving the point back and forth. His gaze followed it. A bead of sweat rolled down his temple.

"I refuse to explain myself."

"That's fine with me," she said. "Y'see, Bardo, I've decided I don't care why you did it. Keep your reasons. What you are going to tell me"—she tapped the bridge of his nose with her dagger point, drawing it down and poking the nub of his nose gently—"is what deal you've made with the bounty hunters. Where, when, and how much."

"You think you can save your lover?"

"No, I think I can save my captain."

"You'll never arrive in time," he snorted.

"I'll be the one to decide when it's too late." She dragged the point over his cheek, blood welling in the shallow cut it left behind. "You might be wise to concern yourself with your own future. There's only one punishment for mutiny. But I'm within my rights to choose the method of your death." She came to a stop in the soft, delicate skin below Bardo's eye. "I hear it's a particularly painful way to die, with a knife in your brain. Blood and convulsions. Very nasty."

The little man was as still as stone. Only his eyelids moved, blinking furiously. "You wouldn't dare."

She pressed her dagger harder. "Try me."

For an endless moment, no one moved. As if time itself were waiting on what would happen next. Kestrel felt as if she'd sprouted roots that sank down far enough to wrap themselves around the keel of the *Thanos*. The men around her had become statues, their humanity betrayed only by the echoes of their stentorian breathing. She couldn't even feel the surge and roll of the waves. Everything had stopped, waiting for one little sailor to let go of the last vestiges of his grab at fortune's spinning wheel.

Finally she felt rather than saw his body slump in resignation. Good thing. She hadn't been looking forward to driving her dagger into his eye. Not because she was squeamish—she'd cut men before, when it was necessary. But killing him in that way would be messy, brains and blood shooting out all over. She palmed the dagger and slid it into her belt. Hanging was so much cleaner. She wondered when she had become so callous. But only for an instant. Moral considerations would have to wait until there was time to ponder them.

The hard edge Bardo had tried to affect was gone from his voice when he spoke. "They're waiting on the lee side of Pecheta, docked in a private harbor."

"Jeremie's estate," McAvrey murmured from behind her.

"How'd you get involved with them, Bardo?"

He shrugged. "I reported to the docks at sunup, like Binns told us, but the *Wolfshead* was already gone. I figured I was out of a job. I went back to the pub for a drink. Nothing better to do, aye? So I hear these fellas talking at the next table, about some pirate who'd escaped them. A woman, black-haired, slippery as an eel, but the only lead they had to find the man they were hunting." He chanced a glance at her. "It couldn't be anyone else but our Kes, could it? So I bought 'em both an ale and offered my services. They were overjoyed to cut me in on their deal. They got McAvery, and I got enough money to set myself up with a nice ship of my own."

They'd offered Bardo an irresistible chance. His ship was gone, the captain he'd hoped to succeed in chains, and his livelihood ripped from his fingers. Possibly he'd have found another ship to join, but he'd have been low man again, and he was a bit old to have to work his way up. That explained why he'd stayed on the docks even under the threat of the guards discovering him. He wasn't being brave or noble—he'd been paid, with the promise of more to come.

"But then, when I was waiting on the docks, this other fellow approaches me. Looks like he's been beat with sticks—leaves in his hair and dirt on his hands. Asks me if I've seen a woman with long black hair and no boots. He's willing to pay even more for her. I was supposed to say no to that?" He snorted. "Trouble was, I couldn't find him again before we rowed out to the *Thanos*. Figured I'd have to sail back to Eldraga and hunt him down later."

Kestrel glanced at her master gunner. "Shadd, I want all the men who were stupid enough to follow Bardo hobbled and tossed below. We'll maroon them as soon as our business on Pecheta is finished."

Marooning was as much a sentence of death as hanging. Each man would be dropped off on some deserted spit of land with a flask of water, a pocketful of biscuit, and a pistol with one bullet. Survival was possible, but extremely dubious. Shadd nodded grimly. "What about this one?" he asked, yanking Bardo's skinny arm.

"He hangs," she said, watching her captive as she said the words. He didn't panic or start fighting. He merely stood, with a tiny smile on his lips. "Sorry to ruin things for you," she said.

"You haven't ruined anything for me," he said. "I'm not finished yet." He raised his voice, not yelling, but loudly enough to be heard across the deck. "You thought you could get away with it, didn't you? Talked your big talk about hating magic, how the only good Danisoban is a dead one. You've given yourself away now, girl."

She raised an eyebrow quizzically. Before she could ask what he meant, Shadd backhanded him. "Stow that racket, little man. Nobody wants to hear your blather."

"You're a fool, Shadd," Bardo growled. "She's a witch. Everybody saw what she did. Kill her now before she does her magic on you."

"Magic? Lad, if ye'd said 'bitch,' I'd likely agree wi' ye," Shadd remarked, tossing a merry wink at Kestrel. She tried to return his grin, but her face had frozen. What was Bardo doing?

"Use your eyes, man." Bardo shook his head toward the weapons in their scattered circle. "She reached out her hand, made our swords fly out of their sheaths."

The men of the day watch were all on deck now, their weapons trained on the dark watch mutineers. At Bardo's words, the other mutineers all began nodding and shouting agreement. "'At's right!" "Jes' reached out her hand, she did, an' it came right to her!" "She's a witch!"

Kestrel paled. She'd been so stupid. How could they have missed a couple dozen swords flying through the air? Defeating one man hadn't been all that hard, but thirty . . . thirty was a war. One with an ending she knew she wouldn't enjoy. She inched her hand toward her weapon, breath tight in her throat as she waited for the onslaught to begin.

Bardo, still gripped in Shadd's hand, was smiling and calm. Damn him. He'd played her for a fool, to gather the ammunition he needed. He was smarter than she'd given him credit. Whether they believed her to be a witch or McAvery, Bardo had found the common enemy for the entire crew to fear. Not one of them was paying any attention to the villainy he'd attempted.

There was a long moment of uncomfortable silence. Why not, indeed? So much simpler, cleaner. Explain to the men who Binns really was, that he'd been in the employ of the crown for years. That they, in serving Binns, had been royal agents as well. If she did that, she wouldn't be the only one to die.

The crew, mutineers and loyal alike, were watching the tableau before them, their gazes hungry for blood. McAvery was watching, too, his face expressionless. And then it hit her, as suddenly as a broadside from a ship in a fog bank. What had worked for Bardo would work for her as well. He turned their attention away from the real problem. She could turn it back again.

"Listen to me, all you men." She squared her shoulders and planted her feet, trying for the most imposing position she could muster. "If it weren't for me, you'd all be sitting on Eldraga pissing and moaning about having no coin in your pocket to buy ale with." She drew her dagger, and tossed it end over end, catching it easily by the hilt. None of the men had moved. "But we never took the time to elect a new captain. Time's tight, but that doesn't excuse me from the articles we all signed when we joined up. So I offer you the choice. Follow Bardo, if you think he'll make a better captain. Don't forget, he could only best me by taking me unawares, and still couldn't keep me for long. And don't be surprised if your shares become smaller, and farther between."

Here and there, men were nodding, glancing at Bardo with glimmers of distrust. A low grumble began in the crowd. Good. She only needed to push them a little further.

"On the other hand, you have me. Most of you have known me two seasons now, some longer. You know how I work. I got you this fine ship. And how'd I manage that? Not by magic tricks and such, but by being the fastest sword. I brought you all this way to rescue one of our own, Artemus Binns. Did any of you ask what Bardo wanted out of his scheme?" She strolled toward the gathered mutineers. "Did he tell you? No? Bardo wants to sail away from Binns, let him die while he's giving the *Thanos* to a slimy pair of bounty hunters for the meager price of a small ship for himself. Himself." She smiled grimly. "I didn't hear him utter a word about the rest of you."

The grumble intensified, and the men shifted nervously. Bardo was watching her, his smug face crumbling slowly into fright. She speared his eyes with hers, ready to enjoy his misery.

"So there's your choice, lads. Bardo, if you want to take a heavy chance on having no ship at all by tomorrow. But if you want to see this to its end, and find yourselves swimming in brass enough to last the whole season, you'll do as I say. Without question."

The grumbling voices eased into interested murmurs. She waited, uncomfortably, while they talked among themselves. It was up to them now. If the decision went against her . . . she cast the thought away.

Shadd was gazing at her, his face changed. Not anger, but not satisfaction either. It was as if he'd only just noticed that she was an adult, instead of a child needing his protection, and though he was none too pleased, he had to accept what he saw. "I don't know about these others, Kestrel," he said, speaking loudly enough to be heard over the entire deck, "but I'm behind ye."

Slowly the interested murmurs became cries of support. Kestrel kept her face grim. Not the time for relaxing yet. But her heart thumped with delight. The crew was choosing her. She hadn't realized how much she feared their decision. Shadd nodded, spreading his hands in a fan before him. "So, Captain," he said, dragging the words out. "What's your orders, then?"

"Make for Pecheta with all due speed. Lee side. Put these men below until we finish our business."

"And him?" He shoved Bardo forward. The smaller man stumbled and fell to one knee in front of Kestrel. Even now, when all his cards had been trumped, he looked her full in the face. Dread flickered behind his eyes, mixed with the last bits of bravado he still had left. Maybe, if things had been different, Bardo could have been something more than a crewman on a tiny pirate ship. But things weren't different. Bardo was a small man who'd reached for too high a star and regret was a killer. She'd just have to hope that in his next life he'd carry the lesson with him.

Bardo was staring at her, pale and shaking. He seemed to know the second before she opened her mouth, and shook his head.

"No," he whispered. Pulling her shoulders back, she met his gaze and gave the order.

"Hang him."

Voices exploded, some in protest and others in cheers. Bardo's men scuffled with their day watch captors, but were easily subdued. Shadd reached down, grabbing Bardo by an elbow and dragging him amidships to where two men were busily looping a noose.

She'd never ordered a man's death before. Queasiness rose in her throat. No choice. Mercy might be a virtue, but on board her ship, it could only be a liability. Even knowing that, her order sickened her. She couldn't watch the preparations, but neither could she let on that her stomach was twisting in nauseous cramps.

Kestrel turned on her heel and marched instead over to where McAvery was still bound. She reached up to the tied-off end of his rope and sawed at it with her dagger until it snapped. McAvery's arms dropped.

"Aahhh," he sighed. "That feels so much better."

Kestrel pointed the dagger at his chest. "I appreciate the help. Do it again, I'll gut you."

"I didn't do anything." A tiny smile played at the corners of his lips. "Though you have to admit it saved your"—he winked—"skin."

Damn his eyes. He'd forced her to use the magic skill she'd denied all her life, and now he wanted her to thank him for it? If it took the rest of her life, she was determined to be the one to leave with the last word. "You're free for now. If you want to stay unbound, keep your mouth closed, your head down, and your tricks to yourself."

He bowed his head obediently. "As you wish, Captain." He sank to the deck, legs crossed, massaging his shoulders.

"Captain!" Kestrel turned toward the call.

A rope had been thrown over the lowest yardarm of the mainmast, and the loose end tied off. At its other end someone had tied a noose. Shadd held it open, while Jaques and Angus forced a bound but struggling Bardo forward. As soon as he was close enough, the big gunner slid the loop of rope over the smaller man's head and tightened it securely. Bardo stopped fighting. He looked suddenly pitiful, visibly trembling, and the mask of bravado he wore was now laced with threads of fear. He'd hardly have been human if he wasn't afraid of what was about to happen to him. Knowing death was at hand, with no way to avoid it . . . she wondered if she'd be strong enough to face a hangman standing on her feet. Kestrel dredged the memory of how he'd talked to her, how he'd treated her, and planted the image firmly in the forefront of her mind. No room for sentiment now.

"Any last words, Bardo?"

"Yeah." He drew a deep breath, then raised his head. Fire blazed in his expression, and he spat with the force of his words. "I'd do it again right now. Any man who follows a woman into battle is a fool who's still hiding under his mama's petticoats." He chuckled, a cold, bloodless sound. "You ain't my captain. Hang me, but you still won't make me do as you say. I'll be looking up at you from the seven hells, and the last thing you hear before they take you down will be me laughing."

Kestrel glanced behind Bardo. Angus and Jaques had hold of the rope and were watching her carefully, waiting for her to give the signal. She raised her right hand. The two men's arms tensed on the rope they held.

"That's right, you'll hear me laughing while they cut you to pieces and take your lovely ship—"

She dropped her hand in the middle of his tirade. Her men pulled, using their bodies' weight to drag Bardo off his feet and into the air. She wouldn't turn away, couldn't. She stood, still as a marble statue, while Bardo's struggling slowed. She could almost feel the tearing of the rope fibers on her neck, the unbearable tightness as her body was starved of air. While she watched, she imagined it was her body in the noose. It very nearly had been.

Twenty-eight

Fly, brother, fly! More high, more high!
Or we shall be belated.
For slow and slow that ship will go . . . .

—SAMUEL TAYLOR COLERIDGE

K estrel split the night into half watches, to let the exhausted
men she had left get at least part of a night's rest. Dreso and
Jaques hustled the mutineers below, but they didn't cause the two
pirates any trouble. The fire had burnt out of them as soon as
Bardo quit kicking.

McAvery moved back to his usual spot by the quarterdeck ladder and was sitting on the deck leaning against the railing. Kestrel
finished arranging the watches, spoke for a moment with Shadd,
then approached McAvery.

He nodded, smiling pleasantly. "All's well that ends well, yes?"

Kestrel waved a hand toward Bardo's body. It swung in the night
breeze, the rope creaking out a gruesome rhythm, the shadow
falling over her face as it broke the plane of the lanterns' light. "It's
over for him. Not for us. We still have work to do. We'll be off
Pecheta by daybreak. I want to sit down with Shadd, Tom, and you,
and discuss the best way to handle this."

He widened his eyes. "A plan? Captain! I thought you wor-
shipped the gods of capriciousness."

Kestrel aimed a kick at him. He grabbed her bare ankle. The
shock of his touch nearly threw her off balance. She tensed her leg,
then thrust her foot forward, hard, catching him in the chest and
pushing him back against the railing. Leaning into her foot with all
her weight, she crossed her arms on her upraised knee. "I'm tired

of your banter. You don't think much of me, of the way I've handled this mission so far. That's your right, but I don't have to hear about it. From this moment, I expect you to keep your opinion to yourself."

"You may not want to hear it," he said, his voice sounding labored under the pressure of her foot, "but you'd do well to listen. Every leader needs a dissenting voice."

"Had one." She shrugged one shoulder backward. "Didn't like what it said, so now it's decorating my rigging."

"Yes, you're very fierce. Bloodthirsty pirate captain, don't cross her or you'll end up dangling."

"Glad to hear my message is coming through."

He rolled his eyes impatiently. "Dissent can be a useful thing. Show you your options."

She laughed bitterly. "Even if it weren't against the code under which we sail, I couldn't allow disagreement. It's another word for suicide."

McAvery coughed, as if trying for breath. "It's not as if your crew is going to argue with you, especially not now."

"Then what are you trying to say?"

"Don't you remember being the voice of reason to your beloved captain, whenever you thought he was being an idiot?"

"Binns was never a—" she began, and stopped. A sudden image rocked her, of wet hair in her eyes, wind and darkness and torn sail flapping above her. And her own words spilling out: *We're in no condition to take a ship . . . what if he's not some fop?* She'd never thought about how she must have sounded. Had she grated on Binns's nerves the way McAvery did on hers? Impossible. Binns had to know she only argued with him because she cared about him. Didn't he?

Without waiting for another word from McAvery, she strode to her cabin door, yelling over her shoulder as she went. "Shadd! To me, now."

Shadd crooked a finger at Red Tom and lumbered across the deck to join Kestrel at her cabin door.

"The dark watch is secured below, Captain," he said. "And Angus is on the wheel."

"Good." She hesitated, glancing back. McAvery had resumed his contemplation of the night sky, but this time she knew his disinterest was feigned. No matter how annoying he could be, she had to admit he was more experienced at this game than she was. As satisfying as it would be to leave him out of things, she couldn't afford to.

"Bring him along."

"What for?" Shadd snorted. "We goin' to use him as a footstool?"

McAvery was a greater thorn in her side than she could have imagined. She feared that she'd want to kill him if she caught his eye again. And this time, in spite of the sweetness of his kiss and the lure he offered, she couldn't think of one solid reason why she shouldn't.

"Just bring him," she said.

"WHAT'S wrong wi' that flower o' yers?" Shadd grimaced.

The bulge in the little potted plant had grown, and seemed ready to explode if they bumped the table. The thin bark that covered its branches was separating, revealing vague glimmerings of red in the spaces between. She wondered for a moment if the plant would bleed if it were pierced, and cast the thought aside.

"Never mind about that," she told him, indicating with a wave of her hand that he and the rest should sit. Shadd and Tom pulled up chairs and sat around the table, but McAvery stood back and leaned against the bookshelves, his arms crossed and his face inscrutable. Kestrel chose to ignore him; he'd draw attention soon enough.

Red Tom reached out to stroke the broad green leaf nearest him. "What's your plan, Captain?"

Kestrel took her own seat. "I trust the two of you. I hope you know how much."

Shadd and Tom looked at each other, then both turned their gaze to McAvery, who shrugged.

"So I'm going to be honest with you. I don't see any other way to accomplish what we have ahead of us. You need to know that some of what I'm about to tell you, you're not going to like."

"I already don't like him bein' here," Shadd grumbled.

Kestrel nodded. "I appreciate you being here anyway." She took a deep breath. "A lot of what Bardo said was right. Binns is being held by Prince Jeremie, on his private estate."

"So ye plan to bust him out? Raid the house and snatch him like a brick of Continental gold?" Shadd pounded one fist into the opposite hand with a satisfied smack. "I like it."

"No good," McAvery drawled. "If it could be accomplished that easily, you could just wait outside for Binns to walk out on his own. Word is Jeremie keeps a dungeon underground, one way in, easily defensible."

Shadd's face clouded. "We missed our chance at waylayin' the ship at sea, before it puts in to the harbor. 'Cause we stopped to chase this bastard," he spat the word, venom in his tone, "instead of lettin' him drown with the sloop he stole." He pushed back from the table and rose, his fists clenched, and leaned ominously toward McAvery. "I have to wonder why he's even in here."

McAvery was inspecting his fingernails, utterly ignoring Shadd's threatening posture. Kestrel stepped between the two men before Shadd could get too close and do something he'd regret. Especially since the regret would have been hers alone; her gunner wouldn't shed a tear if McAvery dropped dead at his feet.

"I'm not ordering you to trust him. Hell, I don't trust him myself," she admitted. "We're sea folk, you and I, Shadd. We charge into battle face forward, swords up and guns blazing. What we're up against now is like a hand of cards in a port where we don't speak the language. It's as Olympia told me. For this sort of game"—she tightened her jaw, despising the need to say it and prove McAvery right yet again—"we need someone who knows the rules on Pecheta, who plays the game as easily as he breathes."

"What are ye sayin'? McAvery's from Pecheta?"

"Yes. He's an agent of the king. They call him the Knave."

Tom snorted. "He's a knave, for sure."

"What guarantee do ye have that he isn't playin' the game right now?" Shadd's ruddy cheeks were darkening, and storm clouds brewed behind his eyes. "They could be waitin' for us this minute, ready to take us into custody. What a party that'll be! All them nice noble families comin' down to the docks with their picnic baskets to watch the pirates hang! Courtesy of that fine upstandin' citizen, Philip McAvery!"

He was holding his side, laboring to breathe after the exertion of shouting, but Kestrel wasn't fooled. She'd seen him in battle countless times, fighting when he should have dropped long before. His stubborn streak was one of the things she'd always admired about him. Lucky thing she was just as obstinate. She speared his glare with her own. "Fine—I was going to break it gently, but what the hell . . . Binns was doing a job for the king. He was working with McAvery until this blasted prince got involved. McAvery works with us until I say he doesn't. The question now is, do you?"

The big gunner didn't move, but her words had struck as sure as an arrow. The redness in his cheeks faded. He finally dropped his eyes and sank, anchor-heavy, into his chair. His voice, when it came, was subdued. "Aye, Captain. I'm still wi' ye."

"Good. I can't do this without you."

Tom cleared his throat. "What is it, exactly, you're goin' to do, Captain? Beggin' your pardon, but between what we know and what McAvery says is true, it don't seem like we got much in the way of options."

She sighed, and sat down herself. Her shoulder was still aching from the binding earlier, and her feet were cold. Hunger gnawed at her belly like a burrowing creature wanting out. The food Bardo had brought to her remained on the table, enticing and repulsive at the same time. She couldn't bring herself to put it to her lips. A sudden hankering for salt fish swept over her, and she nearly laughed at the senselessness. Salt fish, that Binns loved. Loves, she corrected herself. He isn't gone yet.

The men were waiting for her to say something, anything. Even McAvery. She was their captain now, through blood and mutiny. It was her word Shadd would support, but at that moment, she couldn't find one word to offer him.

"Captain? May I make a suggestion?" McAvery interrupted.

The three pirates looked at each other. Kestrel finally nodded.

McAvery clapped his hands together, rubbing them vigorously, and stepped forward to the table. "What you want to accomplish can't be done in the old-fashioned way. Swords and fire and starving them out, that's the stuff of the old days, when the Islands were no more than tribal strongholds."

"Flingo Naile did it," Shadd muttered.

McAvery swung around, his face beaming. "Exactly my point! It's already been done, more times than can be counted. The guard will be expecting that sort of attack. Blazes, they'll be looking forward to it, since it's exactly the kind of thing they've been trained to overcome. Even if you and your crew march in and somehow manage to rescue your captain that way, it would just be the same old thing that Flingo Naile and other pirates of long ago did before. Where's the glory?"

"I don't need glory," Kestrel said. "Just rescuing him is enough." The hairs on the back of her neck were beginning to prickle with apprehension, although she wasn't sure why. Whatever point McAvery was coming to, she had a bad feeling she wasn't going to like it.

"Nothing about this adventure of yours has been usual. So we should go with the flow of it, let the wave of glory take us where it wills. When all ordinary avenues have been exhausted, one should try for the extraordinary."

Gooseflesh rose on her arms. McAvery's eyes were sparkling in the mischievous way she knew too well. Intuition screamed at her to stop him from speaking. Hit him, kiss him, run him through with a sword, the method didn't matter as long as he kept his idea to himself. Because she knew, with a certainty as heavy as the trumps of doom, what he was about to suggest.

Kestrel half rose from her seat, intent on shutting him up, but before she could say anything, Shadd asked, "What do you mean by 'extraordinary'?"

She sank down with a groan that none of them seemed to notice. None but the golden-haired thief. A smirk crossed McAvery's lips. "Exactly what you think, master gunner. Magic."

She braced herself for the onslaught. If McAvery was lucky, Shadd would only cut his throat. The possibility also existed for him to stuff the man down the barrel of one of the cannons and fire him across the horizon.

To her amazement, Shadd seemed neither angry nor frightened. His face grew thoughtful, and he rubbed at his jaw. "I thought you weren't no Danisoban."

"I'm not. Care to shrive me? I'll offer my confession on this point at least." He leaned in close, as if offering his sins to a mendicant priest.

"Shut your mouth, McAvery," Kestrel murmured.

"Up against a real Brother, I'll run like anyone else. But in front of innkeepers, gamblers, and even fine seagoing folk like yourselves, I know enough to pass for one of the Brethren. Enough to get inside the palace, arrange the release of your captain, and escape before the guard takes notice."

Once more, the big gunner shocked her with his calm. He finally nodded, his shaggy hair bouncing. Tom was still for a moment, as if considering the plan, but finally he also nodded. McAvery rubbed his hands together again in satisfied pleasure.

"Hold on one bloody second, the three of you!" Kestrel exploded. "It's all well and good that you boys have come to terms, but nobody does anything until I say they can."

The men started, as if they'd forgotten she was even in the room until that instant. Shadd pulled himself up straight, grimacing.

"Sorry, Captain. We was gettin' ahead of ourselves, looks like."

"Damn right you were." She sat back down, glaring at the three of them. "Magic is out of the question. The mission can't be fulfilled that way."

Shadd interrupted. "Beggin' yer pardon, Captain?"

"What?" she asked, her voice a bit sharper than she'd intended. It wasn't Shadd's fault that McAvery was being an ass, but she couldn't help herself.

"It occurs to me that he's got a good point." He ducked his great head and looked at her from under the fallen hair, innocent as a child. "I mean, the Danisobans is bad and all, but he ain't suggestin' we go to them. The opposite, to my mind. He wants us to use their own devices against them. It's his fault our captain got snatched and our boat sunk, so why not make him use up what he's got before we dig into what we have?"

Shadd meant what he was saying. She looked to Tom; he nodded in silent agreement. Their superstition was being overcome by their pragmatism. She couldn't very well keep arguing without looking like a frightened girl. Shadd was willing to give over his instincts against magic. No Danisobans would be involved. This could all turn out fine. Or it could end up a ragged, bloody mess.

"Because it isn't what he has that he's proposing we use." She hated the look of triumph in McAvery's eyes. "It's what I have. What I am."

Shadd laughed. "What ye are? Ye're a pirate, lass."

Kestrel shook her head, staring at the table. "That's not all I am."

The big gunner squinted at her. "What're ye tryin' to say, Kes?"

Two years. She'd managed to forget it all for two years, sailing with a pirate crew. She supposed she should be grateful for hiding it that long. Nothing went away forever.

"I was abducted back on Eldraga. Fellow named Jaeger put me in a safe house and was going to fetch the Danisobans to pick me up. He was on the docks when we sailed. I don't know who he's told about me. Who might be waiting on Pecheta for the first signs of . . ." She raised her head and looked Shadd in the eye. "I'm a Promise. I can make magic. And the Danisobans know who I am."

The silence in the room was thicker than week-old soup. Shadd was staring at his hands. Tom crossed his arms and leaned back in his chair, eyes lowered. McAvery could have been asleep, he was so still. Except for the dark fire in his eyes, watching her.

"Why didn't ye tell me, girl?" Shadd's voice was a whisper, almost too low to hear. "I'd have kept yer secret."

She reached out to his hands, laying hers over them. "I thought I was protecting you."

As the words left her mouth, she heard Binns's voice in her head. *There's information in there could get you killed, Kes.* He hadn't shared the most important things in his life, and look where it got him. She'd been so angry at him for keeping secrets, yet here she was, doing the same thing.

Kestrel pounded the table, and all three men jumped. She laughed out loud at the startled faces staring back at her. "I can do magic! It's not like I can do it well. Bloody Grace and all her nephews, I've managed to splash water in one man's face, hang another from a tree branch, and fling a couple dozen swords across the deck. That's all, so far. Hardly a record to inspire fear in anyone."

McAvery snickered, and Tom let a tiny smile curve across his face.

"But that's what I am! And what I need to rescue my friend. If you"—she pointed her finger at McAvery—"can give me an idea of how to use my talents to do that, then the gods bless you. If not, I'll do it with my sword." She stopped, breathless, her heart slamming. "So, who's with me?"

Twenty-nine

It raised my hair, it fanned my cheek
Like a meadow-gale of spring—
It mingled strangely with my fears
Yet it felt like a welcoming.

—SAMUEL TAYLOR COLERIDGE

H ard to imagine those ships can float."

"Yup." She'd done her best to avoid conversation with McAvery, but his observation was dead on. The majority of ships that entered and left Pecheta harbor were ostentatious in the extreme, painted in gaudy colors and enhanced with gold and silver where normal ships used iron and lead. Sails sporting intricate, colorful embroideries fluttered and billowed above the decks. They glittered under the red evening sun, looking more like circus transports than anything else.

"If this is how the nobility prefers to live, I think I'll stay with my way."

She bit her lip. He could talk all he wanted, but she wouldn't let him drag her into a friendly chat. Once, when she was a child, someone had advised her never to fall in love with the stray animals that occasionally attached themselves to people. The day might come when that pet was all that stood between herself and starvation. McAvery was just like those strays. He was a tool, nothing more, she reminded herself. Not a friend, not a lover, not even a person. He was along to make sure she got inside and retrieved her captain. Once she had Binns safely in her grasp, she wasn't looking back. McAvery's mission would be his own problem, then.

The sun was setting, staining the waves rust-gold and purple as they sailed past the entrance to the main harbor that served

Pecheta. The rich and powerful owned land all over the Nine Islands—plantations here, farms there, businesses in between, but nearly every noble family preferred to live on the shining streets of the richest island of all. Their beautifully constructed homes crowded as close to the palace as possible, reminding Kestrel of a group of courtiers jostling for position around the throne.

She'd heard it said that when a man offended the Ageless King, he could find himself evicted from his elegant home before sunset. If the offense was not too severe, he might be relocated into a smaller, poorer house farther out from the center of society. The unlucky ones, those who committed truly unforgivable social gaffes, got the rare opportunity to experience the charm of mud-stiffened clothes and hunger so strong dead rats looked tasty. She didn't know if the tales were true. It certainly seemed unlikely that a place as wealthy as Pecheta could have beggars, but the possibility was enough reason to be glad she lived on the ocean. Bad enough to have the roof over your head dependent on the whims of a spoilt, helpless idiot whose power only derived from the good fortune of being born from the womb of a queen.

She focused on the monumental arch carved from white marble that stood majestically guarding the ornate ships sailing in and out. A guard station was carved out of the apex, uniformed men strolling past the glass window that fronted it. Along both sides of the arch, richly dressed sentries climbed continually up and down the steps, greeting each other as they passed and generally making the arch look less like a strategic defense and more like the centerpiece of a strange floating soiree. She could imagine musicians in royal livery arranged up and down the expanse of the arch, while servers balancing trays of dainties tossed their treats to the finely dressed guests sailing back and forth below. Would the cannons installed at the top of the arch actually shoot ammunition at invading marauders, or would brightly colored fireworks explode out in welcome?

After her outburst in the cabin, she wouldn't have been surprised if Shadd had picked her up and lobbed her over the side. Instead, he'd given her a look of such pride, it had almost brought tears to her eyes.

"That's my girl," was all he'd said, before they gathered around the table to try to formulate a plan. She still wasn't sure it was going to work, but for the first time in her life, she didn't feel alone.

A few miles out, she'd struck the tone fork, the curtain of glittering magic falling around their ears and cloaking them in invisibility so that they could sail around to the lee side of the island without being noticed.

The estate dock was shockingly plain. A simple wooden walkway stretched out into the deep water, and two guards walked up and down at intervals. The walls of a huge home rose past the thick tree line, warm lights flickering in the windows. Kestrel ordered the ship to drop anchor some way past the main approach, and assigned Hudee to strike the tone fork every hour until Shadd told him to stop. Shadd and Tom were left in charge of the ship, with orders to sail away if she wasn't back with Binns by dawn. Shadd hadn't liked it, but he had to agree there was no other way. His wound was still too fresh for him to risk a fight.

Once complete darkness fell, she'd gone to her cabin, stripped to the skin, and used bandage gauze to bind the heavy logbook to her back. It was unlikely she'd see the man Lig here, in the prince's stronghold. But Binns had said the book was his only chance, and she didn't want to miss any opportunities.

She and McAvery had climbed into a longboat to be rowed to shore. She'd only looked back once, shuddering at the disorienting feeling of knowing that there was a ship where none could be seen.

"Don't you think it would be wiser to unchain me, at least for the space of the rowing?" He jingled the manacles at his wrists in emphasis. "If I were to fall out, I'd sink right to the bottom of the bay."

"Don't tempt me."

He leaned back against the gunwale, propping his shackled feet up and resting his chained hands in his lap. The plant sat next to him. "About this bounty hunter you're afraid of. Is he a Danisoban himself? A Factor?"

"I don't know. But he told his masters about me. Once we get Binns back, I'll have to stay onboard ship from now on. It's the only place I'm safe."

"Unless he's an ordinary person. Or someone special, like you."

"How did you know about me?"

He shrugged. "Everyone knows what a Danisoban safe house is."

What else did everyone know that she didn't? It was frustrating to feel so stupid about the world she lived in.

"You escaped even though you were dunked in salt water. Makes you special. I can guess why the Brotherhood would pay well for you. If they knew you were in possession of the sanguina, they'd be pissing themselves to lay hands on you both."

She wasn't sure even now that she believed in the supposed power of the sanguina. Men had been searching for ways to hold on to their youth forever. Spells and potions, bathing in hot springs or soaking in vats of crushed ice. There were as many ways to prolong youth as there were people in the Nine Islands. Not one of them worked. If it was truly what McAvery claimed, she could easily see how men would kill to get their hands on such a thing. Kingdoms could fall over the power inherent in the sanguina.

"McAvery. Answer me a question. The king. How old is the man, anyway?"

He pursed his lips in concentration. "He's eaten the sanguina fruit once, when he was well past middle age. Perhaps a hundred years old."

Kestrel couldn't imagine living long enough for her joints to start aching in bad weather, much less over a century. Too long for her, but she'd never hoped to live forever. "What happens if he doesn't get to eat the fruit this time?"

"I'm not sure. I assume he'll start aging normally."

"The Ageless King getting old." She shook her head. "That would be something to see."

She fixed her gaze on the dock, looming closer with each oar stroke. All this trouble could only come from the political scheming of men with too much money and leisure time. Not that it made any difference to her who the king was. She'd be outlaw no matter who sat upon the throne. The trees that lined the dockside area stood black against the midnight-blue of the evening sky, shadow-faced monsters waiting to devour her whole the second she set foot on Pecheta's shore. Let them. Any fear she'd been wrestling with up to now was cast aside, replaced by a cold determination. Men or monsters, she was ready to bleed anyone who tried to stand between her and Binns. Let the Pechetans play their political games as they would, but only as long as they stayed out of her way.

McAvery stayed quiet for the remainder of the trip to shore, but Kestrel could feel his eyes staring holes into her. She'd kept him at arm's length since that dreadful evening in her cabin. She felt a twinge of guilt at the memory. She knew better than to let her body rule her like that. As quartermaster, she hadn't had the luxury of choosing a lover among the crew, for fear of being influenced against any orders the captain might offer. As the only woman aboard, it had been a matter of safety.

But now, as captain, she had even less freedom in that respect. The heat McAvery awoke in her was tempting, seductive, but she would keep her head. He wasn't worth the risk. No matter how fast her blood pounded when he gazed at her.

Kestrel directed her rowers to drop them at the darkest stretch of beach. Once the hull scraped against the sand, Kestrel reached over with a key to unchain McAvery's hands.

"Ah," he sighed, rubbing his wrists. "Sweet freedom."

They made their way through the trees. From the water, it had appeared to be a wild forest, but once within its darkness, it was obvious the trees had been planted deliberately. The ground was flat and easily traversed. Without the usual fallen logs and ground cover, it was not a real forest at all.

Before long, McAvery led Kestrel from the tree line into a shadowed alley between two looming stone walls. The rich fragrance of night-blooming flowers, wafting from the gardens beyond, filled her senses. The tight alley was paved in flatstone, and cleaner than some pubs she'd eaten in, she thought with a tiny pang of jealousy. "This is as good a place as any," he announced. "Are you ready?"

"As I ever will be." She didn't tell him how her stomach was twisted in knots of apprenhension, nor how she felt faint at the thought of letting the magic in. She pushed away the niggling worry. "What do I do first?"

"It's easier than you'd guess," he said with a wink. "Certainly easier than that whistling trick you did back on board the ship."

"You mean the trick you forced me into." She gripped the hilt of her sword, whitening her knuckles with the effort of not drawing it.

"I was merely encouraging." He waved a nonchalant hand. "We can argue semantics later. Close your eyes. You can do this."

Panic fluttered within her like moths.

"It's easier to visualize when your eyes are closed. But if you'd rather end up with Burk's head and Volga's legs . . ."

She sighed. If nothing else about him was true, he did know more about magic than she did. If they were to pull this ruse off, she was going to have to do it his way.

She let her eyes slide closed. The flowers' scent assailed her again, sweet like old honey. Silence reigned in the darkness. For a moment, she wondered how the people who owned these gardens could stay indoors—if they were hers, she'd wander them all night in the moonlight.

"Now picture Burk and Volga." McAvery's voice broke into her pleasant thoughts. "Remember the last time you came face-to-face, and try to recall as much detail as you can. The color and texture of their hair, their body shapes, but also small things. The snake-shaped mole on Volga's neck, or the way Burk's skin burns when he stays out in the sun."

Kestrel thought hard, bringing to mind the first night she saw them, dicing in the pub, shrouded in their dark cloaks. Then the next day with scowls on their sleep-bleary faces. And later that dreadful morning, in the alley, holding her at bay with bloodlust gleaming on their faces.

"Now, do you have a good recollection of how they look? Is one clearer than the other?"

"No, those are two faces I've got securely memorized."

"Good. That helps. You'll be Burk. He's the shorter of the two, closer to your own height, so you won't have to concentrate on too much for your first time."

"First and last time."

"Fine, as you say. Get a solid image of Burk's face in your mind. Color of his hair, shape of his features. When you've got it as clear as you think you can, nod."

She let the memory of the disgusting man fill her mind. Greasy hair, falling in skinny locks over watery eyes, wide nose laced with broken veins. Narrow shoulders, sun-reddened cheeks on skin that was too fair to ever tan. She nodded, once.

"Now start singing."

They'd agreed on a tune the night before, one she knew and could hum easily. She hadn't believed him when he tried to convince her she was capable of something like this.

"You're more than an ordinary Promise. Surely you've suspected it," he'd said. She'd found herself agreeing. Salt water weakened a Danisoban, but it had never bothered her. She could swim in it, even. McAvery had guided her through the process of what they planned, and they'd spent hours practicing until she could make it last a good while. She was different, this proved it. But if she wasn't just a Promise, what did that make her? And would the Danisobans leave her alone now, or want her more? Questions she'd have to deal with later, once she finished the night's work.

She sang softly, the gentle tune in direct opposition to the ugly picture in her mind's eye. Tingling raced along her limbs, electric sparkles that teased her skin. After a verse, McAvery took her right hand in his. His fingers were warm. "You can open your eyes now."

She blinked. "It's done? Already?"

"As if you were born to this sort of thing."

His good looks were gone. Where before he'd been a handsome

rogue, now there stood a broad-built thug, nearly hairless, with several front teeth missing. Scars crisscrossed his cheeks, and his hands were thick-fingered and clumsy. A snake-shaped mole crawled near his ear.

"McAvery?" she asked.

"Good job." He leaned back, one hand cupping his chin as he scrutinized her. "I have to admit I prefer you the other way."

She glanced down at her body. Same breeches, same booted feet, even the same hands. Female hands. As far as she could detect, she hadn't changed at all. He'd assured her the night before that the spell over them both would last until she released it by singing the tune again. "Are you sure? I can't tell a difference."

"You can't see the illusion on yourself. Only those looking at you will see it. Trust me. You're damned ugly right now."

Instead of lurking in shadows, McAvery led her straight down the walks in full view. Kestrel was apprehensive at first, until she realized that there were no patrolling guards wandering by. All this wealth and not a swordsman in sight. Her instincts flared into life.

"You know, a man can tell exactly what you're thinking by the look on your face."

"Arrogant bastard. There's not a man living knows the first bit of what a woman is thinking."

"Never truer word was spoken," he said. "But in this instance, I think there's an exception."

They were passing a brick wall, taller than McAvery's head. Kestrel ran her hand along it, enjoying the velvety softness of old moss and damp brick. "Fine. What was I thinking?"

"No patrols in the paths, because there's no need." He gave her a funny half smile. "Your fellows wouldn't last past the dock."

"You don't know my men."

He shrugged, and motioned her along to the corner they were approaching. "It's a more impressive sight in the daylight," he said, pointing.

Standing in front of it now, Kestrel's breath caught. Enormous walls, carved of rare blue marble mined only on the Continent, towered above the cobbled pavement, splitting into delicate towers that pierced the night sky. Light streamed from stained-glass windows, illuminating the walk below in rainbows. Directly ahead were looming silver doors, tall enough to admit a tall man astride a warhorse without making him duck his head, protected by an immense iron portcullis. Between the doors and them was the porter's shed, a small building that housed the one person who decided which petitioners entered and which were left on the street. Warm candlelight flickered from within.

"Come along," McAvery murmured, wiggling the plant. "We have an appointment." Walking across the cobbles, McAvery rapped at the porter's window.

"A moment, a moment only, please," came a voice from inside. The wooden shutters swung open, revealing an old man. "May I be of assistance to you gentlemen?" he asked.

"The prince is waiting for us."

"It's very late, though. Most of the house is asleep. Who did you say you're here for?" the porter asked, blinking.

McAvery hefted the plant in one hand and rested an elbow on the sill. "I think you know who I'm here to see."

His sleepy manner instantly vanished. "Of course. Please advance to the portcullis." Straightening, he disappeared from the window, the shutters clicked closed. McAvery stepped forward, and Kestrel hurried to join him.

"Master porter knew what he was seeing when I showed him the plant, so Jeremie has alerted him to its arrival. Either way, we're in good shape, wouldn't you agree?"

Kestrel grabbed his sleeve. "We could be walking into a trap."

There was a heavy metallic squeal, and the black bars of the portcullis rose slowly. Each bar was as big around as one of Shadd's arms, and the end of each bore a pointed tip, honed to deadly sharpness.

"As soon as the portcullis is raised, please step to the doors and knock one time only." The porter's voice floated through the night air behind them. "The steward will escort you from there."

The silver doors opened under McAvery's single knock, gliding apart silently into recesses in the walls. Beyond them, the wood-paneled hallway was smaller than Kestrel would have expected, shadowed and dark in an oddly welcoming way.

"Please follow me." Kestrel started at the voice, slithering from beside her like a serpent. The steward stepped forward out of the dimness and bowed. To describe him as a plain man would not be enough. Average height and weight, with a color of hair so dull it defied naming. He was the most unremarkable man she had ever seen in all her life. If it weren't for his bright blue royal livery, Kestrel guessed she'd have missed him standing there, overlooked him as she would an old table.

He turned, fluid in the extreme, and moved down the hallway toward another set of double doors. Wooden this time, and far less tall. She glanced up, suddenly curious. The ceiling was far lower than the silver doors outside had implied. Looking back, they were still silver, but seemed no taller than the hallway ceiling.

"We can return for a tour later, if you like." McAvery's whisper was harsh in her ear.

The steward was holding open the wooden doors, waiting as patiently as a stone. She'd been gawking like a child. Kestrel hurried forward, passing through the arched threshold and into another corridor. This one was brightly lit, sconces at intervals bearing merrily flickering torches. The stained-glass windows she'd admired from the street rose majestically above the sconce line, but their impact was less intense, the colors less pronounced with only the night outside. They passed a number of wide doors, all closed, until the steward finally stopped outside one of them. He opened it and motioned them inside. A sitting room, warm fire crackling in the stone hearth, and several comfortable chairs scattered about in precisely ordered chaos.

"Pray wait here." The steward bowed again and disappeared. Kestrel stared at the closed door and shook her head.

"If I believed in ghosts, which I don't," she said, "I'd swear he was one."

"He's the perfect royal servant." McAvery settled himself in one of the soft leather chairs, his leg cocked over the arm. "Blends in with the scenery. I daresay he could stand right next to His Auspiciousness during some tricky negotiation, and later anyone else who attended would swear there'd been no one there."

The door slammed open. McAvery leaped to his feet. Kestrel's hand fell to her blade as she swung into defensive posture, then stopped in surprise. It couldn't be. Of all the people she thought she might see here, this was never one of them. Not standing up under his own power, at any rate. She'd watched them carry his carcass off her deck days ago.

"Keep your mouths shut and come with me, you two," Cragfarus growled. "You've kept His Highness waiting long enough."

chapter Thirty

It had been strange, even in a dream,
To have seen those dead men rise . . .
—SAMUEL TAYLOR COLERIDGE

He was in a clean uniform, hair slicked back and chin freshly shaved, but his expression was no more pleasant for the cleanliness. And he didn't seem to be suffering at all from his recent skewering at her hands.

"Hurry along. You had to choose tonight to show up, when the whole bloody family's underfoot. Damned weasel of a steward's already gone to fetch Lig."

She gasped, straining to stay in character. Lig! The man she most needed to see, coming right to her. Luck was on her side, finally. Or it would be, if she could stay in this room until he arrived.

"Who's coming?"

He scowled. "Menja Lig. The king's personal Danisoban."

The air rushed out of her lungs, leaving her cold and dizzy. Lig, a Danisoban. And not just any magus, but personal to the king. The man she'd come all this way for, the man who could rescue Binns from certain death. Would he listen to her, take the log and help her friend? Or would he recognize her for what she was, and drag her off to a cell in the Danisoban School, where she'd never see the sun, never feel the spray on her face?

She gripped the back of the chair, trying to get herself under control. There was no way he'd know. All she had to do was remain calm, turn the book over, and get Binns out.

Cragfarus jerked his head toward the corridor. "I can't believe you were so stupid as to come in the front door."

Kestrel snapped a look at McAvery, but he stared straight at the hefty guardsman. He must have known Lig was one of the Brethren, and he'd said nothing. He'd probably excuse himself by saying she'd never asked. She decided to stall for a bit, until the steward returned. Even if he was arriving with a Danisoban in tow, that was the risk she'd have to take. It was what she'd come all this way for. Binns wouldn't have asked her to do this if he didn't believe she could handle it.

"I heard you were dead," she mumbled, looking him up and down for any sign of the injury she'd given him.

"You heard wrong," the soldier snapped, patting his midsection with a sure hand. "It wasn't nothing but a flesh wound."

She couldn't resist digging at him a bit. "The tale was all over Eldraga, how the pirate woman spilled your guts on the deck of that ship you had the keeping of."

"Oh, was it?" Cragfarus sneered. "Did they also tell you how, after I'd killed six of her boys, she tried to snare me into her bed? She was damn near throwing herself at me." He squared his shoulders proudly. "If I hadn't been drinkin' all afternoon, and passed out from the heat, I swear she'd have jumped me right there in front of her men and mine! You shoulda seen her, wailin' over my body, fearin' she'd killed me. Poor little bitch hadn't seen a real man 'til she caught a look at me."

Kestrel's hand was itching to draw her sword. "Poor little bitch," indeed. She'd been a fool not to throw his body overboard and let the deeps claim him. Caution be damned. Before this was all over, she'd finish the job she'd started on board, even if it meant spilling his blood all over the prince's fine carpeting.

Not right now. Killing Cragfarus would have to wait a little longer. But she couldn't resist one final jab. "Then how'd she get the ship out from under you, sir?" Kestrel asked. "Ain't it true she sailed off without you?"

His flabby cheeks reddened. "Shut up," he growled, suddenly reticent. "This ain't no time for stories. Get your arses moving before I move them for you."

McAvery waved toward the door. "After you."

"Ain't we the mannerly gentlemen?" Cragfarus snarled. "You two spend too much time together, I'm thinking. Move."

Maybe they'd meet the steward on their way. She couldn't put it off any longer, or Cragfarus would suspect something. And she was no good to anyone murdered.

Cragfarus closed the door behind McAvery with a gentle *click* and led them farther into the depths of the massive house. Kestrel tried to memorize their route as he took them around corners and upstairs, making note of this painting or that carpet, but she was soon lost—there was just too much to remember. If the evening went badly, she'd have to depend on McAvery for her escape route. The thought was cold comfort. She settled for the stained-glass windows. They, at least, led outside. And she'd survived falls before. Her shoulder throbbed with the memory.

Finally, they stopped outside a set of ornate double doors. Cragfarus opened them, hustling his charges inside, then glanced up and down the hall before he shut them again.

Kestrel looked around, shocked at the opulence. Fabric-hung walls lent an air of softness to the well-appointed room. A crimson velvet couch faced the stone fireplace, flanked by matching chairs and side tables carved from a rich, flame-reflecting wood that must have been imported from some exotic land far from the Islands. On the far wall hung a life-size portrait of a young man, flanked by sconced candles that cast a warm glow over his painted features. He might have been handsome, but for the slight fleshiness at his jawline and the annoyed expression on his too-soft face.

Next to the portrait was a single door. It was closed; beyond it, they could hear muffled voices, one loud and angry, the second cringing. Cragfarus gestured toward McAvery. "Give me the sanguina and I'll let His Highness know you're out here."

Kestrel took a deep breath. Gods help them all if this didn't work. "I don't think so. How do I know you ain't some ghost after all? You *are* supposed to be dead." She cut a look toward McAvery. With his free hand, he brushed his fingers over his thumb. Of course. Money. The one thing men like Burk and Volga would have wanted, and the perfect distraction. "Besides, we got remunerations comin', so unless you got the coin in your pocket now, His Highness can bloody well come out and ask for his plant."

He'd probably wanted to give the plant to his master and leave them in the corridor until some haughty servant threw them out. Or had them beaten. He scowled, and stalked to the single door. Before he could get his hand on the knob, it flew open so hard it bounced against the inside wall. A man came marching out. He was in his early middle years, silver teasing at the roots of his rich mahogany hair, the ease of his life apparent in the softness around his belly and jaw. He was dressed in slops sewn from fine indigo velvet, with a matching velvet frock coat. But it was the ennui he wore like a cloak that was unmistakable. This was the same man from the portrait, with a couple of decades added on.

Cragfarus snapped to attention, eyes firmly locked on some faraway spot. "Prince Jeremie, I've brought the sanguina," he announced.

Prince Jeremie, eldest son of the king, in direct line to next wear the elaborate crown of the Nine Islands. The man most likely to want the sanguina kept far away from the king. The man who stood to gain more than anyone else by getting his hands on the sanguina himself. It was all about sons and fathers, and the eternal conflict between them.

"By Krakel's broken tongue, you're a liar," Jeremie said. His voice was cultured, precise, as if some sculptor had carefully carved his throat and tongue to form words in just the proper way. "You've only just emerged from your sickbed yesterday, and that only courtesy of Brother Lig. What you mean to say, I think, is your men brought the sanguina for you." He sneered at Kestrel and McAvery. "An ugly pair they are. Couldn't you have found servants more pleasing to the eye?" He reserved a look of tender avarice for the plant itself. "Get out, Cragfarus. Guard the door. Let no one in without my leave. And keep in mind what I told you."

The big guardsman bowed stiffly, turned on his heel, and left without a word. Jeremie planted one hand on the velvet back of the chair nearest him. The other he extended, palm up, in a pose elegant enough to impress any portrait artist. He was the very essence of calm. Though it wasn't a peaceful serenity. More like the taut control of a hunting cat just before it attacked its prey. "It's about time you got here."

McAvery shrugged. "Sorry, Your Highness, but the ship—"

"Spare me your tedious excuses," he snapped. "I was expecting you yesterday. Another day and you'd have ruined months of intricate planning." Color rushed into his cheeks. He pushed suddenly, knocking the heavy velvet chair over. Kestrel had to jump backward to keep from letting her toes be crushed. "I have a destiny and you're standing in its way. Hand over my sanguina and let's be done with this business before my beloved father sets his dog of a magus onto your trail and follows it back to me."

"No." Kestrel stepped between McAvery and the prince's grasping hands. "I don't know what kind of men you're used to doing business with, but I want my payment before I hand over the goods."

Jeremie clenched both fists, his arms straining under the sleeves of his doublet. Spittle flew from his lips, his perfect speech marred by his fury. "I demand . . . you . . . give it . . . to me!"

"Demand what you like," she continued. "But you ain't king yet. Which makes what we did high treason. In your name. The least you can do is pay us for our trouble."

The prince glared at her. His hands dropped to his sides, the fingers of his right twitching as if reaching for a weapon that usually hung there. "I am Jeremie, prince and heir to the throne of the Nine Islands. What do you think would happen if I cried out for the guard? Cragfarus wouldn't mind killing you right here on my carpet. Assassins! Help me!" He smiled, cold as a serpent. "No one would challenge my word."

Kestrel thought frantically. She couldn't very well kill the prince outright; if she survived long enough to escape the room, she would still have murdered a member of the royal family. There had to be a way to beat him at his own game. The pot was heavy in the crook of her elbow, as if the plant had grown measurably since they'd entered the palace. She glanced down at it, at the round and swollen sanguina clinging precariously to the thick stem. The one thing that stood between her and pointless, ignoble death. And the best bargaining tool she could hope to find.

Grinning, she reached up to the bulging fruit and wrapped her fingers around it. "Oh, don't it feel smooth and ripe," she said, never taking her eyes off the prince. "I wonder what'd happen if I just went ahead and . . ."

"Stop, man." Jeremie's face, pale to the extreme already, whitened further in understanding. "Don't be an idiot."

"Best watch who you're calling an idiot." Kestrel licked her lips. "I bet it'd taste mighty sweet, even if it ain't quite ready to keep me young forever." She tightened her hand.

Back on the ship, when McAvery finally gave up the secrets of the sanguina, he had stressed that the one crucial detail was the timing. The fact that the plant had survived thus far was a gift from the gods, though to whom was yet to be seen. If she pulled it free of its stem before the moment of peak ripeness, all its life-extending qualities would vanish and it would be nothing more than a snack.

"Cyrus!" the prince bellowed over one shoulder, keeping his eyes on Kestrel's hand. "Bring my cache."

A portly man, easily ten years past his prime, struggled from the open doorway, a large iron-worked box in his arms. Gray-haired and no taller than she was herself, he was dressed in the blue mantle of the merchant class, though the fabric was somewhat shabby and faded, as if he hadn't replaced his gown in far too long. Now that she was standing this close, she realized she'd seen the man before. He'd been at the inn that day, hovering behind Laquebus and the Danisoban when Binns was arrested.

"By your will, Prince Jeremie." Bending at the knees, he lowered the heavy box to the floor and straightened, coming face-to-face with McAvery and Kestrel.

"Open my cache and pay these gentlemen." Jeremie turned toward Kestrel again, his smile false as a paper mask. "I believe the sum was five hundred octavos."

Five hundred? That was all? She cut a look toward McAvery, but he seemed relaxed, a small, pleased smile twitching at his lips. She'd promised herself they would part company the instant she had Binns safely away, but now her curiosity wanted her to buy him a drink, just to get the rest of the story.

Cyrus finished counting out the five hundred coins. He pulled the bag's strings, closing the neck, and tossed it reluctantly toward McAvery, breaking Kestrel's train of skeptical thoughts. Necks . . . strings . . . Binns. The reality hit her like a dead gull falling from aloft. Whatever McAvery was up to didn't matter. No one was going to do anything about Binns. The money was McAvery's part of the deal. Binns's release was hers. Here they stood, in the lair of the enemy. Unless she found a way to turn this to her advantage, and quickly, Binns was as good as dead. And so was she.

"Your Highness," she began, taking a step forward. "Five hundred? I know my partner looks like a simpleton, but neither of us is that stupid."

The startled Jeremie raised a fleshy hand to his chest. "I beg your pardon?"

McAvery was staring at her as well, with an expression somewhere between shock and amusement. So she'd managed to knock him off his feet. It was about time someone did.

Cyrus's face was a mask of surprise. "You forget your place, fellow."

"I don't think so." She thumped the swollen fruit with one finger, setting it to shivering. "I know exactly what my place is. And I think Your Highness does, too."

Silence filled the room. Jeremie was staring at her, as if he couldn't believe what he'd heard her say. Next to her, McAvery had inched backward a little, closer to the door. Kestrel could hear her own blood rushing in her ears, but she felt no fear. Opulent palaces or the deck of the *Wolfshead*, she'd been facing down men no different from this prince for years. Maybe the landlubber's game wasn't so strange after all. Trade the open deck for a sumptuous apartment, and the difference was hard to discern. Maybe her partner in crime was becoming nervous, but she was going to win.

"By Krakel, you certainly are a hard bargainer," Jeremie murmured. "You may bargain yourself into a hangman's noose." He laid one fleshy hand against Cyrus's shoulder and shoved him away contemptuously. "What is it you think you're owed?"

"Two things, Your Highness." She couldn't be too obvious. The log was heavy under her shirt. "Me and my partner, we've taken a fondness for life on the open seas. Thought it'd make our work more efficient if we had our own transportation between the Islands, aye?"

Jeremie poked out his lower lip, nodding sagely. "So, you'd like a ship? I think that's reasonable. After all, you did manage to retrieve what my own agent could not." He cut a glance toward Cyrus. "What if I make you captain of the *Thanos*?"

McAvery was staring at her with a combination of disbelief and admiration. She would have smiled at him, except that she was working so hard to keep her mouth from dropping open in surprise. The *Thanos*! She imagined Binns's reaction when she presented him with the warship.

"You can't!" Cyrus cried. "That ship is mine!"

"Was, Cyrus. You've proven yourself unworthy to act as an agent for me." He waved a dismissing hand in Cyrus's direction. "Begone. Perhaps tomorrow, after I'm king, I'll allow you to give Master Burk a tour of the *Thanos*, help him get used to it now you won't be aboard any longer. I find this fellow refreshingly brash. Just the sort of man I need to helm a ship like the *Thanos*." Jeremie rubbed his hands together. "Cyrus can go back to a life of comfort in the palace. His age has been showing lately," he said snidely, obviously enjoying the discomfort he was inflicting. "Best to let a younger man take the helm."

Shouting erupted outside the door. She tore her attention away from Cyrus to find her cohort. McAvery was busily tying off the coin pouch. He dropped it into his pocket, catching her eye as he did.

"Safekeeping," he whispered.

She snorted at him. If he thought she believed him, he was more of a fool than she could ever be. But she didn't care about his five hundred octavos—she had a ship. A mighty warship. She would see Binns safely rescued, and then she would carve out a place for them in the world. Together, they would become the scourge of the Nine Islands.

Her fantasy was interrupted by the crash of the door flying open and slamming against the rear wall. She started, glancing toward the threshold.

Cragfarus was grinning as he entered. "Sorry, Prince Jeremie, but I figured this couldn't wait." He moved aside, allowing the two men behind him to stride into the room. Kestrel's mouth dropped open in horrified surprise. It all seemed like a sick game, as if the gods themselves were high above snickering over what unwelcome face they would throw at Kestrel next. Bad enough when the formerly dead Cragfarus strolled back into her life. But these faces were going to get her killed.

"Well, well," said Burk, his sunburnt cheeks shining in the candlelight. His clothes were rumpled and sweat-stained, as if he'd been waiting a very long time for someone who was never coming.

"Who might you two be?" he asked pleasantly. Volga loomed behind him, nodding his ugly head. "Because you sure as hell ain't us."

She let out a sigh. Well, damn them all for soft-headed fools. She'd stolen a ship, skewered a soldier, hung her first mutineer, and even let magic have a bit if its own way with her. And not a bit of it had mattered. It'd been an interesting journey, but the road ended here. McAvery wasn't getting whatever he'd really come for. And she and Binns were both dead. Kestrel wondered if the gods would be satisfied now.

Thirty-one

The moment that his face I see,
I know the man that must hear me . . .

—SAMUEL TAYLOR COLERIDGE

Kestrel slid her hand toward her hilt, itching to fight. Enough of this clandestine silliness. Time for an old-fashioned, blood-in-puddles-on-the-floor sort of battle, the kind she understood.

Prince Jeremie had settled back on his heels. "How very interesting." He looked from Kestrel and McAvery to the newcomers, amusement playing over his features. "What gods did your mothers anger in order to warrant such a punishment? Not one set of hideous children but two?" He chortled, as if he'd just made a joke good enough to bring the army to its knees. "So which of you is the original, and which the forgery?"

The real Burk stepped closer to Kestrel, until the two of them were nearly nose to nose. He stank of sweat, stale seawater, and tar, like any other sailor, but worse, as if he hadn't been in proximity to a tub of hot soapy water in a season or more. He raised a fat finger, poked her. "This'un be false. I ain't this ugly."

"No," she sneered, "you're far uglier. But I can make it worse, if you like." She hummed the tune she'd used to create the illusion, and was satisfied to see Burk's stunned face at her return to her own form. "That's better," she said. She flashed her hand to her sword, drawing it with a snick and swinging it up, waving the pointed tip back and forth, forcing Burk's watery eyes to shift in time with it. "Why don't we settle this like men?"

He grinned, revealing stained teeth. "Good idea. Nobody fights like me. You won't last a minute." He drew his own blade and stepped back into fighting stance.

Kestrel settled onto her heels, finding her natural balance, and clinked her sword against Burk's. "You're right—it won't take me a minute to defeat you."

"Stand down, both of you!" The prince's voice snapped like a whip in the tension of the room.

All eyes swung toward Jeremie. He stepped up onto a table and drew himself into a portrait pose. "If there's to be entertainment, I want a perfect view. And I think you should put down my plant before you begin."

Kestrel tightened her grip on the pot, but Cragfarus stepped closer, blade pointed at her neck. "You heard His Highness. Put it down." She sighed, bent, and placed the pot behind her, near the wall, as far away from clumsy feet as she could find.

"Now you may fight," Jeremie announced.

Burk raised his sword and swung at Kestrel. She blocked him easily, sending his steel clanging off to the side. There was no room in the salon to fight properly—she'd have to be tricky to manage this.

Her ugly opponent reared up for another slash. She scooted backward, and hopped onto the bouncy seat of a velvet couch. Burk's sword missed her, the breeze fluttering past her belly. She'd gained a foot of height on him. She spun her sword around and gripped it upside-down. Bringing it up, she slammed the pommel down on Burk's exposed head.

He danced away, holding his head. His eyes rolled back, and he collapsed to the floor.

"You shouldn't get into a fight with a soft head like that," she muttered.

"Stop, you idiot! Let go! You're going to break it!"

The cry got her attention. Across the room, where she'd left the sanguina, McAvery was locked in battle with Volga, and Jeremie and Cyrus were standing close together. Both men's hands were wrapped around the thick plaster pot, pulling it back and forth between each other. The little plant shook and trembled, the heavy fruit wobbling on its stalk, threatening to pop free with the men's yanking.

"You took my ship," Cyrus grunted, his face inches from the prince's. "You're a greedy, whining little child and I'm sick of doing things your way."

"You were happy enough when I was making you rich," the prince snarled.

"You weren't making me anything but your puppet!"

"Better to be the puppet of a king than a trinket-seller on the back streets." He tightened his grip and leaned back, trying to use his own weight to an advantage. But Cyrus wasn't letting go.

"If you end up king because of anything I did or didn't do, I'll be the first to throw myself off a roof. I've been an idiot from the start listening to you." He heaved suddenly, freeing the plant from Jeremie's grasping fingers. "So I'm taking this." He danced backward, brandishing the pot dangerously over his head. "Get used to getting old."

Jeremie roared, and lunged forward. Cyrus skipped out of his reach, Jeremie's fingertips brushing the toes of his boots but missing. The prince fell flat on his belly and banged his soft chin, his teeth clacking audibly.

"Hah!" Cyrus jeered. He backed to the door, sliding a hand behind his back and turning the knob. The door swung open. "You'll never be king," he called over his shoulder as he ran.

Jeremie scrambled to his feet and tore out the door after the escaping man. Cragfarus peered inside curiously, then looked back down the corridor after his master.

"Go," yelled McAvery. "I'll be right behind you."

Kestrel turned on her heel, leaped over the prostrate Burk, and bolted out the door.

KESTREL stopped at the four-way corridor. Which way had they gone? She hadn't been paying attention to where she was, concentrating on keeping up with the surprisingly swift merchant. Not only didn't she know where he'd slipped off to, she didn't know how to get back to McAvery. She bent over, resting her hands on her knees to catch her breath.

The carpet was thick and luxurious, a bloody scarlet that suited the dark wood of the walls and doors. There must have been servants whose only duty was to brush it daily, to keep footprints and dirt from marring its perfect surface.

Except that it wasn't perfect. There, a few steps down the corridor ahead, was something dark, out of place. She moved closer, still bent over. And smiled at the tiny clot of black dirt, lying on top of the red carpet. Right where it had fallen seconds ago.

She straightened up and looked down the corridor. One door to the left, one to the right, and one at the end. All closed. And no more bits of dirt to help her along. "Could have been worse," she muttered. "At least there are only three doors."

Stepping to the closest one, the door to the right, Kestrel pressed her ear against it and listened. No sound beyond. Not that it meant anything. The doors in this place were thick enough to use as rafts. She tried the latch. Locked.

Same with the next door, to the left. *I'll try this last one, and if they're all locked, I'll start kicking*, she decided. The door at the end of the hallway was shorter than the first two, with a plainer latch. Kestrel reached out, certain it would be locked as the others had been. But the latch gave under a gentle squeeze. She tipped the door open an inch and peeked inside.

Flickering shadows showed an empty room, walls of stone with a stone stairway beyond. She pulled the door open enough to let herself in and gazed up. Spiral stairs, so she could only see a few feet. The silence was deafening. This couldn't be the way he'd gone, she thought. It didn't lead anywhere. She turned around.

A gentle clunk echoed down the stairs. Kestrel froze, listening. Had that been a door latch clicking into place? How much higher did the house go? Why would someone bent on escape run into a tower, where he'd be certain to be caught? In answer to her unspoken question, a flicker of weak light revealed another bit of dirt, on a high step near the first curve. Damn him, he had gone this way.

"I hate stairs," she muttered. Not that she had a choice. She started up the stairs, taking them two at a time and not worrying about the clatter of her boots on the stone. At least, Cyrus and Jeremie couldn't go anywhere but down, whether they heard her coming or not. She had them cornered.

The steps became shorter as she neared the top, as if the tower was easing into a point, and her heart seemed to pound harder with every turn around. Finally she reached a minuscule landing, with barely room enough for her feet. A wooden door faced her, unadorned except for the tin and rope latch near its top. She bent to catch her breath, her lungs burning. Back on board ship, she could scramble through the lines like a monkey. This sort of climbing was nothing like that. Her legs were shaking, sweat running in rivulets in her hair, tickling past her collar. If she opened this door and found another pair of stairs, she swore to herself she'd sit right down and wait for one or both of them to get hungry. She grabbed the rope, gave it a good yank to release the catch, then pushed the door open.

CHAPTER

Thirty-two

The harbor bay was clear as glass
So smoothly was it strewn!
And on the bay the moonlight lay
And the shadow of the Moon.

—SAMUEL TAYLOR COLERIDGE

The runaway merchant had stopped running. Permanently. He lay on his side, directly across from her, a puddle of darkness forming under him, the hilt of a dagger poking out from between his ribs.

Next to him, tied hand and foot to a huge wooden cross was Binns. He sagged against the bonds, his face was reddened with sun. His flesh drawn and tight, as if he'd had nothing to eat or drink for days. His mouth was gagged with a tightly tied rag, but his eyes brightened at the sight of her.

"Artie!" she cried.

Jeremie, the sanguina at his right hand, stepped between her and her captain. They were on a turret, probably one of the many she'd admired from the street. The floor was wood, the waist-high outer curtain constructed of a milky stone. Four flagpoles rose at spots equidistant from each other, each sporting fine silk pennants in the royal colors. They snapped and popped in the breeze, sounding like a whipmaster hard at work.

"Who the hell are you?"

"Kestrel," she said. "I serve Captain Binns, who you've got trussed up here. Let him go. You can eat your fruit, live forever, be king of whatever you desire. I'll walk away now."

"Why should I?"

Kestrel slid her sword from its sheath in a velvet motion. "There's nowhere else to go, Highness," she said.

"You can't win," he said, casually setting the sanguina on the curtain wall. The wind caught the door, slamming it. "He's always gotten what he wanted." The breeze shook the plant, and Jeremie reached out to steady the pot. "It's time he had to taste it."

"Taste what?" she asked, confused.

"Defeat. To feel what it feels like to be denied. To never get what you want."

Kestrel took another step, and another. "Who did you hope to defeat?"

Jeremie waved a hand at the city below him. "My father, of course." His eyes burned with hatred. "You think I didn't know? How much he hates me, how he'd rather rule another fifty years than ever let me have a turn at it? I will live my life as a useless prince, nothing more. I am as much as I can ever hope to be, right now. Unless I stop him."

She didn't dare breathe hard, now that he was watching her. Any move she made could panic him, and the fruit was too close to the edge for her comfort. "Why not just throw the plant off the tower? You'd foil his plan."

"Why should I?" he asked, venom in his tone. "He's already lived two lifetimes. I want the same thing. To stay young and handsome while he withers and dies. To rule forever if it suits me."

"We needn't be enemies, you and I," she said slowly. "What care I who rules the Islands? All I want is my captain."

"Your man was sent to stop me. He and the Knave. My fruit would be in my father's hands at this moment. As it is . . . I hope you can see my dilemma. My first act as king will be to strangle the Privateer. You can't have him."

The sky above her was still dark, but the stars had begun to fade. Sunrise wouldn't be long in coming.

Jeremie wrapped his hand around the burgeoning fruit. "So I'll eat the fruit. My father will die, as he should have done long ago.

The world will be as it should be. Perhaps you can finally find some decent work. Something appropriate."

His demeaning tone broke through the wall of misery. A spark flared in her breast. "Appropriate?"

"Of course. A life at sea's no life for a woman. Are you mad? You'd do better seeking a position as a scullery maid, or seamstress." He eyed her up and down. "You're fair enough. You'd probably do well on your back."

The spark flamed into roaring, crackling rage. Kestrel grabbed her sword, the point aimed at the center of his chest. "You're a disgusting little man. I see why your father didn't want to leave his kingdom to you. I don't care about the games landlubbers play. If it was up to me, I'd never set foot on land again. But no one, landbound or not, deserves to be under the thumb of a spoiled infant who thinks he knows how to be a king just because someone gave him a crown to play with."

Jeremie let go of the fruit and crossed his arms. "What do you think you can do to stop me? Kill me and you'll never leave this house alive."

"I don't have to kill you," she said, her mouth drawn tight. "All I have to do is whistle."

She pressed her lips together and blew out a clear note. The plant trembled, its pot clacking softly on the curtain of the turret. She snaked a hand to her dagger, pulling it from its sheath as surreptitiously as she could.

"What in the gods' names are you doing?" Jeremie laughed. "You're no Danisoban."

Kestrel didn't stop. Over the sound in her head, she could hear the prince laughing. She concentrated on the plant in its pot. She sent out invisible fingers of sound, to slide around the pot. She grasped it, lifted it high, drew it toward her.

Jeremie's face fell. "No!" he cried. "Give it back!" He jumped, flailing his arms to try to catch the little pot out of the sky. Kestrel kept up her tune, keeping the plant out of his reach.

"Stop making that sound!" the irate prince screamed. He ran at her, hands bent into claws.

Kestrel dodged when he was inches away and brought her blade up, into Jeremie's belly. It sank to its hilt, as easily as into butter. He spun away, blood spattering in a sunburst pattern all over the turret floor. He fell against the turret curtain, panting.

"My sanguina . . ." he whispered, sliding to the floor. Kestrel was running out of breath. She used her last notes to bring the plant to a rest on the stones of the floor. She leaned over, resting her hands on her knees, and looked into the face of the bleeding prince.

She reached out with her bloodied dagger and wiped it clean on his arm. "How's that for appropriate?" she asked, slipping the dagger into her boot. He coughed, bloody spittle leaking onto his shirt, and closed his eyes.

The fruit hanging from its thick green stalk had changed color, from its earlier faint greenish gray to a bright yellow. When had that happened? She reached out a finger to touch it. Smooth, full of promise. What if she plucked it now, ate it herself, and left them all in her wake?

"It would serve them all," she said out loud, to the birds or whoever might be listening. But it wouldn't be right. And it wouldn't be what she wanted. Living on the sea was a near to perfect life. She'd never worried about having enough time. One lifetime would be plenty. She pulled her hand away from the ripe sanguina.

The world was so quiet, up this high. She almost thought she could hear the sun rising, pink threads of light beginning to play at the very edges of the horizon. She crossed to the wooden cross, and the man she'd come to find. Sheathing her sword, she drew her dagger and sawed at his bonds.

He fell forward into her arms. She settled him on the floor of the turret and cut loose the gag.

"Artie, I'm so sorry."

"Nothing to be sorry for, my girl." His voice was scratchy, dry.

His hand cupped her elbow. "You did just fine, Kes. You're here, aren't you?"

Kestrel leaned over and hugged him tight. "And I brought the log, like you told me to." She laughed, relief making her weak. "I'm so glad to see you."

"And I you, girl. I figured I was a dead man." He coughed, then rolled to his side and tried to sit up. "How'd you get here?"

"There's so much to tell you, but it'll have to wait until we get back to the ship." She slid an arm around his shoulders and helped him to his feet. "I don't know how we're going to get you out of here."

"That won't be a problem," said a voice from the doorway.

Jaeger. It couldn't be, yet there he was. "How did you—"she began.

"Find you? It's what I do." He smiled and lifted the bronze badge around his neck. "I sailed here and reported to Lig that a rogue Promise was on her way here in a stolen ship. He was more than happy to grant me access."

Kestrel helped Binns to lean on the wooden cross and faced Jaeger, one hand on her sword hilt. "I beat you once, when I was tired and hurt."

"I have a proposition for you."

She drew her sword and advanced on Jaeger. "The Danisobans murdered my parents when I was a little girl. I couldn't be less willing to join them, and there is nothing they could offer that will change my mind."

He raised his hands. No weapons she could see, but she kept her own at the ready. "What if I said I'm not with the Danisobans?"

"I'd say you must think I'm a fool with a bad memory. You were going to sell me to them back on Eldraga. You came here with Lig."

Jaeger nodded. "True. That was before I realized what you are." He stepped sideways, away from the door, moving along the turret edge until he neared the unconscious prince. "You know you'll be put to death for this? Killing the prince is treason."

"He's not dead, and if you're trying to frighten me, it isn't working. What do you mean? What do you think I am?"

He smiled. "You're something we've never seen. Only read about. I hunt rogue Promises for the Danisobans, it's true. But I'm also a Eusebian." He pulled aside his collar, showing the tattoo she'd noticed in the pub. Its red and blue swirls were serpents, coiling together. "The sign of my order."

"You're a priest?" It sounded far-fetched, but religious orders sometimes had rules and rituals that bordered on freakish.

"Not exactly. We're researchers. We study ancient texts and family histories. When I was recruited by the Brotherhood, it was a gift from the gods! We've been searching for a lost magical bloodline the Danisobans tried to wipe out centuries ago, and they themselves gave me the means to do that." He nudged the prince with a toe. The wounded man groaned, but did not wake.

"Still not understanding what any of this has to do with me." Kestrel's arm was starting to ache from holding her sword still. She needed to get Binns off the turret and the plant delivered. She didn't have time to listen to Jaeger and his drivel.

"You're what we've been looking for. You're immune to the water. You're not limited to the land. If we could breed more like you—"

"Breed?" She couldn't help the laughter that bubbled up from within at his ludicrous suggestion. Despite the danger, it felt so good to laugh.

Jaeger looked insulted at her reaction. "There's no better way to defeat the Danisobans. You'd be the mother of your people."

"If I wouldn't join the Danisobans, what makes you think a life of servitude with your people would be any more attractive? I'd be a brood mare!"

"Come with me. Let us study you, find out why you can do what you do. You'll live in comfort for the rest of your life, I promise."

Binns was shaking his head, watching her face. He mouthed the word "no," and Kestrel laughed bitterly. "Continual pregnancy doesn't sound like comfort to me."

Jaeger frowned and took a step forward. "Our need is more vital than your stubbornness. I'm taking you back with me whether you want to come or not." He leaped forward, two daggers sliding from his sleeves into his hands, and slashed at her arm.

Kestrel danced back, parrying another strike with her sword. If he slipped past her guard, she was doomed.

"I'm sure you'll see the wisdom of my offer. Menja Lig is somewhere nearby. I went to him first, with my story. He knows about you." He thrust forward, aiming for her belly.

"Won't happen." She swung at him, but he dodged. "King owes me a favor now."

"Not yet. Not until you deliver your little plant. And I'm feeling hungry right about now." He lunged toward the sanguina.

Kestrel pressed her lips together and blew a sharp whistle. The power ripped from her, not in gentle, tingly waves but jagged strikes. It hit Jaeger hard, blowing him back against the turret curtain. He dropped one dagger to grasp, desperately, at the stones.

"You can't," he said. "We're your only chance to put the Danisobans down."

Kestrel didn't look away. She could feel Binns's eyes watching her. She'd come this far, for him. She wouldn't give up now, not for anyone's agenda. She licked her lips, and blew once more.

The power slammed into Jaeger's body, tipping him over the edge. He shrieked, the sound fading as he fell.

She ran to Binns, who was sagging against the cross. He said nothing, but laid an arm across her shoulders. Together they sank to the floor. "I just need to get my legs back," Binns said. Kestrel didn't answer. He was alive, and out of danger. He could sit here and rest all day if that's what he needed.

The turret door slammed open as hard as it had closed. McAvery was through first, his smile for once not making her angry.

"Look at the mess up here," he said. "Missed all the fun, did I?"

She grinned back. "I tried to get them to wait for you. Next time, don't take so long."

He tipped his hand to his brow, as if he were wearing a hat.

Two men were a step behind McAvery, both nobly dressed. The first man strode to the fallen prince and stared down at him, his face impassive. His companion stood quietly, waiting. At last, he waved a hand toward the door, where two servants waited. They bustled onto the already crowded parapet, lifted the unconscious man, and carried him away.

Kestrel looked at Binns. "Is that him?"

He nodded.

"I'm starting to think I should have tipped the plant into the ocean," she murmured. "He didn't even blink when he saw his son bleeding."

"Don't judge him until you've met him, lass. He's a better man than you might assume. Your Majesty," Binns said, "may I present my quartermaster, Kestrel?"

The king stepped toward her, his hand extended. He looked to be in his middle years, not near old enough to have sired a child of Jeremie's age. His chestnut hair was tinged with silver, and his dark eyes were bright. "My lady, you have my deepest gratitude. Not only for your role in the saving of my sanguina, but also for the rescue of my dear friend Artemus."

"The Ageless King. I'm sure it's an honor to meet you, Your Majesty," she said, careful to keep her voice level. "I can't say it's mine."

Binns gasped. The king and his Danisoban looked stunned. Only McAvery continued to smile. She refused to catch his eye. He'd probably say he'd known what she'd do all along. Easing her arm from behind her captain, she got to her feet and faced the king.

"I've been a pirate, in the service of a pirate, for two years. But in the last few days, I discovered that I've been wrong about everything. I've been a bloody tax collector, and the man I admired above all others couldn't even tell me the truth. If I'd known I was working for the lawful end of things, I never would have signed on with Artie."

"Whyever not?" the king managed to choke out.

"Because it's your laws that kept me down. That told me I could be a barmaid or a whore or even a Danisoban, but never, ever a sailor. So here's your plant." She turned and whistled a phrase, lifting the plant and dropping it into the startled king's hands. "You've got your son, and I'll be on my way."

She stalked across the turret to the waiting door. McAvery had shifted his body to block the door. "Move," she said. "Or I'll knock you off this turret."

"Why don't you hear the king out? You might be interested in his proposal."

"You may be willing to be his lackey, but I can't. Not anymore."

"Kestrel, girl, wait." Binns's voice was stronger, and she glanced back at him. He'd struggled to his feet, and was walking carefully toward her. "Let me explain."

Tears welled in her eyes, and she wiped them angrily. "There's nothing to explain, Artie. You lied to me."

He reached her side and took her arms in his gentle hands. "I did, and I'm sorrier for that than anythin' else I've ever done. You've been the daughter I never had. I thought I was protectin' you, keepin' the secret. The life we lived was dangerous enough."

"I don't need protecting," she said.

He laughed. "No, you don't. When I saw you come through that door, you looked like an avengin' angel. And I knew then that I'd made the right choice."

She didn't want to ask, but the words spilled out. "Choice of what?"

Even though he was smiling, a shadow crossed his eyes. "My successor." Kestrel's eyes widened, but Binns held up a finger. "I knew from that first day, when you risked a beatin' just to keep me from losin' my ship. You're a strong one. You can do things no one else can. That's not ordinary, child, and neither are you. You've got a destiny, and it's more than just captainin' a pirate sloop."

Kestrel stared at him, the anger draining from her as quickly as it had flared. All this time he'd been training her to join the strange game he and McAvery played. He thought she was special. She spared a sidelong glance at McAvery. The expression on his face was saying the same thing. As was that of the king. They all saw something about her that she'd never suspected of herself. For the first time, she began to wonder if her magic wasn't a curse, but a blessing.

Until she caught sight of the silent man behind the king. Lig, it had to be. He was watching her, too, with a hunger that made her skin crawl. He'd do whatever he had to, just to claim her for the Danisobans. For an instant, she was the orphan child again, running and hiding in the dark alleys to keep clear of men like him. Lig smiled at her, his eyes cold. As quickly as it had struck, the fear faded. She was special, and she was strong. This man couldn't touch her. She smiled back at him. If he tried to hurt her, he'd regret it.

Binns squeezed her shoulder. "I know it's a great deal to ask, but I can't think of anyone better. Please take my place, and make me proud."

Epilogue

Swiftly, swiftly flew the ship
Yet she sailed softly too:
Sweetly, sweetly blew the breeze
On me alone it blew.
—SAMUEL TAYLOR COLERIDGE

K estrel shaded her eyes against the brilliant morning sun. Huge black sails hung where once were red, like the wings of a monstrous raven, fluttering in the sharp breeze off the water.

The king had been beyond generous—every man of her crew had received a season's worth of gold, enough to keep them up to their ears in rum and wenches for the last six nights. Reward aplenty for the hard labor they'd engaged in during the daylight, overhauling the *Thanos*. She'd considered repainting the big vessel, so it wouldn't stand out so vibrantly on the open sea. But the colors suited her.

Not to mention the long discussion she'd had. By suppertime, she'd not only come to accept his odd system of taxation via piracy, but had convinced the king to make a proclamation allowing women to serve on board merchant vessels. It was a start, and she'd been pleased. *Probably how he managed to talk me into taking on Binns's job,* she thought. She'd negotiated a better cut of the plunder for her crew, at least. Having had a few days to consider, working for the crown didn't have to be the horrible fate she'd thought at first.

Jeremie's treacherous compatriots had all been rounded up and dealt with. She'd particularly enjoyed watching Cragfarus plead for his life. The king packed them all off to work in the salt mines of the Continent, where they couldn't cause any more trouble. The prince survived his wound, but where he was tucked away, no one seemed to know.

The only unpleasant aspect of the day had been her encounter with the Danisoban. Menja Lig was fascinated by her skills, and by her avoidance of the Brotherhood all these years.

"You really ought to join us," he urged. "That traitor Jaeger mentioned your special gift. We could use someone with your strength. You'd be protected from anyone who'd seek to use you."

Except the Danisobans themselves. "I thank you, Brother, but I have a job I'm committed to."

He'd squinted at that. "His Majesty has allowed you to circumvent the law, for now. The day will come, young woman, when you will regret those words. The Brotherhood is not lightly denied."

"I'm not worried," she said. "If you want to take me by force, all you have to do is come to the ocean and get me."

He'd stomped off, his robes whirling. She hadn't seen him again, but somehow she always felt a sensation of being watched. Lig wouldn't give up just like that, so the sooner she was back on the water, the happier she'd be.

"You're not changin' the name?" Binns nudged her.

"No, I like her the way she is." Kestrel turned toward her captain. Former captain, that was. He'd apparently spent a bit of his money to visit a barber and a tailor. His long queue had been neatly trimmed off, and his face was pink and clean-shaven. He was dressed in a frock coat of golden beige, over a plain white tunic and dark brown breeches tucked into shiny black boots. Not at all the way she was accustomed to seeing him garb himself, but it suited him nicely.

"You look like a fine, upstanding merchant," she smiled. "Perhaps even a landlord?"

Binns grinned, nodding. "Aye, well, His Majesty is the soul of generosity," he said. Reaching inside his finely tailored coat, he drew out a folded parchment and brandished it the way he once would have a blade. "Fine man, that king of ours."

Kestrel took the parchment and unfolded it curiously. The formal words scribed within were flamboyantly curled and colored, but she managed to read them despite the ornamentation. "By order of His Majesty, King Manius, in recognition for his allegiant service culminating in bringing a traitor to the Crown to his right and proper justice, the pirate known as Artemus Binns is hereby granted full pardon for any and all crimes committed on land or at sea. Royal gratitude shall be expressed in the grant of a parcel of land and all property standing thereon, located on the gentle isle of Bix."

The document went on to specify the location of his grant. Kestrel laughed. "I'm no navigator, but I believe this bit of land stands right on top of the pub you used to work in."

"Ain't it interestin' how things all come around like that?" he said, a mischievous twinkle in his eye. "I happened to mention my tale of woe some while back, and he remembered. I didn't even think he was payin' attention. Like I said, fine man our king." Binns took his parchment back, sliding it into his jacket, and pulled out another one. "He asked me to deliver this'un to you."

The second parchment was covered in the lacy squiggles she'd spent the last few days learning to scribe. Once written, the letters would hide themselves, but memorizing a magical alphabet had been complicated. "It's my commission," she said. "But you could already read that, couldn't you?"

"Aye, lass." He patted her shoulder. "It took me a sight longer to write than it did you, though. You'll be an excellent Privateer." He sniffed. "So when do you set sail?"

"Today. I'm on schedule. All the repairs have been seen to, my new sails are installed, and food's been stocked. It'll be a short season, but with the bounty added on, I don't think any of the men will have cause to complain."

Before Binns could speak, a horn sounded, and he glanced over his shoulder. "Well, lass, I hate to say good-bye . . ."

"What? I thought you were going with us to Bix." Her heart was suddenly heavy, and the smile faded from her face.

"It ain't a good idea." He quirked one side of his lip—not really a smile, but kind sadness instead. "I been thinkin' about it, so you can't change my mind. Ship like yours can't support but one captain. Best if I leave ye here, to sail into the sunrise on yer own. But I've got you a gift, to remember me by."

She stared, unwilling to believe what she was hearing. Her chest felt heavy, as if bricks were piling on top of her, and she was having trouble breathing. How was she supposed to tell him, in a few fleeting minutes, all the things she'd planned on saying throughout a four-day voyage?

Binns pulled a paper-wrapped package from beneath his coat, proferring it to her. It was hefty and soft. Balancing it on one hand, she pulled at the edges with her other. Under the paper was rich, red fabric, folded into a tight rectangle. She looked at Binns quizzically.

"Keep going," he urged. She tore the last of the paper free and let it fall to the ground. She shook out the fabric and gasped.

It was a flag. A beautiful crimson flag with a black sword across it. A hawk perched on top of the sword, lovely and dangerous. She gazed at it. It was so perfect.

Binns was watching her, turning his hat in his hands, trying to gauge her reaction. "Will it do for you?"

"Do?" She laughed in delight. "It's amazing!"

He grinned. "I just thought you'd need your own colors. Seein' as you're a captain now . . ." His voice faded off. He raised a hand to his face, pinching the bridge of his nose.

Kestrel let the flag fall over one arm. Binns had saved her life as much as she had saved his ship. He'd been the father she'd lost as a child, the teacher she'd never known, the captain who'd given her the chance to shine when all others had spat on her and turned their backs. He'd kept things from her, but only because he wanted to keep her safe. Without him, she'd still be waiting tables on El-draga, hating her life and wishing for better. She opened her mouth, hoping the words would somehow find their way out, but he raised a hand to silence her.

"No, lass." He ducked his head, his cheeks pinking. "You don't need to say it at all. I'm so proud of you I could burst my chest with the swelling of my heart. If I ever wanted to die, it would be so I could find your parents and thank 'em for trusting me with your care." He wrapped his burly arms around her and hugged her tight. "You've always got a home with me, Kes. If y'ever need it, come to me. But now, go hoist that flag and fly her proud. I'll be watching the harbor. Oh, and there's one more thing—" He reached into his pocket and brought out a small silver hoop. "I believe this is yours."

Kestrel took it with trembling fingers and hooked it back onto her ear.

"I never doubted you. Fair winds, my girl," he murmured, releasing her as abruptly as he'd embraced her, turned on his heel, and melted into the crowd.

Tears rose in her eyes. Quickly she raised her arm to her face, wiping it clear before any of the men could notice, then folded the flag and tucked it under her arm. As soon as she got back to the ship, she'd raise it. Maybe Binns would see it fluttering before he shipped out. She hoped so.

"Ahoy, Mad Kestrel!"

He was striding toward her, hair and cloak whipping behind him with the speed of his walking. He'd apparently been shopping already—he was clad in skin-hugging hunter-green breeches, with a black silk shirt. He'd replaced his plain black cloak with a new one crafted from gleaming eel skin. It looked silky, and Kestrel fought the sudden urge to reach over and pet it. She tightened her hands into fists, and kept her arms firmly pressed to her sides. The last thing she needed to do was encourage McAvery.

"Mad?" she asked.

"With a ship like that, you need a fine nickname. Something designed to strike fear into the hearts of your enemies."

"Maybe it'd be better if I earned a name instead, don't you think?"

"Perhaps you're right. So where will you go first, in your fine new ship?" he asked, planting his hands on his hips and striking his now-familiar pose.

"Eldraga—got a new blade I have to finish paying for." She hesitated, then smiled. "What about you?"

"Lidias."

She widened her eyes in surprise. Lidias was a desert island, home to religious ascetics and few others. "I know I'll regret asking, but—"

"Why Lidias?" he finished for her. "I handle many different sorts of business, dear Kestrel. Suffice to say I have a delivery to make on Lidias's sandy shores." He glanced over his shoulder, and back. "I'll be leaving very shortly. The Scion is not a patient fellow."

"Pray tell what do you have that the Scion of Lidias would want?"

McAvery tilted his head, a sly grin creeping over his face. "As if I'd tell you. An agent of the king! You'd slap chains 'round my ankles before I could blink."

"You didn't seem to mind it so much the last time," she said, laughing.

"No, I can't say I did. Perhaps it was the scenery." He reached out and took her hand, drawing it slowly toward him, his gaze locked with hers. He touched his lips gently to the back of her hand, his fingers stroking her wrist. Heat pulsed through her, blurring her vision. Her legs trembled and threatened to drop away from under her. She couldn't pull away. Or maybe she just didn't want to.

Raising up, he released her hand and slid his arm around her waist, pulling her close against his body, his face inches from hers. His eyes were blue now, the blue of the sea on a cloudless day.

"One of these days," she began. McAvery dipped his head and stopped her mouth with his own.

The kiss was warm and soft. She melted against him, closing her eyes and letting herself enjoy him. Finally. She wrapped her arms 'round his neck, sliding her fingers into the silken mass of his hair. His hands pressed against the small of her back, the heat from them burning through her shirt.

All too soon, it ended. She gripped his shoulders for balance, inhaling the warm smell of him through the new clothes. He released her, reached into a pocket, and withdrew a red stone, suspended on a black leather lanyard. Opening it out, he slipped it over her head.

"I'll be seeing you again, Mad Kestrel," he murmured, his mouth close enough to her ear to tickle her with his breath. "We work for the same folks, after all. Until then, wear this. For me."

"Is it magic?" she asked.

"What do you think?" He stepped back, breaking their contact, smiled, and disappeared in the crowd.

She turned to the gangplank and strode aboard her ship. Her ship. Nothing had ever felt so good as the idea of having her own ship. "Quarter!" she yelled.

"Aye, Captain!" Shadd answered, grinning.

"Let's get this voyage under way."

"But, Captain," he said, "there's nowhere near enough breeze to move her along. You want me to arrange for a tow?"

"A tow?" she asked. "Are you mad? Who needs a tow?" Kestrel put her lips together and began to whistle.